Creatures of the Apocalypse Codex

Goeringer • Seedhouse • Robertson • Butler • McAusland

THE MUTANT EPOCH
TABLETOP ADVENTURE ROLE-PLAYING GAME

Created by William McAusland

Published by Outland Arts

"Putting YOU in the Game"

www.mutantepoch.com

'The Mutant Epoch'™ and the 'Outland System' game mechanic™ are all trademarks owned by Outland Arts™
© Copyright 2007-2015 Outland Arts/ William McAusland

OLA1009   ISBN 978-0-9949237-4-5   Black & White Edition   First published December 2015

Outland Arts
1860 Lodgepole Drive
Kamloops, B.C. Canada
V1S IX8

Join the TME Mailing List
www.mutantepoch.com

Introduction to the COTA Codex

Creatures of Apocalypse began to appear as single PDF downloads in April 2013. They were a way to share some nasty new mutants that I've been drawing and throwing at my own players, but so too, were a way to promote the Mutant Epoch RPG to the wider gaming community. We made them available as free downloads on rpgnow and drivethrurpg, plus promoted them on various gaming forums, art sites and other online venues. Whenever they would appear, sales and the fan base grew. They were a hit and inspired us to create the Pay What You Want product lines of One Day Digs and the Wasteland Treasures PDF.

I love monsters. From my earliest days I've always drawn mutant and fantasy creatures. Its one of the huge factors that drew me to role-playing games and writing fiction in the first place, and something I still do when doodling during a long phone call, or sketching while travelling, camping or warming up for a day of illustration work on The Mutant Epoch RPG. I did all the art in this book except for the Wailing Johnny on page 51, which was fully designed, written and illustrated by my friend Camille Robertson. Several other writers gave life to these monsters, including James Butler, myself, Brandon Goeringer, who created One Day Digs one through four, as well as Danny Seedhouse who brought us One Day Dig 5.

Why was this book created? Why not continue releasing individual free creature PDFs? I'll answer that.

I'm old school in many respects, and at times want to take a step back from the digital and online world, perhaps that is why I love to get my hands dirty and stand up at a work bench and create the Handcrafted Dungeons, or break out the pencil and inks and draw art for our Fantasy Clip Inks line of stock art sets - anything to get away from the computer after sitting in front of a screen for 10 or more hours. I don't seem to be alone in this and at a recent gaming expo here in my home town I was quite astounded to learn that a lot of players of The Mutant Epoch do not use PDFs at all, and never heard of Creatures of the Apocalypse or One Day Digs, and wanted to buy the photocopied print outs I had available for some demo games. Like me, some people work at a computer much of the day, so want to get away from all that when gaming and favour print books over ebooks.

I confess that since my wife bought me an ipad, I have embraced PDFs at my game sessions far more. I also use ebook versions when working at a coffee shop and need access to the entire TME library, or else out camping with the family and running test play sessions for an upcoming fantasy miniature game with the kids.

Related to the print or PDF topic is discoverability and access. Many TME gamers discovered the Epoch after coming across the book at a game store or when somebody else ran a session at a convention or home gaming table. While playing it, they never got around to signing up to the Society of Excavators membership, never got onto the mailing list, and don't peruse PDF download stores like rpgnow.com or our gumroad.com store. For many, until they see this book in their local game shop, will have no idea of its existence. To get the Creatures of the Apocalypse in their hands, therefore, required the creation of this mutant manual. A solid, dead tree print book, just the sort of thing I need when I am the game master.

This book includes the free Creatures of the Apocalypse downloads one to thirteen, which we will continue to leave available as individual PDFs. Also found here is the Muto-Harpy, which up until now was a special critter that we will now number COTA 14. The Muto-Harpy was only available to SOE members who snagged it through our members only area of the Mutant Epoch Forum. Creatures fifteen to twenty are new and will only ever be included in this book. At some point we aim to continue on with COTA 21 as a free download but when we get to COTA 30 or so, might create another one of these creature compendiums.

This bestiary was primarily crafted with a print book in mind with both a full color and grayscale version offered to fit different budgets. The full color version is only available through Createspace or Amazon.com as at this time since they are the only print on demand provider who produces high quality color books. In addition, we have also assembled an Adobe PDF variant which contains everything shown in this version, but the table of contents, internal page references and encounter tables are linked for ease of navigation.

In some ways this tome is a selfish creation, as I wanted all these beasties in one handy place, and needed to add some critters that none of my players have encountered before, thus the six all new freaks that won't be offered as free downloads. I hope your players never forget their PC's run ins with these mutated monstrosities.

Kindest regards
William McAusland

Table of Contents

 **Sickle Foot** *Page 5*

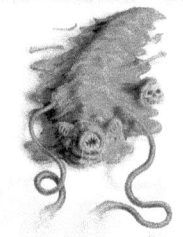 **Red Harvester** *Page 9*

 **Spikeback** *Page 14*

 **Junk-Mobster** *Page 19*

 **Bog-Billy** *Page 25*

 **Scraplurker** *Page 30*

 **Back Hatcher** *Page 37*

 **Quasi** *Page 43*

 **Spiker** *Page 46*

 **Wailing Jhonny** *Page 51*

 **Tyrannosapien** *Page 56*

 **Chest Head** *Page 65*

 **Talontessa** *Page 70*

 **Muto Harpy** *Page 80*

 **Walking Mouther** *Page 84*

 **Rubble Troll** *Page 92*

 **Snaykin** *Page 101*

 **Nubinz** *Page 108*

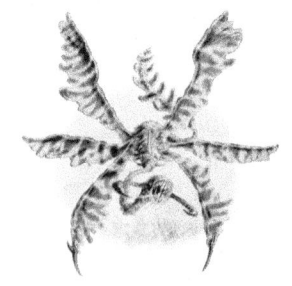 **Apocalypse Moth** *Page 116*

 **Spider Lord** *Page 120*

Encounter Tables *Page 126*   **Player Handout Versions** *Page 129*

CREATURES OF THE APOCALYPSE: 1
SICKLE FOOT
By William McAusland

Sickle Foot

Defense Value: **-17**

Endurance: **60+3d20**

Movement: **9m**

Initiative: **+2**

Attacks: **3: Bite and 2 sickle claws**

Strike Value: **01-70**

Damage: **d12+6 each**

Strength: 64

Agility: 82

Accuracy: 71

Intelligence: 12

Willpower: 43

Perception: 69

Valuables: nil

Experience Factors: 84

Morale: Excellent

Size: 2.1m long

Weight: 40+1kg per point of endurance

Mutations: 23% chance of 1 (see description)

Relics: nil

Implants: nil

A sickle foot is a nasty, nightmarish pack hunter of about the size of a black bear. Territorial, cunning, and needlessly cruel, this mutant predator can be found in both remote ruin areas as well as along well traveled trade roads and woodland paths. In an attack, sickle feet charge out from cover, often from multiple directions, and go directly for the nearest prey animal or person, leaping up at the last second and extending their rear, yellow clawed feet to rend the target open, often eviscerating the hapless victim in the process. Besides attacking with their terrible sickle clawed rear feet, they can deliver a horrendous bite in conjunction with their claws, going for the throat of their intended prey.

Although considered an animal by those forced to live near sickle foot territory, new era scholars and bioengineers adamantly insist that these new mutant beasts are at least a quarter human. Besides DNA testing, which proves some human lineage, experts also point out that sickle feet can speak to each other in the area's old world language, although what they say sounds more like grunts and growls. Witnesses claim they have overheard these things discussing an attack on an approaching refugee caravan, and during the attack, swore at defending humans who were putting up a good fight.

Those sent to study the sickle foot also discovered that some individuals exhibited mutations. In one case, a specimen was met that had a pair of human arms as well as its regular forearms

and rear clawed appendages; the beast using its human arms to fire a bow from a distance and kill the research expedition's guide. Other mutations have also been documented, ranging from extra sickle limbs, throwing spines, plated bodies, multiple heads, enlargement, and even a bat winged variant.

A rumor also persists of several humanoid species using sickle feet as guards or tracking animals, and in one instance, of skullocks riding these beasts into battle.

While speculation, rumor and second hand accounts are often dismissed by those who haven't encountered sickle feet, what is known is that they are entirely carnivorous, quick, observant, hard to approach unawares, and merciless. Accounts of their attacks on travelers, villages and looting expeditions repeatedly state that they do not differentiate between ripping apart men, women or children, regardless of their pleas for mercy. Worse, whatever humanity exists inside these beasts, they seem to have utterly no awareness that the humans they prey upon are related to themselves. The notion that sickle feet could crossbreed with regular humans has only been reluctantly guessed at, likewise, speculation on where these beasts came from is also discussed cautiously.

Without a doubt, sickle feet are genetically engineered, as opposed to a purely randomly evolved mutant species. The reason for this claim is that several excavation teams reported that they encountered these monsters, in concentration both above and below ground near ancient bio-industry facilities. The fact that these ancient sites often had robotic and fixed relic defensive measures in operation, along with electric power, points to some intelligence behind the occurrence of these beasts. Sickle feet, in conclusion, seem to have their dens near these high tech ruin sites, and whether operating under their own volition or not, are highly territorial and attack with extraordinary zeal and fight to the death on home ground.

Who or what their creators are, is still a mystery, as so far, no dig team has been able to defeat the sickle feet and the automated and robotic defenses of their lair. New era communities sitting near these high tech, beast infested sites, are hesitant to delve too deeply into who created the monsters, nor move against the sites in force. Clearly, since the mysterious bioengineers have the ability and technology to create such hellish beasts, what else could they unleash if provoked?

A sickle foot has excellent morale and will stay in a fight at least until half their own number are defeated without inflicting equal casualty numbers among their targets. They seems to favor the flesh of humanoids over horses or oxen, as when attacking travelers, ignore these herbivores in favor of men and women. Riding dogs, on the other hand, are attacked equally as often as humanoids, but left uneaten on the field of battle. For their own part, riding dogs and all other carnivorous mounts, pets and guard beasts seem to have a special hatred of sickle feet, and go beyond their normal aggressive tendencies to try and go after these strange, leaping, swearing mutants.

Beastial humans can smell the distinct, putrid odor of a sickle foot from hundreds of meters away, if the wind is favorable, and can alert human comrades to the presence of the threat, negating the normal initiative bonus of the predators.

Sickle Foot Mutation List   Roll d20
23% of all Sickle Feet exhibit a mutation, determined from the following list:

1. Humanoid: This specimen is the product of a sickle foot and human crossbreeding experiment. The subject's face, while still hideous and toothy, protrudes less and has a more recognizable man or woman's face (appearance score 3d6). The beast-man also has a pair of rather regular looking human arms growing from its shoulders, and in battle, hangs back and fires a missile weapon (**roll d6: 1-3.** bow/**4,5.** longbow/ **6.** a pump shotgun with 2d4 shells loaded. This creature has an intelligence of 20+d20, can speak the local language well. Although a man eater, this freak will try to negotiate the surrender of the most tender travelers (women and children) and let the less appetizing (mutants, cyborgs, androids, beastial humans, etc.) go free, or it will speak to warn strong units of humanoids away from the sickle foot lair.

2. Screamer: This sickle foot shouts when within ten meters of prey, screaming so loud that those not wearing ear protection or a combat or better relic helmet, must make an agility based type A hazard check to cover their ears in time or be deafened for d20+20 minutes,

3. Extra sickle foot appendage, growing between regular pair, adding one extra attack.

4. Two extra sickle appendages, growing from back, adding two more sickle attacks per round.

5. Bone knobs cover this specimen, increasing its defense value by -10 (now DV -27).

6,7. Gland sacks grow along the sickle foot's back and rump. If the creature is struck, there is a 50% chance the impact ruptures one or more of these defense glands, which pop and ejaculate mist-like spore. Fellow sickle feet are immune to this fine spray, but other creatures caught within the 6 meter radius of the fine mist must make a type D perception based hazard check to spot the cloud and cover their mouth and nose with a sleeve or some other breathing protection. Those who inhale the spore suffer a dramatic affliction, known only after inhaling. Each person can experience a different result: **roll d6: 1.** Victim becomes nauseated and begins to vomit and heave uncontrollably for d10+10 minutes. In that time, he or she is -1 movement, -10 Strike Value and +20 Defense Value easier to be hit. The retching causes 2d6 stun damage to the victim, as well./ **2.** The spore has a narcotic effect, making the subject intoxicated and unmotivated. He or she must make a type E willpower based hazard check or stagger drunkenly away from the battle and seek a peaceful place to contemplate infinity. Duration 2d6 +20 minutes./ **3.** The spore causes hallucinations. The character happens to see the skin dripping off his or her comrades and self, like wax, exposing living muscles, organs and the skeletons beneath. The victim is allowed a type D intelligence based hazard check to shake it off and convince him or herself it is all an illusion. If so lucky, the subject can get beyond the visions to fight normally, otherwise, stranger visions overlap the first and make him or her temporarily hysterical. If made hysterical, the victim will run off in a random direction, screaming, for 3d6 minutes and very likely attract all manner of other predator./ **4.** Mating pheromones, which were not meant as a defensive measure, force the character to make a type C willpower based hazard check or become abnormally aroused. Of course the sickle feet hold no attraction for this amorous character, but those of the opposite sex of his or her own kind, do become an obsession for this unreasonably frisky person. As far as this individual is concerned, the appearance score of any nearby member of the opposite sex is double for the next d6 hours, plus, the victim of these pheromones will be distracted, and +5 easier to be struck in combat (thus a +5 penalty to his or her DV) and he or she will be -10 strike value when trying to engage others. These modifiers last until the hot and bothered victim has had his or her lust satisfied or else the d6 hour pheromone duration has passed./ **5.** Spore is casuistic and burns the subject's throat and lungs and inflicts d6 lethal and 2d6 stun damage on the subject./ **6.** Spore is actually a fungal growth and a symbiotic life form which thereafter resides in the inhaler. While having no obvious outward effects, the fungus growing inside the character protects its host from harm as best it can, improving the character's immunity against all diseases, toxins, venoms and other contaminants, but not including radiation, by allowing the PC two hazard checks from any of these threats. For example, if the PC is injected with a scorpion's poison, he or she gets two tries to make a successful hazard check from table TME-3-1, page 118 of the Hub Rules book.

8. Poison Bite: This sickle foot's saliva contains a numbing toxin. The victim of a successful strike must make a type C endurance based hazard check or succumb to a debilitating numbness in his or her limbs, making the subject half movement rate, half the strike value for any physical attack, and half the rate of attacks for the next 10+d10 minutes.

9. Wings: This specimen has a pair of massive, fur lined bat wings with a total span of 7 meters. The creature can take to the air and fly 15 meters per round, and while in the air, improves its defensive value by -23 (DV now -40). It makes passing dive attacks using only its two rear claw feet to rake over the heads and backs of its intended prey.

10. Throwing Spines: This sickle foot's entire back, shoulders and rump are covered with rows of 30cm long dagger-like yellow spines. During combat, it will hang back 9 or more meters and whirl about to shoot d6 spines per round, with all the spines in one burst directed at one target, determined randomly. Spines: max range 18m, rate d6, Strike Value (SV): 01-50, Damage d10 each. This specimen has 60 throwing spines available to it per day. Once exhausting is supply of ammo, it will rush in to join any close quarters fighting.

11. Giant Mouthed: This freak has an extra-large, elongated mouth. Any successful bite from this maw will inflict double damage (2d12+12).

12. Armor Plated: Armadillo DNA has clearly been injected into this specimen. Although slower (moves -3 meters per round, thus 6m), this deviant's Defense Value is increased by 23 points (now -40).

13. Telekinetic: This sickle foot has developed potent telekinetic powers, with which is has perfected a hunting technique involving the hurling of stones and other heavy debris. Each round, it can throw one fist sized stone or chunk of rubble at a random enemy target, SV 01-70, damage d12, range, 24 meters. This creature will try to hang back behind cover, overlooking a hunt, and hurl objects from the safety of rubble and tree trunks, gaining -20 DV (now DV -37).

14. Electrical Charge: This specimen goes into a fight only after spending two rounds charging itself up. It crackles and sparks with energy as it moves and if in dark conditions, is visible by its aura of surging power. Anything to hit it or be hit by it in melee has a 70% chance of receiving a powerful jolt of electricity inflicting d20 lethal and d100 stun damage. This unique mutation can only be used once per hour by this sickle foot, and once the charged is delivered, to one victim, it is spent.

15. Two Headed: This sickle foot swears twice as much and is allowed a second bite attack per round.

16. Harpoon Tongue: This mutant can shoot its tongue out 9 meters and impale victims. Often used on birds, rabbits and other small prey, which the sickle foot can then drag back to its hungry mouth, this creature will also employ this appendage on humanoids. If struck, a person is tugged toward the waiting sickle foot at a rate of 1 meter per round and if brought to the thing's mouth, will be hacked and chewed upon by the beast at +20 SV per attack. Of course, a heavier target (more kilograms weight than the sickle foot) cannot be pulled. The victim can hack the tongue off (tongue DV -5, Endurance 6). The tongue attacks at SV 01-80, damage d12 and has a 9m range.

17. Robust Build: This sickle foot is much bulkier than the rest and has an additional 2d20+20 endurance.

18. Mind Crusher: As the mutation mind crush, number 55, page TME-70. Summery: range Willpower x3: 129 meters/ rate 3 times per day/ damage d20 END and d6 Intelligence/ victim allowed type B intelligence based hazard check to avoid harm.

19. Cybernetically Enhanced: While not mutated, this specimen is clearly unique. Somebody somewhere modified this sickle foot to be a cyborg variant. It boasts areas of partial alloy plating (DV improved by -23 (now DV -40), sports solar collectors on its back, and is fitted with a laser pistol on the left side of its head where its eye once was. It can shoot its onboard weapon 20 times per day, range 500m/ SV 01-83/ damage d20+10.

20. Freakish Horror! This specimen features one additional mutation from this table, and is also massive, having and extra 100 endurance, moves 3m faster per round, and each bite or sickle claw attack does d20+6 damage instead of the normal d12+6 damage.

CREATURES OF THE APOCALYPSE: 2
Red Harvester
By William McAusland

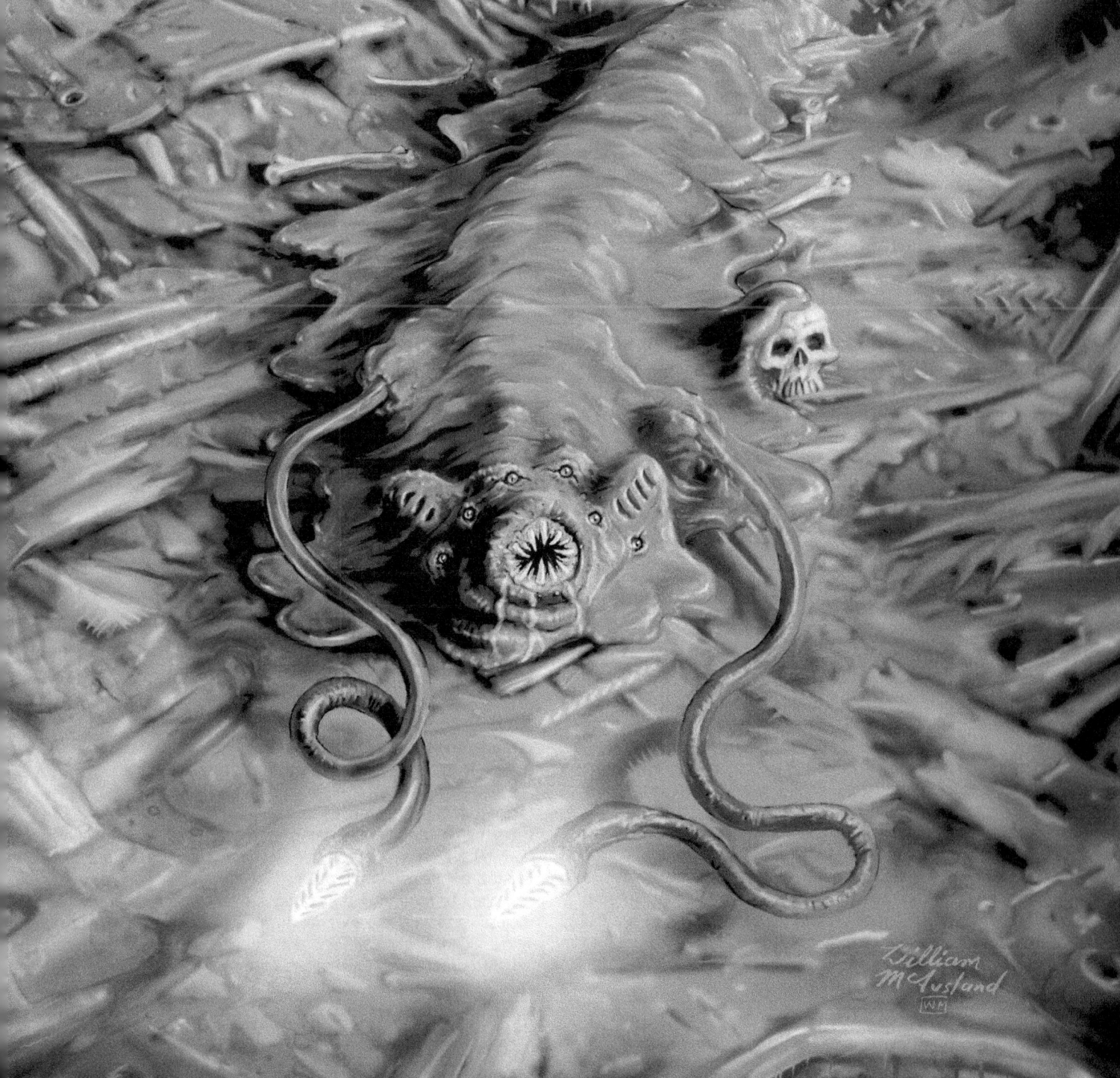

Red Harvester

Defense Value: **-0 (tentacle -30)**

Endurance: **70+d100 (tentacle 26)**

Movement: **5m**

Initiative: **+3 camouflaged or -3 once engaged**

Attacks: **3: Bite and 2 Energy Blade tentacles**

Strike Value: **01-80**

Damage: **Bite d8+8+ Digestive Enzyme/ Energy Blades d6+6+ Neurological Affliction**

Strength: 72

Agility: 16

Accuracy: 44

Intelligence: 6

Willpower: 72

Perception: 81

Valuables: nil

Experience Factors: 120

Morale: Excellent

Size: 2m +1cm per point of END in length

Weight: 200+1kg per point of endurance

Mutations: 17% chance of 1 (See Red Harvester mutation list, page 13)

Relics: nil

Implants: nil

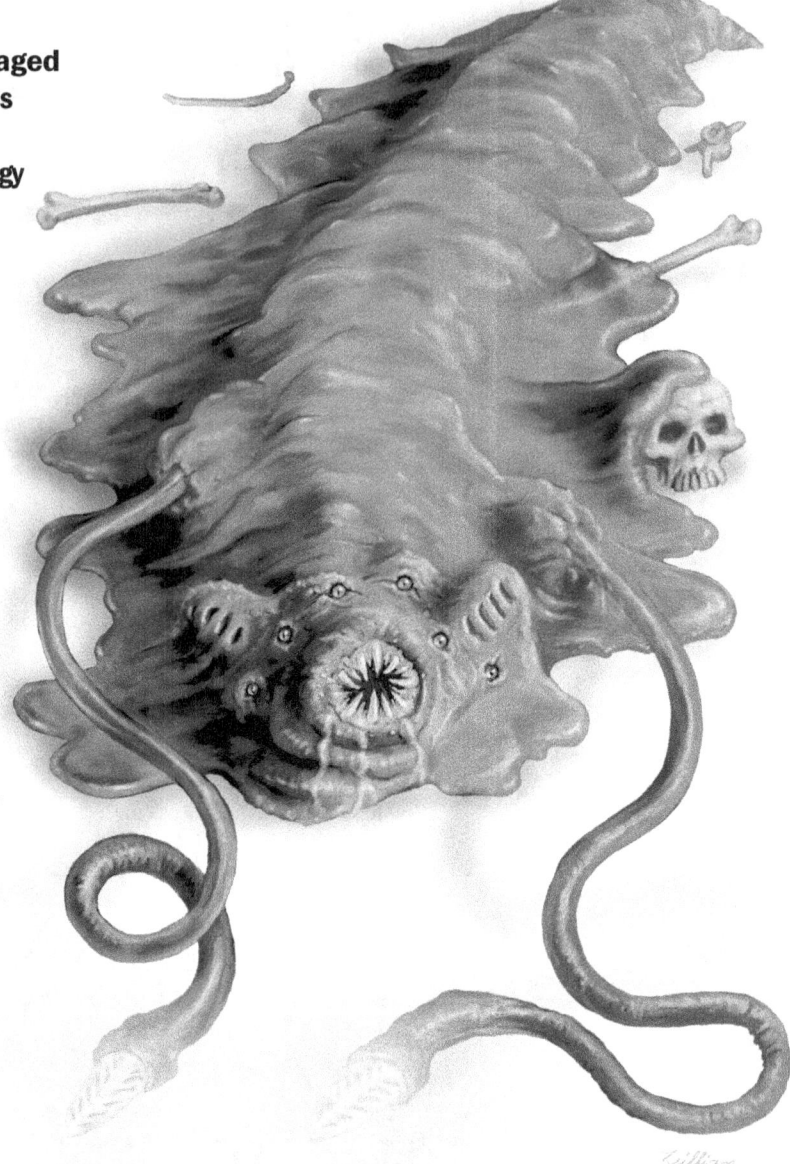

The red harvester is so named for its ability to appear from seemingly nowhere and reap a bounty of flesh.

This odd, hideous worm-like creature inhabits dense terrain areas were it can conceal itself from the sun and larger creatures, but so too, ambush passing prey. Although called a red harvester, its natural coloration is whatever surrounds it, as it has chameleon like powers and can go entirely undetected into the vegetation and junk.

When hungry or its territory is intruded upon, this ferocious, slithering monster becomes a brilliant red color, its eyes gleam brilliant blue, and two or more long, slick purple tentacles erupt from its sides and extend toward its next potential meal. At the tips of these disgusting, oily tentacles are brilliant emerald colored, perforated bone wedges, which glow when the creature is excited and give off a neon green light, illuminating everything within a 9 meter radius of the beast.

Because it is slower than most other animals, including unarmored humanoids, the harvester relies on concealment and surprise to get close enough to targets to strike. Additionally, older, more experienced specimens have learned to employ dead end corridors, ravines and wooded hollows to allow prey creatures to pass by before it reveals itself, cornering its victims before advancing on them.

Its bite can inflict a terrible wound, and the saliva from its yellow, ring-like mouth expels digestive enzymes. These enzymes begin to break down flesh after a successful bite attack is made; the victim suffering two points of endurance loss, due to tissue degeneration, for d6 rounds, per bite inflicted.

The red harvester's truly unique and most dangerous attack mode is, of course, its tentacles. These purple, snake-like tubes can extend up to 9 meters out of the harvester's bloated body. The gleaming green tips of these appendages are used to stab and slash at creatures. Adversaries of the harvester can elect to try and use a bladed weapon to hack off the tentacles, especially the gleaming green tips, which are defense value -30 and can take 26 endurance damage before being severed and thereafter useless to the creature. Although dangerous and lethally sharp, the energy blades also discharge some sort of shocking, neurological disruption charge. Anyone hit by one of the green blades must make a willpower based, type D hazard check or suffer a random affliction from the following list. The same victim can experience multiple afflictions, however, re-roll duplicated results.

Red Harvester Energy Blade Afflictions List   Roll d100

01-04. Insanity: The victim immediately begins to suffer a random insanity from page 126 of The Mutant Epoch Hub Rules (if using a different game system than TME, see hallucination, roll 71-75, this table). The insanity commences at once and will remain in effect each day thereafter, with the subject allowed a daily type E willpower based hazard check to shake the affliction.

05-09. Heart Attack: The shock of the attack put too much strain on the character's heart, and he or she suffers a heart attack which inflicts 10+d20 damage on the victim, plus, the subject must make a type D endurance based hazard check or succumb to the attack and drop dead on the spot. Note: If a medical robot or relic field medical kit is used on the fallen victim within 1 minute (20 rounds) then the subject can be revived and made stable. Also, if a character doesn't have an organic heart (such as some plantoids, robotic or android characters or cyborg's with mechanical hearts, then the shock of this attack is limited to the damage only (d20+10).

10-14. Mental Attack: The subject suffers d20 willpower and intelligence damage to each trait, which heal at the PC's normal healing rate. If reduced to zero or less in either trait, the PCs is considered unconscious and in a coma until healing.

15-19. Radiation: The red harvester expels a burst of radiation into the victim's wound. This dosage is cumulative with any previous radiation exposures and should be noted on the character sheet. Radiation Intensity received: roll 2d6: 2,3. Mild Exposure/ 4-7. d3 Mild Exposures/ 8-11. Medium Exposure/ 12. Strong Exposure. Consult page 125 of the TME hub rules to review any results.

20-24. Electric Shock: The victim is given a powerful jolt, tossed back d6+1 meters, taking d20 lethal damage and 2d20 more points of stun damage.

25-29. Trait Drain: Similar to an electric shock, this character is hammered with a mysterious charge of energy and thrown back d6 meters. He or she is permanently drained of one point from each trait.

30-33. Paralysis: The character's muscles spasm and lock up. He or she must make an agility based, type E hazard check or fall over and remain motionless like a manikin, unable to do anything physically except watch and listen in horror as the red harvester either comes to feed on him or her, or engage the paralyzed subject's comrades. If attacking the immobilized subject, the red harvester will only use its mouth attack making +40 SV strikes at the fallen, hapless morsel. Fortunately, this paralysis will only last for 2d6 rounds.

32-35. Rash: Immediately after being struck by the energy blade, the afflicted area of the subject, even if armor was worn, puffs up into a terrible, itching, pussy rash. The bleeding, sticky and agonizing rash will remain for 3d6 days and in that time the character is always at a 10% diminished endurance trait value, even if otherwise totally unharmed and healed up. For example, if the subject normally has 36 endurance, he or she is depleted by 3.6 endurance for the duration of the rash, and thus at only 32 points now (36 -10% = 32.4, rounded down to get 32 END)

36-38. Deafness: The character's hearing simply ceases to work. The duration of this affliction is 2d6 days. Exposure to any sonic attacks in this time, however, have no affect on the character.

39-41. Blindness: The character's vision fades to black for d6 days. See the blindness on page 122 of the TME hub rules, but to summarize, the PC is at a -50% penalty to strike values, and is +40 SV easier to be attacked by enemies.

42-46. Limb Frozen: A random limb simply stops working and hangs limp. If a character's main weapon arm goes limp, he or she can switch to the off hand and take a -20 SV. If a leg goes limp, and the character is a biped, the PC is reduced to half movement, while a quadruped is reduced by 25% speed. This limb freeze lasts 2d100 minutes before feeling comes back, painfully. Limb frozen, roll d4: 1. Right Arm/ 2. Left Arm/ 3. Left Leg/ 4. Right Leg.

45-48. Speech Impediment: The character's mouth and tongue feel weird, as if the tongue has tripled in size and his or her lips gone loose and lopsided. For 3d6 days the characters drools and spits when talking and the sound coming from the person is nonsensical gibberish. Those listening require a type D intelligence based hazard check to accurately understand the subject when he or she speaks.

49-52. Bleeding Pores: Almost instantly, the subject's skin becomes covered by red dots as blood leeches to the surface, mingles with sweat and then runs freely. Although serious looking, and giving off the scent of blood which is compelling to scavengers and predators alike, the bloody character's endurance is only reduced 10% by this weird injury. The affliction remains for 2d8 days.

53-56. Loss of Continence: The shock of the energy blade afflicts the character in a most embarrassing way. Without warning, the character's guts churn and heave painfully as he or she has an uncalculated bowl movement, and simultaneously urinates. This bizarre, gross, and alarming affliction may make the character lose temporary focus on the fight with the harvester, and must make a type C willpower based hazard check to pay attention fully to the fight. Failure to pay attention means that for d6 rounds the PCs is unable to use mental mutations. Even worse, the soiled victim is -20 SV (strike value), while any attacker, such as the red harvester, finds it +20 SV easier to hit the incontinent subject. The victim suffers no long term physical effects from this attack, although his or her pride might be stained.

57-60. Numbness: All at once, the character has near total loss of feeling and control of his or her toes, fingers, tongue and any other smallish body parts. Unless using enormous force of will, the character will drop anything it is holding in its hands or other appendages. Objects include things like machetes, guns, bows, grenades, ropes, and shields. Each round of the affliction, a successful type C, willpower based hazard check must be made to allow the subject to clench onto whatever he or she was holding, and continue to use the object or hold onto a ladder rung, rope or the reins of an animal mount, etc. The affliction lasts only 3d6 rounds.

61-65. Hair Loss: The shock is painful and knocks the wind out of a living creature, however, if surviving the fight, the character begins to notice his or her hair or fur coming out in patches when touched. Within 4d6 hours, the subject loses all his or her hair completely, including body hair, fur, manes, or a full pelt. It will take a month before hair begins to grow back.

66-70. Personality Alteration: If the game master is an SOE member (Society of Excavators member, free with ownership of the TME hub rules) he or she can download the d1000, 273 personality matrix found at http://www.outlandarts.com/member-sonly/TME-SOE-personality-matrix.htm . Use the 'Random' personality column to determine which new personality this character has adopted, which replaces previous personalities for 20+d20 days before the old, familiar nature of the character gradually returns. Without access to the personality table, a GM can roll d10 here for a quick new personality, which manifests at once: **d10: 1.** Blood-thirsty/ **2.** Catty/ **3.** Docile/ **4.** Fearless/ **5.** Immature/ **6.** Lawless/ **7.** Nagging/ **8.** Prankster/ **9.** Show-off/ **10.** Wimp.

71-75. Hallucination: The game master should not disclose that this is a mere hallucination, but rather something the afflicted character actually experiences. The vision can be relayed to the player of a hallucinating character by passing him or her a note, or taking the player aside and describing the scene. Of course, the following random selections are just a sample, and the actual setting and layout of the encounter area might require a different description. The all-convincing imagery remains for 10+d20 rounds and the GM may want to add more than one occurrence. Random hallucinations, **roll d10: 1.** Dead comrades, as well as long gone family friends and pets start to erupt from the ground and walls and stare back at the hallucinator, saying nothing./ **2.** Another red harvester is on the scene, range 3d6 meters and closing fast./ **3.** The area around the character is filling up with blood, raising 1cm per second!/ **4.** Bones, either already present on the surface, or else buried in the ground, begin to burst up and assemble into animated skeletons and stomp toward the viewer in a threatening fashion, trying to strangle and grapple the character./ **5.** The character's skin begins to melt and peel off, dropping away and revealing bones beneath. Strangely, there is no pain involved in this quick rotting process./ **6.** Comrades, pack mates or other allies begin to turn into rotted corpses, complete with maggots encrusting their peeling skin. The stench is awful, and the decaying allies moan like plague victims./ **7.** The character's legs and arms erupt into flame! The pain is excruciating!/ **8.** The character sees his or her loved ones behind the red harvester, calling the hallucinator to come closer to them, pleading with outstretched arms, yet their voices muffled and their words inaudible./ **9.** The character happens to notice huge, 5 centimeter long, bright blue ants all over his or her body! Looking down, the PC see's that he or she stands on some sort of ant nest. Hundreds of the insects bite and sting the character. After the duration of the hallucination, the ants fall away and disappear into the ground. / **10.** An angelic being, made of gold, white feathers and light, smiles back at the PC from just the other side of the red harvester. It calls the character's name, promising him or her all the bliss of heaven, to stop fighting and come home to God. The harvester seems to disappear as the glow of the divine, loving radiance sweeps forward and caresses the character. The illusion fades if the character is struck again, or, after the duration has passed.

76-79. Hear Sounds and Voices: The wounded person notices no other immediate affliction and may fight on or flee as desired. A minute after, though, he or she then hears something unexpected. Audible hallucinations continue for 3d6 minutes, **roll d6: 1.** In the distance, the character discerns the sound of trumpets and the voices of shouting men approaching./ **2.** From someplace unseen, behind the red harvester the

character can plainly hear a baby crying, then the sobbing of a woman!/ **3.** The character's parents are heard telling him or her just what a failure he or she has become, how disappointed they are with the PC's career choice, companions and mates. They scold the character so relentlessly that he or she is put at a serious disadvantage in a fight, being -10 strike value to attack others, while being sloppy in his or her defense and +10 SV easier to hit./ **4.** Somebody, most likely a fellow character, is shouting "Flee! Retreat! Run for your lives!" If the character is alone, then it is from somebody nearby, but out of sight, possibly a parent or former officer./ **5.** As if things weren't bad enough! Somebody is shooting at the character and his or her comrades! Every round, the sound of a gunshot goes off and the din of an occasional ricochet as bullets come inbound at the PC's position. The character can't see a shooter or actual bullet impacts. / **6.** The red harvester taunts the character, even using his or her name. The thing seems to be speaking as its circular, sphincter-like mouth spits out foul threats, cuss words and promises to make the character suffer the worse, slowest death imaginable.

80-83. Amnesia: The character seems to notice nothing during the fight with the red harvester, but after, can't seem to recall the names of comrades, where they were going, where they came from, the mission at hand, or even loved ones and family members back home... wherever home is. He or she does know that comrades currently on scene are allies and not to be harmed, but anybody else is now a stranger. This condition lasts d12 days.

84-87. Agony: For 3d6 rounds, every joint, muscle, organ and ounce of tissue on the character throbs and aches painfully. It is as if the PC's body is held in a vice and then being twisted and scratched. Only by sheer force of will (type D, willpower based hazard check) can the PC stop from dropping to the ground and writhing in pain, screaming at the top of his or her lungs and generally being useless in a fight. If a dropped character is actively being attacked, he or she is at a disadvantage, being -20 SV to strike others, and +20 easier to be hit.

88-91. Nausea: The character ain't feeling so well, and a round after being afflicted begins to wretch painfully, possibly filling up a closed helmet and drowning him or herself if unable to get the visor open or remove the helmet. So violent is the puking session that unless a type D willpower based hazard check is made, the PC will have to drop to his or her knees and dry heave, being +30 SV easier to strike, and -20 SV to strike at others. This affliction lasts 3d6 rounds.

92-95. Crushing Headache: From the moment of impact onward, the character's head throbs in agony as a inescapable, all-over migraine assails the victim. While horrendous, the only real consequence is that this character cannot use any mental mutations should he or she possess them. This headache lasts for 2d6 days.

96-00. Delayed Side Effect: A day after the engagement with the red harvester, this victim experiences an assortment of side effects. Each day, for 4d6 days, with duplicated results allowed, **roll 2d6** to determine that day's side effect: **2.** For just a second, the character sees a parent standing a few meters away before he or she fades away in a puff of green smoke./ **3.** The character swears he or she sees another red harvester creeping closer, but well away in the distance, and disappearing behind cover. / **4.** Terrible nightmares disturb the character's sleep, making him or her wake repeatedly in the night and exhausted and agitated by day./ **5.** When with others, the character occasionally thinks he or she hears somebody say something insulting to him or her. If only surrounded by comrades, then a random fellow character is the one who made the slur, otherwise a stranger./ **6.** The character has a spider in his or her shirt and can feel it crawling up his or her back and going around the front! If exposed, there is nothing found. / **7.** Constipated./ **8.** Back door trots (diarrhea)./ **9.** Pounding headache all day, inability to use mental mutations/ **10.** Terrible gut aches and inability to hike more than a kilometer, and then at half speed. Lasts all day./ **11.** Can't keep food down all day. Feels nauseous./ **12.** Character passes a strange, elongated bright purple 'cone'. If the cone is investigated, cut open or otherwise studied, an undeveloped, pale white harvester is discovered inside. The embryo is harmless, and dies once the egg is opened. If allowed to hatch, it does so in 10+d20 days and out emerges a 15cm long red harvester, which while harmless to humans, will commence to eat small insects, reptiles and rodents. It will grow into an adult within 2+d4 years, depending on food supplies, but can never be tamed.

Red harvesters are normally found alone, and seem to be intolerant to others of their kind. The exception to this is during the fall when they gather to spawn and move as a pack to exploit new food supplies, lay eggs, and claim new territories for their kind. They lay eggs in both living and dead flesh, which grow to adulthood in about 4 years. Also see result 12 of Delayed Side Effect on the Red Harvester Energy Blade Afflictions list, above, for a disgusting example of how these creatures can replicate.

Although a worm, the red harvester is very much like a pit slime in some respects. It is able to squeeze through holes much smaller than its bulky form would normally permit, with a 30cm opening all that is needed for this beast to wriggle in after prey. Although able to fit in such small openings, including most ventilation ducts, its tentacles cannot deploy unless it has at least a meter in diameter to occupy; however, it can still bite those it overtakes.

Because of its chameleon-like powers, the red harvester can remain hidden with ease, and if full, might not even wake when excavators or other food animals pass by its location. If hungry, and it initially wins the initiative roll, consider the harvester to be met at point blank range, such as right alongside the character group, or even amid the party as they step over what they initially thought was a mound of rubble or rotten log. Once engaged, a harvester will become brilliant red, and thereafter lack any initiative bonus and suffer -3 initiative.

While these creatures are little more than mindless eating machines, and have no use for treasure or relics, they do tend to drag away the corpses of humanoids, especially ruin explorers, and stash the cadavers in dark, subterranean lairs. These body dumps, which stink terribly, are rich deposits of salvageable loot and the occasional wondrous item of old. Found in such lairs are 3d6+6 humanoid skeletons, along with the remains of dozens of other animals as well as 3d100 silver coins, 2d20 gold coins, d6 suits of scrap relic armor, d6 rolls on the Possessions Carried Classification A ('Adventurer', from page 208 of the TME hub rules) and d6 random, low rank relics (from table TME-8-1, page 210 of The Mutant Epoch hub rules).

Red Harvester Mutation List   Roll d10

17% of all Red Harvesters exhibit a mutation, determined from the following list:

1. Additional d2 energy blade tipped tentacles.
2. Mouth and eyes at both ends of the beast, making it able to make a second bite attack if surrounded, or forced to pursue creatures who get passed it and into a very narrow passage of 30cm or more in diameter.
3. Glue-Backed: This specimen oozes a glue like substance all over its back, which over time has allowed rocks, rubble, scrap metal, bones and other hard objects to adhere to it and give it even better camouflage (now +5 initial initiative) but also extra armor protection of -30 DV.
4. Covered in Thorns: Similar to the thorns on a rose bush, this specimen is covered in black bony ridges that are razor sharp and strong as iron. The animal gains -10 defense value, and if bit by another creature, the biter is considered attacked at strike value 01-70 for d8 damage.
5. Poisonous Flesh: If successfully bit, the biter receives a gush of toxic blood back into its mouth and must make a type A, endurance based hazard check, or pass out after d6 rounds and die 2d6 rounds thereafter. Administration of an anti-toxin injector will be 84% likely to save the victim's life.
6. Spring Jumper: This oddly shaped red harvester has several lateral, stubby appendages which with it can spring off the ground once every fourth round, travelling 9 meters horizontally to either es-

cape, or go up and over prey to corner them. It can also spring directly up, such as when trying to leap a wall or project itself into a second story window. Its vertical jump distance is 6 meters high. If landing on a target, the subject is considered attacked at SV 01-80 and suffers 3d20 stun damage. However, a clever target might extend a spear, sword or other pointed object to try and impale the oncoming harvester, with any successful strike on the beast having a 33% chance puncturing the red harvester's brain stem and instantly killing it.
7. Shooting Spines: When not deployed, these mismatched, grey, 30cm long spines lay flat along the animal's back and look like grass or old wires. When the harvester is on the attack, however, it will hang back from initially going into melee to fire d8 spines each round, all at one random target within range. Each spine has a strike value of 01-50 and inflicts d10 damage on a hit. The red harvester can fire a total of 60 such spines per day with a range of 24 meters.
8. Sword Tailed: This especially long red harvester has a meter long, serrated bone blade at its tail. It can arch its rear over its main body and, much like a scorpion's stinger, use it to hack and stab at targets. The sword has the same SV as the thing's bite (01-80), but does d20+8 damage on a strike.
9. Big Fella: This red harvester is bulkier than normal, having an extra 50 endurance and its bite inflicting d12+12 damage on a successful bite.
10. Huge Harvester: This monster has 100+d100 extra endurance points, moves +3m per round faster, an extra pair of energy blade tentacles, and its bite does d20+20 damage on a strike.

CREATURES OF THE APOCALYPSE: 3
Spikeback

By William McAusland

Spikeback

Defense Value: **-30** (enraged -0)

Endurance: **80+2d20**

Movement: **8m**

Initiative: **+3**

Attacks: **3 on separate targets (bite and 2 claws)/ or 1 combined maul for 1 attack**

Strike Value: **3 separate attacks 01-70/ or 1 combined maul attack 01-95** (or enraged maul 01-110)

Damage: **Bite and claws d10+8 each/ Maul 2d20+16** (or enraged maul 3d20+16)

Strength: 74 (+8)

Agility: 88

Accuracy: 78

Intelligence: 11

Willpower: 69

Perception: 108

Valuables: nil

Experience Factors: 95

Morale: Excellent

Size: 2.4m tall

Weight: 100+1kg per point of endurance

Mutations: 15% chance of 1 (See Spikeback mutation list, page 17)

Relics: nil

Implants: Rare

Spikebacks are large, hunched animal-like humanoids of low intelligence and wicked disposition. When standing fully erect they are well over two meters tall, although they prefer to scuttle about on all fours like a chimp or bear. They are so named for a series of black, lethally sharp bone spikes growing from their backs, with some specimens bearing meter long protrusions. While impressive looking and remarkably effective in dissuading larger beasts from feeding on them, these vaguely human monsters do not employ their spikes when hunting. Should a large predator try to bite a spikeback, or anybody leap upon one of these mutants, the deviant's horns will automatically serve as a counter attack on the attacker at strike value 01-80 and inflict 2d20 damage. This counter attack is made on the aggressor's turn and merely a passive protective measure on the spikeback's part.

These creatures are thought to be genetically engineered combat beasts which have changed little since their creation centuries before. The common belief is that they live as long as an average human, grow to adulthood in about 6 years, have a gender division of about 55 percent male to 20 percent female, with another 25 percent being either sexless, hermaphrodites, or of rotating, seasonal gender. While having human DNA, they don't see fellow humanoids as anything other than food. Their diet is entirely carnivorous, and even when well fed, spikebacks are known to kill and mutilate other living things for mere sport.

These creatures exhibit a camouflage skin pattern and coloration that is best suited to their surroundings, yet if migrating to a new terrain type, switching pigmentation after six months. They come in woodland green and brown camo when found in forests and swamps, mottled tan and gray in desert and scrub areas, or mingled grays, rust brown and concrete dust white when encountered in the ruins. This camouflage allows them to remain concealed when either hunting or evading larger predators. On account of their ability to hide and remain out of sight until desired, they are prone to ambush tactics, and if winning the initiative (+3), are considered to have been spotted too late and met in melee range, with one or more spikebacks leaping from concealment within three meters range.

When attacking, these monsters use a series of two frontal claw slashes and one bite, either directing their attacks on three separate adversaries if the prey animals are in a group, or instead, combining all their attacks into one furious maul against foes larger than themselves, or when multiple targets are not closely packed.

The spikeback is known to have an incredibly bad temper. If struck by a single, identifiable opponent and the hit does 10 or more damage to the spikeback, then the beast will go berserk and direct subsequent attacks as maul attacks solely on the person who struck it until killing it or being killed. These enraged maul attacks are enhanced and delivered with extra aim (+15 SV to total SV 01-110) and additional strength and inflicts an extra d20 damage (new total maul damage while enraged is 3d20+16). However, while enraged, it completely throws caution to the wind and neglects to dodge, sidestep or wheel about while focused on the subject of its rage, and is reduced to DV -0 instead of -30. Even those using missile weapons are able to take advantage of the spikeback's inattention, and fire on the thing as if it were unmoving and unarmored.

Once the beast's victim is killed or unreachable, it will shake off its blind rage and either flee the scene, or engage another target.

Although its claws and bite are terrible in themselves, the bite of a spikeback often coats the victim's wound with a rare, terrible disease. Anyone bit by and survives the encounter is potentially infected by 'meat-rot', a sort of necrotizing fasciitis or flesh eating disease, around the afflicted wound. Each successful bite on an organic limb is 8% likely to result in the rot. This rot will begin to appear 12 hours after the initial bite, and turn the afflicted area into a pus weeping, purple, throbbing sore. Not only does the wound ache pitifully, but becomes swollen and extremely painful to the touch. Worse, twenty four hours after the meat-rot appears, the tissues surrounding the injury begin to corrupt, turn black and decay. The subject suffers 3 points of damage per day, per wound, plus, permanently loses 1 point each of endurance, strength and appearance per rotting wound, per day.

The mutation of heal touch can be applied to this wound, and will repair the damage and hold off further rot, if the mutation is used each day. Unfortunately, heal touch will not cure the ailment, which will commence to eat the subject once the daily use of the mutation is not applied. Deviants exhibiting the mutations of body regeneration, limb regeneration and disease immunity (immunity mutation, roll 3,4) are immune to meat-rot.

Relic medical devices, such as an anti-toxin injector, field medical kit or treatments from a medi-bot, are the best bet for a cure, but the outcomes of their use depend on the sort of patient treated. As most relics were designed for pure stock human physiology, the odds of a medical relic being able to cure a person of meat-rot varies. The table, shown at the bottom of this page, presents the percentage chance of a successful cure based on the patient's species. If the treatment is unsuccessful, the meat rot will continue until either another attempt can be made, with one attempt allowable per day, or the victim is consumed the meat rot illness.

Spikebacks hunt either alone or in small packs of up to twelve members. While highly territorial toward other animals and humanoids, they are strangely tolerant to other, unfamiliar spikebacks, and will overlap their territories and even exchange pack mates when two groups temporarily merge together.

Another aspect of these ferocious beasts, which is both bizarre and troubling, are the rumors of them serving as attack-patrol monsters for mysterious, high tech enclaves. Specimens have been found fitted with cybernetic control collars, eye pieces, headcams and brain augmentation and control-chip insertion, as well as submachine guns and assorted mutational enhancements. Just who might be using these grizzly sized mutants as guardians, and to what extent they direct the beasts, is yet unknown.

Beyond their meat-rot contaminated mouths, multiple or single maul attacks and defensive spikes, 15% of these creatures can also appear on the scene boasting a mutation or other cybernetic implant. The table on the following page offers a random list of potential add-ons, however, the GM can easily pre-create unique spikebacks with implants by using table TME-1-62, page TME-84, using creatures set 1, or add a mutation or two from table TME-1-58, page TME-59 of the Hub Rules.

Meat-Rot Cure Table

Percentage chance treatment or dosage cures subject, one attempt per day

Life Form	Anti-Toxin Injector	Cure Tab*	Medi-Bot	Field Medical Kit
Human, pure stock	95%	97%	96%	99%
Human, clone	91%	93%	95%	97%
Human, trans-human	94%	96%	95%	98%
Human, bioreplicant	90%	93%	94%	95%
Human, ghost mutant	82%	89%	88%	90%
Human, mutant, mild	78%	84%	81%	85%
Human, mutant, typical	74%	81%	79%	83%
Human, mutant, severe	62%	67%	65%	76%
Human, mutant, freakish	35%	41%	52%	69%
Bestial human, chimp	48%	59%	56%	73%
Bestial human, mammal	32%	39%	44%	61%
Bestial human, bird or reptile	26%	35%	41%	59%
Bestial human, spider or scorpion	13%	18%	32%	41%
Bestial human, cockroach, mantis	14%	20%	36%	45%
Humanoid, skullock, etc.	59%	64%	61%	72%
Animal, mammal	29%	36%	41%	58%
Animal, bird or reptile	24%	31%	37%	56%
Animal, insect	11%	13%	16%	26%

Spikeback Mutations and Unique Features Table Roll d100

01-12. Cybernetic implant: Video camera and transmitter fitted onto side of spikeback's head. Who or what is viewing what the creature sees and hears, is not immediately known. By Killing this spikeback, the characters might anger unseen, and powerful controllers such as a Mecha robotic cell, holdover bunker dwelling corporate sleepers, or worse.

13-22. Cybernetic implant: subcutaneous alloy plating. This specimen is slow and moves only 5 meters per round, but it is sheathed in relic body plating and has a defense value bonus of -30 (now -60 total).

23-29. Cybernetic implant: Somebody, or something, has fitted this specimen with a **shoulder mounted submachine gun turret.** The weapon will be empty 36% of the time, otherwise loaded with 10+2d20 rounds of belt fed standard pistol ammo. This freak will hang back and use a built-in optic enhancement to target and shoot apart its adversaries. If dispatched, looters can salvage any remaining ammo as well as the parts to assemble a handheld submachine gun. Anybody with the gunsmith skill, or, has the junk crafting or mechanical technician skill of 3 points or higher, can do this modification in the field with minimal tools within d3 hours.

30-41. Spike thrower: This beast has five rows of meter long, thin black spines on its back instead of the usual large, fixed spikes. With these, the specimen can whirl about and using muscle contraction, shoot one spike per round, with up to 6+d6 such spikes available to it per day. These organic javelins have a range of 24 meters, a strike value of 01-70, and inflict d20 damage each.

42-47. Elongated neck: This bizarre mutant has a neck that is three meters long, and like a giraffe, can thrust it about with remarkable ease and allow it to peer around corners, over walls, into small openings and generally stretch out and bite at things it wouldn't normally reach. This specimen has an improved initiative of +2 (now +5).

48-54. Multi-headed: This spikeback's chest sprouts d3 extra heads. Each head will add one more bite attack, complete with the extra potential of infecting a victim with meat-rot (8% chance per wound inflicted). When adding these bites to its maul attack, simply make extra bite attacks as normal in conjunction with the maul. Due to its many heads, it is very alert, hard to surprise and gains +1 initiative (now +4)

55-61. Winged: Growing from this mutant's shoulders are massive, leathery bat wings. While half speed when moving about in cramped hallways and other narrow spaces, this spikeback can fly at a rate of 15 meters per round, plus, in melee, adds two buffeting, club like attacks that do stun damage (SV 01-70 each, damage d12+8 stun each).

62-68. Poisonous bite: Any bite attack or successful maul attack allows this spikeback to inject a dose of paralysis venom into its prey. Those failing a type C endurance based hazard check will collapse and lose all physical abilities. The subject will of course feel everything normally, including being eaten alive, yet, if able could employ any mental mutations. The duration of the paralysis is 10+d20 minutes.

69-76. Hulking brute: This specimen is over-muscled, hunched, and stands a meter taller than regular spikebacks. Due to its impressive size, it has an extra 50+d100 endurance, and a strength score of 115 (+18 damage). If making multiple attacks, add 10 (for a total of d10+18 each) to the damage of each strike, while add 15 to the maul attack damage (now 2d20+21).

77-86. Ballistic skin: Genetically engineered to have ballistic cloth-like skin, this spikeback is hard to puncture with bullets, thus having a DV -20 extra against gunfire (total -50 DV vs. bullets).

87-92. Screaming summoner: Having a much deeper chest, sagging, sac-like neck and wide mouth, this freak can call upon others of its kind. If entering a fight against challenging prey or intruders, this spikeback will spend a round hanging back from melee and instead puff itself up to three times its normal girth. If not shot or otherwise struck, it will spend the next turn screaming out a deafening, deep howl. This summons can be heard for many kilometers, and is 78% likely to bring 2d6 other spikebacks to the vicinity within 4d6 minutes. If victorious characters have defeated the summoner and other spikebacks with it, any reinforcement beasts will easily pick of the scent of the humans and commence to hunt them down, going as far as 20 kilometers from their lair before calling off a chase.

As an attack mode, the screamer can direct its mouth toward oncoming attackers or prey and blast them with a sonic attack. Those not protected by some sort of sonic screen or other defenses, are assaulted and must make an agility based type C hazard check to leap aside or suffer d10 minutes deafness plus d20 stun damage.

This screaming summoner can unleash 6 bellows per hour, range 15 meters

93-00. Brain: Having a massive, almond shaped skull, this odd looking spikeback will hang back when encountering intruders and use a series of mental attacks to weaken or distract enemies. Other spikebacks that might be with this deviant will busy themselves in normal melee attacks. For every turn the brain spikeback gets, roll d6 to see what random mental mutation it unleashes on a random target. It cannot, however, use a mutational power if engaged in melee range combat. Consider the brain spikeback to have 30 intelligence and 90 willpower. The mutations can be found in The Mutant Epoch hub rules book: roll d6

1. Coma Inducement, *page 63*
2. Electrical Pulse, *page 65*
3,4. Mind Crush, *page 70*
5. Stun Ray, *page 74*
6. Telekinesis, *page 75*

CREATURES OF THE APOCALYPSE: 4
Junk-Mobster
By William McAusland

Junk-Mobster

Aka: Mob-Mutant, Rubble-Gangsta, Junker

Defense Value: **-10**

Endurance: **120+d100 body/ 20+d20 per head** (d3+1 heads)

Movement: **9m**

Initiative: **+1**

Attacks*: **club and net or 4 claws plus 1 random mental attack per round**

Strike Value: **01-80**

Damage: **club d20+8 stun/net** see description **/claw d12+8 each**

Strength: 74 (+8 DMG)

Agility: 34

Accuracy: 52

Intelligence: 5+d12 per head

Perception: 42 (+1)

Willpower: 76

Appearance: 2d4

Valuables: Most carry only d4 rolls on the Junk-Mobster loot table, however 1 in 6 are heavily laden with loot and carry 3d6 items from the included table on page 4

Experience Factors: 270

Morale: Firm

Size: 2.2m tall and 3m across

Weight: 400kg +1 kg per point of starting endurance

Mutations: Each turn during combat, including melee range fights, a Junk-Mobster will unleash one random mental mutation per round at a random opponent. This freak has unlimited use of these mutations. See random mental mutation table, page 22, this document.

Relics: If it carries any relic valuables that it can employ, such as guns and grenades, it will use them in combat, otherwise none.

Cybernetics: 9% chance of d3 from set 2, table TME-1-62, page 84 of the The Mutant Epoch hub rules book.

It is advisable that the GM pre-determine what items of loot each Junk-Mobster carries before unleashing this mutant monster on characters. Many of the items can be used as weapons, or add excellent gaming detail to the encounter.

Junk-mobsters are nomadic, multi-headed, multi-limbed flesh eating mutants. They get their odd name from their many heads which form a gibbering mob atop their hideous, misshapen bodies. These heads, of which there are usually between two and four, shout, swear, spit, mumble and laugh together like an insane crowd, keeping itself company as it haunts the junk mounds and rubble heaps near ancient cities. They are also called mob-mutants, junkers, and rubble-gangstas.

Normally solitary, these fearsome creatures are known to periodically gather into gangs. Once grouped, they mate, trade slaves, share meat animals, and barter with assorted relics and looted treasures. On some rare occasions, when eight or more get together, they will sally forth to make a raid on a particularity promising humanoid lair, caravan, farm or village. These assaults are designed to either rid them of a troublesome enemy, or merely to find mating slaves, flesh and booty.

Clearly having human DNA in them, as evidenced by their man-like arms, feet and many heads, they do not see themselves as human, nor show empathy, pity or mercy to related beings. In spite of their outward inhumanity, they are reliant on humankind for their continued existence. They are incapable of mating with each other directly and instead reproduce with humans of the opposite sex, with the offspring of the union always being a small, globular junk-mobster which takes 6 years to reach adulthood. Once the mating slave concludes its part in the act, either by giving birth after a 3 month gestation or fertilizing the beast, the prisoner is either traded to another Junker or eaten.

The main purpose for their standard club and net attack mode is to capture a potential mate of the opposite sex, and will use these tools to direct both the net and bludgeon at the object of their desire. 7 in 10 rubble-gangstas are male, the rest being either female, or of these, 20% are hermaphrodites exhibiting both male and female heads and sexual organs. Hermaphrodites will try to capture both a good looking male and female whenever possible, and, being more prolific breeders, produce a greater number of young than single sex variants.

When attacking humans, then, the mob-mutant will direct non-lethal attacks on the most attractive target person of the opposite sex, and employ its claws and lethal attack modes on everybody else. Even while engaged in melee combat, the mob-mutant can unleash one mental mutation per round, with the mutation being randomly determined, and the target also randomly selected each turn. The exception to this is the mutations of *coma inducement* and *stun ray*, which it will always direct on a member of the opposite sex that it has not yet knocked out with its club or ensnared in its lead-weighted net. These random mutations are shown on the table on page 22 of this document.

The **net attack** of a junk-mobster is used by sweeping it around a likely target, up to 9 meters away, with a strike meaning the lead balls fling around the back of the person and wrap into the net openings on the other side. Once a hit occurs, the victim is allowed an agility based type C hazard check to leap, summersault or hop clear of the net before it is pulled tight. If the person is successful, the net can not be redeployed for two turns. If the target is unsuccessful, the net is yanked tight. An ensnared person must make another type C agility based hazard check each round to stay on his or her feet, otherwise he or she is pulled over and dragged to the monster's side, where the victim is pummeled by the Junker's club at +30 SV. If able to stay upright, a snared person can still fight, but at a strike value reduction of -20 and is unable to move or use the dodge skill. The mob-mutant's club will also be used normally against an ensnared but upright target, gaining a +10 strike value (SV) bonus.

If the rubble-gangsta is successful in knocking out a likely mate early on in the fight, and another potential reproductive partner is within sight, the beast will be 88% likely to go after the person, too, instead of attempting to merely kill and dismember him or her.

During a fight, and forced to deal with undesirable humanoids, the junk-mobster will unleash both a mental mutation per round plus all four of its claw tipped arms, aiming to slash, crush and mutilate victims. If able, it will employ one claw-arm against separate opponents while in melee range. The beast's arms can reach 6m away, and can easily pluck defenders off walls or second story windows of buildings.

When assaulting large groups of humanoids, particularly skullocks for which these horrid beasts have a particular hunger, junk-mobsters will collect up to a half dozen of their dead targets and wrap them in their nets and carry them off to their most recent lair to feed. Mating captives will be bound by gut-string or relic cables to the underside of their captor and also transported to the mob-mutant's lair for 'courting'.

Rubble-gangstas are able to talk to each other, as well as among their many heads, but so too, to their reproductive or work slaves. Likewise, they enjoy tormenting human prey during a fight, especially if they've treed a person or forced a humanoid down a hole where they can't reach it. They speak the common area language, although often in confusing, wordy sentences, with one head interrupting the others.

Of low intelligence, with each head having a different trait value, junk-mobsters are just smart enough to use most relic weapons, but aren't witty enough to employ traps, build structures, or utilize wealth to bribe or recruit other intelligent species as mercenaries. Thus far, no specimen has been encountered which could read or do even rudimentary math and so they see no value in books, high-tech devices, ancient facilities, robotics, nor even gold or silver, which they haphazardly discard along with most everything   else from the corpses of their victims.

Junk-mobsters seem to dislike all other life forms and only on the rarest occasions employ slaves to do work for them excavating a new lair or performing some other tedious or dangerous tasks. Additionally, they are almost never seen serving more powerful beings, yet, the instances of them being killed and found to be exhibiting cybernetic implants attests to their being in the service of some high-tech group. Whether their masters are machines or men, is as yet unknown. In addition, their original method of creation has not yet been proven. Like so many beasts in the Mutant Epoch era, where they came from is of less concern than where they will strike next, or how to rid the countryside of their presence.

Many communities, both stationary and nomadic, which are forced to contend with these evil, disgusting and nightmarish beasts, will offer sizable rewards for the killing of mob-mutants, sometimes paying as much as 1000 silver coins per specimen slain. Mercenaries and bounty hunters alike are keen to organize hunts for these beasts when the reward is generous, sometimes hiring excavation teams as extra muscle, but at other times kidnapping attractive youths to use as bait to lure amorous junk-mobsters into open ground where snipers can deliver killing shots on individual mob-mutant heads.

Those in the know have long since realized that killing a junk-mobster in a close quarter fight is no easy task. Instead, a team needs to get the things out in the open and, from a safe height, rain down well placed (called-shots) on the separate heads of the lumbering mutants. Each head has a separate endurance score of 20+d20, and if all its heads are killed, the beast is blinded and deaf, and unable to locate prey beyond the normal melee range. Without any active heads, the monster will flee, usually after smashing into trees, ancient structures and rusted automobiles several times before getting away from sniper fire. New heads will emerge from a headless specimen after a month. These new heads are said to be the faces of past victims which the aberration has eaten, having inserted the heads into its bloated body as spares. This gruesome speculation implies that the heads already present on a junk-mobster are past victims, and that it might be possible to see the faces of long lost loved ones and comrades peering back at a person when encountering these hellish creatures.

When a game master introduces one or more junk-mobsters on the scene, he or she might want to pre-roll what loot each specimen carries since some of the many possible items will either add to the encounter's look and feel, or else be a weapon that the mob-mutant will employ against its adversaries. Each will have d4 rolls on the junk-mobster loot table, while 1 in 6 are extra laden with loot and carry 3d6 rolls.

Junk-Mobster Random Mutation List   Roll d100

01-12. Beam Eyes (TME pg. 61): Range 118m/ SV 01-65/ damage 10+d6

13-21. Blurred Movement (TME pg. 62): For the next d6+1 rounds, this creature gains an extra -20 to its defense value (DV), thus -30. If this mental mutation occurs again while already in effect, simply add an extra d6+1 rounds to the duration.

22-27. Coma Inducement (TME pg. 63): Range 76 meters/ see table on page 63 of the hub rules for his mutation, with the subject allowed a type B willpower based hazard check to avoid a coma.

28-41. Earth Thump (TME pg. 64): Range 76m/ SV 01-101/ Afflicts up to 3 man sized beings if in a group/ DMG 3d10

42-53. Electrical Pulse (TME pg. 65): Range 76m/ SV 01-96/ DMG d20 to organic beings or 3d20 to mechanical beings including cyborgs.

54-62. Light Burst (TME pg. 69): All beings in a 10 meter radius, including other Junk-Mobsters or creatures allied to them, must make a type C agility based hazard check or become partially blinded for 2d6 rounds. Within those rounds, the victim is +20 easier to be struck and itself penalized -20 SV to make outgoing attacks.

63-80. Mind Crush (TME pg. 70): Range 228m/ Target must make type B INT (intelligence) based hazard check or suffer d20 endurance damage and d6 Intelligence damage.

81-86. Radioactive Pulse (TME pg. 72): Range 76m/ SV 01-90/ DMG d20 plus mild radiation contamination, and forced to make a type B hazard check using the target's current endurance value, or suffer medium radiation instead!

87-00. Stun Ray (TME pg. 74): Range 152m/ SV 01-90/ DMG 2d20 stun or 4d20 to machines including cyborgs. This specific stun damage fades after an hour.

NOTE: TME pg.72 or pg.74 etc. Means the page number in The Mutant Epoch (TME) hub rules book where more details on this mutation can be found.

Junk-Mobster Loot Table   Roll d100

01. Magazine for assault rifle with 0 to 18 (d20-2) rifle rounds loaded
02. Baggy of 3d6 standard pistol rounds
03. Pair of black wrap around sunglasses, worth 50+d100sp
04. Mini grenade
05. Bottle of red wine, recent vintage
06. Fragmentation grenade
07. Baggy of d6 shotgun shells and one shotgun slug
08. Battle rocket, without launcher
09. Communicator, battery drained
10. Shotgun pistol in ornate leather holster, empty
11. Headset communicator
12. Bag of dried human hands
13. Sack of 4+d6 human, skullock and warmort skulls
14. Solar calculator, worth 100+d100sp
15. Relic extension cord, 5m long, worth 70+2d20sp
16. Solar powered personal hand held fan, worth 60+d100sp
17. Map of the Crossroads Region (or GM's own region)
18. Plastic pail of 12 like-new sidewalk chalks, worth 12+d20sp
19. Pocket-bot, battery drained
20. Thermometer, oral, worth 20+d20sp
21. English flag (white with red cross, Saint George, worth 100+d100sp
22. Spiderbot, battery drained
23. Lamp shade, worth 5+d10sp
24. Power cell, fully charged
25. Fake flowers, roses, dozen, worth 24+d20sp
26. Mini power cell
27. Paint brush, for house painting, worth 10+d12sp
28. Belt of standard rifle ammo, 20+d20 rounds
29. Glasses, prescription, worth 25+2d20sp
30. Pocket pistol, empty
31. Tattered but serviceable yellow 'Don't Tread on Me' Libertarian coiled snake flag of old, worth 100+d100sp
32. Baggy containing hundreds of humanoid teeth
33. Nylon delta kite with eagle printed on it, and 100m twine in plastic tube, worth 50+d100sp
34. Gasmask
35. Woman's hot pink thong underwear, worth 12+d12sp
36. Pump shotgun, empty
37. Ice cube tray, blue, worth 15+d20sp
38. Automatic pistol with d6 shots remaining in magazine, used by Junk-Mobster (SV 01-92/ rate 2/ range 250m/ DMG d20)
39. Nail file, worth 3+d6sp
40. Safety goggles,
41. Buckle, for belt, silver with gold details, motorcycle image, worth 140+d100sp
42. Red-scanner, battery drained
43. Pool cue, worth 20+d10sp, can be used as staff or club, or turned in to a javelin
44. Baggy of 3d10 .22 cal ammo rounds
45. Box of 2d6 unsharpened HB pencils, each worth 10+d12sp
46. Flashlight, large, half drained of power
47. Plastic handled box cutter, like new, worth 30+2d20sp, treat as knife in combat

48. 2d4 rolls of toilet paper in original packaging and like new, worth 5+d6sp each

49. Anti-toxin injector

50. Six inch tall super hero action figure, worth 30+d20sp

51. Napoleonic War figure set, plastic, hand painted, 12+3d6 figures, 20mm (1/72nd scale) tall, each worth 10+d10sp

52. Single round of .50 cal ammo

53. Pepper spray, full

54. Handcuffs, with 2 keys

55. Tear gas grenade

56. Filter mask

57. Riot shield

58. Landmine (The Junk-Mobster doesn't know what it is and uses it as an idol)

59. Leather belt pouch containing d6 pistol, 2d6 rifle, and 3d6 .22 rounds of ammo)

60. Pump shotgun with folding stock, sling and barrel flashlight (drained and empty of ammo)

61. Pair of alloy surgical scissors, worth 20+2d20sp

62. Green coffee shop apron with mermaid logo on it, worth 3d6+6sp

63. Leather pouch containing dried, strong smelling herb/ 50+d100 grams worth 10sp per gram if sold in a large trade town)

64. Leather wine skin containing curdled blood

65. Small plastic box containing 3d6 high calibre pistol rounds

66. Leather wineskin filled with vodka (d3 liters)

67. Nail clippers, relic worth 18+2d8sp

68. Tattered copy of the Purist Bible printed in Pure Hub City

69. Doubled headed eagle flag of the Dominion of Aberratia, red with black eagle insignia (see The Crossroads Region)

70. Map to a ruined site of the ancients, showing overland route on one side, and a more detailed, zoomed in version of the entrance to the dig site on the other.

71. Pair of binoculars

72. Magazine for a submachine gun, with 3d6 pistol rounds inside

73. Rifle scope

74. Baggy of human fingers, spiced in herbs, dried and crunchy

75. Rifle bipod

76. Submachine gun, magazine empty

77. Magazine for automatic pistol, containing 3d6 rounds ammo

78. Switchblade knife

79. Relic hockey mask (treat as sports helmet, which this beast will wear on one head for -3 DV improvement

80. Plastic wrapped box of 24 relic tampons, worth 4sp each

81. Gold wedding ring with sapphire and diamond arrangement. Worth 500+3d100sp

82. Plastic spray bottle, filled with a yellow liquid, bottle worth 3+d6sp

83. Plastic clipboard, worth 12+d20sp

84. Plastic High level security ID pass card. Can be used to swipe through active ancient doorways and try to open them. Worth 300+d100sp

85. Female patterned android, service industry model, tied to the back of Junk-Mobster's body. Unit survives by signing Christmas Carols to the beast and cooking its victims.

86. Track and field medal with blue ribbon. First place, worth 25+d20sp

87. Stainless steel travel mug, with lid, 500ml capacity, marked with green mermaid faction symbol, filled with human and animal eyes, dried and apparently a snack. Worth 20+d20sp

88. Plastic garbage bag filled with human feet, arms, legs and assorted choice organs. Fresh.

89. Bright red and purple fake Mohawk haircut with chin strap, worn by one of the beat's heads

90. Chainsaw with d100 rounds use of fuel remaining. Junk-Mobster will employ this instead of a club and net.

91. 10 liter drum of ethanol fuel. DV -10. If struck by a bullet, beam weapon or flammable projectile or mutation attack, the drum has a 90% chance of exploding in a 6m radius, forcing an attack on all those in the area of effect (SV 01-70/ DMG 3d6) but as it is strapped to the beast, will blow it apart doing an automatic 2d100 DMG.

92. Flame unit, lacking ethanol fuel.

93. Light laser cannon, but power pack is drained. Used as a tent pole when the Junk-Mobster camps at night.

94. 2d6 human and 3d6 skullock skins, dried and sewn together to forma tarp 6m across.

95. Cage strapped to the monster's back, made of aluminum, bones and wicker. Inside are d3 human children and d6 skullock children. Part of a mobile larder.

96. Partially buried in the rolls and skin of this specimen is a radio transmitter and flexible antenna. The device has been surgically implanted in the Junk-Mobster and is broadcasting its location to some unknown source. Worth 50+d100sp if removed and sold as a curiosity in a large town.

97. Large plastic drum filled with barely drinkable water, 3d6 liters remaining.

98. A rope is lashed to the back end of this specimen, and tied to it are 2d6 sheep, d6 goats, 2d6 pigs and 2d6 skullocks. All are in bad shape and have witnessed their fellows being devoured day after day. The skullocks will be so thankful to be rescued that they will serve as porters and guards to their liberators for 3d6 days, but will not enter human settlements nor approach caravans and the like.

99. Power pack with cables. Fully charged but otherwise not attached to anything.

00. Between the central heads of this Junk-Mobster is a cybernetic implant. There seems to be an eye, audio receiver, broadcasting module and antenna. Somebody or something has been observing this beast from an unknown location, and watching and listening to the characters. If dissected after being killed, the implant is discovered to have subcutaneous wires running to the brains of each head, suggesting that perhaps this monster was being controlled by unknown operators. The value of the implant, if sold in a large town, is 100+d100sp.

CREATURES OF THE APOCALYPSE: 5
Bog-Billy
By William McAusland

Bog-Billy

Aka : Nailbiter, Floor Devil
Caused by William McAusland

Defense Value: **-10**
Endurance: **30+2d20**
Movement: **4m**
Initiative: **+0**
Attacks: **2: 2 fingernails & 1 toxic bite**
Strike Value: **01-70**
Damage: **fingernail d12+6 or bite d6+2 and toxic saliva**
Strength: 63
Agility: 18
Accuracy: 67
Intelligence: 3+3d6
Willpower: 78
Perception: 31
Valuables: None Carried
Experience Factors: 45
Morale: Moderate
Size: 1.3m long, 1m wide but can squeeze through 30cm holes
Weight: Kilograms as starting Endurance value +20kg
Mutations: 18% chance of 1
Relics: Hoarded but rarely used unless a mutant specimen with human arms.
Implants: Usually none

Just who originally named these hideous, malicious humanoids 'bog-billies' is undocumented as the original discoverer was assumed to have been eaten while researching them. The common assumption by those who live near these creatures claim that they were supposed to be titled after hillbillies. Although known to inhabit swamps, especially the thickest parts and making their homes under the roots of great Bald Cypress trees and other swamp vegetation, they are also perfectly at home amid arid ruins, deep underground industrial complexes, the ventilation ducts of old malls, and even beneath new era human shantyburgs.

Bog-billies, sometimes called nailbiters or floor devils, like to hunt in-between layers of rubble, junk and crushed vehicle mounds. Their horizontal, low height habitat is perfect for over-taking, ambushing or cornering other animals and humanoids, which often crawl into such spaces looking for ancient loot on their hands and knees. Humanoids who move on their all fours are half speed and suffer a -20 SV penalty when using two handed weapons..

Nailbiters are cunning, cruel and calculating adversaries, and will sprinkle their hunting zones with items which will entice

tall folk to get down in the dirt and wriggle into the tight confines between fallen concrete slabs and other cramp spaces. Often bog-billies will scatter a few ammo rounds, a power cell, or some well preserved mundane item such as a magazine, security swipe card, coffee mug or article of clothing. Besides this main bait area, they will then litter a trail deep into an ambush point with increasingly more valuable items. Use the table on page 27 for a list of bait items found strewn about the mouth of a low ceiling opening, and then individual items spaced about 3 meters apart along the trail of 'crumbs'. The included map on page 29 can also be used to give an idea what a bog-billy lair might look like.

When attacking, bog-billies like to get in close and make a frenzied flurry of melee strikes, slashing with their enormous index fingernails, as well as biting at the prey with its saliva dripping mouth. While the dirty, yellowed nails of a bog-billy are nasty enough, and leave both a bloody wound and week long inflamed rash in those they hit, the bite of this mutant is much worse. The saliva of a floor devil contains an unsavory blend of neurotoxin, digestive enzymes and hallucinogenic agents. Anyone successfully bit must make three separate hazard checks (HC). The first, a type C strength based HC must be made to avoid the neurotoxin. The second, against the digestive enzyme, is a type B hazard check and made using the victim's current endurance score. The third hazard check, a type E using willpower, is made to attempt to avoid succumbing to hallucinations. The effects of each of these afflictions are described below.

The **neurotoxin** takes effect at once, and begins to shut down the victim's muscles causing a -5 drop in his or her strength score, per minute. Once the subject reaches zero or less strength, he or she collapses and is entirely paralyzed for 3d6 hours. If the bog-billies are able, they will make every attempt to track down the incapacitated morsel and eat it alive and conscious.

The **digestive enzymes** of the saliva begin to break down the tissues around the wound. See table TME-2-7 page 106 of the The Mutant Epoch (TME) hub rules for body location of the wound. The enzymes will turn the flesh around the injury into partially digested goo, causing 1 point of damage per hour for 3d6 hours. Worse, if this wound occurs on the subject's face or head, this trait deduction also applies as a permanent loss to the victim's appearance score. The application of the mutation 'heal touch', or administration of an anti-toxin injector (see Relics page 199, TME hub rules) will stop this enzyme.

Hallucinogenic agents injected into the victim's blood will commence to mess with the afflicted person's head within 3d6 minutes after taking the wound and failing the hazard check. The game master will be able to hint that something is wrong by describing things to the PC's player such as the character seeing or hearing noises that nobody else does. Hallucinations will occur once per hour for the next 3d6+6 hours. For a quick random suggestion, roll or pick from the following samples:

Suggested Hallucinations   Roll 2d6

2. The calls of birds, rodents, insects, along with the rustle of leaves or grass begin to sound like words. After a few minutes, the PC begins to hear whispered proclamations from one calling itself God. The voice orders the character to form a new religion and spread it to the infidels by converting new adherents by sermon or sword. The religion is to be named after the character, adding 'ism' after the PC's name.

3. Either in a crowd or among the rubble or foliage of the wilderness, the character looks up and for a second sees his childhood sweetheart standing there. The apparition steps from view, bidding the PC to follow.

4. Somebody in the distance shouts the character's name.

5. Companions and strangers around the PC suddenly begin to speak in an utterly incomprehensible language. This weird event ceases after a minute.

6. The nearest person to the PC is overheard saying he or she is going to murder another companion at the first chance.

7. One of the character's companions suddenly turns into a bog-billy and looks at the PC menacingly, laughing and mocking the afflicted character for a full minute before assuming his or her normal form.

8. If the character has a spouse or significant other, not currently with the characters, then that loved individual is heard calling for help from 100+d100m away. If the PC has no lover, then instead he or she hears comrades mumbling that they want to expel the PC from the party for being a coward and a know-it-all.

9. For the next hour, the sky, or interior lighting if occurring indoors, keeps changing color.

10. The character feels ants and worms under his or her clothing and armor, their wriggling, biting and burrowing is next to impossible to resist. The victim must make a type G willpower based hazard check or else stop whatever he or she is doing and strip down to rub the vermin off.

11. The character believes he or she is dying of thirst and can't seem to get enough water or other fluids. He or she will guzzle water rations or even drink from tainted, radioactive pools if not stopped. This mania lasts for 3d6+6 minutes.

12. The character is convinced that his or her skin is melting off in a puddle on the ground, and forming into a new bog-billy! Only by great self control can he or she disbelieve the feelings and vision, and must make a type J willpower based hazard check... otherwise run away screaming at the top of his or her lungs. This illusion lasts 3d6 minutes.

Bog-billies are frequently exposed to mutagenic agents, radioactive hot spots, and a myriad of other deviation causing compounds. Those that survive to adulthood, at age 12, are those that were not born with severe life shortening flaws. Of these, there is an 18% chance that each boasts at least one random mutation from the Bog-Billy Mutation list starting on page 28.

Bog-Billies do not see fellow humanoids as distant kin, but merely as a source of food and cruel sport. They hunt alone or in groups, but nearly always share a lair with others of their kind with packs numbering as many as thirty individuals. While some have human arms as a mutation, most do not, nor do they have any use for relics except as bait to lure skullocks, warmorts and human excavation teams into traps. Although dim witted by human comparisons, they are clever enough to know not to leave out bait relics that are favored by humanoids as weapons, therefore, items such as grenades, blades, bows, crossbows, and firearms are either buried in the rear of their lair, crushed or thrown down deep pits. They do not see the leaving out of ammo as a bad idea, assuming interlopers who tote guns will already have ammo, and if anything, see the presence of unattended cartridges as an irresistible lure for their next meal.

About the only creatures bog-billies will associate with, are Man-Slugs*, however, some tribes will also form alliances with nearby clans of moaners, and even work alongside them to entice humans into ambushes and together, attack them in unison.

Bog-billies speak the local area language, but in such deep, wet voices that their words are hardly discernible. They do not value gold or silver, and when not on the hunt or torturing captives, seem to be preoccupied with sleeping in a trance-like state which they can maintain for up to three weeks at a time, conserving calories and remaining hidden from predators and prey alike.

Most new era communities have a policy of eradicating floor devils and even offer a 250sp reward for each one dragged into town, dead or alive. Because bog-billies tend to stick to one area, they do not provoke the same hatred as do skullocks or other humanoids, as they aren't known to attack a human settlement on mass or ally themselves with powerful overlords and threaten whole regions. Still, they are much feared by excavators, who, in the narrow crawl spaces beneath a toppled skyscraper, are at a distinct disadvantage when on their all fours and coming face to face with one of these ugly, vicious killers.

*Society of Excavator (SOE) Members can download the Free PDF of The Man-Slug, as well as dozens of others. SOE membership free with purchase of the TME hub rules.

Bait Items Scattered by Bog-Billies
d4+1 items at cave mouth and another item each 3m up to the ambush point. Re-roll duplicated results, except for ammo.

01,02. Baggy of 2d4 standard pistol rounds
03,04. Golden wedding band, men's, worth 150+d100sp
05.06. .22 caliber round of ammo
07,08. 15cm tall toy robotic Tyrannosaurus Rex. Uses a pill battery to run for 30 hours. Can walk, roar, detect obstacles and follow simple voice commands. Battery drained, worth 200+d100sp
09,10. Standard pistol round
11,12. Owl tea pot, ceramic, clean and like new. Worth 70+d20sp
13,14. Standard rifle round
15,16. Small stack of silver coins of recent minting. 3d12+10 coins
17,18. Shotgun shell
19,20. Empty 30 round magazine for an assault rifle
21,22. Shotgun slug
23,24. Stapler, with 2d100 staples loaded, worth 70+d100sp
25,26. Toilet cleaning brush, bright purple, worth 10+d10sp
27,28. Pair of pink and white cartoonish cat earmuffs. Worth 40+2d20 sp
29,30. High calibre rifle round
31,32. Anti-toxin injector (see relics on page 199 of the TME hub rules).
33,34. High calibre pistol round
35,36. Safety goggles
37,38. .50 cal round
39,40. House painting brush, in plastic sleeve worth 6+d12sp

41,42. Toy Samurai sword, 150cm long, hollow plastic, cheaply made, worth 8+d12sp
43,44. Lingerie, deep red one piece nighty, sealed in original plastic and worth 90+d100sp
45,46. Mini power cell, drained
47,48. Mini power cell, with d40% charge remaining (d4 x10%)
49,50. Power cell with d60 % charge remaining (d6 x 10%)
51,52. Ballpoint pen, blue, half full of ink
53,54. HB pencil, 20+d60% (20%+d6X10%) remaining length
55,56. Porno magazine, tattered worth 80+d100sp if sold in large town.
57,58. Filter mask
59,60. Combat helmet, with old human skull still inside
61,62. Communicator, standard handheld, power drained but in good shape
63,64. Calculator, solar, yellow and black, worth 200+d100sp
65,66. Stainless steel coffee mug with plastic lid, worth 50+d20sp Starstruck Coffee logo on side.
67,68. Baggy of 25 plastic straws, never opened, worth 1sp per straw
69,70. Bright orange roadside pylon, makes for a stylish hat, worth 20+d20sp
71,72. Plastic milk jug, filled with sour wine, jug worth 10+d12sp
73,74. Land mine, in plastic seal and like new
75,76. Plastic model kit containing 24 Napoleonic, 28mm French line infantry, still in shrink wrap, on sprues and perfectly preserved. Worth 100+d100sp in large town where curiosity collectors frequent relic markets.
77,78. 20cm tall plastic fashion goddess idol, with moving head, arms and legs, blond hair and in prom dress, worth 100+d100sp
79,80. Blue apron with Starstruck Coffee logo on front. Stained but remarkably well preserved for something just laying exposed where it is.
81,82. Head of a gorgeous woman, laying on its side. When PCs approach, she opens her eyes and calls to the PCs in a strange language. GM note: Any PC who happens to speak Japanese will understand that she is saying. "Masters, stop! This is a trap! Go back the way you came! Dangerous sub-human cannibals have placed me, and other merchandise, in your path to lead you close to them! Run away masters! Save yourselves!"
83,84. Bottle of unopened red wine. The label shows it is from a winery of the nearest large farm town, the date readable as 3d6 months ago.
85,86. Head lamp flashlight, battery drained.
87,88. Ceramic piggy bank with 3d6 dollars (Pounds, Euros or other currency from that world location) in old world coins inside. Piggy worth 3d6+20sp, coins worth a silver each as curiosities
89,90. Swipe access card, for nearby ancient underground facility.
91,92. Scary Halloween latex mask, very realistic and nasty, from horror movie and in excellent condition and worth 90+d100sp
93,94. Pair of nylon tube socks in original plastic bag, worth 15+d20sp

95,96. Contemporary leather coin pouch made in nearby village, previous owner's initials sewn in, containing 3d6 silver coins.

97,98. Hand made child's doll of recent crafting. If PCs are from nearby village, they might know the identity of the doll's owner, who went missing several months ago.

99,00. Random cybernetic implant From table TME-1-62, page 84, freshly torn from some poor cyborg. Blood and muscle stuck to the hook ups and nerve nodes.

Bog-Billy Mutation List   Roll d100

18% will exhibit a mutation determined from the following list:

01-05. A third long nailed arm grows beside one of the others, adding an extra melee attack. The extra arm also assists the bog-billy to crawl, adding +1m movement per round.

06-09. Two extra long nailed slashing arms grow along with the others, adding +2 meters movement and two extra claw attacks per round.

10-16. A pair of frail, skinny human arms grow along the bog-billy's side, one each behind the clawed limbs. Although weak and useless in melee, this specimen can use tools in these arms, including relic weapons. This nailbiter uses a random weapon with a base strike value of 01-50.
Relic roll d6: 1. .22 caliber auto pistol with 2d6 rounds (rnds) left in magazine./ **2.** Pocket pistol with d6 rounds remaining,/ **3.** Shotgun pistol with d2 shot shells loaded and another d6 in a pouch./ **4,5.** Automatic pistol with 3d6 rounds in mag./ **6.** Stun pistol with 3d6 shots left in power cell.

17-23. Two headed, can make an additional bite attack per round.

24-30. Mind mangle: Similar to the mutation mind crush, this power has a range of 90 meters and forces the target to make an intelligence based type D hazard check or suffer a piercing headache as well as 3d6 endurance damage and 2d6 intelligence damage. Once the victim is mentally harmed, he or she continues to take d6 endurance and d2 intelligence damage automatically, so long as the attacking bog-billy does nothing but focus on the target, and its hold is not broken by itself being struck physically or mentally. This mutation can be used 10 times per day by this creature.

31-34. Regeneration: Any depleted traits heal at 1 point per round.

35-41. Mimicry: When ready to ambush approaching prey, this bog-billy will cry out in a voice or animal sound to attract the desired target species. Normally this mutant needs to first get a look at the approaching quarry before selecting the most promising cry. For example, when trying to call in coyotes, it will make the chirps of marmots or prairie dogs, while to fool human males, it selects the pleaful cries of a young woman in distress. Other mimic sounds include a baby crying, the whinny of a distressed horse, a kitten's meow, or laughter of a playing child. The range of this call is about 200 meters and the specific bog-billy must have heard the sound it mimics at least once in its life.

42-45. Attraction odor: A gland in this bog-billy's abdomen can disgorge an aroma into the surrounding vicinity which in mammals will often illicit an illusionary olfactory stimulation. In short, when exposed to the scent, the subject smells his or her favorite food. Many mammals, such as dogs, cats and deer have narrowly escaped this trick in the past and now detect the overpowering stench of the waiting bog-billy as well as the mouth watering food smell, and thus avoid the ruse, but newcomers to nailbiter turf are rarely so vigilant.

Each character exposed to the odor must make an intelligence based type F hazard check or fall for the trick and honestly believe that their favorite dish is being prepared nearby. Those who don't believe the trick are aware that it is a ploy, and can try to hold back less skeptical comrades. Once falling for this fake scent, and surviving, a character will never fall for it again. The attraction odor travels on the wind and can drift as far away as a kilometer, drawing in the gullible and dim witted, often into a well prepared ambush involving a half dozen bog-billies.

46-53. Armor plated in articulating bone shell, moves -1, but DV improved by -20 (now -30).

54-57. Stinger tail, similar to a scorpion's tail, arching over the floor devil, but made of flesh and tipped with a black bone spike. This extra attack inflicts d12+5 damage but also attempts to inject coma inducing venom. Victim must make a type C Endurance based hazard check or drop into a coma for 3d6 days. The bog-billy will drag the inanimate victim to a deep larder, a place filled with other unconscious men and beasts, as well as heaps of skeletons and discarded personal items, including many abandoned and potent relics. The entire pack of bog-billies will dine from this larder after a few days of poor hunting.

58-62. Covered in a long fur pelt, this floor devil looks like it is wearing an ancient sniper's ghillie suit and identical in color to the grass of the bog-billy's local habitat. The thing, if remaining motionless, can go undetected by passing travelers, or attack from otherwise open ground. If it wins the initiative, which it now gets +2 at due to its pelt, and if not yet seen, it is considered to be right along the trail side and attacking at melee range. Besides keeping this mutant warm, the fur also offers protection increasing the thing's defence value by -5 DV.

63-66. Gills and flippers. This specimen can breath under water as well as swim 8m per round.

67-72. Reflective mind: There is a 77% chance that any mental attack against this deviant bounces off its mind. Of those assaults that are reflected, there is a 50% chance it returns to the instigator as if projected from that individual.

73-76. Ballistic hide: Against bullets, this bog-billy has an extra -20 DV bonus.

77-80. Junk sheathed: The skin of this mutant exudes a paste-like yellow goo, which over the years has managed to become thoroughly encrusted in junk, shredded clothing, bones, dust, pebbles and twigs. The end result is that the bog-billy is virtually indistinguishable from its natural ruin habitat. This freak is thus +3 initiative and if it chooses, can remain motionless and let more dangerous creatures pass it by. The secondary benefit of the junk coating is that it offers some armor protection and increases its DV by -10.

81-83. Suction cups: The entire underside of this floor devil is covered in suction cups like those on an octopuses' tentacles. When desired, it can crawl upside down along the ceilings of ruined structures, as well as up the sides of even the most slippery surfaces, including glass.

84-88. Big fella: This specimen is bigger and tougher than others, and +30 Endurance and inflicts an extra +3 damage to any physical attack it makes. It can't, however, fit into 30cm holes like normal variants, and is restricted to 50cm or larger passages.

89-93. Huge bog-billy: Easily twice the size of a regular floor devil, this one has +60 endurance, moves +1m per round, has a +20 strike value bonus and any physical attack it makes is an additional +5 damage. It is able to fit into 100cm or larger openings, and simply can't go where others of its kind can.

94-96. Spits glue: Once every round, for up to ten rounds per hour, this bog-billy can hork out a disgusting glob of phlegm. Range 12m, SV 01-80, however the armor of the target doesn't help the wearer from being struck, although, any modifiers caused by the target's agility, dodge skill, or use of cover do still apply.

Anyone hit will have one limb fused to his or her body and made useless. Roll d8 for the struck limb, with the same limb possibly hit more than once. Limb hit by glue **d8: 1,2.** Right arm/ **3,4.** Left arm/ **5,6.** Left leg/ **7,8.** Right Leg.

If one leg is glued, the target is reduced to half speed. If two legs are glued, the character can move only 1m per round by pulling him or herself along the ground. If one arm is glued, no two handed weapon use is possible and any attacks or items used by the glued arm are also fused the subject's body. If both arms are fused, then pending the existence of some other attack mode on the target's part, he or she is unable to counter attack against the bog-billy.

Characters with more than two arms or legs will have to have the GM's input on what setbacks the target experiences, and which limbs are hit. One coating of glue can be scraped off in 5 rounds. Thus, if an arm is hit by glue twice, it will take 10 rounds to clear off and make the arm useful again. A Type F strength based hazard check, per limb, can also be made to snap free of the glue on the target's first round, too, but for small creatures, this is a difficult thing to achieve.

The bog-billy's objective with the glue spit attack is to render the target immobile enough to tackle on its own, or make it easier for others of its kind to close in and make the kill.

97,98. A random prime mutation from either the TME hub rules or another source at the GMs discretion.

99,00. Roll two mutations from this table.

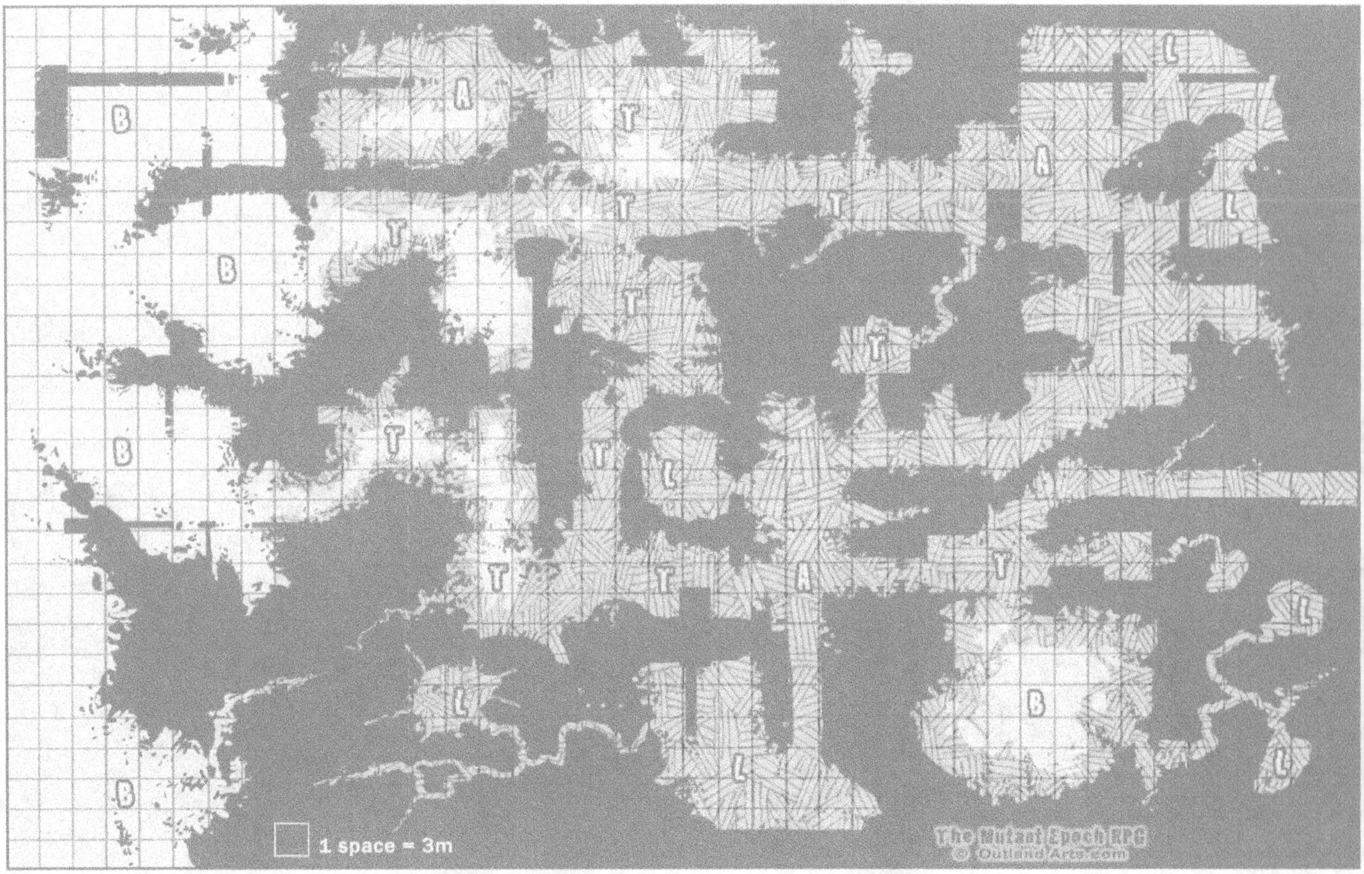

1 space = 3m

The Mutant Epoch RPG
© Outland Arts.com

Map Key

Open Air Areas	**B** Bait Zone, with d4+1 bait items
Buried Passage Areas	**A** Ambush Area, with d3 Bog-Billies in wait
	T Tunnel, with 1 bait item spread every 3m
Solid Concrete and Packed Rubble	**L** Larder, Relic Stash, & sleeping hole

Scraplurker

By Brandon Goeringer aka @SavageGM

Scraplurker	Juvenile	Adult	Brute
Defense Value	**-16** -2 (no debris)	**-38** -10 (no debris)	**-45** -18 (no debris)
Endurance	**10+d12**	**30+d20**	**60+3d20**
Movement	**4m** 5m (no debris)	**4m** 6m (no debris)	**3m** 6m (no debris)
Initiative	**+1**	**+2**	**+1**
Attacks	**bite**	**bite & 2 claws**	**bite & 2 claws or back slam**
Strike Value	**1-35**	**1-55**	**1-70 / 1-50 back slam**
Damage	**d10+2**	**d12+6**	**d20+12 / 3d20+10 back slam**
Strength	36	59	92
Agility	43	62	57
Accuracy	38	52	48
Intelligence	11	13	15
Willpower	28	36	53
Perception	52	66	74
Valuables	d3 items*	d4+1 items*	2d6 items*
Experience	24	40	80
Morale	fair	average	excellent
Size	1 meter tall	1.6 m tall	2.8m tall
Weight	64kg 52kg (no debris)	81kg 67kg (no debris)	302kg 198kg (no debris)
Mutations	11% / 1	14%/1	18%/d2

Items are rolled on the table on page 34 of this creature description. These are the valuable items stuck to the fleshy back of the specimen.

The dreaded scraplurker is a formidable foe of excavators and scavengers alike. This pink flesh colored aberration is vaguely human in appearance except for the bulbous putty-like skin that covers its entire body. The backside of this ruin dwelling monster appears to be hunchbacked due to a large mound of pliable flesh. It has, white shaggy hair, dark red globular eyes, a sharp toothed maw and retractable claws that serve as its main source of offensive weaponry.

An infant scraplurker, with only a thin layer of putty skin, will start to collect small rocks and pieces of metal only hours after birth. It begins applying these items into its skin which hold fast, quickly hardening into a thin outer protective shell that also aids in camouflaging the beast whilst it conceals itself in destroyed buildings. Only vicious when cornered, infant scraplurkers quickly run from intruders or other predators.

As the scraplurker becomes a juvenile, it turns more hostile, and exhibits longer claws and fangs, as well as its improved debris armor. During puberty the young horror molts away its putty-like exterior only to regrow even more putty as it gains in size. This increased skin allows for larger pieces of debris and scraps to fuse with its body. Its slowed down metabolism now allows it to stay completely motionless for long periods of time as it awaits prey to come within striking distance.

Having a shell of possibly worthwhile relics and other trinkets attached to its frame, its hide also serves as bait; a dangerous ruse for the foolhardy excavator or scavenger with an eye for shiny things. Once the curious prey is close enough, the scraplurker lunges forward attempting to shred the prey with its sharp claws and teeth.

A juvenile of this species will eat creatures of relative human size or smaller, and, as it is growing extraordinarily fast, is always ravenous from hunger and will attempt to immediately consume its defeated foe. Juvenile scraplurkers have 2 Stealth skill points and an 11% chance of a mutation from the table on page 33 of this creature listing. A defeated Juvenile will have d3 loot items fused to its back (see the scraplurker loot table on page 34, this document. They can be found hunting alone or in packs of 3d6 in number.

Once scraplurkers are of adult size, they will often join others of their kind in a mixture breeding den and killing zone. A typical ruined building with an infestation of scraplurkers will house anywhere from 7 to 16 (3d4+4) adults. They each spread out amongst the fallen structure, staying within 3 meters of one another, using their camouflaged backs of relics to enhance their stealth. This allows for gang sized take downs of numerous prey at one time or the chance to tackle larger meals that are too far big for a single scraplurker.

Though they only make hissing snarls as they attack they do appear to have a form of communication amongst themselves. Their large claws are tapped on concrete, brick or wooden flooring in a pattern that seems to mimic a crude form of Morse Code. Response tapping has been heard from survivors of scraplurker ambushes right before the attack, seemingly a signal that is one of the last things the poor souls hear before their own shrieks of horror. Adult scraplurkers have 3 Stealth skill points, a 14% chance of a mutation, and offer up d4+1 items from the loot table on page 34 of this document.

Rumors from many regions tell of larger brute scraplurkers. Supposedly, this strain of scraplurker have a genetic mutation that allows them to grow to huge sizes with increased strength and thick hides with massive amounts of debris attached to them. Tales of relic vehicles and ancient fire hydrants springing up on top of a mound of teeth and claws, slashing whole excavator groups to shreds are not too far fetched. Their huge size has made them slower on account of the amount of kilograms of debris these beastmen now collect, cladding them in an almost impenetrable husk of junk. This shell of rock, trees, metal bars, relics, pipes and other large scrap has also become a terrible weapon as the scraplurker has learned to slam its back and massive weight down on prey, squashing them onto a pile of rubble. Excavator bodies that meet this grisly fate are often kept in the debris to further lure potential meals.

Brutes can stay motionless for months at a time due to their remarkably slow metabolism. These enormous scraplurkers have 3 Stealth skill points, an 18% chance of having a mutation, and carry 2d6 items of interest fused to their backs.

The origins of these humanoids are unknown, although it is widely believed they were made as a bioengineered weapon to retake lost buildings and fortifications. During these ancient wars, scraplurker units would slowly sneak into these destroyed positions and help in the counter assault to reclaim the area by ambushing hostile combatants, lessening their numbers, and terrifying those who remained. Although clever hunters, they are dim witted otherwise and have no concept of trying to employ the relics they adhere to their backs.

Scraplurker Mutation List   Roll d20

1. Poison Bite: This scraplurker's saliva contains a numbing toxin. The victim of a successful strike must make a type C endurance based hazard check or succumb to a debilitating numbness in his or her limbs, making the subject half movement rate, half the strike value for any physical attack, and half the rate of attacks for the next 10+d6 minutes.

2. Increased Girth: This specimen has a larger frame than the rest and has an additional d20+10 endurance, plus an extra loot item stuck to is back.

3. Two-Heads: This aberration has an additional bite attack per round.

4. Mimicry: The vocal cords of this scraplurker have mutated to allow it to recreate the sounds of other prey it has fought against in previous attacks. The sounds of excavators yelling for help or screams of pain are expertly reproduced, luring nearby quarry closer to give aid or investigate. The range of this sound is 200 meters.

5. Long Legged: This freak has longer than normal legs and stays on all fours when walking or running adding +3 meters to movement.

6. Illuminated Tongue: This scraplurker has a light-bulb-like tongue tip that glows with the intensity of a flashlight. This enhanced mutant uses its tongue to lure prey by moving the tongue around to simulate scavengers or excavators. If severed, it will give off continuous light for 20+d20 minutes before fading.

7. Sticky Spit: The saliva of this scraplurker is extremely viscous and sticky. Instead of a normal attack, the mutant can hock a huge loogie at its foe with a SV 01-60 and a range of 12 meters. No damage is dealt but the movement of the struck enemy is reduced by -3 meters as the scraplurker will aim for the target's legs. To remove the spit takes 1d6+2 rounds.

8. Foul Glands: This specimen has smelly glands that it can express to cover a 10m wide diameter in a putrid funk. All inside this stench cloud must succeed at a type C Willpower based hazard check or be at -20 SV and -15 to DV. The cloud disperses in 2d6 rounds and can be expelled only once per day.

9. Reflective Mind: There is a 77% chance that any mental attack against this deviant bounces off its mind. Of those assaults that are reflected, there is a 50% chance it returns to the instigator as if projected from that individual.

10. Regeneration: Any depleted traits heal at 1 point per round.

11. Suction Cups: The entire underside of this scraplurker is covered in suction cups like those on an octopuses' tentacles. When desired, it can crawl upside down along the ceilings of ruined structures, as well as up the sides of even the most slippery surfaces, including glass.

12. Extra Arms. This specimen has d4 extra arms with which to claw opponents. For juvenile scraplurkers, add one extra bite attack for every pair of arms the creature has. This creature also has d3 skill points in climbing and will go up buildings or trees after fleeing prey.

13. Screamer: This scraplurker shouts when within ten meters of prey, screaming so loud that those not wearing ear protection or a combat or better relic helmet, must make an agility based type A hazard check to cover their ears in time or be deafened for d20+20 minutes.

14. Giant Mouthed: This freak has an extra-large, elongated mouth. Any successful bite from this maw will inflict double damage.

15. Telekinetic: This specimen has developed powerful telekinetic powers, with which it has perfected a hunting technique involving the hurling of stones and other heavy debris. Each round, it can throw one fist sized stone or chunk of rubble at a random enemy target, SV 01-70, damage d12, range, 24 meters. This creature will try to hang back behind cover, overlooking a hunt, and hurl objects from the safety of rubble and tree trunks, gaining -20 DV.

16. Jumper: this freak can leap once every 4th round to a height of 6m, or horizontally 12m, allowing it to either escape or pursue up a ledge or between ruined skyscrapers, etc.

17. Harpoon Tongue: This mutant can shoot its tongue out 9 meters and impale victims. Often used on birds, rabbits and other small prey, which the scraplurker can then drag back to its hungry mouth, this creature will happily employ this appendage on humanoids. If struck, the person is tugged toward the waiting scraplurker at a rate of 1 meter per round and if brought to the thing's mouth, will be hacked and chewed upon at +20 SV per attack. Of course, a heavier (more kilograms weight) target cannot be pulled, in addition, the victim can hack the tongue off (tongue DV -5, Endurance 6). The tongue attacks at SV 01-80, damage d12 and has a 9m range.

18. Extra Mutie: Roll twice on this list, re-roll duplicate rolls.

19. Prime Mutant: A random prime mutation from either the The Mutant Epoch RPG's hub rules on page TME 58, or another source at the GM's discretion.

20. Freakish Horror! This specimen features one additional mutation from this table, and is also massive, having an extra 100 endurance, moves 3m faster per round and does +12 more damage per bite or claw.

Scraplurker Loot Table   Roll d100

Although dozens, if not hundreds of bits of scrap, gravel, twigs, weeds, and unidentifiable junk adhere to the backs of each of these humanoids, several valuable or curious items can also be found. The GM can use the following random table, but, if the excavators defeat several of these beasts, other treasure table might need to be consulted to keep the variety fresh. **Roll d100**, but re-roll duplicated results or pick the result below a reoccurring number.

01. Landmine, that, when the scraplurker fell dead, has had its firing mechanism depressed. The individual looting this body is permitted a type A intelligence based hazard check to recognize that the landmine is even a threat, let alone respond to it. If failing to recognize the explosive, the device detonates (blast radius 3m, SV 01-90, damage d20+15). If the device is recognized, the character is allowed an agility based type C hazard check to leap aside, letting the beast's corpse drop back onto the relic before it explodes in a gruesome, yet harmless, gory fountain.

02. Golden pen, with plenty of blue ink, worth 60+d100sp

03. Skateboard, worth 70+2d20sp

04. Plastic baggy containing 3d6 standard pistol rounds

05. Anti toxin injector

06. Shotgun slug

07. Gold chain, ancient construction, worth 80+2d20sp

08. Baseball cap, LA Dodgers, faded but wearable, worth 40+d20sp

09. Clown idol of old, Golden Arches faith, plastic, 20cm tall, worth 40+d20sp

10. Mermaid insignia Coffee Cult green apron of the faithful, tattered, worth 10+d12sp

11. Iron manhole cover, 16kg in weight, curiosity and worth 10+d10sp

12. Pump shotgun, folding stock, pistol grip, sling and barrel light, yet empty.

13. Baggy of shotgun shells, 2d4

14. Deck of old world playing cards in stainless steel tin, image of nude woman on facing side of all cards. Worth 30+d20sp

15. Relic crossbow bolt with explosive arrow head, unarmed

16. Plastic ID card, military, maximum access to restricted area at a specific bunker, but location not denoted.

17. Stainless steel canister with lid. Contents are dried powder that smells like coffee. Worth 10+d10sp

18. Baggy of standard rifle rounds, 3d6

19. Poly-poster, 30cm wide by 60cm long, rolled in plastic shrink-wrap. Shows old world, classic movie star in scanty bathing suit. **Roll d6: 1.** Pamela Anderson circa 1992/ **2.** Arnold Swarzenegger, as Conan, circa 1982/ **3.** Marilyn Monroe, circa 1951 / **4.** Scarlett Johansson, circa 2014/ **5.** Bettie Page, circa 1953/ **6.** David Hasselhoff with the word 'Baywatch' written under his name. Any of these Posters worth 20+d20sp

20. Magazine for automatic pistol, containing d20 standard pistol rounds of ammo.

21. Cybernetic implant weapon arm attached to skeletal upper arm and part of a rib cage. See page 92 in the TME hub rules for a random weapon arm, plus whatever ammo it might come with.

22. Power cell, drained

23. Steering wheel from an ancient car, worth 6+d6sp as a curiosity

24. Bottle of locally brewed red wine from last year, worth 4+d8sp

25. Battle rockets, 1d2, operational

26. Baggy of dried ears, fingers, toes and other small body parts.

27. Saltshaker, crystal with silver top, worth 10+d20sp

28. Pocket flashlight with the battery half drained

29. Leather pouch and belt of recent construction. Pouch contains 3d6 silver and d6 gold coins.

30. Recently made rag doll, worth d4sp

31. Fragmentation grenade

32. Quiver of 3d6 arrows, recent manufacturing

33. Baggy of marijuana, 3d6+10 grams

34. Plastic ruler, 6" long, clear, worth 2+d6sp

35. Plastic folder, black, with 12 pockets inside. Filled with tattered, yellowed ancient tax receipts and related forms. Folder worth 6+d8sp

36. Plastic model dragon with moveable head, arms and tail, 9" tall, worth 60+d100sp

37. Plastic box with snap seal lid. Contains d6 standard pistol and d12 rifle rounds along with d4 shotgun shells and 2d20 .22 cartridges.

38. Skullock child, half dead and unconscious, has d6 endurance remaining.

39. Squeezy bottle of hardened caramel syrup, worth 7+d10sp

40. Small statue of odd ancient metal tower (Eiffel Tower) 25cm tall, and of silver, worth 70+2d20sp

41. Canister of pepper spray

42. Pocket-bot, intact, badly scratched, but operational should its power source be recharged.

43. Vietnam style US army helmet, SV -5, Move - 0.25m, worth 210+d100sp

44. Hula dancer dashboard figure with grass skirt, plastic, 20cm tall, suction cup on feet, faded but in good working order, worth 30+d20sp

45. Rubber chicken, slightly faded and bashed up, but worth 20+d20sp

46. Nylon belt with huge brass buckle depicting a man riding a leaping bull. Worth 20+d20sp

47. Pink plastic handcuffs with attached set of keys. Type A strength based hazard check to break free. Worth 30+2d20sp

48. Never opened plastic package of woman's fishnet stockings. Worth 20+2d20sp

49. Pocket pistol in original nylon ankle holster, d6 rounds in magazine and spare, empty magazine in holster compartment.

50. Mini grenade

51. Assault rifle, d2 shots left in magazine

52. Machete, rusted but usable

53. Small snake, still alive and pissed off, but its lower half is fused to the husk of the scraplurker. Looter must make a type A perception based hazard check to notice the snake in time to leap back out of the reptile's bite range.

54. Ancient diamond wedding ring, set in gold, worth 400+2d100sp

55. Old world flag, worth 20+d20sp or more, depending on locality of adventure. **Roll d10: 1.** United States of America/ **2.** California/ **3.** Union Jack (UK)/ **4.** China/ **5.** Mexico/ **6.** Canada/ **7.** Japan/ **8.** Texas/ **9.** Italy/ **10.** New Jersey

56. Stovetop Espresso brewer, 4 cup capacity, operational and worth 50+d100sp

57. 100cm tall, four sided plastic safety pylon, stating 'CAUTION FLOOR WET', bulky, 2kg, worth 10+d20sp

58. Never peeled bumper sticker showing a cartoony picture of the earth with the phrase 'Love your Mother' beside the icon. Worth d4sp

59. Compound crossbow

60. Advanced fragmentation grenade

61. Communication headset, battery drained.

62. .50 Caliber rifle round

63. Baggy of assorted ammo: d20 .22 rounds, d6 shotgun shells, d6 standard pistol rounds, d3 high caliber pistol rounds, 2d6 standard rifle rounds, d6 HC rifle rounds, and 1 shotgun slug.

64. Pistol shotgun with 1 shotgun shell loaded

65. Solar charging pocket music player with 1000 old world songs loaded, plus, fold open back and set of ear buds. Worth 200+2d100sp. Player can be loaded with another 5000 songs or pictures.

66. Small pure gold statue of Buddha, 500gm, worth 130+d100sp

67. Ammo belt, holding d6 high caliber rifle rounds, but belt can hold 100 rounds of ammo in total.

68. Self inflating olive drab colored sleeping roll, rolled up, worth 40+2d20sp.

69. Pair of old world eye glasses in crush-proof case. Worth 30+2d20sp

70. Ancient sheriff's cowboy style hat, stained and a bit tattered, but can be reshaped and look half decent. Worth 20+d20sp.

71. Book light, slides into spine of book and gives off faint yellow illumination in a 40cm cone, shake for one minute to yield 2 hours light. Worth 120+2d100sp

72. Rare double barrel over and under rifle-shotgun combo. Lower barrel a standard shotgun and the upper being a high caliber rifle loaded with one of each ammo type. Break action, takes a full round to load each barrel. If sold, worth 900+d1000 sp

73. Hand mirror, made of bright pink plastic with faded cartoon cat chasing mouse around the edge. Worth 30+d20sp

74. Pair of scissors with red handles, worth 15+d12sp

75. World War One replica 'Pickelhaube' German spiked helmet. Made before the Apocalypse. DV -4 move -0.25m. Worth 100+2d100sp

76. Ceramic owl piggy bank, ancient and miraculously unbroken and worth 30+d20sp. Plus, there is a 71% chance that inside are old world coins totaling 3d100 dollars (Pounds, Euros or other game locations old world currency). Other than a curiosity, such coins may have no purchasing power in the GM's setting.

77. Kitten, still alive and mewing pathetically. If pulled free of the scraplurker, it will purr and nuzzle its savior and make a great pet. There is a 4% chance this kitten is actually a robotic variant and requires a mini power cell once a year, and if so, 13% likely is a Mecha controlled scout with a type D death poison bite, and if cornered, self destructs as an advanced frag grenade.

78. Tube of odd shaped black dice with red numbers. There is a four, six, eight, 2 tens, a twelve and twenty sided dice. Set worth 80+d100sp

79. Plastic coat hanger worth 4+d4sp

80. Brightly painted, yellow toy civilian automobile of about 6 cm in length made of plastic and metal. Worth 14+d12sp

81. Silver colored wind-up clock, with alarm and worth 70+d100sp

82. Bright red T-shirt folded up and still in original plastic wrap. If opened it reveals writing, **roll d8: 1.** A large arrow pointing to the left saying 'I'm with stupid'/ **2.** An arrow pointing right and the words 'I confess. He did it' / **3.** Words saying 'Mr. Wrong'/ **4.** Words saying 'I may not be Mrs. Right but I'll f–k you until she shows up' / **5.** An image of an automatic pistol and beneath it the words 'Gun Control Means Using Both Hands' /**6.** Words saying 'Sunny Acres Rehabilitation Resort'. / **7.** A group image of Stalin, Hitler, Castro and some US president with their hands up or out in a weird salute. The caption under the images says 'All in Favor of Gun Control put up your Hands'. / **8.** Curvy writing saying 'Your Mom was here'. Shirt worth 18+d20sp

83. Deflated blowup nude woman, life size and worth 24+2d20sp

84. Small metal button-pin with the writing on it, **roll d6: 1.** Vote YES for Texas Independence 2118 /**2.** Ask me about Erectovisil natural male enhancement / **3.** Say NO to mutants getting citizenship/**4.** GOD hates human clones. Say NO to one in your home! / **5.** Save your marriage! BAN sex robots and pleasure clones today! /**6.** God never made 'em! Vote NO to citizenship and benefits for non-humans!

85. Sealed plastic box with automatic pistol inside, nylon holster and 2 mags. No ammo.

86. Aluminum Yard stick, worth 4+d8sp

87. Unopened box of 20 standard pistol rounds, shrink wrapped and like new.

88. Nerve gas grenade

89. Shrink wrapped box of 24 condoms, glow in the dark and box full worth 24+3d20sp

90. Magazine for a .22 cal semi-auto rifle, drum style holds 10+2d20 rounds, max capacity 100 rounds.

91. .22 caliber revolver with 10 shot rotating cylinder and loaded with 4+d6 rounds of ammo

92. Holographic picture frame, solar powered. When turned on it will start a slide show of 4000 family photos from some ancient household. Buttons on the side allows for folder selection plus importing of images from other devices and robotics. Worth 200+2d100sp

93. Strange pink tubular object made of studded, flexible plastic and with battery compartment at wide end. Uses one mini power cell (drained). If turned in all it does is warm up and vibrate. Doesn't seem like much of a weapon but worth 90+2d10sp

94. Spiderbot, stuck fast and switched off. If turned on there is a 57% chance it is in the service of a local anti-human Mecha hive and will attempt to kill humanoids on sight.

95. Relic Bayonet stabbed into the scraplurker's hide

96. Plastic box containing twelve 20mm (1/72nd scale) Napoleonic French *cuirassiers* cavalrymen with horses, unpainted in blue plastic. Each worth 5 silver coins if used as currency.

97. Tattered real paper book on a subject, **roll d6: 1.** Dictionary / **2.** Bible / **3.** The Hobbit by JRR Tolkien /**4.** Field combat medic's handbook. GM may allow any medic with this book at hand to be +2 skill points using the medic skill./ **5.** Vegan cooking complete with 300 receipts for meatless, dairy and egg free dishes./ **6.** Computer repair and programming manual. GM can allow a PC with the computer technician skill to be +2 skill points higher in that skill when having this tome with him or her while reprogramming or repairing a computer or robot.

98. Unopened, shrink-wrapped box of facial tissue, in floral Hawaiian print box, worth 4+d6sp

99. A remote video camera, operational, flexi-antenna, bolted to the scraplurker's head and apparently transmitting all the audio and video to some unknown observation station. Detaching the surveillance system deletes all files and breaks transmission. Camera has a bank of d6+1 mini power cells, half of them drained. Camera can be helmet mounted and will record and broadcast continuously to an advanced receiver within 1000km above ground and 20km below ground. One mini power cell runs the device for 3 months. Worth 500+4d100sp

100. Fifty caliber sniper rifle with scope and fold out bipod, sling, cleaning kit. Magazine can hold 10 rounds, but presently has d2 remaining.

CREATURES OF THE APOCALYPSE: 7
Back Hatcher

By Brandon Goeringer

Back Hatcher
By Brandon Goeringer aka @SavageGM

Back Hatcher	Clinger	Adult Spawner
Defense Value	-0	-18
Endurance	d6	100+3d20
Movement	1m	4m
Initiative	N	+2* or N
Attacks	bite	bite
Strike Value	1-35	1-80
Damage	d4	d12+6
Strength	11	82
Agility	21	30
Accuracy	24	36
Intelligence	3	5
Willpower	14	57
Perception	20	48
Valuables	nil	nil
Experience	3	70
Morale	fair	average
Size	30cm	2 wide, 3m long
Weight	1.5kg	180kg
Mutations	nil	11%/1

* +2 Initiative when remaining motionless, but Normal once discovered or engaged.

The moment that an excavator realizes that he's encountered the dreaded back hatcher he instantly knows that he took a wrong step. Found in marshes, bogs, swamps and other muddy foliage covered quagmires, the back hatcher is a nasty surprise for anyone that is not watching where they're going.

This giant green or brown, flat frog-like creature uses its legs to cover itself in mud, sludge and reeds. Once concealed, it remains motionless, its exposed, large lidded eyes are barely open as it watches for predator or prey alike. A wide maw of sharp teeth is its main weapon but is often not needed to kill; that sloppy work is often taken care of by its young. Upon its large flat back are d12+8 fleshy holes of skin, 30cm deep. Inside these holes rests an equal amount of hatchling young that are normally dormant and waiting for a meal. When someone steps on the spawner's back, receptors in the parents skin trigger a reflex that sends a slight electric jolt to the brood in the location stepped on, immediately the eyes of d6+3 of the young pop open, locate the offender, and with the aid of their back legs, jump up to 80 cm in the air, attacking the potential meal with their sharp toothy mouths. These 'clingers' attack like piranhas, biting and trying to grab on with their small legs, rending flesh with incredibly voracious appetites.

Any other movement by the unlucky soul, other than to jump off of the Back Hatcher, will trigger another clutch of young to join the frenzy. Whatever meat is torn off is quickly devoured by the brood while larger parts of a slain victim are consumed by the adult. The parent allows its children to feed first, only eating after they have had their fill. The parent will attack if it takes more than 10 endurance points of damage itself, or if half its young are killed. It has no use for valuables and any on a victim are discarded, left in the mud or in dung. These unconsumed articles are often a sign that the predator could be in the area.

Spawner's have 2 Stealth skill points and an 11% chance of a mutation that only develops fully after it has left its parent, usually after a year from birth.

Though their origin is only speculated at, a back hatcher's zoology is known to a few excavators who are curious enough to study its behavior. Shockingly the spawner is actually a male specimen of its species and female versions take no part in young rearing. Females are identical to males in terms of physiology but their manner of breeding with males is most unique. After normal copulation, the female jumps onto the back of a receptive male and drops her fertilized eggs into the male's back holes. Therein, the eggs hatch and the young are cared for by the male while the female looks for another mate.

Back Hatcher Mutation List   Roll d12

1. Acid Holes: This specimen has acidic skin that actually kills the young and breaks down the brood's bodies in their holes. Each hole contains a volume of acid that when the spawner is stepped on, it sprays the acid up into the air in small watery geysers. SV 1-40/ damage d8+2 / 2 damage each round for 6 rounds unless washed off with at least one liter of liquid.

2. Hidden Barbs: Under the spawner's back are hidden barbs that spring out along with the electric shock that awakens the brood. These barbs are meant to spear the prey's feet and hold it fast for the impending hatchling feast. SV 1-40 / damage d6 and the victim must succeed at a type C Strength based hazard check or be immobile.

3. Mimicry: The vocal cords of this back hatcher have mutated to allow it to recreate the sounds of other prey it has fought against in previous attacks. The sounds of sheep, hogs, crying babies, hysterical farmers and lost excavators are all reproduced to lure in potential meals. The range of this sound is 200 meters.

4. Venomous Bite: The bite of this back hatcher is toxic and injects Type C paralysis venom. The subject must make a type C endurance based hazard check of begin to pass out. During the first 4 rounds after exposure the victim drops whatever he or she was holding, moves half speed and is +20 SV easier to strike. On the fifth round the subject collapses and can do nothing but use mental mutations if available. The unlucky victim can see, hear and feel everything that happens thereafter and remains immobilized for 3d6 minutes.

5. Increased Girth: This specimen has a larger frame than the rest and has an additional d20+10 endurance.

6. Two-Heads: This aberration has an additional bite attack per round.

7. Regeneration: Any depleted traits heal at 1 point per round.

8. Screamer: This back hatcher shouts when stepped on, screaming so loud that those not wearing ear protection or a combat or better relic helmet, must make an agility based type A hazard check to cover their ears in time or be deafened for d12+12 minutes. There is a 2 in 6 chance this cry attracts d2 other adult back hatchers within 3d6 minutes.

9. Jumper: This specimen can leap once every 4th round to a height of 6m, or horizontally 9m, allowing it to either escape or pursue up a ledge or tree.

10. Fire Glands: In this mutants throat has two glands that can spew fire from the critter's mouth once every 4 rounds up to 6 meters away. SV 1-40 / d20 damage on the first round and d8 automatically each round thereafter for d6 rounds or until the flame is put out by water.

11. More Freaky: Roll d10 twice on this list.

12. Freakish Horror!: This specimen features one additional mutation from this table, rolling d10, and is also massive, having an extra 100 endurance, moves 3m faster per round, carries an extra 2d6 hatchlings in its back, and does +12 more damage per bite.

Back Hatcher Discarded Items Table   Roll d100

Valuables littered around Back Hatcher hunting grounds or found in debris or dung. **Roll d100**, but re-roll duplicated results or pick the result below a reoccurring number.

01. Burritos, white plastic bag containing d6 wrapped burritos that still look and smell edible. Unfortunately they each cause explosive diarrhea for an hour after being consumed inflicting d3 damage, worth d3sp each

02. Children's book, worth 2+d4sp. **Roll d6: 1.** "Mommy, Who Is That Man?"/ **2.** "Time To Sleep!"/ **3.** "Duke the Daring Dog"/ **4.** "Everybody Poops"/ **5.** "Pajama Time"/ **6.** "Green Eggs and Ham"

03. Dog collar, black with metal studs worth 8+d6sp

04. Sweet potatoes, d4 worth 2+d3sp

05. Plastic batarang, toy weapon used by a popular crime fighting superhero, worth 5+d4sp

06. Shotgun shells, d12+2, 12 gauge

07. NES video game, plastic grey cartridge with worn label, has the name "Jason" written on back with permanent marker, if working NES console is found, blowing on cartridge gets it to play after some effort, worth 15+d10sp. **Roll d6: 1.** Super Mario Bros. 3/ **2.** Mega Man 2/ **3.** The Legend of Zelda/ **4.** Castlevania/ **5.** Contra/ **6.** Skate or Die

08. Red boxing gloves, worth 15+d12sp

09. Pocket pistol, no ammo

10. Small brown pouch containing 40+2d20sp

11. Leather football worth 10+d6sp

12. Plastic spray bottle, holds 1L, currently holds a blue liquid in it, worth 8+d6sp (blue liquid is window cleaner)

13. Remote control, no batteries, worth 10+d8sp

14. Chainsaw with broken chain and only 1L of gas left in tank

15. Black fedora, worth 4+d3sp

16. Fanny pack, black worth 8+d6sp containing d12 scrap pieces of paper and 2d6sp

17. DVD case with movie, worth 20+d12sp. **Roll d6: 1.** Ghostbusters 2/ **2.** Windy City Heat/ **3.** Tootsie/ **4.** The Goonies/ **5.** The Monster Squad/ **6.** Dune

18. Ring of keys, 2d20 assorted keys on a brass ring, worth 20+d10sp

19. Laser pistol, pristine condition, fully charged

20. Mini grenade

21. Baseball cap with 2 drink holders and elaborate straws that hang down to wearer's mouth, worth 15+d12sp

22. Magic shop disguise kit, fake nose, mustache, fake teeth, glasses, worth 26+d8sp

23. Junk armor, slightly dented and very smelly. **Roll d6** for smell: **1.** Body odor/ **2.** Vomit/ **3.** Blood/ **4.** Poo/ **5.** Unknown smell but very offensive, -10 SV to wearer from stinging eyes and nausea/ **6.** Skunk spray

24. Iron cap

25. Pool stick, collapsible, worth 16+d10sp

26. Black tote bag, empty heavy duty tote bag with shoulder strap, worth 20+d12sp

27. Machete

28. Battery powered piano keyboard worth 30+d20sp

29. Standard shield covered in blood and some sort of viscous green goo

30. Switchblade knife

31. Snow globe, depicts the San Diego Zoo, worth 10+d6sp

32. Large blue foam hand, fits over wearer's hand with the words "Go Team!", the index finger is pointed up, worth 8+d6sp

33. Plastic folder, contains d10+2 issues of MAD Magazine, worth 8+d6sp each

34. Leather cowboy hat, brown and well worn

35. Container of antacids, 50 extra strength tablets of various colors, worth 20+d12sp

36. Bag of nacho flavor Doritos, chips are crushed but still edible, worth 2+d4sp

37. Astronaut Ice cream blocks, d6 squares still in packaging with the word NASA written on them, worth 40+d20sp

38. Fondue set, electric pot with 6 steel forks, well used, worth 50+2d20sp

39. Black boots, leather and water resistant, worth 8+d8sp

40. Chinese wok, burn marks at the bottom but usable, worth 20+d12sp

41. Sub-machine gun, with 2 full 50 round clips, needs to be cleaned of mud

42. Tent, 2-man, green

43. Rad scanner (see page TME-199, battery drained).

44. Instant tea, 1L of instant sweet tea with scoop, just add water, worth 4+d3sp. **Roll d6** for flavor: **1.** Lemon/ **2.** Green/ **3.** Peach/ **4.** Raspberry/ **5.** Ginger lemon/ **6.** Apple

45. Fishing gear

46. Ramen noodle packet, d4 packs of noodles, worth 2+d3sp each. **Roll d6** for flavor: **1.** Oriental/ **2.** Chicken/ **3.** Pork/ **4.** Beef/ **5.** Spicy/ **6.** Creamy chicken

47. Bow with d12+8 arrows

48. Summer sleeping bag

49. Bag of balloons, 50 round balloons of various colors, worth 4+d3sp

50. Lawn darts, d4+2, worth 6+d4sp each (treat as knives if thrown or stabbed at someone)

51. Robotic dog, small robot dog 12cm tall, can bark and do flips, uses battery pill which it currently is missing, worth 20+d10sp

52. Baby food pouches, d6 pouches of various flavors, worth 2+d3sp

53. Fragmentation grenade

54. Nerve gas grenade

55. Mini power cell, half charged

56. Portable cooler, red and empty with flip locking handle, worth 8+d4sp

57. Green visor with electric fan in bill to cool face, uses pill power cell, d100% charged, each pill will operate fan for 100 hours, worth 6+d4sp

58. Bottle of red wine. **Roll d6** for location of winery: **1.** France/ **2.** Italy/ **3.** California/ **4.** Arizona/ **5.** Spain/ **6.** North Carolina.

59. Planet of the Apes action figure, worth 8+d4sp. Roll d6 for character: **1.** Cornelius/ **2.** Dr. Zira/ **3.** Dr. Zaius/ **4.** Taylor/ **5.** Nova/ **6.** General Ursus

60. Assault rifle, no ammo

61. Fuzzy dice, 2 six sided dice connected by a string, red, worth 2+d3sp

62. Battle rocket

63. Exploding arrow heads, d8

64. Toenail clippers, worth 2+d2sp

65. Novelty glasses, plastic eyes on springs attached to glasses frame, worth 10+d12sp

66. Crowbar

67. 6 pack of Jolt cola, worth 2+d4sp each

68. Paddle attached with rubber band and ball, worth 1+d2sp

69. Sports padding armor in surprisingly good condition

70. Silencer for standard caliber automatic pistol

71. .50 caliber bullet

72. Pocket flashlight, battery half charged

73. Jar of popcorn kernels, worth 3+d3sp

74. Banker's lamp, green and slightly cracked, still works, no bulb, worth 6+d4sp

75. Pocket fart machine, electric device that fits on key chain with various fart noises, uses pill power cell, d100% of charge remaining. One charge produces 1000 fart noises, worth 16+2d4sp

76. Alcohol flask filled with random booze, worth 12+d4sp. Roll d4 for type of hooch: **1.** Vodka/ **2.** Whiskey/ **3.** Gin/ **4.** Moonshine

77. Wooden case with 4 souvenir shot glasses in it, worth 12+d8sp

78. Yellow plastic whiffle bat, worth 2+d3sp

79. Black leather jacket with a large stylish scorpion on the back, very nice quality.

80. Carpentry saw

81. Wooden flute

82. Bent bayonet

83. White gold ring with missing jewel, worth 200+2d20

84. Box of 100 .22 caliber rounds

85. Swiss Army knife with corkscrew and scissors, worth 40+d20sp

86. Pouch of Capri Sun, tropical punch flavor, worth 2+d2sp

87. Smashed moon pie in plastic bag, "The Original Moon Pie", worth 2+d2sp

88. Cans of soup, d6 various soups with no labels, worth 3+d3sp each: **1.** New England Clam Chowder (roll d2: 1 Red, 2 White)/ **2.** Chicken Noodle/ **3.** Cream of Mushroom/ **4.** Tomato Basil/ **5.** Chicken n' Rice/ **6.** Butternut Squash

89. Wooden picture frame with an original ink drawing from a fantasy role playing game piece of art, priceless to some, worth 200+3d20 to others

90. Laser carbine in a black case. Pristine condition, 1 shot remaining.

91. Ballistic shield with the word SWAT written on it, some scratches.

92. Cardboard box with "Judy" the blow up female companion, worth 50+d20sp

93. Land mine, not armed

94. Compass

95. Random roll from TME-1-62 Implant Determination Matrix page TME-84, the implant is in a black metal lockable box from an unknown cybernetics manufactory, perfect condition with all needed wires and connections, but lacking any power cells or ammo that might be required.

96. Bottle of shampoo, worth 3+d4sp

97. Dead excavator wearing usable riot armor

98. Binoculars

99. Sniper rifle with full clip

100. Hatchling back hatcher that is still alive on its own. Having somehow survived without its parent, this hatchling has a strong survival sense. It is not hostile to approaching individuals and will act much like a pet if given some meat, showed compassion and cared for. This hatchling will answer by name with time, food, training and care. It will grow up to be of normal size with an 11% chance of one mutation on the previous list. It will in all purposes be a dog-like pet to its master.

Clinger

CREATURES OF THE APOCALYPSE: 8

Quasi

By James Butler

Quasi

By James Butler aka @Clock_punk

Defense Value: **-15**

Endurance: **40+2d12**

Movement: **8m**

Initiative: **-1**

Attacks: **2 slaps, or grapple** (skill level 2)

Strike Value: **01-60**

Damage: **d8+3** (slaps), **d12+6** (bear hug – every three rounds held)

Strength: 71

Agility: 55

Accuracy: 53

Intelligence: 6+d3

Willpower: 25

Perception: 38

Valuables: 15% chance of a random item carried (focus of obsession)

Experience: 35

Morale: Poor

Size: 1.4 m long, 1m tall

Weight: 180 kg (+/ 2d12 kg)

Mutations: 16% chance of 1

Poetically named after the literary character of quasimodo, with whom they bear more than just a passing resemblance, these creatures are believed to have once been the unfortunate victims of early genetic therapies that have since developed into a completely new race. Their basic form is comprised of a bulky, muscular frame beset with odd oversized limbs and a rigid humpback, whilst their faces – although extremely misshapen and bedraggled – were once unmistakably human. They are capable of basic, broken speech, but this is limited to a form of babbling about current obsessions – which change almost day by day, as some new item or creature catches their playful interest. For although their bodies are physically developed, their minds and emotional control are nowhere near fully formed, and they live in a perpetual state of blissful ignorance to the savagery of the world, instead existing solely for a series of temporary fascinations and fleeting curious wonderment.

All quasis possess a highly inquisitive nature, and are likely to try and steal any items which arouse its curiosity (and is 80% likely to become a source of obsession for which quasi will do anything to acquire), and subsequently suffer a high likelihood of breaking it through boisterous manhandling. If any current item of obsession is forcibly removed, its loss will send the creature into a berserk rage. The quasi will stop at nothing to get its item back, no matter how worthless it is, which can unfortunately give the impression to others that these items may have inherent value.

Despite their bulk, quasis are quick, nimble, and very good climbers – a survival requirement given their reduced intelligence. As such, the dens they prefer tend to contain numerous objects they can climb, swing or scurry across, and otherwise form rudimentary obstacle courses, which they innately learn to traverse quickly without issue. This provides each creature with a climbing skill level of d3+1 points as standard.

If hurt, they will go into a rage and lash out at everything around them, even their 'pets' and items will be destroyed, and dens can be completely trashed. Any objects within tend to betray the signs of serious abuse, looking battered and bashed to excess. If seriously injured they will openly cry out in pain, burst into an animalistic sobbing, and likely curl into a protective ball, as befits their diminished mental capacity hoping to elicit sympathy so they can either flee, or strike any opponent who gets close enough to investigate.

A quasi will attack using a combination of brutish slaps and attempts to grab an opponent in a bear hug, ostensibly meaning to hold it at bay until it can calm down and may be taken back to its lair, but the strength of these beasts invariably crushes anything held in this manner.

Quasis are not maliciously evil creatures, rather they are entirely incomprehensive of their strength and manner of playfulness; for they possess a childlike understanding of the world, where all they desire is simple mental stimulation to ward off boredom. This is manifest in their frequent attempts to capture a 'friend' - typically a wild beast which is caught when crippled by traps, then caged, 'played' with, neglected, mourned briefly, and subsequently replaced. As a result, there is an 80% chance of a single, randomly determined wild creature, in a poor state of health, being kept within the quasi's den. This 'friend' can be any creature, no matter how dangerous, to which a quasi is usually completely oblivious. Likewise, their neglect is not purposeful, but an unfortunate effect of their wandering fascination. However, given their juvenile state of awareness, any humanoid creatures of the opposite sex are much more likely to become the object of a quasi's fascination, for which they may try to 'woo' through the gifting of random debris acting to lure the individual to their den or – much more likely – just try to kidnap outright. Unfortunately, such quarry is treated in the exact same manner as are captured pets.

One particular affinity quasis do possess is setting plenty of basic traps around their dens; simple mechanical ones are preferred and are treated like toys. Prey captured in these implements are 'played' with for hours, expending much of the quasi's day.

Fish, no matter how mutated, form a large part of a Quasi's diet, which they can capture bare handed with a high level of skill. Also on the menu are creatures killed by their traps and discovered in time before scavengers locate the snared or crushed beings; quasi's check their traps only sporadically, if remembering to check them at all.

These creatures do not plan for anything beyond the immediate future in terms of survival preparation. If impeded in their simple everyday routine, however, such as being blocked from using their favoured den exit, or barred from their usual water source, their tempers can flip. They go from being calm to a destructive tantrum instantaneously, with little warning (physiological or psychological), and vice-versa.

Always desirous of holding the dominant position, quasis reside alone (outside of the favoured 'pets'), and if they believe they are being forced into subservience in any capacity, will do anything to reverse the roles – even if the circumstances are to their best interest (such as a character trying to help them escape a dangerous situation), and revert to their basic lifestyle described above. Long-term imprisonment and other abuse faced is quickly forgotten, just like their passing obsessions, and so resentment and acts of vengeance will only span a brief period immediately following any treatment that would elicit such a response.

Quasi offspring, produced by brief and savage one-off dalliances, will be treated exactly like their pets. Only infants who are strong and wily enough to survive, and escape their mother's neglect and find their own den, will go on to live their own isolated existence.

Quasi Mutation List Roll 2d8

2. Furred Pelt: Clad in long fur of natural coloration, this mutation allows a quasi standing still to go undetected – typically while it scans its surroundings looking for something interesting, and provides +2 to the creature's initiative if it launches into an attack from such a situation.

3. Spitter: Once every six rounds, this creature can expel a huge glob of saliva with surprising accuracy, range 6m, SV 01-70, in an attempt to temporarily blind an opponent. If eye or facial protection is not being worn, this attack (made in lieu of one slap) results in penalties to the target's movement (-3m), SV (-14) and Defense Value (+8) until the sticky spit is removed (taking d4+2 rounds).

4. Extra Arm: This mutation adds one extra attack per round, allows a single attack whilst bear hugging an opponent, or improves the grappling skill of the quasi by one point (now 3).

5. Two Heads: increased babbling and arguing with itself, allows for a +12 bonus to perception, and each head will have a separate obsession and desire for a different pet.

6. Spined Hump: Dozens of sharpened protruding bone spikes cover the back of this quasi, providing it a -5 defense value bonus in addition to causing 2d10+5 damage on a back slam, which can be attempted instead of a bear hug when grappling (at -12 SV due to the awkward shape of the creature).

7. Mimicry: This quasi has the ability to recreate the sounds of any creatures it has previously taken in as pets (d6+2 randomly determined creatures), which it can switch between at will. It typically conducts crude conversations between these different voices.

8. Slough Skinned: The creatures body is extra large, and covered in layers of fatty tissue that reduce any inflicted damage by d3 points, and can absorb d10+20 points worth before being shed and eaten by the creature (once every 72 hours).

9. Jumper: Already reasonably skilled at acrobatics, this creature can leap every third round to a height of 8m, or horizontally 12m, allowing it to adopt even harder to reach dens.

10. Gills and Webbed Limbs: This Quasi is capable of breathing underwater (for up to 2 hours at a time), and can swim at 8m per round.

11. Foul Gland: This mutant constantly exudes a stench of rotten matter, but once every 24 hours, upon being surprised, it can release a concentrated cloud of putridness, spanning a 10m diameter around it that causes all others within to make a type C Willpower hazard check or suffer -15 SV and -20 DV. This disperses in 3d4 rounds.

12. Extra Long Limbs: The arms and legs of this creature are even more oversized than found on a typical specimen, and adds +2m movement, in addition to being able to strike targets at a distance of 2 meters.

13. Absorptive Mind: There is a 60% chance that any mental attack against this creature is simply absorbed without any ill effect.

14. Extra Mutated: Roll twice on this list, re-rolling any duplicates.

15. Ghost Mutant: A random ghost mutation from either The Mutant Epoch RPG's hub rules (table TME-1-59 on page TME-59), or other source at the GM's discretion, which will be activated randomly whenever the Quasi is excited, and is never purposefully controlled.

16. Freakish Horror: This mutant beast features an additional mutation from this table, in addition to being grossly oversized. It possesses +60 endurance, moves 1m faster per round, and does an additional +2 damage to slaps and +4 to bear hugs.

Sample Quasi Obsessions Roll 2d20

Note: For a forgotten pet that may still be alive, re-roll until one is determined.

2. Pet - weasel
3. Item – Box of d12 highly polished copper high caliber pistol bullets, bearing ceramic symbols in the four playing card suites, worth 60+d20sp ea.
4. Pet – jack rabbit
5. Pet – skullock, d2 dislocated limbs
6. Item – battery powered lava lamp, pill-battery drained, worth 100+d100sp
7. Pet – wild boar
8. Item – old light bulb painted in array of colors, worth 3+2d6sp
9. Item – bright orange flick-knife, worth 90+d100sp
10. Pet – calf, bearing a brand
11. Item – broken miniature RC helicopter, without power or corresponding remote, worth 6+3d8sp
12. Pet – skunk
13. Pet – spotted scorpion

14. Item – miniature disco ball, worth 5+d10sp
15. Item – pack of brightly colored vacuum-sealed coffees of different flavors, worth 20+2d20sp
16. Pet – venomous lizard
17. Item – video game console joystick, worth 8+d10sp
18. Item – laser sword, that flickers into action for three rounds before shorting out, worth 2000+d1000sp in this state. To fix costs 1000+d1000sp
19. Pet – gutter rat
20. Item – hula doll ornament, worth 3+d6sp
21. Item – mostly unbent slinky, worth 2+d4sp
22. Pet – medium snake
23. Pet – cockroach
24. Item – tatty and moldy pink bear, worth d3sp when cleaned and repaired.
25. Pet – highly-irradiated frog (treat as venomous, but with radioactive attacks, each bite inflicts a dose of mild exposure)
26. Item – small metal suitcase, broken catch, filled with poker chips of various denominations, worth 250+d100sp
27. Item – fluttering toy butterfly in a jar, powered for 400 years by a single power pill, worth 30+2d20sp
28. Item – old watch, motion-wound, skeleton style with moving parts and luminescent hands and face, worth 300+3d20sp
29. Pet – wild dog (randomly determine sort)
30. Item – plastic golden trophy, worth 5+d6p
31. Pet – black bear cub (half stats of full sized)
32. Item – broken cuckoo clock with carved bird dangling from open doors, worth 10+2d6sp
33. Pet – two-headed wolf
34. Pet – ground hawk
35. Item – rad scanner, cracked screen, but still operational, worth 1200+2d100sp
36. Item – 6 x 8 foot Canadian flag, worth 100+2d1000sp
37. Pet – moaner, plague-infected
38. Item – sealed toy fish aquarium, worth 120+2d20sp
39. Pet – mud worm
40. Item – small ceramic tile decorated with a painted bottle of wine, chipped, worth 5+d6sp

CREATURES OF THE APOCALYPSE: 9
Spiker
By Danny Seedhouse

Spiker
By Danny Seedhouse

Variant	Wild Spiker	Armored Spiker
Defensive Value	**-10** (thick hide)	**-43** (thick hide and combat armor with helmet)
Endurance	**90+3d20**	**100+4d20**
Movement	**7m**	**5.5m**
Initiative	**+1**	**+1**
Attacks	**2 spike launchers** firing 2d4 spikes each per round, or **2 melee slams** with spike launcher appendages, **plus 1 Bite**	**2 spike launchers** firing d4+1 spikes each per round plus use of **1 automated turret** or if in melee range **2 slams** with spike launcher appendages plus **1 Bite** (or kick if wearing a gasmask)
Strike Value	**Spike launcher: 01-80/ slam or bite 01-85**	**Spike launcher: 01-80/ Turret: Base SV of 01-80 + weapon SV modifier/ spike appendage slam plus bite 01-85**
Damage	**Spike launcher d12+2 each** (range 150 meters)/ **Spike slam d20+14**/ Bite d10+14 and poison type B weakness.	**Spike launcher d12+2 each** (range 150 meters) / **Turret: Varies by weapon system** / **Spike appendage slam d20+10**/ **Kick d8+10 or Bite d8+10** (and poison type B weakness)
Strength	101	84
Agility	34	32
Accuracy	90	90
Intelligence	8	10
Willpower	68	52
Perception:	45	51
Appearance	d4	d4
Experience	228	322
Morale	Excellent	Excellent
Size:	2 meters tall 1.5 wide	2 meters tall 1.5 wide
Weight	300kg	420kg
Mutations	Poison bite, poison blood, radiation absorption, low light vision, and a 20% chance of random mutation from the wild spiker chart.	All have a poison bite (type B weakness), poison blood, radiation absorption and low light vision.
Relics	None	Turret weapon system and see valuables
Cybernetics	None	Communication and control implants
Valuables	2d10 spikes equivalent to a relic bayonet, and a 30% chance of 1d3 un-looted corpses found nearby (type UC, page TME 209).	2d10 spikes equivalent to a relic bayonet. Armor can be scavenged and made into man sized scrap relic armor, over sized combat helmet with night vision targeting optics, gas mask and digital video camera.

Spikers are bio-weapons leftover from a forgotten pre-fall war. These terrors are walking anti-infantry assets, possessing biological weapon systems or even relic augmentation. A spiker is a major threat to anyone unfortunate enough to stumble across their hunting grounds or designated patrol zone.

They come in two main varieties: wild and armored. The type encountered depends on the terrain they are met in, with a 70% chance of armored spikers met in ruins, but only 22% of the time in other environments. Wild spikers, therefore, are more commonly spotted by farmers, trappers and nomads, and so inflict more devastation on human populations, eliciting rewards for the hunting and killing of these monsters.

All spikers are omnivores, however, wild variants tend toward the flesh eating side and can consume an entire human in a single feeding. Engineered to be able to reproduce naturally to help maintain combat numbers, half are female and able to give birth to small litters of d4+1 'pups', every 6 months.

Both wild and armored variants have a poisonous bite, which forces anyone chomped on by one of these beasts to make an endurance based type B hazard check or suffer weakness – victim at 50% all traits, including the SV of all attacks, rates of fire and damage from mutational or physical attacks. Firing guns will inflict the same amount of damage, but the strike value is halved. This toxin remains in effect for 3d6 hours. Their blood contains this same poison, with anything biting a spiker also forced to make a type B hazard check.

Thankfully, wild spikers are usually found without their battle armor and high tech weaponry, either because they shed it upon going feral, as they find it uncomfortable, or else they were born wild and never served a human, Mecha or other master. These brutes hunt for food, rarely for sport, and usually avoid people unless they have been attacked by humanoids before, or haven't fed in a few days. They are territorial and with brain patterns borrowed from dogs, tend to form packs with there own kind or any canine that will accept them. In rare instances, wild spikers have adopted small groups of people – usually those containing ghost mutants able to talk with them mentally – or canine bestial humanoids.

Each wild spiker is 20% likely to appear with one random mutation from the following list.

Wild Spiker Mutations   Roll d12

1. Its a **big one:** This spiker is unusually large for its species standing half a meter taller, weighing an extra 40+1d20kg. Add 30+2d20 END, 20+1d20 STR and 0.5 meters to their speed.

2. Spike overgrowth: Additional spikes grow haphazardly from this specimen's entire body giving it an extra layer of armor and increased damage in combat. Its DV becomes -20, spike launcher ROF increases to 4+d6 per round with +5 to SV, slam damage is increased +10 (now d20+24) and anything striking it in combat with a natural attack self-inflicts 1d8 damage on itself per successful strike.

3. Deadly poison: This spikers bite and blood deliver type B death poison.

4. Poison spikes: The spiker has poison glands in its spike launchers. Each gland holds enough poison for 10 shots before being depleted for 24 hours. **Roll d8** for poison type. **1.** Type A weakness/ **2.** type B weakness/ **3,4** type B sleep/ **5,** type C sleep/ **6,** type B paralysis/ **7,** type C paralysis/ **8,** type B death.

5. Fast on its feet: The spiker moves at +2 meters faster and gains an extra -2d6 to defense value. It also possesses the burst of speed mutation called 'sprint', see page 73 of the TME hub rules.

6. Flesh eater: This spiker has gone extra feral and entirely carnivorous and hunts meat wherever it can find it. Its jaws are larger having a SV of 01-90 and doing 2d10+20 damage. Worse, it will attempt to grapple a target with its over-sized jaws (with 3 skill points in the grapple skill) and savage the victim with spikes and teeth. Luckily, a feral spiker tends not to use its spike launchers unless the prey is out-running it, as the creature prefers to taste its prey's flesh, and feel it die in its mouth.

7. Ghost mutation: This spiker has 1d3 ghost mutations generated from the standard ghost mutation chart (page 59 of the TME hub rules). If three mutations are rolled one is always advanced mind (mutation number 3) giving it 3d10 extra intelligence.

8. Alpha: Better then its fellows, this spiker is a natural leader. Improve DV by -6, END is increased by 50+1d20, all SV's improved by +10, plus it now has +2 to initiative. The beast's speed is increased by +1 meter per round and improve both intelligence and willpower stats by 10+1d10.

9. Sniper: This spiker has an extra spike launcher on its back employed as an organic sniper rifle. SV 95/145*, rate 1 or ½*, damage 3d20+20, range 2.5 km, with a clip size of 10 rounds. Additional spikes are regenerated at a rate of 1 per hour.

* Carefully aimed shots take two full rounds to train on a specific target.

10-12. Alternate weapon mutation: Replacing one of its two launchers, this spiker instead has a different bioengineered weapon. **Roll d8** on the fallowing chart for a replacement appendage:

1. *Flame projector:* This hose-like appendage belches burning oil. The bio-weapon has a strike value of +20 and expels flame in a 6 meter long cone that is 3 meters wide at its end. Burn damage is 2d20 on the first round and thereafter inflicts 1d10 for the next 1d6 rounds. The creature holds 100 rounds worth of fuel in various gland sacks that are refilled at the rate of 1 round an hour. This spiker's skin is fire resistant allowing it to ignore the first 10 rounds of flame and heat exposure. After 10 rounds of exposure, in a 10 hour period, the creature takes 1/2 damage.

2. *Beam projection:* This beast has multiple shiny disks along its arm that allow it to shoot beams of focused light, much like a pulse laser. SV 01-105, rate 5, damage 1d20 each, and range 1km. The creatures skin is also reflective and 70% of every laser, stun or other beam weapon to strike it actually bounces off. It can fire up to 18 bursts per 24 hour period.

3. *Blades:* Large bone blades replace the usual dagger-like spikes on one thrower. These yellowish swords fire at a rate of 1 per round, SV 01-95, DMG 2d20+20, range 200 meters, with a maximum of 8 swords available per day. Each is a +1 SV / +2 DMG saber if harvested, and sells for 50+d20sp.

4. *Pincer:* A massive crab like pincer has replaced one spike launcher. SV 01-90, damage 2d20+20.

5. *Electrical Arcs:* One of this spiker's launchers has mutated to project electrical pulses out to 60m range. SV 01-100, rate 1, damage is 2d20 stun to primary target and 1d20 stun to 1d4 targets within 2 meters. Machines and cyborgs suffer double stun damage. This power can be used 12 times per hour.

6. *Acid Spitter:* A conical tube grows from this launcher complete with massive liquid bladder. 6 times per hour this spiker can disgorge a liter of flesh eroding acid, range 30m and potentially harming up to three man-sized beings if they are grouped together, SV 01-90, those hit will dissolve taking d8 damage per round for 2d4 rounds. Immersing oneself in at least 2 liters of water will neutralize the acid. This particular spiker is immune to all acid attacks.

7. *Dual Alternate Weapon:* Roll d6 on this list and instead of replacing one spike launcher, both limbs are replaced by new alternate appendages.

8. *Telekinetic:* This spiker has small mostly atrophied limbs (melee range slam attack only: SV 01-75 doing 1d4+5 damage). To compensate for this, the spiker has the Telekinesis prime mutation (#84) its willpower is increased to 80 as well, and it is sheathed in a constant protective aura increasing DV by -10. It can lift 240kg and move it 12m per round, possibly throwing a large man out a window or off a cliff*. It will hurl stones and rubble as 'large rocks' at a rate of 1 per round range 80m, SV 01-160, DMG d12+3, uses: 16 times per day.

*GM: Give the unfortunate PC a chance to grab onto something to avoid being heaved off to his or her doom!

Armored spikers are usually under the control of an organized, high-tech military force. This can be good or bad as an unknown faction sets the spiker's mission parameters; which means the tank-like monsters are under supervision and if one's luck holds out then the controllers could be negotiated with. Spikers are genetically programmed to respond to certain types of chemical and verbal commands. Controlled specimens are fanatically loyal to their designated handler and anyone he, she or it introduces them to as friends; the spiker acting much like an armored, bone-knife throwing, bear-sized watch dog.

They react violently to the death of their master and tend to go berserk unless immediately sedated; this has led to some escaping into the wilds. This berserk rage can last for days (1d4+1 days) after which the beast acts in a generally depressed manner for 1d4 weeks during which it avoids all contact with people or anything that looks humanoid, though it will seek out others of its kind.

These alloy and relic encrusted spikers are a deadly menace to anyone its controllers wants to drive off or kill. Thankfully they are not usually found wandering in the wilds, but are sent out for surgical strikes and as part of major military deployments on the part of high tech enclaves. If encountered in a defensive roll they will usually announce a pre-recorded warning from helmet mounted speaker and allow intruders to retreat, unless the trespassers are in a 'kill on sight' zone – then all bets are off.

The turret system on the armored spiker carries one of the following weapon systems:

Armored Spiker Weapon System List   Roll d6

1. Anti-Armor Battle Rocket System: Holds 6 Advanced Battle Rockets, SV: 01-110, Rate: 1, Range 9km, 2d100+40 damage on a direct hit, blast radius within 10m SV: 01-80, 2d20+6 DMG. The precious rockets are primarily used for anti-armor, counter-robotic and anti-heavy cyborg purposes; rarely used against soft targets.

2. Ripple Pack Grenade Launcher: Holds 24 grenades in two rotary magazines of 12 with the fallowing load: 16 advanced frags, 4 smoke, 4 tear gas. SV: 01-90, Rate: 4, Range 100m, DMG varies by grenade (grenades covered on page TME 195).

3. Sniper System: .50 cal Sniper Rifle, SV: 01-100 / or 01-150*, Rate: 1 or 1/2* DMG, 3d20+20, Range 3km. Telescopic sight linked to helmet optic system, and an active camouflage system that gives the spiker 3 skill points in stealth. Box magazine holds 30 rounds of ammo.

4. Twin Flame Units: SV: 01-100, DMG: 2d20 initial burn then 1d10 damage thereafter for d6 rounds. Range 20m tank holding 200 rounds of flame ammo. Both Units are able to engage targets independently. This spiker is immune to fire attacks.

5. Light Laser Cannon: SV: 01-110, Rate: 1, DMG d100, Range 20km, power pack provides 50 shots

6. Chain Gun and Anti Personnel Shotgun. Chain Gun SV: 01-90, Rate: 10, DMG: d20, Range 220m, Drum holding 200 rounds. Anti personal Shotgun SV: 01-100, Rate: 2, DMG: 3d10, range 30m. Drum holds 40 shotgun shells.

*Carefully aimed shots take two full rounds to train on a specific target.

Insignia of the 3rd Spiker Battalion

Wailing Jhonny

By Camille Robertson

Wailing Jhonny

Written and Illustrated by Camille Robertson
website: realdealcamille.com or Deviantart:ProfessorParsec

Defense Value: **-20**

Endurance: **80+2d20**

Movement: **9m**

Initiative: **+2**

Attacks: **Bite and 2 claws**

Strike Value: **01-80**

Damage: **bite d8+10 / claw d12+10 each**

Strength: 81

Agility: 36

Accuracy: 42

Intelligence: 4

Willpower: 67

Perception: 77

Valuables: d3 discarded items in nest per adult in pack.

Experience: 85

Morale: Excellent

Size: 3 meters long, 2.2 meters tall.

Weight: 500 + 1kg per point of END

Mutations: 17% / 1

Predominantly a creature of the night, the wailing jhonny is aptly named for its haunting howl which is used to locate prey. With large front legs and laughably small back legs, one might think it to be a clumsy runner. This is often the first mistake made by past victims. Through a combination of driving pushes from the hind legs and unfurling their wings, these monsters can pull their heavy bodies into fast sprints and glides. These winged quadrupeds roam in packs with searching cries that can detect prey up to 100m away. Using their generously proportioned ears and sensitive noses, the jhonny can search out even the smallest of creatures.

Due to their fiercely territorial temperament, it is never encouraged to seek out an encounter with these beasts. Unless on the hunt or taken by surprise, a wailing jhonny will typically screech out a warning to trespassers. If continually provoked, members of the pack will employ echolocation to hunt down threats. Their cries can be up to a deafening level 130 decibels. Jhonnies favor more primitive methods of attacking, such as charging and biting. In addition, they may use their wings to surround and trap prey.

However, strength can be turned into weaknesses. Strong-scented sprays can repulse most jhonnies, aside from berserkers, who are prone to blind rage. Loud, constant noises can create confusion, but may also provoke an enraged charge; game masters should roll a d6 each round that the player characters are making sustained noise, with any result of 1 or 2 resulting in a charge by the jhonnies for that turn, after which the animals back off and scurry about in confusion. Berserker variants (see mutation 4, next page), of this species always attack regardless of distracting scents or sounds.

Although they possess thick hides, wailing jhonnies underbellies aren't as well protected and anyone to shoot or stab upwards from beneath one of thee creatures gets a +20 Strike Value bonus and inflicts double damage.

While they are a fierce creature to behold, jhonnies rarely attack without specific a reason such as invasion of territory or protecting their young. Travelers wishing to avoid said encounters should look for telltale signs of territories such as sign-post indicators (bark stripped from trees), scent marking and thoroughly trodden flora and fauna.

Wailing jhonnies typically reside in covered areas and avoid large plains, as they provide little prey or information for echolocation. With logging, agriculture and the growth of new era communities taking over some forested areas, packs of wailing jhonnies may attack smaller settlements at night for food and shelter.

Nests are built from anything found in the area, although most forest-dwelling males will grind down a mix of wood and bones into chips to create a soft nest, with females choosing to reproduce with the male who provides the most appealing nest. If the pack happens to inhabit ruins or abandoned settlements, males will gather items and attempt to chew all into a pile. For the lucky traveler, such nests may contain various intact treasures, including ammunition and power cells.

Packs have been sighted with anywhere from 3-18 (3d6) members, all ranging in age. Cubs come yearly in small litters, at a maximum of three. While food is gathered by the pack, designated caretakers will look after cubs.

The diet of wailing Jhonnies is strongly dependent on location. As they are omnivores, Jhonnies will consume anything from plants to people. Specimens who dwell in lush territories will most likely be well fed from what the forest offer. In ruins or territories where a pack must fight for survival against nearby settlements or other large predators, they will feed upon whatever sustenance is available. A starving jhonny will not think twice about attacking any living being if it will feed the pack and further the lives of their brood.

The average wailing jhonny has low level intelligence, which shows potential for domestication.

However, a cub is often already set in its primal behaviors 4 weeks after birth. Even with constant socialization, jhonnies are not reliable as working animals or mounts unless raised away from their pack from birth.

Due to communication and sight being heavily dependent on echolocation, wailing jhonnies may acknowledge bat-like humanoids as non-threatening. Therefore, a bestial human bat or Night Wing (Bat-Folk from page 75 of the Mutant Bestiary One) may be able to go throughout this creature's territory without invoking aggression. However, they will not accept any humanoids as a member of their pack.

Each wailing jhonny is 17% likely to have one mutation from the following list:

Wailing Jhonny Mutations   Roll d12

1. Silky Saliva: This mutation, which can be used four times per hour, creates cement-like saliva. When wailing, the saliva can spray 6 meters from its mouth and can coat one human sized adversary. If successfully making a hit, the severity of limits on movement range from fingers to the whole body. Strike value 01-70. **Roll d6** for result to a humanoid if struck: **1.** One random hand fused and useless except as a club or fist attack, unless already on the grip or trigger of a weapon. / **2.** A random foot fastened to the ground. Takes a strength based type D hazard check to free and allow movement. / **3.** Knees of victim fused together, stopping movement, although a type E strength based hazard check is allowed to snap the bond. Individuals with knees stuck together must make a type B agility based hazard check to avoid falling face first. / **4.** One random arm is fused to the torso of the target, making it useless, however a strength based type C HC can be made to snap the arm free of the cement and return it to use./ **5.** Target's face is covered over, blinding the subject (who now fights at half SV to all its non-mental attacks and is +40 SV easier to be hit by the jhonny)./ **6.** Both of the victim's arms are fused to its body. Each arm is permitted a type C strength based hazard check to snap free and made useful again.

The cement deteriorates quickly in the air and after 3d6+10 rounds, can be broken free of and later dusted off completely.

2. Shrieking Jhonny: The lungs of this monster are shaped for shorter, higher pitched screeching, which without ear protection or advanced relic helmets that offer such defense or a successful agility based type

A hazard check to cover one's ears, the shriek will deafen a person for d20+30 minutes.

3. Whisperer: These types tend to mix in with regular packs, as wailing directs a prey's attention away from these silent skulkers. A mutation has rendered their shoulder blades more independent, creating an ease of sneaking locomotion. Additional +2 Initiative (now +4), +10 agility, +5 accuracy, +10 perception. This specimen has 4 skill points in stealth and will pounce from unexpected locations, or infiltrate the camps and lairs of humanoids to hunt the young of such beings.

4. Berserker: With an extra helping of blind rage, this beast has a propensity of charging at anything loud, including gunshots or shouts, doing so 6m faster per round than usual when enraged (moves 15m per round). Successful claw attacks by this freak will also smash objects and man sized or smaller beings into the air, tossing them d6m away in a random direction.

Anyone within a 10m radius of this thing's attack or rush must also make an agility based type B hazard check to dodge debris. Failure to dodge the junk, logs and rocks it churns up result in an 'attack' from a stray projectile: SV 01-60, DMG d20 stun damage.

5. Tree Hugger: This specimen has long claws for grasping onto tall objects as well as making an extra d12 damage when attacking (now 2d12+10 per claw attack). Tends to swoop down on prey for the first strike with 4 stealth skill points and gains an extra +2 Initiative on its first attack (now +4). Can climb trees as well as structures with holes or uneven faces.

6. Mother of Jhonnies: Queens of this species are large and overly protective of their brood. This one has the ability to call in d6 regular wailing jhonnies as reinforcements who will arrive 3d6 rounds after any encounter occurs. This very large wailer is slower than regular specimens and moves only 6m per round. It has an additional +50 endurance as well as a much larger mouth which inflicts an extra 2d8+10 damage per bite (now 3d8+20 DMG).

7. Plated Roller: With shorter front limbs and numerous plates (additional -20 defense) that cover its body, this variant tends to go into death rolls, wherein it neatly tucks itself into a ball and will roll about until it hits its intended prey or loses momentum. These are an extra 200kg in weight and gain +30 endurance. When attacking, they will line themselves up to impact the maximum number of targets as possible, and employ the roots of trees, rubble and rocks to plan out their bounce over numerous victims.

Each person in its path is allowed a type G agility based hazard check to try and leap clear, or else be lined up for potential collision. A regular attack is still required for the wailing jhonny to impact the target, but is a single crushing attack SV 01-90, doing d20+10 regular and d20 extra stun damage on a person and prey animal struck. The dodge skill of a character, who might possesses such a benefit, is applied as usual to his or her defense value, for ease of game play, and not connected to the original agility based attempt to dodge the incoming ball of flesh and bone. The roll attack can be made only once per attack, and after being attempted, the creature reverts to a regular jhonny's bite and claw attacks.

8. Typhoid Mary: Infected from birth, this specimen is a carrier of a disease that is characterized by a seal-like cough and blind, red eyes that weep yellow gunk. Although weaker in strength by -10 points, depleted of -20 endurance and only having 20 agility, with each cough comes a black mist that if successful against a target's type D agility check, will render the character blind for d20 rounds. Blind characters fight at half their strike values and are +40 SV easier to be hit. The disease carried by this mutant is up to the game master, but could be one from the Mutant Epoch hub rules on page 127, including white plague, rose pox or bio-toxin 1 or 2.

9. Toothy and Tusked: This mutation gives a Jhonny a second set of teeth (+10 damage per bite) as well as elephant-like tusks from which, if it makes a bite 'hit' on an opponent, has a 5 in 10 chance of also sweeping and hurling any creature that weighs less than it to some random fate: roll d10: **1,2.** Flips then tries to gore the target: allowed another attack as if a bite but at +20 SV doing double damage on a strike!/ **3,4.** Flips the target end over end, forcing it to drop anything it holds in its hands, and dropping it hard for d20 extra stun damage./ **5,6.** Hurling the target to one side d6+2m away to a hard landing for d20 stun damage./ **7,8.** Scoops the target up in the air high above the Wailing Jhonny which raises its tusks ready to impale the creature when it falls. Treat impaling as a separate attack the same round, SV +20, inflicting whatever the Jhonny's bite damage is, adding +5 extra DMG. / **9,10.** Topples and stampedes over the target. The victim is trampled and takes d20 extra stun damage and allowed a type C agility based hazard check to avoid having its head stomped. If stomped, an extra d100 stun damage occurs. GM Note: Remember, stun damage heals at a character's base healing rate, but per hour instead of per day.

10. Regeneration: This specimen heals one lost trait point per round.

11. Two headed: This specimen makes two bite attacks per round.

12. Hairless and Sticky: This species has no fur or spinal spikes, but secretes a sticky goo from its bare skin to protect itself from the elements. A variety of debris is usually caught upon its skin. Its territory is often marked by strange placement of objects on trees that it scratches itself upon. If threatened, it will roll up into a ball and roll up creatures or characters onto its sticky hide. Its roll attack is SV 01-90 and inflicts an initial d10 stun damage. Those struck by the creature as it rolls over or even brushes by them must roll a type C strength hazard check or be stuck on the creature's body for d4 rounds. Those stuck to this monster in subsequent rounds while it is rolling around, suffer d4+10 stun damage per round until catapulted free of the creature. If this specimen is defeated, it will be found with d4 discarded items stuck to it, rolled from the following table:

Wailing Jhonny Discarded Items Table Roll d100

d3 discarded items in nest per adult in pack.

01. Mini grenade
02. Paint-by-Numbers set, worth 10+d12sp. **Roll d6: 1.** Unicorns with lasers / **2.** Dogs playing Canasta / **3.** "Hang In There" inspirational image with a T-Rex biting onto a tree root on a cliffside. / **4.** Kittens in teacups / **5.** Flamingo on a skateboard / **6.** Robot monkey
03. Aviator glasses, worth 3d20sp
04. Machete
05. Flattened top hat
06. Fragmentation grenade
07. Cast iron pan, usable, worth 10+d20sp
08. Magnifying glass, usable, worth 20+d12sp
09. Large metal flashlight, no power cell
10. Gasmask, hot pink
11. Child's walkie-talkie with batteries (range 1km in ruins, hills, city or up to 5km on the sea or open terrain. Batteries are a mini power cell in each unit, 50% charge, with a full charge running them for 18 days. Set worth 200+3d100sp.
12. Bottle of moonshine, age and origin questionable.
13. Metal file
14. A can of Numberghetties, worth 4+d4sp
15. A match box, half-used, 10 matches remain
16. Heavy book worth 20+d20sp. **Roll d6 for type: 1.** Old mapbook / **2.** Giant book of I Spy / **3.** Medical Illustration book / **4.** "Germs and You" / **5.** Cats / **6.** Android repair guide
17. "Unwelcome" mat, worth 2+d6sp
18. Pepper spray, half used
19. Alloy scalpel, treat as a knife in combat, worth 15+1d20sp
20. Rubber duck, worth 5+d4sp

21. A steel canteen filled with lighter fluid
22. Pith helmet (-4 DV/ MV –0 /500g weight) value 3d6+12sp
23. Submachine gun, containing 4d6 rounds of ammo
24. Heavy nylon rope, 3d6m
25. Rifle scope
26. Winter sleeping bag
27. Leopard print leotard in fabulous condition, worth 20+d6sp
28. Switchblade knife
29. Relic baseball cap, worth 6+d6sp. **Roll d4** for team: **1.** Sluggers / **2.** Whitecaps / **3.** Bluejays / **4.** Ninjas
30. Anti-toxin injector
31. Pocket-bot, full battery
32. Handcuffs, with one key
33. Dirty wig, worth 2+d6sp
34. Bear spray, full
35. Hatchet, dull
36. Oversized foam cowboy hat, worth 7+d6sp
37. Assault rifle, no ammo
38. Battle rocket
39. Bo staff, relic alloy, can be disassembled into three lengths, worth 40+4d20sp. Treat as regular staff but inflicts d12+6 damage and is +5 SV.
40. Red plastic handled paring knife with the phrase "Baby's first shiv" scrawled on the handle in marker. Worth 3d6+20sp
41. Mini power cell with d100% charge remaining
42. 10m of parachute cord
43. Worn hiker's backpack with an empty sawed off shotgun and 3 packaged snack cakes inside.
44. 2 cans of creamed corn, each worth d6+6sp
45. Pair of blue binoculars
46. Large orange tarp, worn but usable, worth 3d4sp if sold.
47. Filter mask
48. Miniature metal unicorn, worth 10+d6sp
49. Submachine gun, empty
50. Magazine for auto pistol, containing 2d6 rounds inside
51. 10+d6 old superhero comics contained in a plastic folio. Worth 3+d6 each
52. Bottle of white wine, recent vintage
53. Helmet with flames on the sides. Treat as relic riot helmet. Mildly used.
54. Headless stuffed animal covered in drool.
55. Carved skull, worth 12+d6sp
56. Carved golden skull, worth 100+2d100sp
57. Burlap sack, usable
58. Rusty knife, worth 2+d3sp
59. Plastic recorder. Playable. Worth 4+d6sp
60. 4 mini power cells, fully charged.

61. Rocket launcher with 1+d3 battle rockets

62. Hunter's knife, mint condition

63. Five cans of chili and a gas mask. Pure coincidence. Cans worth d8+6sp each.

64. Jeweled skull, worth 200+4d100sp

65. Two submachine guns and an assault rifle, each containing d6 rounds ammo.

66. Compass on thin steel chain necklace

67. Steel baseball bat, giggle stick inside. Usable as a 1 or 2 hands, inflicts extra +3 DMG and is +2 SV over a regular club.

68. Wooden jewelry box, worth 10+d3sp

69. Chainsaw with a half tank of gas

70. d6 packets of dry soup. Each worth 3+d6sp

71. Skeleton in usable riot armor

72. 2 nerve gas grenades

73. Tent, 1-man, blue, worth 20+d20sp

74. Rubber boots, water resistant, worth 10+d8sp

75. Packet of 20 relic soldier toys, worth 8+d8sp

76. Welding mask, very used. Worth 10+d20sp treat as a full helm if worn

77. Basketball, deflated with giant teeth marks

78. 2 rolls of gauze

79. Crowbar with painted blue flames

80. 7 packets of very dry beef jerky. Each worth 2sp

81. 2 unarmed land mines

82. 1kg bag of jasmine rice in airtight foil bag, worth 5+d12sp

83. 50 assorted relic cardboard chips in a plastic bag labeled "POGS"

84. Blue ballistic shield with a large dent in it. The word POLICE written on it in faded, scratched lettering.

85. Rusty pail with "HEnRy" scrawled on it. A hole has been haphazardly patched on the side.

86. A sweater vest carefully wrapped in plastic, worth 3d6sp

87. Lime green keytaur, worth 60+4d20sp, uses a standard power cell, missing.

88. Worn out, faded backpack, both straps broken, but is filled with 2d4 mini grenades.

89. A bottle of relic rum. Worth 30+2d20sp

90. Cooler with wheels, plaid. Filled with swamp water and two cans of lemonade. Worth 100+d100sp

91. Gold flecked relic tennis racket. Worth 40+3d20sp

92. Four jars of fireflies, tied up to poles.

93. Body bag. Filled with 2 clean sets of riot armor.

94. Relic mirror. Gold and highly ornate, worth 200+2d100sp

95. Male patterned service industry android. Missing an arm from a large bite, but in working condition. GM: 17% chance it is a Mecha controlled spy, and try to murder pure stock humans.

96. A sword heavily embedded in a rock. Roll d20. 5 or below sprains arms for 2 turns. 6-18 pull the sword free. It appears to be a newly forged long sword in good condition. 19-20 Pull the sword free and the holder discovers it is a relic razor sword.

97. Survival kit, containing three anti-toxin injectors, two rolls of gauze, two half liter bottles of water, half liter of rubbing alcohol.

98. Assault shotgun, d8 shells in drum.

99. Advanced frag grenade. A soggy box filled with 12 cans of condensed soup and a gnarled wooden staff with the words "You shall not pass" scrawled on it.

00. Rocket launcher loaded with one battle rocket and a furry, talking relic robotic toy bear with 2 relic mini power cells inside, (drained), robot worth 150+3d100sp.

CREATURES OF THE APOCALYPSE: 11
Tyrannosapien
By William McAusland

Tyrannosapien

By William McAusland

Defense Value: **-10**

Endurance: **300+4d100**

Movement: **12m**

Initiative: **+0**

Attacks: **Trample** or **Bite and 2 claws**

Strike Value: **01-90**

Damage: **Trample 2d20 stun + d20 lethal** or **bite 2d20+20** and 2 **claws 2d12+10 each**

Strength: 270

Agility: 24

Accuracy: 38

Intelligence: 10+d10

Willpower: 88

Perception: 26

Valuables: nil

Experience: 375

Morale: Excellent

Size: 4 meters tall, neck can reach up to 7m

Weight: 3400 + 1kg per point of END

Mutations: 22% / d4

Tyrannosapiens are among the largest, most fierce mammalian creatures of the new era. They weigh in at 3800 kg or more, stand 4 meters tall but with their long necks extended, can reach as high as 7 meters and are able to snatch arboreal animals right out of most trees. Although they can move about on all four appendages, they refer to walk in a bipedal fashion and use their clawed, front arms to slash and dismember other creatures.

When on the attack, this enormous creature will always employ any offensive mutations it might posses, first. Once any mutations are expended or prove ineffective, the animal will make a thunderous, ear splitting bellow. This roar is so intense, and overwhelming, that any creature smaller than the Tyrannosapien must make a morale check, failure means the creature is frozen in horror and for d2 rounds can do nothing but stare in shock at the giant predator as it charges toward them at full speed. For characters with no morale rating, each player character is allowed a type C Willpower based hazard check or lose d2 rounds of action. Those who are successful at their morale or hazard check can fight or flee as usual.

The tyrannosapien has two main modes of attack, either a combination of a bite and two claws, or a trample. The later is used when facing off against groups of smaller creatures, including humans, and involves simply charging clear through their ranks and stomping them as it goes. The T-sapien seems to enjoy this act, and makes what witnesses have described as a joyous, belly laugh as it wades through its victims time and again until subduing about a dozen. Each person in the path of this giant beast is considered attacked, with the damage being 2d20 stun and d20 lethal. If the tyranno sapien cannot run through the prey animals, perhaps due to the targets being among large trees, rubble or some location where the area behind is a solid barrier, river or cliff, it will instead resort to biting and clawing. The trample attack can only be made if it can get some speed up, and must start at least 24m away from the intended targets. After each trample pass, it must stop, 24m away again and turn and come back, taking four rounds, often giving humanoids a chance to either break and run in different directions, or fire upon the monster with missile weapons and mutational powers.

When attacking humanoids, Tyrannosapiens have their own critical hit tables with separate outcomes for trample, bite and finally claw attacks, as follows:

Critical Hits from Trample Attacks　Roll d6

1. Maximum damage (40 stun and 20 lethal)
2. Curbed! The victim's head seems to take most of the T-sapien's weight and is crushed. Take regular random trample damage (2d20 stun and d20 lethal, as well as brain damage with permanent loss of 3d6 Intelligence to a minimum of 1 point).
3. Drop kicked. The victim takes regular damage from the trample attack, but is also scooped up and kicked into the air, thrown 4d6+10 meters and lands hard for an extra 3d20 stun damage and a 23% chance of impaling him or herself on a sharpened branch, length of rebar, tent pole or other protrusion. This impalement is treated as an attack SV 01-80, damage 2d20 lethal.
4. Double damage, plus, one of the victim's legs is broken (d6: 1-3 right/ 4-6. Left) and takes 3+d8 months to heal. Half speed.
5. Double damage plus the victim's arm (d6: 1-3 right/ 4-6. Left) is snapped in several places and takes 2+d6 months to heal.
6. Flattens the target, shoving the victim's head down into its chest cavity, and the legs driving up into the subject's abdomen. Death occurs within d3 rounds regardless of medical attention.

Critical Hits from Bites　Roll d6

1. Maximum bite damage (60 points)
2. Mash up! The character is hauled off his or her feet, thrown in the air, chomped a few times and then spit out. The chomping removes any belts and back packs or objects held in the subject's hands, worse, the extra attention has inflicted an additional d20 stun and d10 lethal damage. When spit out, the T-sapien will hork the character out at another random adversary, using the spit coated victim as a projectile (SV 01-80, damage d20 stun and d10 lethal damage).
3. Shaken and thrown! Regular damage, however the T-sapien lifts and shakes the victim viscously before throwing the limp body 3d6 meters away to one side. The subject takes an extra d20 stun damage from being shaken and is severely disorientated and -4 initiative and half speed for the next 3d6 minutes. Likewise, all non-mental attacks it conducts are down to half their usual strike value.
4. Chomp! The character's arm is severed at the shoulder (d6: 1-3 right/ 4-6. Left) and swallowed. Regular damage, plus the loss of the arm and a subsequent blood loss of d4 endurance per round thereafter until the wound is pressed, cauterized or a tourniquet wrapped on the stump.
5. Snapped up, chewed and spit out! The character takes regular damage, but is severely mauled and coated in saliva and digestive enzymes before being spit 3d6 meter away for a hard landing. The impact is treated as a separate attack (SV 01-80, damage 2d20 stun).
6. Big gulp! The victim takes no bite damage, but... is enshrouded in the beast's mouth, gripped by the tongue and swallowed whole and alive. Half way down the T-Sapien's neck, the ingested person becomes temporarily lodged and the shape of the victim's body visible to anyone watching from outside. Here, litres of saliva and digestive juices wash over the character, making the subject well lubricated for the final swallow.

If the character has a hand mounted relic, mutation or implant, or a mental or other non-handheld mode of fighting back, he or she can do so at this point for d3 rounds. Each gulp by the monster sucks the victim deeper and finally into the animal's highly acidic stomach. In the stomach, the subject dissolves rapidly taking d8 damage per round, as well as suffocating and suffering 10 points of stun damage until slipping in to unconsciousness. If the tyrannosapien is killed by the swallowed character, he or she can cut free of the guts and survive. Likewise, if comrades can kill the beast and cut out the victim before he or he expires, then the hapless casualty might also survive the ordeal.

Critical Hits from Claw Attacks   Roll d6

1. Maximum claw damage (34 points)!

2. Laceration! The claw slides down through the character's face, neck, chest and onward to the ground. The claw does regular damage plus permanently scars the character and reduces his or appearance by 10+d10 points to a minimum of 1 point.

3. Snagged! The tip of one claw hooks through a strap, belt or some other harness on the target, cutting his or flesh deeply as a regular claw attack, but also dragging the victim about for d4 rounds. During this time, the T-sapien becomes furious with the thing stuck to its paw and shakes the clawed hand vigorously, making no further attacks with it. The shaking is so sever that the casualty is unable to do anything but scream or use mental mutations. Everything he or she looks out upon is a blur, and after becoming unhooked, the subject tumbles in onto the ground taking an extra 2d20 stun damage and having dropped anything he or she had previously been holding.

4. Tripped! The curved claw comes low, catching the character behind the knee and besides doing regular damage from the gory wound, the claw snags and yanks the character off the ground and tosses him or her 3d6m away. The subsequent fall is treated as an attack: SV 01-80, damage d20 stun and d10 lethal

5. Severed arm (d6: 1-3 right/ 4-6. Left). Besides regular damage, the claws take off the subject's arm just above the elbow. Blood loss occurs rapidly and the victim takes d4 damage per round until death, or until somebody uses a tourniquet to stem the flow of vital fluid.

6. Decapitation! A claw cleaves through the neck of the target, neatly slicing the head off the body. Instant death occurs unless the victim is an android, has other heads, or some other arrangement.

Although its name is inspired from the prehistoric dinosaur, this freakish giant has no reptilian DNA and in fact is a humanoid. While technically able to crossbreed with giant humanoids such as garnocks, and some mad scientist could theoretically blend the genetic material of these beasts with regular humans, tyrannosapiens by nature see all other animals solely as food.

Given their massive bulk and hot blooded cardiovascular systems, they require an enormous amount of flesh to maintain themselves. They quickly exhaust an area of large prey animals and must constantly wander to new feeding grounds, particularly those featuring lush agricultural land with plenty of cattle, sheep, hogs and farm labourers to ingest.

Although tyrannosapiens sometimes gather to mate, and females with a single offspring can be encountered, they are most often seen alone. Researchers suspect that these monsters do not commingle well with their own kind, except during mating season in the fall. Females experience a 22 month gestation period and give birth to one live offspring at a time. Growing fast, a youngster will reach adulthood at age six, and over the next year, wander in and out of its mother's life for the following year before being driven off or establishing its own territory.

T-sapiens cannot swim and dislike deep water where they cannot see the bottom. They will cross rivers and streams, however, but only at low points or where there is plenty of rubble or vegetation to clasp onto. While they fear fire, a small cook fire, mere hand held torch or bright electric light will do little more than attract their attention and make them think a meal is someplace near the illumination source. A bonfire or large brush fire on the other hand, will keep them well away. Villages established in the territories of one or more of these giant hunters will have prepared fire pits, spike filled trenches or deep moats surrounding their settlements, plus employ catapults loaded with bales of burning hay to fire at the creatures and drive them off.

Occasionally, packs of mutant dogs, wolves and other scavengers will follow along behind tyrannosapiens, feeding off the entrails, gristle and shredded carcasses of the giant's victims, and may even attack those who manage to slip away from the enormous humanoid's raids.

Unsubstantiated, but persistent, reports of tyrannosapiens being used as colossal mounts for travel and warfare have circulated into the saloons, digger forts and barter towns of humanity. These accounts supposedly tell of warmort raiders from the wastes employing the creatures after having built enclosed, armor plated platforms on the backs of these giant deviants. The notion is scoffed at. Having such a beast serve as a mount for a powerful post-apocalyptic warlord is fanciful enough for most new era thinkers, and if it were true, they claim one would have to raise such a fiend from its 'childhood' to have any hope of controlling it, unless some sort of cybernetic control node was implanted into the monster's brain.

While the basic shape of a regular tyrannosapien is terrible enough, documented accounts of mutated specimens have circulated. 22% of all encountered specimens are deviants with d2 mutations from the following list: Roll d20

Tyrannosapien Mutations   Roll d20

1. Extra arm: Although the appendage ends with a massive human hand with which it uses to hammer other beings as a regular claw attack (doing stun damage), it can also throw boulders, rubble and stumps at distant foes. Range 80m/ SV 01-70/ DMG 2d20+5/ rate: once every second round.

2. Rhino-like overlapping armored plates: DV improved by -20 (now -30), plus add +30 endurance points, how ever, the creature is slowed by -2m movement per round (now 10m).

3. Spike and scale covered: Increase the endurance of this specimen by +50, reduce its movement by -4 (now 8m per round), however its defence value (DV) is bumped up -30 (now DV -40).

4. Two headed: Makes two bite attacks per round.

5. Multi-eyed: Growing all around the deviant's head are d6 extra eyes. Altogether, the eyes give this specimen +2 initiative and +20 perception (now 46).

6. Covered in sacks of acidic sweat: Like dozens of saddle bags, this mutant is covered in shingle-like fleshy bags filled with bright orange goop. If struck, an acid sack erupts and spits out a stream of offensive smelling liquid 6 meters in the direction of the successful attacker, SV 01-70, Damage d6 per round for 2d4 rounds. Drenching the victim in two or more litres of a neutral liquid, like water or beer, will stop the acid from burning further.

7. Mental defence lobe: Someplace in the tyrannosapien's skull is a section of the brain that scrambles 92% of all incoming hostile mental attacks and controls, making this specimen virtually immune to such attacks and intrusions.

8. Regenerates: This beast heals 2 endurance points per round. If killed fully however, and not merely unconscious, its circulatory system shuts down and will not regenerate.

9. Sticky mess: This monster exudes a sap-like pus that over the years, has allowed objects from its environment to adhere to it and both conceal and armor plate the thing. It gains -10 DV (now -20), is slowed somewhat by -2m (now 10m per round) but gains +2 initiative, and, if it wins the initiative, can remain motionless and hidden and therefore allow prey or larger creatures to wander right passed it without noticing the tyrannosapien laying in wait. There will be d4+2 treasure items from the included table festooned onto this specimen.

10. Spits glue: Once every fourth round, this tyrannosapien can hork up a glob of dark purple, glue-like phlegm and spit it at one or more grouped targets. The ball of glue opens into an adhesive net once in the air, and can cover a 6 meter area in the sticky mucus. Those in the path of the gob are only allowed their agility and dodge skills as far as avoiding the gross projectile. Anyone struck (SV 01-80) is fastened to the goo for d4 rounds. While trapped, the victims are +30 easier to be attacked by the tyrannosapien, plus, all physical strikes made by bound victims suffer a -20 SV. Movement while glued is possible, but only at half rate.

11. Shooting spines: Covering the back and shoulders of this specimen are hundreds of long bright blue spines. When first encountering prey animals or enemies this tyrannosapien will unleash d6 spines per round, range 30 meters, SV 01-80, DMG d12+2 each. Besides being able to fire these half meter long darts, the countless undeveloped spines growing on its skin serve as armor, improving the DV of this specimen by -10 (now -20).

12. More robust: This freak is built tougher than normal specimens, and has an extra 70 endurance, inflicts another +4 damage per strike, has thicker skin (DV improved -5 so now -15), but is somewhat slower at 11m per round instead of 12m.

13. Radioactive bite and flesh: Anything this creature bites, or if some other person or animal bites it, the subject is potentially exposed to a dose of medium radiation. (Make a type A END based hazard check per successful strike on or from the tyrannosapien to avoid the dose. Successive doses can occur from multiple contacts with the animal).

14. Toxic flesh: Anything to bite this mutant must make a type D endurance based hazard check or succumb to a strange, debilitating toxin. Victims suffer a 50% loss to their movement, hallucinate, are +20 SV easier to be stuck by any attacker, and break out in a horrendous body covering rash for a week (-50% appearance trait). The toxin's symptoms, except for the rash, fade after d6 hours.

15. Howl of doom: Once every fifth round this tyrannosapien can bellow in a specific direction, range 18 meters, emitting a cone of wind and sound so deafening and powerful that only the largest, most courageous beings can stay and face the beast. Anyone in the 6 meter wide blast zone must first make a type D willpower based hazard check to shrug-off the fear or else flee for 3d6 minutes. Secondly, the intensity of the wind forces targets to make an endurance base type E hazard check or be blown off their feet and driven back 2d6 meters. If blown back, the unlucky victim is prone to injuries from objects on the ground, and attacked twice: SV 01-60, damage d12 lethal and d20 stun.

16. Shock tendrils: Growing from this specimen's back are 4+d4 long, meat colored tendrils. Each tube is 12 meters long and able to lash out and slap one or multiple targets: SV 01-70, Damage d20 stun. The tendrils can be shot or hacked off by adversaries (DV -20/ END 12 each).

17. Electrical field generation: This tyrannosapien can put a powerful charge of electricity into the ground and air around it, range 9m radius. All within the radius, either flying or on foot are jolted and take d8 damage automatically. This power can be used three times per hour.

18. Immunity to poison.

19. Runner: This tyrannosapien has longer legs and a leaner build. Its endurance is reduced by -50, however it can run 14+d6m per round, easily overtaking horsemen and most every prey animal it comes across. It stands 6m at the shoulders.

20. 'Rex', a Monstrous specimen: This tyrannosapien is a true giant of its kind, weighing twice as much, having an extra +200 endurance, inflicting an extra +10 damage per attack, and covered in bony lumps, spines and sheets of bone giving it a -20 DV bonus (now -30) yet reducing its movement rate to 6m per round. The creature stands 7m tall at the shoulders and can extend its studded, scaly neck out 12m. Slow and lumbering, it relies mainly on ambush tactics, or else scavenging the kills of other beasts.

Tyrannosapiens do not value relics, coins or anything man made, however, they do like to carry fresh kills to specific eating spots. These sites are often out of the sun, protected from the wind, and a place where they can slowly munch on the dead and dying from recent hunts. On many occasions, a tyrannosapien will have merely stomped over a group of humanoids, and after subduing several, will let the unhurt quarry flee while it turns its attention to the fallen. If hungry (86% of the time) it will straight out eat about six man sized victims before grabbing one more in each clawed paw, and two more in its mouth and bring the morsels to one of its feeding spots.

It will try to keep living beings alive for as long as possible, imprisoning them in a dead end, pit, ruined building, or steep ravine, to maintain freshness, but so too, to enjoy taunting them in a sort of cat and mouse game whereby it pretends to let a victim flee, only to rush out from a hiding place, run down and grab and maul the escapee afresh, only killing and eating a 'pet' prey animal or person after the victim becomes too damaged or uncooperative to play further.

The feeding site of a tyrannosapien is often located by smell long before it is sighted. Here, the macabre bone and gut mounds of these flesh eaters reveal a mix or animal and humanoid remains, as well as the still living, maimed victims of the beast. As the creature does not value relics, it will leave them and any valuables and gear exactly where they drop, either as the victim is crushed and swallowed and hard bits spit out, or items pass clear through the digestive track of the monster and end up in meter tall fecal stacks. Many of these stacks, reduced by time, rain and worms to mounds of shredded fur, bone, horn, clothing and equipment, can be easily poked through to uncover valuables.

The following table supplies a d100 random listing of items found in a tyrannosapien feeding site, with 3d6 rolls allowed, re-rolling duplicated results. For the searching of a simple feces stack, roll on the same table but use a 2d20, d3+1 times.

Tyrannosapien Feed Site Discoveries   Roll d100

01. Pair of fuzzy six sided dice, attached by string.
02. Magazine for an automatic pistol with d12 rounds remaining
03. Fragmentation grenade
04. Roll of camo duct tape, 3d6+6m remaining on roll, worth 1sp per meter
05. Tattered blue Starstruck Coffee™ barista apron, worth d20+20sp
06. Shotgun shell
07. Anti-toxin Injector
08. d3 standard rifle rounds
09. Jaw worm, which wriggles up and out of the decaying heap to attack whatever disturbed it.
10. Pocket flashlight, battery has 3d6 minutes of illumination remaining
11. Steel alcohol flask filled with vodka, 500ml
12. 6+d6m of old world, bright yellow nylon rope
13. Human skull of a cyborg with a random optical implant still fused to the left side. A robotics technician could remove the parts and sell the item in a major town for 400+2d100sp.
14. Magazine for an assault rifle with d4 rounds loaded inside
15. Pocket pistol, empty of ammo but magazine still attached
16. Spring-spike, closed
17. Power cell, drained
18. Human skull, partially dissolved, wearing an intact dark green relic army helmet.
19. Pair of handcuffs, with two keys on a wire loop
20. Skeletal human arm and hand with communicator wristwatch still attached and having a half year's charge remaining.
21. Night vision headgear, battery down to 30 minutes operation.
22. A single fifty caliber round of ammo
23. A drum magazine for an assault rifle, loaded with 2d4 rounds of standard rifle ammo.
24. Zippy bag containing 3d6 .22 caliber rounds of ammo.
25. Binoculars, standard
26. Plastic pouch with zipper, bright pink with flowers on it containing d6 gold coins and 3d6+6 sliver coins. Coin purse worth 16+d12sp
27. Pewter miniature of some pig faced, fantasy humanoid with an axe and shield. Worth 6+d6sp
28. Standard hand held communicator with 3d6 minutes of power left on the battery.
29. d6 pistol rounds
30. Ballistic vest wrapped around the skeletal remains of a human rib cage.
31. Bright green plastic horse, kid's toy, cartoonish design. Worth 22+2d20sp
32. Stainless steel coffee cup with a plastic flip lid and a blue star logo on it, worth 3d6+6sp
33. Skeletal human hand with a gold wedding band on the ring finger, worth 60+d100sp
34. Stainless steel woodworker's C-clamp, old world manufactured, worth 10+d20sp
35. Lockblade relic folding knife, 13cm (5") blade. Treat as regular knife but +2 SV and +2 DMG, alloy, worth 200+2d100sp if sold

36. Large glow in the dark plastic star, hand sized, worth 6+d8sp

37. Small plastic pill bottle with tinfoil seal intact. Anyone who can read notes contents as '48 male enhancement pills. Guaranteed to add between one and four inches to one's member and allow for multiple intimate moments per day'. Pills worth 4sp each if sold in a major town.

38. Advanced fragmentation grenade

39. Plastic box of 24 individually wrapped, antique female hygiene pads. Each worth 2sp if sold in a major town.

40. Rotted human face and skull attached to a serviceable gasmask.

41. Men's solar charging electric shaver, complete with 3 body grooming settings and fold out handle for shaving one's back. Will fully charge in one hour of sunny exposure and offer 5 hours of shaving. Worth 200+2d100sp

42. Quiver of 12+d12 arrows along with d6 special arrows tipped with relic exploding arrows heads (TME hub pg. 196).

43. Compound crossbow with stock mounted bolt holder and fitted with d6 relic quarrels. These relics are tipped with expanding tips (see page 197 TME hub rules).

44. Landmine, disarmed.

45. Recently forged machete in a bloody leather sheath

46. Battle rocket

47. Bottle of red wine, half consumed, bottled in nearest large farm town.

48. Leg of a human, decaying, but strapped to the thigh is an empty drop-leg style holster with a magazine pouch on it. There is one automatic pistol mag inside loaded with d12 rounds of ammo.

49. Pepper spray

50. An ammo belt of 6+d6 rifle rounds.

51. A shredded, blood stained suit of scrap relic armor. Requires an hour to clean and reassemble.

52. Silencer for auto pistol

53. Small metal tin with latched lid. Inside are 12+d12 glow in the dark condoms still in their original packages. Each worth 5sp if sold in a major town.

54. Tiny solar charged music player with white ear bud headphones. Contains 10,000 songs from all old world genres dating back to the earliest recordings of the twentieth century, including Metallica. Worth 300+3d100sp if sold.

55. Tactical helmet with drained power cell for mounted headlamp and communicator, otherwise in good shape.

56. Shredded, mechanical weapon arm ripped from some hapless cyborg. Bone and some decaying flesh present. The weapon is chewed beyond use, but it does have a drum magazine for an assault rifle filled with 3d6 rounds of ammo.

57. Ballistic shield, scratched up but in good order with the word POLICE written across it.

58. Shredded poncho made from relic digital pattern camo, complete with hood. Torn open from claws along the back, but only needs a half hour's stitchery work to make it wearable. Anyone trying to hide in the wilderness wearing this poncho gains 2 skill point in 'conceal self' and 'concealed movement' (see skills in the hub rules, page 51).

59. Tear gas grenade

60. Assorted, broken and dismantled robotic parts. It looks like something destroyed the unit at that location. Any character with the robotics technician skill will recognize the parts as belonging to a heavy combot, and could gather and resell the parts to collect 200+d1000sp, although the items would weigh 250kg and require a wagon, cart of horse to pack out.

61. Location beacons, 6 in a bright yellow plastic case. Pill batteries are loaded in each but a plastic slip-sheet has kept the batteries from being activated. Even so, the cells are ancient and will only run the beacons for two years.

62. Large shoulder carry water skin filled with three liters of drinkable water

63. Small olive drab plastic box containing five .50 caliber rounds of ammo.

64. Small chrome desk globe. Solar powered base makes the thing turn and light up showing different old world countries. Fist sized weighs 1kg, and worth 200+2d100sp

65. Power cell, fully charged and protected in bubble-wrap.

66. Skeletal remains of a human wearing a motion powered digital wrist watch. Worth 300+2d100sp

67. Magazine for a submachine gun, loaded with d12 rounds of standard pistol ammo.

68. Pocket-bot, coated in slime, slightly chewed and laying half buried in the dirt. Its battery is intact but drained.

69. Empty assault rifle magazine

70. Zippy bag filled with 2d6 standard rifle, 2d6 standard pistol, d6 shotgun shells, 3d6 .22 cal rounds, and d6 each of high caliber rifle and pistol ammo.

71. Torn leather backpack containing smelly work clothes, comb, pig's bristle tooth brush and a baggy of 3d6 high caliber rifle rounds

72. Small leather pouch on broken belt. Pouch contains 30+d20 silver coins and a braid of blonde hair tied at both ends with pink ribbons.

73. Torn open backpack with straps missing. Clothing strewn about along with some woman's plastic slippers, an ancient, zippered pink bag filled with old world makeup (worth 100+2d100sp), and a night vision headset, half charged.

74. Small wooden box, stained dark green with brass fittings. Recent construction. Inside is a small horde of 100+d100 silver coins, 3d6 gold coins, gems worth 200+d100sp, and bits of brightly colored plastic, fashion doll heads and other curiosities worth another 200+2d100sp. Also in the box are d12 standard pistol rounds. The box itself is worth 50+d20sp and has the initials F.B. carved ornately inside the lid.

75. A short, skeletally thin, gray skinned humanoid with a skull-like face. The thing is covered in scratches and a few large tooth punctures, but is breathing. It raises its head when approached and mumbles something intently. Its legs and one arm are broken and it cannot move.

GM: This is a skullock and just one lone survivor of a large band of peskies who happened to come under attack by the Tyrannosapien. If calmed down and talked to, it could relate some important information, such as that two of the things attacked their tribe, or that the monster, If not already slain, is nearby watching from the shadows of trees or a ruined structure.

The pesky could be put out of his misery, which it will thank the PCs for as he sees what they are about to do, or else, if carried off and given medical attention, could be saved and is 78% likely to become a loyal servant of his saviors, for life. If not becoming a loyal attendant, it will simply steal what it can from the PCs and slip away back to its territory.

76. Plastic tub containing hundreds of tiny gray model parts for at least 48 hard plastic Viking war gaming miniatures. They have been cut from the sprue and all their skin tone painted, but the rest of the incomplete models are merely primed. Set worth 70+d20sp if sold in a major town.

77. Small hard plastic sculpture of a life size chickadee bird. Sings like the real thing whenever the top of its head is touched. Solar powered. Worth 70+2d20sp

78. Antique SCA Roman Legionnaire's helmet, crafted from historically accurate metals and treated as an iron helmet if worn. If sold, would fetch 150+d100sp

79. Bright yellow twenty sided dice, worth 20+d20sp

80. Faded, torn and dotted by a few bullet holes, is the national flag of the former country that once ruled the pre-devastation area the characters now stand in.

81. A roll of plastic coated bright white wire, 10+d20 meters in length and if sold will fetch 1sp per meter. The wire is strong enough to hold an average man's weight if used as a fine rope.

82. Leather pouch containing 2d4 mini grenades

83. Clear plastic dispenser and 20+d10m of clear household tape, worth 18+3d6sp

84. A half eaten man in ragged leather, commoners clothing. He wears a bone handled dagger at his belt as well as a fine pair of tire tread sandals.

85. Bright purple plastic ruler, 30cm long with the alphabet and numbers running down the middle as open stencils for lettering, worth 10+d20sp

86. Large plastic heart, bright red, has hinges on one side and a simple latch on the other. Inside the 30cm wide container are hundreds of ancient, faded, yellowed valentines cards, all with cartoon characters and photos from various old world movies and TV series. Collection and case worth 80+d100sp

87. Canister of ethanol fuel designed for use with either a chainsaw or flame unit relic. 2 liters. Completely full.

88. Book wrapped in clear plastic. **Roll d6: 1.** Ancient bible, worth 400+2d100sp/ **2.** Army Medic's Manual, worth 500+3d100sp (any PC with the medics skill already, and who can read, and studies this manual nightly for 30 days, will gain 1 skill point extra as a medic. / **3.** 2218 AD Comic Buyer's guide worth 100+d100sp/ **4.** Purist Bible, written by hand recently and worth 50+d20sp if sold to a devout, mutant-burning purist cultist, otherwise no value. /**5.** Guide book to Tanks and Armored Vehicles of the 4th World War, worth 200+2d100sp/ **6.** Compendium of an ancient series of graphic novel regarding zombies. Over 300 pages of wonderful ink artwork. Worth 300+d100sp.

89. Mostly eaten, maggot encrusted horse still wearing its saddle and saddle bags. If inspected, the characters find d6 liters of water, 3d6 kilograms of grain, a saddle bag holding 3d6 days dried rations as well as a leather gun boot-holster thingy containing some sort of firearm! **Roll d6: 1.** Musket rifle, loaded, and comes with 20 rounds of shot, wad and powder./ **2.** Twenty-two rifle, lever action sporting rifle. This old west influenced gun holds d20 cartridges in its 20 shot capacity tube magazine./ **3.** Twenty-two semi-automatic rifle with a 30 round box magazine loaded with 3d10 .22 cartridges./ **4.** Survival rifle with d10 rifle rounds in its standard ten shot mag. / **5.** Pump shotgun with d8 shells in its 8 shot tube magazine. / **6.** Assault rifle with 3d10 rifle rounds in its 30 round magazine.

90. White plastic comb filled with greasy hair and visible head lice.

91. Assault rifle with magazine, empty

92. Compound bow with a broken bow string.

93. Pump shotgun with d4 shells in tube

94. Small, putrid smelling sack containing 3d6 small, clawed gray hands (skullock hands).

95. Hunting rifle with bipod and standard scope. Treat as sniper rifle but bolt action and has only a 5 round magazine with d4 HC rifle rounds inside). Complete with nylon sling.

96. Blood stained canvas sack with a shoulder strap. If opened, inside are d6 dead rabbits, d6 bloated marmots, 2d6 maggot coated rats and a young, still living hell-cougar kitten (treat as a domestic cat while young).

97. Automatic pistol, high caliber with d6 HC pistol rounds loaded in mag.

98. A near dead human child wrapped in some sort of backpack rig that must have been worn by one of her parents. The child is no more than four years old and once revived, will be in shock for 2d4 days. While accepting food, water and blankets, will not speak of what happened until after the shock fades. Once remotely normal, the child will treat the PCs as her new family, with all of them being her parents and calling them mommy or daddy depending on their gender.

99. A human woman in a ragged, blood flecked woolen skirt and poncho. She is alive, but only barely, with a broken arm, severe bruises and a few obvious tooth punctures. If given water and medical attention she will say that she was taken from a migrants camp nearby, where a great monster came and fed on her people. She will not leave the character's side and begs them to let her be their cook and housekeeper.

She is a non-combatant by nature, but an accomplished healer with 1 skill point as a medic. There is a 66% chance she is a deviant with d3 minor mutations, otherwise a pure stock, aged 17+d12 and goes by the name of Flora.

100. Fifty caliber sniper rifle with d6 rounds loaded in magazine. No scope.

CREATURES OF THE APOCALYPSE: 12
Chest Head
By Brandon Goeringer

Chest Head
By Brandon Goeringer

Defense Value: **-20**

Endurance: **70+d20**

Movement: **6m**

Initiative: **+3**

Attacks: **1 weapon** (battleaxe / spear) **& bite**

Strike Value: **01-80**

Damage: **d20+12 battleaxe/ d20+11 spear/ d6+10 bite**

Strength: 83 (+10 DMG)

Agility: 68

Accuracy: 76

Intelligence: 8+d6

Willpower: 62

Perception: 90

Appearance: d8+2

Valuables: very poor (See page TME 208, 4 rolls for tribe leader) / 23% chance of each having 1 roll on the included loot table on page 68

Experience: 70

Morale: Excellent

Size: 2.7 meters tall

Weight: 205kg

Mutations: 14% of 1

Relics: 11% each has WC-R

Implants: nil

Hunger is a primary driving force in the plains, forests, swamps, and ruins of the wastelands. This is even more true for the barbaric marauding tribes of chest heads. These tall, long limbed mutants are easily recognized by their two heads. Though unlike many other mutants in the 24th century which have side by side, neck mounted additional heads, the second head on these brutes sits squarely in their chests, thus giving them their somewhat blunt name.

Most chest heads have dirty pink skin with protruding bone spikes running down their arms or spine. Tuffs of hair sprout from large boils, moles or warts that afflict their epidermis. Both of the unique heads of a chest head are monstrous in appearance, with long sharp teeth, small upturned noses and bloodshot bleary eyes. The head set into the chest is situated very close to its digestive organs. This unique anatomy layout produces a strong desire in the humanoid to eat vast quantities of food due to flawed nervous system pathways and hormonal imbalances. This craving leads the head in the chest to bite during combat, attempting to tear off a hand, nose or ear for a mid-fight snack. They speak in a crude form of the language of the ancients, with both heads often talking in stereo, grunting out the same words in unison.

They make and wield deadly archaic melee weapons with remarkable skill; these implements made from various scrap materials. It is reported from surviving raid victims that chest heads don't use relic weapons or tools, although this might not be factual due to the small number of survivors. Thankfully, none of them have been encountered possessing cybernetic implants, though a rare few have showed signs of mutation. Chest heads have 2 stealth skill points, a 14% chance of a mutation, and have 23% chance of having an item from the table on page 68 of this book. If one head is destroyed the other head is also incapacitated.

Chest heads live in a tribal community where the war party is the primary force for raids, protection and gathering food. Warriors, d4+3 in number, are often sent out to pillage small settlements or attack caravans and farms at night. Possessing twice the number of eyes as most of their prey, and linked nervous system brains, they are excellent at observing hazards, enemies and potential meals. They don't take slaves but do adorn their bodies with the heads and skulls of their kills. They will hack and dismember their victims after battle for transportation back to their tribe and readily eat pure stocks, mutants and cyborgs alike. Many of their spoils are consumed as "road snacks" whilst returning to their community due to lack of self control. The presence of discarded body parts make travelling chest heads easy to track by animal predators or hostile hunting parties looking for revenge, with the trail of these tall, two headed brutes often littered with blood, discarded cybernetics and indigestible bits.

Most chest heads encountered are males, as females tend to stay behind in their communities and take care of the young. They usually make ancient ruins their tribal homes though some have fashioned crude wooden huts when no ruins may be located. Their community normally consists of d8+8 females with an equal amount of offspring and d10+10 male warriors. They're always led by a tribal leader that is taller, stronger and tougher than regular warriors, and possesses four times the amount of valuables. Tribe leaders are a half meter taller, do an extra +14 damage and have 20+3d20 more endurance.

Their origins are not much studied or contemplated. They are believed to just be the mutated descendants of bioengineered frontline shock troops, created sometime during the ancient wars. They are feared by all inhabitants of the wastelands due to their brutal butchery, voracious hunger, skilled fighting prowess, and rigorous constitutions. Rumors of chest heads being spotted and consuming still living captives will freeze the hearts of towns people with fear until the monsters have been driven off or killed. The recruiting of mercenary or excavator squads to deal with these freaks is standard procedure by most community warlords, mayors, clergymen or councils.

Chest Head Mutations Roll d12

1. Bad Breath: The head in the chest has horrible breath. When it makes a bite attack at a target, striking or not, the target must make a successful END based, type C hazard check or spend 2 rounds vomiting, becoming +30 easier to strike, with the victim's own SV being reduced to half, rounded down.

2. Spines: -16 to DV, unarmed strikes to the creature deal d10 damage to the attacker.

3. Puke Attack: In lieu of all other attacks per round, the head in the chest may, once per combat, vomit up to 9 meters away, at a single target. SV 0-86, inflicting d6+2 acid damage on a successful hit per round for d6 rounds.

4. Two Heads in Chest: This mutant gets an additional bite attack in melee combat.

5. Huge Maw: This freak has an extra-large, elongated chest mouth. Any successful bite from the chest maw will inflict double damage.

6. Regenerate: Any depleted traits heal at 1 point per round.

7. Decap Attack: This truly unique mutant may, in lieu of all attacks, detach and throw the head on its shoulders, range 15m, SV 01-80, inflicting d12+10 damage on a success-

ful hit. The head grows back at incredible speed at the beginning of the next round. The freak may make this attack any amount of times per day it desires, but at a cost: this attack inflicts 5 END damage to the Chest Head.

8. Spitter: Once every six rounds, this creature can expel a huge glob of saliva with surprising accuracy, range 6m, SV 01-70, in an attempt to temporarily blind an opponent. If eye or facial protection is not being worn, this attack (made in lieu of all attacks) results in penalties to the target's movement (-3m), SV (-14) and Defense Value (+8) until the sticky spit is removed (taking d4+2 rounds).

9. Suction Cup Hands: This chest head has the Climbing Suckers mutation per TME Hub Rules page 63.

10. Long Legs: This freak has longer than normal legs and stays on all fours when walking or running adding +3 meters to movement.

11. Ghost Mutations: This dangerous freak has d3 Ghost Mutations rolled on Table TME-1-59 page 59 of the TME hub rules.

12. Freakish Horror: This specimen features one additional mutation from this table, rolled using a d10, and is also massive, having an extra 100 endurance, moves 3m faster per round and does +12 more damage.

Chest Head Loot List   Roll d100

The following items may be found on a chest head body or in their community. Roll d100, but re-roll duplicated results or pick the result below a reoccurring number. If the item would not be carried on a chest head's person, re-roll.

1. Silver bullet, rifle caliber, worth 100+d20sp
2. Bottle of hot sauce "Texas Peter", 16oz, worth 20+d10sp
3. Cloth pouch of 13 gold teeth, worth 120+d10sp
4. Jade Buddha necklace on leather cord, worth 100+2d20sp
5. Cardboard tube with plastic top, full of crumbs, says "Sour Cream & Onion" on tube, worth 12+d4sp
6. Box of 20 candles, worth 4sp
7. Sickle
8. 3d6 steel Shish Kabob skewers, worth 1+d2sp each
9. Sling for a long gun made with unknown purple colored leather, worth 3d6sp
10. Metal chain, 2m
11. Plastic bag of wine corks, 6+d6, worth 1sp each
12. Jar of misc. eyeballs in green solution, various colors, worth 12+d6sp
13. Black metal case with malleable plastic 'face', the face can be applied in 2 minutes and gives the wearer +1 skill point of Disguise Artist, worth 400+d100sp
14. Wooden flute
15. Quiver, leather, bottom contains 8 dead rats
16. Metal red urn of ashes, tightly sealed, worth 30+d8sp
17. Leather holster, empty
18. Box of "Barkies!" dog biscuits, worth 14+d6sp
19. Pink bottle of child's bubbles, worth 4+d2sp
20. .22 Caliber pistol, loaded with 0-7 cartridges (d10 -3)
21. Whip, stained with blood
22. Baby food, d4 jars, worth 3+d4sp. **Roll d6: 1.** Peas / **2.** Green Beans / **3.** Apples / **4.** Squash / **5.** Carrots / **6.** Prunes
23. Power cell, fully charged
24. Screwdriver set, worth 90+d100sp
25. Inflatable beach ball, still in plastic bag, worth 5+d4sp
26. Blood soaked leather pouch containing d12 misc. fingers and toes, worth 3+d2sp
27. Knife with green stain on blade, will not wash off
28. Cast iron pot, may be used as junk helmet, smells like vegetable soup, worth 12+d10sp
29. Brass doorknob, worth 14+d10sp
30. Bark armor, dark brown

31. Leather spiked choker, -1 DV, worth 8+d6sp
32. Backpack with small plush creature peering over wearers shoulder, creature is green with pointy ears, empty, worth 20+d12sp
33. Stun stick, empty mini cell
34. Dart gun, 6 darts
35. Android head, gold skin and eyes with brown hair, worth 1000+2d100
36. Box of 100 cocktail umbrellas, worth 25+d10sp
37. Pump shotgun, empty
38. Plush oversized slippers, brown with black animal nails, resembles a bear's paw, worth 14+d6sp
39. Simon Says™ electronic memory game, uses mini cell which are currently missing, worth 30+d10sp
40. Stained wooden spoon
41. Toy ray gun, makes 4 different sounds, uses mini cell which it has but drained, worth 16+d4sp
42. Large nylon sack containing d4+2 misc. mannequin body parts, worth 10+d8sp each
43. NES Advantage video game controller, worth 60+d12sp
44. Hip sack
45. Laser carbine
46. White cut off t-shirt with the work "LICK" written across the front, worth 8+d2sp
47. 12m of green hose pipe, worth 50+d20sp
48. Foam football, orange, worth 12+d4sp
49. Junk armor made from street signs
50. Necklace of mutant ears, various colors and shapes, worth 4+d2sp
51. Mesh sack containing a woman's shoulder length wig: **Roll d6: 1.** Blonde / **2.** Black / **3.** Brown / **4.** Red / **5.** Blue / **6.** Purple
52. Resin figurine, mouse sitting on a mushroom, worth 20+d10sp
53. Plastic doll, mutant girl with 3 arms, no clothes, worth 8+d6sp
54. Portable electric mini fireplace, uses power cell which is fully charged, heats up 4 meter diameter space, worth 400+d100sp
55. Pick axe
56. Bag of plastic costume jewelry, rings, necklaces, earrings, tiara, worth 2+d2sp each
57. Musket pistol, no powder or shot
58. Flint spear
59. Bottle of oil
60. Salt and pepper shakers, both half full, ceramic pigs, dispenses out of nose, worth 20+d10sp for set.
61. Rope, 15m
62. Saw with blood and gore

63. Hula-hoop, pink, worth 7+d4sp

64. Electric nose shaver, uses mini cell which it has but is drained, worth 40+d12sp

65. Stress alien, little rubber alien for alleviating stress by squeezing it by hand, makes eyes and ears pop out, worth 3+d2sp

66. Mace with grey matter caked on it

67. Box of shotgun shells, 2d12

68. Wheel barrow full of gibs and body parts, will never be clean, worth 9+d6sp

69. Padlock, large

70. Necklace of 6+d4 shrunken heads, various character types the size of an apple, due to its uniqueness, worth 50+d20sp

71. Basketball, inflated, worth 30+d10sp

72. Blue phone booth keychain with the word "TARDES" written on it, d4 various keys, worth 12+d4sp

73. Hand drawn map on heavy parchment, leads to hidden cache, if true worth 400+d100sp

74. Binoculars

75. Glass container of 2d20 robotic fireflies, may provide light equivalent to a torch, very unique of unknown design or origin, lasts for 200 years, fireflies will scatter and flee if jar is opened, worth 2000+3d100sp for all including container.

76. Plastic ruler, worth 10+d4sp

77. Hand vacuum, has drained power cell, worth 70+d20sp

78. Piece of alien metal, strange symbols cover the light durable piece of 15cm x 15cm metal, worth 50+d20sp

79. Fold out plastic square table, beige, worth 25+d10sp

80. Happy Fun Ball, wrapped in plastic with following disclaimer on it:

Warning: Pregnant women, the elderly, and children under 10 should avoid prolonged exposure to Happy Fun Ball.

Caution: Happy Fun Ball may suddenly accelerate to dangerous speeds.

• Happy Fun Ball contains a liquid core, which, if exposed due to rupture, should not be touched, inhaled, or looked at.

• Do not use Happy Fun Ball on concrete.

• Discontinue use of Happy Fun Ball if any of the following occurs:

- • *itching*
- • *vertigo*
- • *dizziness*
- • *tingling in extremities*
- • *loss of balance or coordination*
- • *slurred speech*
- • *temporary blindness*
- • *profuse sweating*
- • *or heart palpitations.*

• If Happy Fun Ball begins to smoke, get away immediately. Seek shelter and cover head.

• Happy Fun Ball may stick to certain types of skin.

• When not in use, Happy Fun Ball should be returned to its special container and kept under refrigeration.

• Failure to do so relieves the makers of Happy Fun Ball, Wacky Products Incorporated, and its parent company, Global Chemical Unlimited, of any and all liability.

• Ingredients of Happy Fun Ball include an unknown glowing green substance which fell to Earth, presumably from outer space.

• Happy Fun Ball has been shipped to our troops in Saudi Arabia and is being dropped by our warplanes on Iraq.

• Do not taunt Happy Fun Ball.

• Happy Fun Ball comes with a lifetime warranty. Worth, 15sp

81. Sealed box of 5 teeth whitening strips, use once per day for up to 2 hours, worth 90+d20sp

82. Compound bow, and full quiver of 20 arrows

83. Reflective Suit

84. Cybernetic Eye with Targeting optics as per the implant on page 89 of TME Hub rules

85. Roll of 20 meters of barbed wire, worth 100+d20sp

86. Bladed shield

87. Plastic bag full of pure stock hair, various colors and lengths, worth 13+d4sp

88. Fake dog poop, good for a laugh, worth 6+d2sp

89. Rotisserie poles, worth 20+d12sp

90. Box of 4 power cells, drained.

91. Handcuffs, has severed android hands still in them

92. Headlamp with mini-power cell, 100 hours left

93. Honey baked ham, wrapped in plastic and mesh, worth 12+d6sp

94. Charm bracelet, 3+d4 charms are small vials of blood from "donors", worth 28+d6sp

95. Box of 8 title drink coasters, worth 16+d4sp

96. Sub-machine gun, no ammo

97. Javelins, 2+d3, well used

98. Large headdress, contains feathers, hands, feet, tuffs of hair, fingers, toes, eyeballs, teeth, etc., worth 10+d4sp

99. Spandex pants. **Roll d6** for color: **1.** Red / **2.** Blue / **3.** Green / **4.** Black / **5.** Purple / **6.** Camouflage

100. Pure stock head fused with golden chalice, shriveled flesh with mouth open and tongue sticking out, inside is a black liquid, which replenishes once a month, enough for 4 "drinks" poured from the head's open mouth, each consumption gives the drinker +20 to all traits, except for Appearance and Intelligence. Willpower is halved, rounded down; these trait adjustments last for 2 minutes (40 rounds). The consumer will have a hypnotic or possessed look and will act in a cruel or bloodthirsty way. They will mumble, "Kali ma... Kali ma... Kali ma, shakthi deh!" Any fire damage done to the consumer will instantly stop the affliction and return the subject's traits back to normal. Worth, 5000+3d100sp

CREATURES OF THE APOCALYPSE: 13
Talontessa

By William McAusland

Talontessa

By William McAusland

Defense Value: **-30** (Junk, Agility, Dodge Skill)

Endurance: **20+d20**

Movement: **9m**

Initiative: **+2**

Attacks: **2 foot claws** and **2 weapons**

Strike Value: **Claw 01-70, weapon base 01-60**

Damage: **Foot Claw 3d6+2** or **by weapon**

Strength: 38 (+2 DMG)

Agility: 113 (-18 DV)

Accuracy: 77 (+10 SV)

Intelligence: 20+d20

Willpower: 66

Perception: 68 (+2 Init.)

Appearance: 20+2d20

Valuables: See Loot table, page 77

Experience: 35

Morale: Firm

Size: 1.3m tall

Weight: As END in kilograms +10kg

Implants: Normally none

Mutations: 15% chance of one, See mutations, page 75

Skills: 2pts Dodge, lying 3pts, Climbing 4pts, Erotic Arts, Grapple 2pts, Pick Pocket 3pts, Stealth 2pts, Tracking 3pts, Wilderness Survival

The bio-engineered, mutated race of talontessa is cruel, beautiful, and vain. They are short, tan skinned, lean muscled, multi-limbed humanoids with four regular human arms, and slightly wedged shaped, attractive faces. They exhibit green, amber or violet colored eyes and black or dark purple lips. Their long hair occurs in many bizarre colors, including streaked with several pigments, but most often a raspberry reddish hue. Perhaps their most striking feature is the source of their many names, being four well toned legs which instead of ending in a foot with regular toes, sprout a remarkable, deadly sharp black velociraptor's talon. Not only can these beings run surprisingly fast upon these legs, but in melee range, rear up on two of the limbs to attack either forward, backward or side to side. Besides these nasty clawed foot attacks, they also wield a mix of ranged and melee weapons, and employ relic armaments when possible.

Depending on the region, these all-female creatures are known by different names, including Junk Jezebels, Sickle-Sues, Hook Hussies, Bloody Babes, Blood Brides, Hook Girrrls and Claw Maidens. Epoch era zoologists, historians and military thinkers believe that the race of talontessa were created long ago, like so many other humanoids and crea-

tures, to serve as genetically engineered troops. While many suggest they have mutated well beyond whatever original configuration and coloration they may once have exhibited, they are certainly peculiar and one of the x-breeding humanoid species. Halfies do not seem to exist. 82% of all births produce new talontessa 'sisters' while all other births appear to be stillborn variants of their father's species, complete with mutations. In short, they can mate with members of the opposite sex from other human based entities, yet produce only females as viable offspring. Warmorts, incidentally, who are one of the sworn enemies of sickle-sues, are also x-breeders and the bulk of their surviving offspring are males. Like skullocks, their prime enemy, talontessa reproduce and mature rapidly, with a pregnancy lasting only 5 months and 1 in 6 births producing twins. Talontessa were created to reach combat readiness far sooner than human troops, yet age quickly. By age 7 they become teens, and reach adulthood at age 9. The oldest known talontessa reportedly died at 39 years old.

Talontessa Weapon Table   Roll 3d6

3d6	Weapon	SV	Damage	Rate	Range	Ammo
3	Stun pistol	01-75	2d20 stun	1	200m	2d20 shots
4	Pump shotgun**	01-80	3d10	1	30m	2d4 shells
5	Spear	01-60	d20+3	1	16.5m	1 spear
6	Javelin	01-60	d12+2	1	22m	1 javelin
7	Machete	01-60	d12+3	1	melee	-
8	Knife	01-60	d8+2	1	3.3m	1 knife
9	Dagger	01-60	d10+2	1	3.3m	1
10	Dagger, poisoned*	01-60	d10+2	1	3.3m	1 dagger
11	Knife, poisoned*	01-60	d8+2	1	3.3m	1 knife
12	Saber	01-60	d20+4	1	melee	-
13	Bow**	01-60	d12+2	1/2	44m	20 arrows
14	Crossbow**	01-68	d20+3	1/3	66m	20 quarrels
15	Pocket pistol	01-65	d20	2	120m	3+d3 rounds
16	Automatic pistol	01-72	d20	2	250m	2d10 rounds
17	Shotgun pistol	01-75	3d10	1 or 2	20m	2d4 shells
18	Submachine-gun	01-70	d20	5	250m	5d10 rounds

*Poison type determined randomly after first successful strike on a victim, **roll d6: 1.** Death type A, administer anti-toxin injector or other medical procedure within 3d6 rounds or subject drops into a coma for 2d6 hours, at the end of which must make another END based type D HC or slip away and die. If surviving coma, victim loses d4 to each trait permanently./ **2,3.** Sleep poison. Type D END based hazard check or collapse after 2d6 rounds and pass out for 3d6 hours/ **4,5.** Paralysis poison, victim must make a type E END based hazard check or collapse immediately and be unable to move physically. Victim can continue to see, hear, feel and use mental mutations. Duration of paralysis is 2d4 hours. / **6.** Bliss poison, victim must make a type D intelligence based hazard check or succumb to pleasant hallucinations and sensation and collapse someplace soft and experience pure bliss. If attacked and taking any damage, bliss is instantly cancelled and he or she becomes normal again. Any pleasant experiences, such as sexual intercourse, maintain the bliss for another two hours. Normal duration of bliss is 2d4 hours.

**Two handed weapon, which employs one of the talontessa's non-attacking hands, and still allows for a second weapon attack. If a bow or crossbow or other ranged weapon is used in two hands, the talontessa will stow it during melee and draw a dagger to replace this weapon attack.

Typically, talontessa cannot read or write and manage only simple math on their many fingers. For language, they speak whatever was the pre-devastation tongue of the area, however, with often shrill, rapid speech when excited, or lower, throaty and sexy tones when trying to be seductive or seeking assistance from travelers.

Talontessa are excellent climbers (4 skill points) and enjoy the safety of heights in virtually inaccessible skyscrapers, cliff faces or the canopy of mutated woodlands. They construct well concealed 'tree forts' with interconnecting rope bridges and sturdy net-like climbing grids of vine, rope or old wires. Individuals live in small sisterhoods; usually with the grandmother being the ruler of the household and all her adult daughters living in huts adjoining her shelter. Any captive or voluntarily visiting males are kept in their own huts which hang below the talontessa who owns, or is beloved to, the male in question. The 'man huts' are more heavily built than regular shacks to both support the weight of a full grown human man, as well as to serve as a jail for any man kept against his will.

Although living high above the ruined streets or beast infested forest floor, talontessa do not restrict their activities to these heights and will hunt, harvest crops and patrol all terrains types except watery areas, as they seem to be poor swimmers in spite of having so many limbs.

Members of this all female race live as savages, existing in tribal sisterhoods ruled by a queen and her court of most popular, most beautiful, and ferocious hunters. They spend their days hunting small game, harvesting fruit and vegetables, fishing, looting ruins for items to employ or trade, or else defending their territories from much larger, more belligerent species. Another activity they delight in is the finding, seducing, dominating and fornicating with ideal males. To this end they strive to make themselves as beautiful and enticing as possible, and have developed a strange culture around the acquisition of relic beauty products and symbols of glamour and womanhood. They will spend days in search of old shopping malls, seeking beauty salons, fashion outlets, and drug stores, eager to uncover usable makeup, shampoo, hair dye, skimpy outfits, bikinis and jewelry.

In their pursuit to be the best looking in their tribe, and catch the eye of handsome young men, they will often resort to vicious in-fighting, theft, gossip, savage jalousies and occasionally fights to the death to secure a prize 'stallion' or scratch their way to the supreme hut and status of tribe queen.

Although many men joke how nice it would be to be the love slave to a band of talontessa, anyone who has actually survived the ordeal can attest to the nightmare of such a fate. They claim that the hook hussies were indeed frolicsome, but also petty and would beat the captive, threaten to kill him if they couldn't have him, bartered and bickered over him for days on end without sleep. The physical punishments were also unendurable, so too the bland food, unpredictable and often ferocious moods of their mistresses, and ever present fear of falling to one's death from the towering hidden villages of the sickle-sues. If not escaping of their own luck and skill, many men who have been so entrapped have instead been simply dropped off outside the gates of the nearest village, naked except for the garish makeup, miniskirt and feather boa the claw maidens left him in.

These junk jezebels, as they are called by those who don't much care for the creatures, are intolerant to slavery insofar as they don't like being slaves themselves. Somewhere, either in each tribe's recent history or somehow imprinted on them genetically, is the memory of being slave-soldiers. While it is true that certain humanoid species consider owning a talontessa as a sign of status and wealth, and many human slavers do pay hundreds of silvers for the acquisition of a these multi-limbed mutant women, they do not actually make for ideal slaves. For one thing, they are deadly fighters and must have their foot claws sawn and sanded off. Secondly, they are fiercely independent and willful, and for most hook hussy captives, no amount of threatening or beating will make one do what a master wants. Turning one into a submissive bath attendant or gardener simply doesn't happen, although many have been left claws-intact and successfully made to entertain the crowd in a fighting pit.

Indeed, their hatred of slavers is so strong that they will butcher them on sight and free all their captives - except for any skullocks, and the like, who they also cut down with glee. The hypocrisy in their anti-slavery stance comes when they decide to capture other beings and make them do their bidding. For the most part, they only take attractive males of 30 or higher appearance as breeding stock, preferring pure stocks or only mildly mutated humans for this purpose, and then only for a few months until the man is so frazzled, worn out, bruised and half mad that his usefulness has run out and he is either sold to some other talontessa household, or merely transported back to a human community and left at the gates. The other sort of slaves more ruthless tribes of hook hussies keep are workers, whom are beaten and whipped into performing agricultural or rubble excavation chores. These slaves can be males or females, and include even unattractive captives.

The collection of captives is conducted along known trade routes, but not all talontessa tribes participate in this. Typically only tribes that have been first attacked by humans and mutants will undertake slave taking or the robbing or killing of travelers, as other tribes have formed generation-long ties with local human villages and go so far as to unite with them during times of trouble, natural disaster, of to defend their territories from invaders.

Generally, when a group of huntress talontessa comes across excavation teams, traders or nomads, they will evaluate the strangers for numbers, weaponry, visible relics, factional allegiances, races and notable castes. The junk jezebels will typically eliminate purists of any stripe, and do their utmost to wipe out most barbaric humanoid species. Their hatred for skullocks and warmorts runs especially deep and it is surmised that these sickle-sues were originally engineered to seek and destroy skullocks in particular. In fact, to this day, peskies and talontessa wage a war of extermination upon each other, with both sides attempting to enlist other species as well as travelling mercenaries to fight on their side. Because of this war with most sub-humans, these female mutants are prone to mistreating any ugly mutants, bestial humans or exceedingly mangled cyborgs. Likewise, as they are obsessed with external beauty, they are cruel and often dangerous to unattractive prisoners, basing their encounters with groups of travelers more so on their looks than the perceived value of any loot they can steal off them.

When capturing beautiful human or mutant women (of 30 or higher appearance), there is some risk that the lead talontessa huntress must make a willpower based type D hazard check to avoid acting on her jealousy and beating the good looking human-

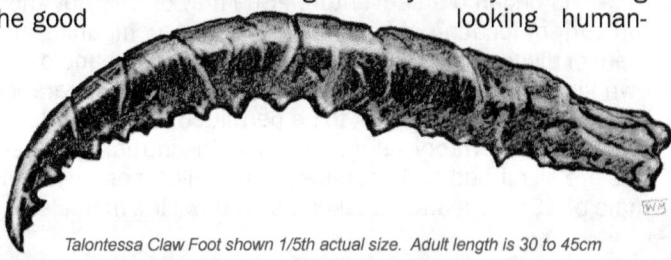

Talontessa Claw Foot shown 1/5th actual size. Adult length is 30 to 45cm

oid severely on the spot (for 2d20 stun and d8 lethal damage). If held as a work slave, The attractive captive female is also at risk of having her good looks ruined by vicious members of the hook hussy tribe, and must roll her appearance score or higher on a d100 each day to avoid being slashed and suffering a permanent d4 appearance loss. For the most part, talontessa's hate females of other races regardless of their looks, and if not keeping them as laborers, will merely rob them and send them on their way with any other undesirables.

As previously mentioned, any intruders into talontessa controlled turf will be appraised from a distance. If the travelers are not exceedingly numerous or well armed, then a single talontessa huntress may present herself to them with hands outstretched and empty, smiling as she draws near and investigates the newcomers. This envoy will first look for any familiar traders and nomadic peddlers, scavs or others with which they have had prior barter sessions. If the strangers seem to be ruin looters, and have little in the way of trade goods, the talontessa may ask if they have any alcohol or sweets to trade for wire, pelts and glass or other salvage materials used as trade items. This invitation to trade could be a ploy to lower the intruder's guard, or genuine, it all depends on the mood of the hook hussy tribe, as well as past incidents with recent interlopers, and the objectives of the talontessa tribe.

As there are so many variables as to the outcome of an encounter with these humanoids, the following disposition table can be used by a game master to determine the nature and actions of a talontessa huntress party. As a guideline however, add +3 to the 2d6 roll if the talontessa group outnumber the characters by at least 2 to 1.

Talontessa Disposition Table　　Roll 2d6
Note: Add +3 if talontessa outnumber PCs 2 to 1

2. The talontessa are encountered as they flee an oncoming skullock invasion. There will be 2d6 elderly, 3d6 young and another 2d6 regular but very badly wounded talontessa in this group, being tracked by a large warband of peskies who have driven the hook hussies from their territory. These multi-limbed mutant women will be very eager to enlist a strong excavation team to assist them in defeating the skullocks, possibly supplying the characters with relic weapons to aid in the battle, plus the promise to all the men to wed the best looking talontessa ladies.

3, 4. A single talontessa walks up to the characters, unarmed and smiling. She directs all her attention to the best looking male in the PC group and asks if the team is looking for a guide to the nearest ruins, perhaps a place to sleep that is safe and off the ground. Her intentions are good 75% of the time; otherwise this is all a ruse. If the PCs do stay in her people's village, the sickle-sues will drug their food. When the PCs wake they are all robbed and left in loin cloths. Any male over 30 APP is made a love-slave to the most powerful talontessa's while the rest are put into chains and made to dig in nearby ruins excavating an old department store in search of the cosmetics department.

5, 6. The talontessa failed to see the PCs and are instead observed several dozen meters away harvesting fruit from some low bushes. The hook hussies can be bypassed or approached.

7-9. Talontessas leap up from all around the PCs, range 15m meters, ranged weapons at the ready and demand the

PCs drop their own weapons and hand over all their belongings or die. If fired upon, the talontessa flee if outnumbered, otherwise will stay and fight until either the PCs surrender or are killed, or the hook hussies lose half their number and thus flee.

10, 11. Talontessa warriors emerge all around PCs, but have their weapons lowered and appear relaxed and flirty. Their leader will approach the front of the character line and asks if the PCs have any booze, dried fruit, candy or smoked salmon to trade for either several jugs of drinking water, dried meat, or info on a relic-rich skullock lair in nearby, well hidden in an old military bunker.

12, 13. Vengeful and ruthless. This tribe of talontessa have been routinely mistreated by slavers, purists and other human war parties, not to mention warmorts and skullocks. They attack the PCs on sight and will first target any women, cyborgs, mutants and men with appearance scores below 30. If they are clearly winning a fight, the sickle-sues will propose the characters surrender and forgo their property. If the PCs surrender and submit to having their belongings taken there is a 68% chance that the talontessa will also take the characters as slaves.

14. Jovial and confident. The talontessa pop up from all around the PCs, weapons at the ready but not firing. In fact, the hook hussies grin broadly and wink and make flirtatious gestures toward any attractive male PCs. The lead talontessa approaches and demands that the PCs do something for them, **roll d6: 1,2.** Join them in a raid on a nearby warmort hideout. The PCs can keep any relics they find, these ladies just want the barbarians eliminated from their turf./ **3,4.** That the PCs join them in their village for a few days of feasting, amatory delights, and the discussion of joining forces to deal with a band of chest heads* that have recently taken up residence nearby./ **5.** That the best looking male in the PC party join the talontessa leader in the nearby bushes for a half hour of love making. The travelers are free to go immediately after./ **6.** The PCs are ordered to strip down to their underwear and walk back the way they came, or else 'become food for the worm and crow'.

15. The talontessa are prepared and have lined the pathway ahead with net traps and leg snares and all carry bows with arrows tipped with paralysis poison. They will harry the PCs for d4 kilometers and only rush in with clubs and nets when the travelers are reduced to half their number. All those captured are divided into attractive male concubines (30+ APP) and work slaves.

See Creatures of the Apocalypse 12 by Brandon Goeringer, page 66.

As mentioned above, skullocks and sickle-sues exist in a state of permanent war, and with skullock numbers on the rise everywhere, these female x-breeders are always on the look out for a team of gullible heroes to join them in their fight against the skullies. The terms of a truce are differ widely, and the moody, unpredictable talontessa can't always be relied on to hold up their end of the deal. Still, numerous accounts exist of talontessa units joining in on an already running scrap between excavators and skullocks, with the hook hussies jumping in to drive off peskies and save otherwise doomed diggers. Once rescued, the remnants of an excavation squad are nursed back to health amid the heights of a talontessa village, either in the forest canopy or ruined, sheered off skyscrapers. Convinced to aid the claw maidens, the dig team is offered half the loot in return for waging war on the enemy skullocks. After a successful raid, the talontessa may indeed be as good as their word, and split the relics of the enemy and let their new friends go in peace, but on other occasions, reports tell a different story. Deceived by unscrupulous talontessa queens, some teams explain that they were then robbed and humiliated, or their best looking men taken away in bondage to serve as the unwilling mates to dominant hook hussies. Others relate of worse betrayal, whereby the team was all but wiped out over a simple dispute at the time of loot distribution.

Where talontessa are a menace, and prone to killing those they rob, humans will treat them just like any other humanoid barbarian species, and eradicate them. In other areas, however, especially where talontessa have never been encountered and a solitary specimen appears, they are often considered to be just another unique mutant human, and let into a mixed barter town along with every other odd looking freak. Only when bands of these x-breeders are spotted together do people realize they are observing a separate species of humanoid, and then their initial interactions with each other determine relations in the years ahead.

Talontessa are usually content to live among their own kind, regardless of their feuds, all-night shouting matches, duels and competitive and jealous natures. Occasionally one will however be found as a loner, or in the company of other intelligent beings. These individuals have either split from their tribe after committing some offence, or been bullied and driven out, or even the sole survivor after some sort of calamity which has befallen her people. Very rarely a hook hussy is simply unique and yearns for a different life, to be with other humanoids of similar disposition, seek adventure, wealth, power and less severe or competitive living circumstances. From these few come excavator talontessa. These mutants crave nothing more than to be part of a mixed race team of adventurers and try their luck in the ruins, travelling to new lands and learning the truth of their creation.

Talontessa Player Characters

Game masters can decide to allow a rogue talontessa to become a player character or merely occur as a NPC. Should a player want to have one as a character, the following stat block and rules can be applied. Keep in mind that skullocks hate these mutant woman and will always attack them on sight, often bypassing humans, cyborgs and mutants to get at a talontessa first. Also, the starting caste of a talontessa, randomly determined on the next page, reveals much about how this particular specimen became isolated from her tribe and became an adventurer. She may or may not know the current location of her people. If she accompanies and team of diggers and the group is confronted by a band of her own kind in the wilds, she must then make an appearance based type C hazard check to be permitted to lead her team through their territory safely, otherwise the intruding characters are all robbed and left naked in the wilderness, with any male of 30+ appearance taken as an unwilling mate.

Talontessa Player Character Stats

Endurance	10+2d20
Strength	10+2d20
Agility	80+3d20
Accuracy	20+3d20
Intelligence	10+3d20
Willpower	40+2d20
Perception	30+2d20
Appearance	20+3d20

• Base DV -10 (before armor and agility modifiers)
• Base movement 7m (before agility modifiers)
• Base Strike Value before Mods 01-50 for weapons or 01-60 with talons
• Starting age 14+d6
• Mutations: 65% of PC Talontessa starts with d2 mutations from their own racial listing plus a 30% chance of d3 ghost mutations Implants: very rarely encountered as augmented, but there is a 5% chance PC variants have been modified and appear with 1 each of offensive, defensive and miscellaneous implants from table 1-62, page 84 of the hub rules.
• Rank gain bonus as 'Mutant'
• Besides having the talents and skill points listed in their creature stats, all player character talontessa's start game play as one of the following random castes with all the skill and trait benefits as regular characters:

Talontessa Starting Caste   Roll 2d6

2. *Slave, Gladiator*
3. *Street Thug*
4-5. *Hunter*
6. *Nomad*
7. *Raider*
8. *Draftee*
9. *Militia*
10. *Watchman*
11. *Infantry*
12. *Mercenary*

Talontessa Mutations   Roll d20

There is a 15% chance of each talontessa having one mutation from the following list:

1. Extra set of claw legs, allowing this specimen to make two additional Claw Foot attacks during melee. Also, she can climb at one skill point higher (now 5 pts) and move an extra 3m per round.
2. Extra arm, adding one more weapon attack per round.
3. Two heads, add +5 overall endurance, +1 improved initiative.
4. Mind crusher: As the mutation page 70 of the TME hub rules. Overview: Range 198m, uses per day: 6 (or 3 times per day/rank if a PC talontessa). Victim allowed type B intelligence based HC or suffer d20 END damage and d6 intelligence damage.
5. Poison bite: Add an extra melee attack per round SV 01-60, damage d4 plus victim must make a type F endurance based hazard check or drop unconscious after d4 rounds.

Unconsciousness lasts variable duration depending on weight of subject: creatures lighter than 50kg remain asleep for 3d6+10 hours, creatures 51 up 99kg unconscious for 3d6 hours, creatures 100 to 199kg pass out for d4 hours, and victims over 200kg pass out for only 3d6 minutes.
6. Upper body and back covered in bone plates: reduce movement -2m per round however she gains -20 DV.
7. Back, shoulders and outer edges of arms covered in bone spikes. Her movement is -1m slower, but her defense value increased by -20. Anything to bite or grapple this talontessa is simultaneously attacked: SV 01-70, damage d12.
8. Shoulders and upper back covered in 50cm long black throwing quills. Rate 4 per round at same target, range 60m, SV 01-70 inflicting d12+2 damage each. She can fire up to 20 per day.
9. Electrical bolt: three times per day (or per rank if a PC), this talontessa can charge up and shoot a bolt of lightning from her forehead. Range 120 meters, strike value 01-80, Damage 3d12+4 to living beings, but 3d20+4 to cyborgs, electronic beings, vehicles, structures and robots.
10. Scream of rage: This talontessa will shriek once every ten rounds, or whenever taking damage or things don't go her way. This cry is so high pitched that most animals, especially dogs, cats, bears and such, will call off an attack and turn and run off whining in pain. For humanoid foes, at least those not wearing ear protection or a relic helmet that protects the wearer's hearing (such as a combat helmet), the scream causes damage and disorder. Anyone within 18 meters of the scream must make a willpower based type C hazard check or drop whatever they are holding, including the edge of a cliff, rope or weapon, plus, stop dead in their tracks and try to cover their ears. All those within the area of effect (except other talontessas) If not covering their ears by the second round, suffer d4 damage per round that the scream persists. Only by hitting or covering the mouth of the talontessa screamer can the shriek be stopped. The screamer needs to inhale on the 8th round after starting the cry.

Those who failed their type C willpower check must continue to cover their ears and cannot shoot at the screaming talontessa unless they have more than two appendages with which to do so, or some eye-based or mental attack modes,

During the scream of rage, other talontessa's will make missile or melee attacks on the intruders or prey.
11. Winged! A pair of bat-like, flesh colored wings grow from this talontessa's back. In spaces wider than 6m these appendages allow her to fly at a rate of 22m per round and while flying, gains a -20 DV bonus. This specimen will attempt to fire missile weapons from above during any combat, including dropping rocks like bombs (SV 01-60, DMG d20 stun, carries up to four rocks per flight), or else, make fly-by attacks with all four claw-feet, raking the throats and faces of enemies. If taking a hit during a fly-by attack, there is a 19% chance that she will spiral out of control and crash into the ground taking 3d6+10 stun damage and a 23% chance of breaking one wing.
12. Telepathy: Besides coordinating attack or defense with her sisters by way of telepathically messaging her comrades, this talontessa can employ this power to send impressions, images and suggestions to other humanoids to

initiate trade dealings, threaten them away, enlist them as mercenaries, or suggest more playful dealings with a particularly attractive male. To mentally intrude on a stranger, the subject is allowed a willpower based type C hazard check to block the mental transmission.

13. Larger specimen. This talontessa is fully human sized, has an extra 10+d12 endurance and is stronger (+10, so now 48 STR) and so inflicts +4 damage from strength based attack modes including her claw feet.

14. Poison blood: Anything to use its mouth or other feeding orifice to break the skin of this talontessa will be rewarded by a gush of toxic purple blood and must make a type D endurance based hazard check or begin to convulse and die. Death will occur d3+3 rounds after ingesting her blood.

15. Immunity: This specimen is immune to poison, disease, radiation and metal intrusions, controls, or attacks such as mind crush, coma inducement and the like.

16. Beauty enhancement: This talontessa's body and face are exquisitely well formed and for straight male human-based beings, she is the ideal of beauty. Unless the viewer is directly being attacked by this exquisite specimen, he will not be able to bring harm to the gorgeous talontessa. Worse, he will be forced to make a type G willpower based hazard check to avoid letting her go free if she is a captive, or, to even intervene if the talontessa is doing something wrong like stealing from his comrades or otherwise up to a clearly undesirable, but not life threatening, act. Female humanoids will not share this ridiculous infatuation and awe at the sight of the extreme beauty, unless of a sexual preference which inclines them toward other females.

This talontessa's Appearance score is 100+3d20. Over the years, her unnatural good looks have attracted the attention of others, some who are jealous of her stunning beauty and wouldn't mind if she were 'disappeared'. Others, such as barbaric male humanoids including local warmort chieftains, skullock warlords, and even human slavers, will be desirous of possessing her as a prize. Being aware of these perils, this talontessa may conceal her appearance with a mask or face paint, or else strives to become the Queen of her talontessa tribe, going so far as to employ the devotion and prowess of an attractive, champion–lover, to help her assume dominance.

17. Ghost mutation from the list on page 59 of the TME hub rules.

18. Illusionary shape shifting: This talontessa can project a mass hallucination of her shape. She will normally use this to turn herself into a regular human woman, a tree, a block of old concrete or some harmless woodland animal such as a deer. The form she assumes acts like a shell around her, so she cannot become smaller than she really is, although can curl into a ball and appear as a fairly convincing rock. All those who see her are allowed a type E Intelligence based hazard check, with failure meaning that she appears to them as she desires, while those who succeed see the illusionary form as a ghostly, semi-transparent image around her true form. This talontessa is not aware who does and does not fall for her illusionary form, except when they react to her presence with alarm.

While in this form, she can move about if desired, but if touched, her true form then becomes fully apparent to the person or creature touching her, but others continue to see her illusionary visage if previously doing so. In most cases this mutant will take on the forms of rocks and trees to hide while unintelligent beings pass her by. If assuming this form as part of an ambush, however, she will choose to hide herself as an inanimate object until the target gets within range or falls for the illusion and has been drawn out into the open for other talontessa's to launch their attack. This power can be used twice per day (or once per rank if a PC talontessa) and the illusion can be maintained for one minute per point of her intelligence score, or until she attacks from it with any physical modes. She can launch continued mental attacks from this illusionary form if possessing any.

19. Regeneration burst: this specimen can heal herself 3d6 trait points once per day in a burst, but so too, heals an extra 2 trait points per hour.

20. Beguilement: Using a combination of mind attack, suggestive gestures and body language, this talontessa will attempt to seduce a male humanoid and not only make him feel amorous toward her, but so too cease attacking either this mutant or her kind. The subject of this Talontessa's beguilement must be within 12 meters or less and see her fully. The male subject is allowed a type F willpower based hazard check, and if failing that, will stop any aggression and simply stand in place, dumbfounded and love struck. The talontessa will then try to ensnare his mind and convince him he is in love with her and her obedient servant. To gain full control and convert the male to her will (and the GM's control) the man is allowed a type E intelligence based hazard check.

This seduction will remain in effect for as long as the talontessa maintains the link to this one male, whom she might control for weeks or months. If the man is attractive (say of 30 or higher appearance), there is some chance that after 24 hours she herself will fall in love with him and genuinely seek to protect and empower her new concubine, selfishly keeping him away from her sisters and perhaps even dropping the beguilement little by little to gradually allow the man to wake up and hopefully accept and maintain a real relationship with his former controller.

A beguiled man will not harm comrades, although will not allow his teammates or other beings to harm the talontessa who controls him, and if possible, will also see to it that no other hook hussy comes to harm.

Valuables

All talontessa will carry a pouch with 2d6 days dried fruit, veggies and meat, d3 litres of water in either an oiled skin or ancient bottle or milk jug, as well as a sleeping fur, knife, sheet of plastic for a personal shelter, assorted scalps, tusks, teeth and other trophies of the hunt. Also packed are shreds of old fashion magazines, primitive makeup made from oils, crushed berries and charcoal, plus appropriate seasonal clothing or sandstorm protection. Unless encountered in very remote areas of the wasteland, they all have a handful of 3d6 silver coins, d6 -2 (0-4) gold coins and one roll on the following table:

Talontessa Loot Table   Roll d100

01. Pink plastic comb, worth 4+d6sp

02. Bright pink swimming goggles, worth 3d6+10sp

03. Brilliant purple plastic flip flop-style sandals worn as a bra, worth 4d6+10sp

04. Neon-green fly swatter, worth 8+d8sp

05. Clear plastic rain poncho with flowers and cartoon bunnies on it, worth 4d6sp

06. Set of bright pink polyhedron gaming dice in original tube, worth 50+d100sp

07. Small, pink, plastic rod with a knobby texture along its shaft, If shaken for a minute, will vibrate for thirty minutes, worth 70+d100sp

08. Faded pink phone case, no communicator, worn as jewelry and worth 4+d8sp

09. Data stick, bright pink with polka-dots, contains ancient photos of a spring break holiday by a dozen ancient pure stock women in their very early twenties at beach and pool parties. Very sordid imagery. Much booze and buff boys involved. Worth 50+d100sp

10. String of fashion doll heads worn around talontessa's neck. 3d6 heads, each in varying degrees of disintegration and worth 3sp each.

11. Necklace of ammo and one advanced fragmentation grenade as central pedant. All items tied on by fishing line, however, this talontessa could yank and throw the grenade as needed if losing a fight or dying (whereby she will pull the pin and roll over onto the grenade, the relic detonating when she is searched after a battle. Ammo on necklace includes 3d6 standard pistol, 2d6 standard rifle, 3d6 .22 rounds, d4 high caliber pistol and d4 high caliber rifle rounds.

12. Baby Talontessa strapped to her back in a leather and bone infant carrier. If raised by humans, this talontessa could grow up to be a fearsome warrior or digger.

13. Leather bag containing the dried faces of d4 skullocks and one warmort.

14. Bright yellow extension cord, 20m, makes a great rope and worth 40+d20sp

15. Makeup kit, relic, with dozens of eye shadows, false nails, false eyelashes, lipsticks, blush, application sponges and tiny brushes. Worth 50+d100sp

16. Golden chain with tiny, ornate old world crucifix on it. Worth 200+2d100sp

17. Zippy bag of 300+2d100 grams of marijuana, along with d8 pre-rolled joints.

18. Handcuffs with two keys attached.

19. Pair of costume angel wings, adult size, stained but otherwise in good order. Pair worth 60+d100sp

20. Lingerie magazine in protective sleeve. Worth 10+d20sp

21. Wedding dress magazine in plastic bag, in good order and worth 30+d30sp

22. Nerve gas grenade

23. Zippy bag containing 2d6 shotgun shells

24. Zippy bag containing 3d6 standard pistol rounds mixed with 3d6 gold coins minted in the nearest Purist factional lands.

25. Skullock baby, alive and wired to the talontessa's head as a headdress. The skullock's mouth has been stitched shut to stop it from crying and the thing is more dead than alive.

26. Skull of a warmort worn as a helmet, adding -5 DV but concealing the appearance of the talontessa and making her look very fierce.

27. Collection of skullock hands, genitals and scalps worn as a belt, worthless and stinky.

28. A gorgeous, tiny clip winged humanoid tied to a wooden X and worn as a pendant on a leather strap. The humanoid is a pink skinned, blonde haired female Devilkin (see Mutant Bestiary One if owned by a gamer at the table). The humanoid is well fed and kept clean and lovely by its proud master. At night, the pretty, 15cm tall captive is kept in a wooden cage and made to sing and perform exotic dances for the talontessa and her comrades. If freed from this servitude and allowed to join an adventure party, she will be most grateful and very useful as far as scouting. If her tiny dragonfly-like wings are not clipped, they will grow back in 30 days and allow her to fly 12m per round.

29. Spotted scorpion in a glass canning jar. The talontessa has been feeding it crickets and cockroaches. If threatened, she will open the jar and thrust the scorpion at an adversary, range 9m (spotted scorpion stats on page 169 of the TME hub rules).

30. Leather pouch containing 20+d20 silver coins, a glass flask of 500ml vodka, 3d6 skullock ears, an anti-toxin injector and 3d6 .22 cartridges.

WM

31. A shoulder satchel containing 3d6 ancient fashion magazines lovingly protected in UV resistant archival poly sleeves. Each issue worth 10+d10sp.

32. Plastic sun hat, bright pink with large fake flower on it. Worth 20+d12sp

33. Ancient book: The Joy of Sex, poly-paper and plastic cover construction and only slightly faded and stained, worth 3d6+30sp

34. Ancient Book: Kama Sutra, tattered and stained, worth 20+d20sp

35. Leather bag containing an assortment of newly forged torture tools, all of them blood stained. In the bag are 3d6 skullock ears, dried fingers, toes and other parts, including an entire peeled off face.

36. Cloak made from the skinned faces of skullocks, a warmort, and at least two moaners

37. Bloody leather pouch containing cybernetic parts torn from recent victims. Bits of meat and bone are still fused to the parts which include d3 optical enhancement implants, an artificial heart, hypodermic tendril, and laser pistol weapon arm. All power cells are drained.

38. Magazine for a submachine gun, empty

39. Assault rifle magazine with d6 rounds remaining inside

40. Bog spider in a clear plastic box. The thing is alive and angry, worn on a steel chain around the talontessa's neck. If dying or about to be captured by skullocks, warmorts, chest heads or other humanoids, this sickle-sue will grab the spider and stuff it into her mouth to ensure she is bitten, and then hope that some humanoid discovers it accidentally when looting her corpse.

41. Fragmentation grenade worn on a bright pink string about her neck.

42. Poster tube on a leather strap. Inside the plastic tube is, roll d6: 1-3. a huge poly sealed poster of a shirtless, blonde haired ancient man (Fabio Lanzoni) dressed as a pirate, worth 4+d8sp/ 4-6. Poisonous snakes, d4+3 small snakes with type D sleep poison bites.

43. Box of 20 shotgun shells

44. Bottle of red wine from the nearest farming community. There is a 3 in 6 chance it has been laced with a crushed, tasteless herb that induces a slight narcotic effect lasting 3d6 hours. The drug makes the victim docile, optimistic, and preoccupied with love, affection and carnal inclinations. Worth 16+d20sp

45. In a leather sack is the dried out husk of a wrapped, baby talontessa baby. The thing looks like it has been dead for years. If the Talontessa carrying this cadaver is still alive when this bag is inspected by the characters, she will sob pitifully and beg the PCs to return her baby to her at once.

46. Tied to the talontessa's back is a human baby girl, gagged and blindfolded but otherwise seems unhurt and well cared for. The talontessa who carried it will insist it is her adopted child, that its original mother had died and made her promise to raise it as a talontessa huntress.

37. Pistol grip shotgun that is loaded (six shells) but hopelessly jammed and won't pump. Only a person with the gunsmith or mechanical technician skill can repair this weapon, doing so with a half hours work so long as he or she has the tools and gun oil to perform the needed repairs.

48. Large glass pickle jar filled with d4+1 furious venomous bats. This talontessa's plan was to hurl the jar into an enemy camp then run for it.

49. Leather pouch containing strange looking, rather large seeds. If any talontessa captive is alive to explain what the plants are, or a bio-engineer is available, the seeds will be identified as 3d6 blood weed, d6 constriction vines, and d4 jaw plants (see plants in the hub rules, page 165).

50. United States of America flag, a bit tattered and with several bullet holes through it, but folded perfectly and sealed in a plastic sleeve. Also in the sleeve is a poly-paper copy of the ancient US Constitution. In a small village, these items won't fetch terribly much as people don't know their historical value or importance and may only get 30+d20sp. However, in a large trade center or to a Resto-rationist, will earn at least 1776+3d100sp.

51. Hot pink dog collar with tiny studs, worn by talontessa, worth 15+d10sp

52. Baggy of fake glass diamonds and gems, many with peel and stick backings for kid's crafts. Also, a glass vial of pink sparkle glue. There is a 1 in 6 chance that one of the diamonds is actually real and if the PC who discovers these is perceptive and smart, this 1000+d1000sp valued stone will go unnoticed. The odds to spot the real diamond is a type D hazard check using a combined perception and intelligence hazard check, although add both traits together and divide by two to get a unique trait for this HC purpose.

53. Pistol-like bright orange spray nozzle for a garden hose. Could be used to trick dumb humanoids into believing it is a real gun (INT based type C hazard check). Worth 30+d20sp

54. Bottle of vodka, 750ml, brewed recently in a nearby trade town. Worth about 20+d20sp

55. Zippy bag of d8 standard pistol rounds, d4 standard rifle rounds, 2d6 .22 cartridges, d3 shotgun shells, and a 1 in 6 chance of d4 fifty caliber rounds

56. Small leather pouch containing 4d6 standard rifle rounds

57. Necklace made mostly of skullock, moaner and warmort teeth, but hanging from it are also d4 mini grenades and a military ID access swipe card. If questioned, the talontessa who owns it says they found it at a hidden series of ruined bunker hatches only a few kilometers away, but skullocks infest the place. She will add that her tribe would be passionately thankful to the PCs for helping eliminate the peskies, and suggests a truce and peace treaty.

58. Plastic banana, worth d3+4sp

59. Box of 20mm (1/72nd) scale miniatures, unpainted and on the sprue, figures are Napoleonic era British line Infantry, modeled in red. Still in shrink wrap and never opened. Worth 3d6+12sp

60. Ancient Confederate battle flag from the first American Civil War. Value varies depending on size and type of community sold in. Could be worth as little as 20+d20sp, and as much as 1000+d1000sp to a true collector of old world history.

61. Communicator, hand held, battery drained.

62. Power cell, drained

63. Pouch containing bluish gray skullock scalps along with d3 eight gauge shotgun shells (Mall of Doom adventure TME-1 contains several chances to find an 8 gauge pump shotgun).

64. Hand drawn map on a square of human skin. Map seems to show the correct path through ruins and to a door into a place called 'The Spire of the Cyborg God' (see One Day Dig 3 'Beneath the Spire'
http://www.rpgnow.com/product/143928/One-Day-Digs-3-and-4-Double-Feature).

65. Skirt made from the finger bones and dried hands of skullocks.

66. The head of a mannequin worn above the talontessa's own head. While not an android, the head is solar powered and makes various facial expressions, including smiling, making kissy faces, winking and its blue eyes following the movements of people nearby it. If talked to, the head will only say. "Please ask a sales associate for more information on this or other merchandise I am wearing." Worth 200+d100sp

67. Bright pink lacy bra, made of nylon, ancient manufacturing and worth 3d6+10sp

68. Pair of fishnet stockings in original plastic packaging, worth 50+d20sp

69. ID swipe card, Bank Managers, worth 30+d20sp

70. Three pack of woman's panties, pink, black and red wine colored, set in original packaging, worth 50+d20sp

71. Holo-train-set. When activated this device displays a meter wide by three meter long floating, illuminated model train set. The 1920's themed steam engine and freight cars move through a town, over a bridge, through a tunnel and other scale details with lively sounds, animated people, and music. Every time the device is activated, an entirety new N scale layout presents itself. The palm sized device uses 1 standard power cell and will run continuously for 400 hours on a charge. Worth 400+4d100sp

72. Solar charging BBQ lighter. When charged (takes an hour of full sunlight) this hand held, red unit will expel a 5cm long flame up to 100 times, ideal for lighting a traditional barbecue. Worth 200+2d100sp

73. Zippy bag of dried skullock eyes, along with a mix of 3d6 silver coins, and 3d6 standard pistol rounds.

74. Ancient print magazine in plastic sleeve, roll d6: 1. Transgender Today/ 2. Big Breast Fiesta/ 3. Survivalist Strategies Monthly/ 3. Concealed Carry Quarterly/ 4. Robotic Erotica Monthly/ 5. Android Companion Illustrated/ 6. Mutant Rights Now. Any of these magazines are worth 3d6+20sp. Tattered but readable.

75. Stuffed cat hanging from a pink plastic leash, worth d3sp

76. d4+2 fifty caliber rounds wrapped in a bright pink sleeping eye mask.

77. Fashion doll wearing a prom dress, wrapped in plastic and worth 40+2d20sp

78. Roll of bright pink doggy poop baggies, each with a purple poodle silhouette on one side. Roll of 100 bags worth 40+d20sp

79. Roll of zebra print duct tape, 50 meters length. Worth 60+d100sp

80. False 'bald' wig with 50cm tall Mohawk of fake pink hair. Worth 40+2d20sp

81. Rear view mirror from an ancient Porsche automobile, worth 20+d12sp

82. Blue plastic hand mirror, worth 18+3d6sp

83. Classic novel from the old world, worth 30+2d20sp, roll d6: 1. Howard Pyle's The Story of King Arthur/ 2. Mark Twain's Tom Sawyer/ 3. R.L. Stevenson's Treasure Island/ 4. Sir A.C. Doyle's Sherlock Holmes/ 5. Jack London's The Call of the Wild and White Fang/ 6. M. Shelly's Dracula.

84. Pink feather boa, missing about half its feathers but still very flamboyant, worn around talontessa's neck, worth 3d6+6sp

85. Faux-leather black mini-skirt, worth 16+d20sp

86. Elbow length white glove, one, worth 12+d12sp

87. Spare, empty magazine for an automatic pistol

88. Empty 10 round magazine for a fifty caliber sniper rifle

89. Empty 50 round drum magazine for an assault rifle (will also fit a survival rifle).

90. Pocket-bot, battery drained. 21% chance that if activated, is actually a Mecha controlled spy and will make live-feed transmissions back to a nearby robot hive, plus work to bring doom to any human masters. Will transmit coordinates to position of PCs when in ruins and summon 2d6 light combots.

91. Ancient corset, hot pink with black lace, worth 40+2d20sp

92. Pack of 3+d3 anti-toxin injectors in original plastic shrink wrap.

93. Pack of d6 flares (see page 201 TME hub rules)

94. Barrel flashlight, battery has 100+d100 hours of illumination remaining.

95. Night vision headgear with d12 hours operation remaining in battery

96. Pocket pistol in waistband concealed holster, has d4 rounds of ammo loaded in mag.

97. Power cell, fully charged

98. Proximity mine, not currently armed (pg. TME 196).

99. Filter mask

100. Belt of d20+10 rifle rounds on ammo belt that would normally hold 200 rounds.

Muto-Harpy

by Danny Seedhouse

Muto-Harpy

Aka : Spire Harpies, Ruin Hags, Winged Watchers

By Danny Seedhouse

Defense Value: -16 or -36 flying
Endurance: 20+d20
Movement: 3m/20m flying
Initiative: +2
Attacks: 2 wing claws or 2 spears or 2 hand weapons
Strike Value: 01-56 base SV or 01-62 with spears
Damage: wing d12 each/spear d20+5 each
Strength: 32
Agility: 81
Accuracy: 64
Intelligence: d20+3
Willpower: 43
Perception: 65
Appearance: 2d8
Valuables: Braves and Bird-Heads poor (P)/ Patch Wings VC-A
Experience Factors: brave 50/patch wing 50 +25 EFs per rank above 1st/bird-head 100
Morale: Firm
Size: 1.3m tall with 2.6m wingspan
Weight: 40kg
Mutations: Ambidextrous, plus, regular muto-harpy braves have a 6% chance of 1 random mutation/ patch-wing 36% chance of d2 mutations/ bird-head 17% chance of 1, plus berserker rage (mutation no. 14, page 61 of the hub rules). See muto-harpy mutations, page 82.
Relics: braves and bird-heads have a 1 on 20 chance (5%) of WC-R, patch wings have a 22% chance of a weapon (WC-R)
Implants: Patch wings have a 5% chance of 1 from set Implants set 2 (page TME 84).

Muto-harpies are another product of the long wars which cumulated in the fall of civilization. Created in labs to serve humanity's hard pressed military, muto-harpies were engineered to be urban aerial combat and recon units. They are agile flyers, excellent climbers (5 skill points with a climbing speed of 6m), sharp eyed (twice as effective as a human's vision) and cunning.

In the dark times of the pre-collapse, they were released on enemy cities to sow terror with hit and run raids, all the while scavenging food and weapons, lairing in out of the way nooks and crannies, and reproducing quickly to replenish combat losses. While they had little chance of success against heavily fortified and prepared troops, or lumbering battle robots, they resorted to hit and run attacks on softer targets, including supply lines, leadership assets and civilian run facilities.

When their human controllers died, or were dispatched by their muto-harpy slave-soldiers, these 'winged-watchers' spread rapidly and adapted to the reality of the Mutant Epoch era. By the time the fall came they had already moved to the high places of the world. It is there they can still be found, hunting and raiding the surrounding areas and guarding there aeries with savage ferocity. They can often be found on the edges of sheer cliffs, within the highest reaches of mighty skyscrapers, or nesting on the steep edges of craters and junk mountains. Although able to wear clothing or scrap and junk armor, they often go entirely naked, their skin colors ranging from dark brown, to orange and all the way to albino white. Their hair color also varies, and for females is worn long and free flowing, while males tend to shave their heads bald.

When not in their junk and stretched leather nest-villages, they are busy hunting for game, raiding travelers, looting nearby ruins, or tending to dozens of scattered, well hidden vegetable gardens. While livestock and meat slaves are often kept in secluded pen areas in and around their lairs, they occasionally manage flocks of birds for both food and hunting companions, especially if the tribe includes any 'bird speakers' or 'bird-heads'.

Muto-Harpies can be negotiated with if human explorers approach, but do not enter, their skull and feather totem marked territories. Additionally, traders and others seeking to converse with muto-harpies must be willing to stand a few near misses as young braves test the stranger's courage with dive-bomb style swoops, a few spear tosses, and cuss-filled, threatening shouts. After 1d4 such 'attacks', and if the exuberant winged youths are not violently assaulted in response, a 'patch wing' will approach to open talks. Like most human-headed muto-harpies, Patch wings speak a crude, trimmed down version of the area's pre-devastation language.

There are 3 distinct castes within a muto-harpy tribe. The vast majority are the common braves each armed with a minimum of 4 spears, of which two are dropped on or thrown at targets to soften them up before the brave closes for the kill. All adult muto harpies have two skill points in weapon expert with spears (+6 SV/ +4 DMG), and 2 points in junk crafting, however, 1 in 10 harpies will be a patch wing veteran with 1d4+1 ranks of experience and gain 'rank up bonuses' as a bestial human on table TME-1-22, page 34 of the TME hub rules. Patch wings are so called for the numerous, stitch tracks and patches in their wings, a result of many fights with enemies, predators and each other; features which these humanoids take great pride in.

Patch wings will also be equipped with a junk crafted alloy saber which is +4 SV and inflicts d20+8 damage. Tribes with 5 or more patch wings will tend to be better armed than more primitive flocks, employing junk bows and crossbows and complicated hit and run tactics. A typical patch wing has 54 END a base SV of 01-72 an extra -8 DV and 2 spear attacks at SV 01-80 doing 1d20+12 and will carry 6 spears in a special harness. Each patch wing is also 22% likely to carry a relic weapon from WC-R, page 207 of the hub rules.

1 in 20 muto-harpies is born with a bird head and the ability to talk with and control birds, often called a 'bird-speaker'. They possess a beak (SV 01-74, Damage 1d12+4) and claws (2 attacks at SV 01-71 doing 1d12+2 damage each) are stronger (STR 40 +2 damage included in attacks) healthier (END 40+1d20) but are less intelligent (INT d10+2). These bird-headed specimens are savage, possessing the Berserker Rage Mutation (-5 DV, +10 SV, +10 damage with muscle powered weapons and double the number of melee attacks. And if 'killed', fight on for 1d6 more rounds regardless of wounds before falling). Defeating a bird-head-harpy rewards 100 experience factors plus that of any bird companions it controlled. Roll d8 to see what a bird-head had at its disposal:

d8	Bird Companions
1-3.	3d6 Ruin Vultures
4-6.	3d10 Skal Birds
7.	Black Owl
8.	Great Eagle

All muto-harpies have vicious hooks and spines on their leathery, bat-like wings, and if disarmed or having spent all their spears, will readily stab and lacerate opponents for d12 damage per wing in hand to hand combat.

They are omnivores, but prefer meat, and while the smartest among them recognize that, long ago, they were created by humans and are related to them, they do not consider it cannibalism to devour other humanoids. While crossbreeding with humans is possible, the idea is repulsive to muto-harpies, who want to keep their species pure.

If not attacking humans for food or territorial reasons, a tribe of muto-harpies might give hints that they are interested in trading relics, pelts and assorted ancient junk for hard to acquire items, such as beer and wine, spices, dried fruit, tobacco and pot. They have no use for silver and gold and discard it as trash.

Very occasionally, a outcast harpy will be encountered who doesn't fit in with his or her tribe. These loners often seek the companionship or other humanoids, and either serve as a mercenary scout, body guard, or adventuring companion to human, skullock, or other intelligent beings. Player character muto-harpies are possible and start as a 'hunter' from table TME-1-5a Pre-Game Caste Determination. In addition, they always have 1 mutation from the muto-harpy mutation list, and a 50% chance of a ghost mutation from table TME1-59, page 59 of the TME hub rules.

For whatever reason, either on account of inter-tribal death duals among males or some genetic, chromosomal aberration, 70% of all muto-harpies are female.

Muto-Harpy Mutation List   Roll d100

01-05. Enlarged Wings: Flies +8m per round.

06-11. More Humanlike Body: Instead of this specimen's arms growing where its legs were, it has actual legs, plus, arms growing from normal shoulders and the wings coming out of the back. All in all, the individual is rather more attractive with a total app score of 20+2d20.

12-14. Dual Wings. This harpy has a second set of wings growing from its back. It flies much faster (+5m) and adds several more hooks and spines to its two wing attacks making them do d20 each instead of d12 damage on a hit.

15-18. Bladed Tail: A long, 3m tail hangs down from this specimen. The tail ends in a meter long serrated black blade which adds an additional melee attack at +10 SV and inflicts d20+6 damage.

19-24. Two Heads: Extra hard to surprise. Now has +4 initiative. Won't shut up.

25-31. More Robust: This specimen is somewhat larger, more muscular, and toned. Add 10+d20 strength and 10+d20 endurance.

32-36. Extra Arm: This muto-harpy has one extra arm and wields an extra two spears into battle, throwing one, and then using the next in melee.

37-42. Two Extra Arms: This harpy uses its two spare arms to fire a longbow. It will hang back from melee, attempting to use cover, and shoot all of its 30 arrows before rushing in with spears. Longbow using muto-harpy: rate ½, range 70m, SV 01-61, DMG d20.

43-48. Electrical Pulse: Shooting from its forehead, this freak can unleash three lightning bolts per day, range 43 meters, SV 01-76, damage d20 to organic beings or 3d20 to machines, including cyborgs.

49-55. Massive Jaws: Having a face like a baboon, an elongated neck and jaw, massive yellow teeth and powerful jaw muscles, this harpy can add an extra bite attack per round which is SV 01-70, damage d20. Abysmally ugly, this muto harpy's appearance is 2+d4.

56-60. Bone Studded Hide: This hideous harpy has bone knobs covering its torso, head and main wing bones, giving it a -10 defense value bonus.

61-66. Thorn Covered: Covering this muto-harpy are hundreds of small, hooked black thorns, giving it a -20 defense value bonus. Also, anything to bite this specimen suffers an attack at SV 01-80 for d6 damage.

67-72. Poisonous Blood and Flesh: Anything to bite this harpy is rewarded with a gush of poison: **roll d6** for type: **1,2.** Type B death/ **4,5.** Type C sleep/ **5,6.** Type E paralysis.

73-77. Manticore Tail: This freak has a bloated, bulbous tail growing from its lower back. The end of this tail is covered in hundreds of purple spines, some of which are 40 cm long and ready to fire. Each day, this harpy can shoot up to 10 mature spines, rate 1, range 30 meters, SV 01-60, damage d12+2 each.

78-84. Spits Acid: Four times per hour, this specimen can hork a blob of highly acidic gob up to 12 meters away, SV 01-80, damage to those in non-acid proof armor or other protection is d6 per round, for d6+2 rounds. Dousing oneself in at least a liter of water, or leaping into other water-like liquids will immediately stop the acid's burn effect.

85-89. Shell: Crab-like shell covers this harpy's body, making it -5 movement in the air and -1m on the ground, but very hard to damage, being -30 bonus to its defensive value (DV -46 ground and -66 when flying).

90-96. Huge: This specimen has a 6 meter wingspan, an endurance value of +100, and each wing attack does d20+3 damage instead of d12, plus, it uses 4 meter long tree saplings or lengths of rebar as spears, which it can throw 120 meters and do 2d20+12 damage on a hit. Its SV for either attack mode is 01-80.

97-00. Random Ghost mutation from table TME-1-59, page 59 of the TME hub rules book.

Walking Mouther

By William McAusland

Walking Mouther

Also called an Osmu, Hop Jaw, Gorger or Tooth-Head
By William McAusland

Defense Value: **-14**

Endurance: **70+2d100**

Movement: **9m** plus hop every 4th round 12m

Initiative: **-1**

Attacks: **1 bite**

Strike Value: **01-80**

Damage: **2d20+8**

Strength: 122

Agility: 22

Accuracy: 54

Intelligence: 2 to 12 (2d6)

Willpower: 42

Perception: 19

Valuables: None carried, but their lair is littered with gear from past victims.

Experience: 102

Morale: Firm

Size: 2.9m tall, 3.2m long

Weight: As END in kilograms +300kg

Implants: Normally none

Mutations: 19% chance of one, See Walking Mouther mutations list, page 87

The Walking mouther is a somewhat comical looking mutant beast, but for those who have encountered them before, there is nothing funny about these flesh gorging, fast moving, ravenous eaters of men. Tooth heads, as they are called by many, can be encountered either alone or in packs of up to eight members (2d4). Although big, bulbous and somewhat clumsy when in a full run, they can still easily overtake most humanoids in a straight out chase. In addition, once every fourth round they can add a hop to their run, or do so when standing still to leap to a higher level or down into a ravine or cavity in the earth to get at something delicious. This hop adds 3 meters to their regular movement rate when giving chase, or allows them to leap upwards 4 meters, often sufficient to jump up to a higher level of a ruined building, or over the walls of a human village. Although sufficiently fast to feed on dig teams, skullocks and other slow creatures, these freakish brutes are inherently lazy. They instead rely on their natural camouflage and use ambush tactics to wait for prey, lurching up from junk holes, behind old automobiles, rubble mounds and scrubby vegetation to snap up their victims.

Although not limited to inhabiting the ruins, they do seem most prevalent in the streets, junk strewn flats and wastes around ancient cities. For the most part, they don't do well above street level or in the tight quarters beneath the earth, yet make their lairs in burned out structures, including those many levels underground so long as the access points are wide enough to accommodate their massive, bloated bodies.

Generally, their coloration is a good match for whatever environment they routinely inhabit, and after only one generation of living in a given terrain type, newly born gorgers will take on the pigmentation and color patterns that best suit their surroundings. In ruins then, they are typically a dull gray, green or rust color, with many having mottled, spotted or striped patterns to their leathery hides. Although they are slow witted when met out in the open and not expecting other creatures, so having a normal initiative of -1, yet when in an ambush mode and hunkered down patiently waiting for a meal to happen by, they gain +3 initiative and will often leap out from only 2d6 meters and attack the middle prey creatures in a passing herd or marching line.

Greedy and always hungry, each walking mouther will pursue a separate prey animal. If there is insufficient food for a group of these monsters, they will then latch onto a single victim and tear it into junks, with the two biggest pack members often fighting savagely to get the largest portion and establish dominance of the pack. When hunting humanoids, the gorger will think nothing of splitting up to give chase to those that flee in different directions. Skullocks, interestingly enough, have been known to use captives as bait to draw out an annoying pack of walking mouthers, and then when the prisoners flee in panic and split up, leading separate osmu off in different directions, the skullocks will spring their attack on solitary tooth heads to bring them down one at a time.

On occasion, young osmu are captured and raised as battle mounts by human savages, raider tribes and several species of humanoids, including chest heads found on page 65 of this book.

The meat of a walking mouther tastes like bitter mud and 1 in 6 times is contaminated with a dose of mild radiation, and 1 in 8 times is so polluted with toxic agents that any human to eat the flesh must roll his or her body weight in kilograms or less on a d100 or become violently ill and succumb to chills, nausea, and weakness for d6 days (victim is half speed, -30 SV and +20 DV easier to be struck).

Walking mouthers are unable to swim and will drown if immersed in water deeper than their 2.8m height. They will enter pools or cross streams so long as they can easily touch the bottom and the current isn't too strong, and they are already in the midst of a chase or themselves being hunted by a much larger foe.

Osmu have a lifespan of about 18 years, with young reaching adulthood at 1 year of age. These monsters exhibit unsettling human-like features, including oddly

human ears, toes and organs, including reproductive features. They do not, however, see humans as anything other than their next meal, and can neither understand them, nor make their own barking, belch ridden chatter understood by people. In truth, these beasts were bio-engineered long ago and indeed have about 10% human DNA. Their original ancestors were much smaller, walked upright, had powerful arms and were engineered to serve as anti-personnel troops and laborers. Whatever contaminated their DNA, they were forever changed between batches, with the new, all-carnivorous, giant jawed specimens consuming both their masters and previous variants.

The bite of an osmu on a man sized or smaller target is often lethal, however, when a critical hit occurs, roll 3d6 on the following table to establish what extra gruesome fate awaits the victim. Larger creatures who suffer a crit from the walking mouther merely suffer double random damage. A critical hit usually means the mouther has torn off a limb from a humanoid victim.

Critical Hits on humanoids by Walking Mouthers   Roll 3d6

3. Decapitates one head (instant death to most targets).
4. Right arm*
5. Left arm*
6. Right hand*
7. Left hand*
8-13. Chomp, crush, shake and throw. Victim badly mauled. Drops anything held in hands, suffers 2d20+8 damage but is hurled 3d6+6 meters away and must make a type D willpower based hazard check to drop into unconsciousness for 3d6+10 minutes. If victim is alone, the osmu will consume the person entirely and within 3d6 hours excrete any non-digestible items and armor.
14. Left leg below knee*
15. Right leg below knee*
16. Entire left leg*
17. Entire right leg*
18. Severs target in two at waist. Usually instant death occurs.
*Victim must withdraw from combat at once to tie a tourniquet above the stump of the lost limb (unless a cybernetic or

otherwise non-living appendage) or else bleed out taking d8 damage per round until passing out and dying.

All fumbles by a solitary walking mouther means it bites at rubble, junk and rocks and hurts itself for d20 damage. However, if another mouther is near it, it bites into its pack mate doing maximum damage.

Every walking mouther is 19% likely to have one mutation from the following random list:

Walking Mouther Mutations   Roll d20

1. Lateral saw toothed bone blades on flexible arms; each adds an extra attack SV 01-70, damage d20+8 each.

2. Two headed, side by side allows it to make an extra bite attack per round.

3. Huge brute, add +5 bite damage, +10 SV (SV 01-80), +1m movement, and a whopping +40 Endurance extra.

4. Thick rhino hide, improves defense value by -16 (now -30 DV), but -1m movement.

5. Coated in viscous, **protective slime**. Flame, acid, sand storms and most other area effect attacks, including from killer bees and army ants, do only half damage to this glistening freak.

6. Junk fused: This specimen is coated in a thick glue, which over the years has resulted in all many of pebble, scarp of junk, bone, dead weed and other small item to adhere to the creature's hide. If not moving, this collection of adhered matter serves as excellent camouflage allowing the osmu to gain +3 initiative if laying in ambush. Furthermore, this outer coating is hard, and offers the specimen an extra -10 defense value (now -24 DV).

7. Sharked toothed, with rows of extra teeth. Bite does an extra +5 damage on a strike.

8. Acidic saliva: After a strike, the victim's flesh begins to bubble and turn to goo as digestive enzymes do their work. For the next d6+1 rounds, the victim suffers 3 points of automatic damage, unless he or she can immerse the afflicted area in one or more litres of liquid.

9. Paralysis venom bite: The victim must make a type D END based hazard check or experience a body numbing surge. If succumbing, the subject has 2d6 rounds before all his or her limbs stop working and he or she falls to the ground, able to see, hear, and feel everything thereafter... but not move. The subject can still use mental mutations or any head mounted cybernetic implants. Duration of paralysis is 3d6 minutes.

10. Bone plated monster, defense value improved by -24 (now -40 DV), increase endurance by +20, but -3 movement due to weight.

11. Belch of suffocation: Once each hour, this walking mouther can belch out a hideous, deafening burp. Humanoids in the path of this howling rush of sickening digestive gases must make a type D strength based hazard check to remain on their feet, likewise, willpower based type C HC to avoid growing horribly ill and vomiting painfully for d6 turns. If reduced to vomiting, the victim is +30 easier to be stuck, and makes any attacks at half SV. This painful retching will also inflict d6 damage on the unfortunate.

This belch has a cone-like attack and will affect up to five man sized beings out to 9 meters.

12. Spits digestive gobs: Once every third round, this osmu can hork up a luggy and shoot the spittle up to 24m away, SV 01-80. Anything hit must roll its kilograms weight or less on a d100 or be knocked back d6m, plus, must make an agility based type F hazard check or become coated in the digestive gob. If coated, the subject's skin, clothing, hair and non-metallic objects begin to dissolve, taking 2 End damage per round. This dissolving continues each round, with a 2 in 6 chance per round thereafter of ceasing its destructive process.

13. Mega jumper: The legs on this specimen are elongated and ripple with extra muscle. Once every fourth turn it can leap 16 meters if getting a run at it, or 9m up or horizontally if standing still. It will try to leap onto groups of humans or other prey animals with this maneuver being treated as an attack on a random PC within range. SV 01-90, Damage 3d20+10 stun.

14. Gas emitter orifices: This particularly bloated, baggy freak can emit a type of gas, usually once per encounter (or every two hours). The gas is often released when it feels threatened, needs to escape or is extremely frustrated such as when prey has lodged itself just out of reach, either up a tree or in a crevice. The gas is always the same for the specimen, but there is no telling what sort of gas an individual walking mouther will employ until it unleashes a cloud around itself from a dozen blowholes that run along either side of its body. The cloud will cover a 6m radius around the creature and in non-windy areas remain for 2d6 minutes, while in exposed windy areas, dissipate after 3d6 rounds.

Gas type **roll d6: 1.** Smoke screen, although bright green and smalls like bleach, is actually harmless. Obscured creature gains -20 DV while in cloud. / **2.** Spray paint, although looking toxic, this bright pink cloud coats everything in a quick trying, oily coating of paint. Removing this substance is laborious and its presence on skin, hair, clothing and gear will most likely make the subject easy to see by enemies and predators. / **3.** Skunk spray. Identical to a regular skunk's spray, this putrid smell coats those in the area around the creature, and although can be washed off skin, will taint gear and clothing for six months or more. (GMs can learn more about skunk spray from the skunks listing on page 101 of the Mutant Bestiary One)/ **4.** Irritant, while not harmful, those who breathe this gas suffer from horrendously painful irritation of the lungs, eyes, mouth and nasal passages. Each victim must make a type D endurance based hazard check or also cough so hard that they must cease all actions except for fleeing from the area of the cloud. The coughing fit will last as long as the subject remains in the cloud, or for 3d6 rounds after leaving the purple fog. / **5. Sleep gas:** All those not wearing a gas mask, and who breath, must make a type C endurance based hazard check or start to pass out. This check must be made each round while staying in the cloud area, regardless of successes or failure. For each failure of the hazard check, the victim is reduced by -10 perception and -1 movement. If either trait reaches zero or less, the victim is considered to have toppled over and fallen into a deep sleep for 3d6 minutes. If the targets are all knocked out in this way, the gorger, and any young or companions, will feed on the victims while they sleep, swallowing man sized victim's whole, head first. Other osmu are immune to this gas. / **6. Death gas!** Each round that a living creature remains in this black cloud, he or she must make a type A endurance based hazard check or suffocate and begin to die, taking 2d20 damage each round. If remaining alive and able to flee the gas, the damage will heal at 1 END point per round. Other osmu are immune to this poison.

15. Bone harpoons: Growing from the upper back of this specimen are d4+1 large bone spikes. These are each attached to a 24 meter long meaty tentacle. If chasing down, or trying to reach elusive prey that is smaller than itself, this mutant can fire one of these bone spikes at a target per round, SV 01-80, DMG d12+7. Any hit means the victim is punctured and can be yanked back to the mouth of the osmu. The tendril has a DV of -15 and can be severed after suffering 30 endurance damage. Those pulled back are chomped at by the creature's mouth at +20 SV (now SV 01-90).

16. Mental deflector: This walking mouther's mind is protected in a complex sub conscious defense mechanism which allows it to deflect 87% of all incoming mental attacks and controls, with an 8% chance of any bounced off attack returning to the sender!

17. Swallower: This brute is nearly double the size of a regular walking mouther, having an extra 50 endurance and double the weight. It also has a huge mouth and half dozen long red tongues. When attacking man sized or smaller creatures it will attempt to latch onto and simply swallow a victim. Any bite by this specimen does only d20+7 stun damage as the thing's tongues latch around and crush the victim. The target is allowed a single type G strength based hazard check to yank and spin free - missing his or her next attack but getting d6+2 meters away. Failure to get free means the subject is swallowed whole and lands in the thing's acid filled stomach. Besides suffocating, the subject begins to dissolve and take d8 damage per round, plus a -1 reduction to his or her appearance score, permanently, from the digestive juices.

Suffocation rules are covered on page 121 of the TME hub rules, but in brief a person can hold their breath for 2 minutes (40 rounds) but when swallowed, only 5 rounds before forced to make a willpower based type D

HC each round thereafter to not gulp for air, and in this case, fill one's lungs with acid and pass out from the agony and inability to breath. The swallowed victim can use a one handed weapon or some implant or mutation to cut his or her way out. The DV of the inside of the osmu is -10 and inflicting 40 damage will allow the victim to cut its way out the belly of the thing and slip free amid a pool of digestive juices, and bones of recent victims. Remarkably, the gorger can survive this cut in its gut and will continue to hunt, its underbelly healing within hours.

18. Pukes garbage: Once every 4th turn, this walking mouther will aim itself at a target and spit out a gooey mouthful of crushed concrete, metal, bones, glass, plastic and rocks. Range 15 meters, SV 01-90, damage d20+15 stun, plus the target must roll his or her kilograms in weight or less on a d100 to remain on his or her feet. If knocked over, the subject will fly back 2d4 meters and miss its next turn. GM: There could be a slight chance that a random relic could be spit out, too, but keep it modest such as a empty assault rifle magazine, a few shot gun shells, a unexploded frag grenade, drained power cell, army helmet, or gasmask with the dissolved head of its previous owner still attached.

19. Frothy foam: This thing will spit out a stream of yoke colored frothy foam once very 4th turn, attempting to coat the ground around potential prey animals or enemies. The walking mouthers seem to have no problem walking on this sudsy, 30cm deep froth, but other creatures must make a type D agility based hazard check every round to remain upright on the coated floor. Those who fall are -30 DV and so easier to attack, but also, -20 to their SVs when attacking the osmu. This foam covers a 6m wide by 12 m long swath and dissipates after 10 minutes.

20. Sonic scream emission: If hurt and suffering 10 or more points of damage in a single round, this specimen will open ridges along its sides which emit a wave of flesh peeling sonic attack. The specific harmonic vibration of this emission will dislodge loose building materials, and can cause collapses and landslides, but so too will inflict d8 damage per round, automatically to all those not wearing shell class armor. This osmu can maintain this scream for 6+d6 rounds, or until taking a hit and breaking its concentration. It can unleash up to five sonic attacks per hour. Other waling mouthers are also harmed by this emission.

Although these flesh eaters don't use or carry valuables, they do tend to feed on sufficient numbers of humanoids that they inadvertently acquire a vast treasure trove of loot in their regular feeding spots. After a few generations of a pack of osmu inhabiting the same lair, they will accumulate the gear and remains of many dozens of human excavators, as well as hundreds of scavs, nomads, savages, skullocks, warmorts, moaners and countless other equipment using beings. Some of the items are excreted in their walking mouther's feces, while other items, including full suits of armor, are deposited in the bone pits after the body is dragged back to the nest for later consumption and thereupon stripped bare of flesh. Young osmu will typically pick clean a corpse leaving an intact skeleton, using their long, acid covered tongues to lick the flesh and skin from the bones even inside the plated limbs of their victims.

For every adult tooth head in a pack, the game master can allow for two rolls on the included loot table. In addition, assume that the treasure hunters will also find d100 silver and d20 gold coins per person searching. Likewise, each looter will uncover enough leather armor to make a serviceable protective suit, as well as d3 machetes, d6 daggers, d12 arrows, d12 crossbow bolts and a 24% chance of working crossbow and 36% chance of an intact bow. A game master who has access to *Wasteland Treasures Set One* can also allow each searcher a roll from table WT-3 'Loot, Trophies and Curiosities found on Wasteland Savages' on page 16 of that document.

Random Loot Table for a Walking Mouther Lair
Roll twice per osmu in pack   Roll d100

1. Razor sword in original nylon sheath
2. Slightly chewed pistol grip pump shotgun with sling and d3 shells loaded in tube.
3. Mangled and useless cybernetic weapon arm, complete with shoulder blade and several ribs. The old assault rifle is utterly useless; however the rifle-arm's magazine is still attached and salvageable and contains d10 standard rifle rounds.
4. Goo covered ancient action figure from some comic series, worth 3d10+20sp if sold.
5. Large stainless steel commuter coffee cup with plastic lid, filled with vodka, 750ml, worth 20+d20sp
6. Candy apple red wig with built in pigtails, worth 10+2d20sp
7. Human arm, rotted and mostly bone, attached to forearm is a wrist laser with d6 shots remaining in battery.
8. Tattered plastic zippy bag filled with an assortment of relic ammo, including 3d6 .22 cartridges, d8 standard rifle and d12 standard pistol rounds, d6 shotgun shells, and d6 high caliber pistol rounds.
9. Handmade, leather ammo bandolier worn on the hip bone of some past victim. Belt can hold up to 50 rifle or pistol rounds, currently carries 0 to 8 standard rifle rounds (d12 -4).
10. Alloy hubcap which somebody turned into a shield (treat as junk shield but without a movement penalty and better -8 DV bonus.
11. Torn open leather backpack containing a plastic canteen (with d2 liters of water inside), and d6 days dried rations of rather recent creation. There is also a 1 in 6 chance that a spare, fully loaded 30 round magazine for an assault rife is inside.
12. Ripped open human rib cage. Across the skeletal chest is a strap leading down to a satchel filled with soiled clothing, a silver flask filled with 500ml of rum, along with a pouch containing 2d100 silver coins, 3d12 gold coins and d8 high caliber pistol rounds.
13. A cyborg's severed head, the right side has a optical implant (roll on page TME-89 for the random variety). Power supply detached. If salvaged, could fetch hundreds of silver coins.
14. Bright red swipe card. Writing on it simply says Level Five Authorization. Worth 10+d20sp as a colorful piece of plastic, but way more to somebody who knows the value of this card.
15. Skeletal human hand, with a gold ring on the wedding finger. Ring has a gemstone set in it and in total is worth 400+3d100sp
16. Never opened extra thick, clear, plastic drop sheet, for painting. Folds out to 4 x 4 meters. Worth 20+d20sp if sold unopened, half that if opened.
17. Pump shotgun, broken into scrap metal and rusty, but does have d8 shotgun slugs in tube magazine.
18. Tangled heap of guts, covered in maggots. Protruding from it is the butt end of some sort of gun. If pulled free from the disgusting pile **roll d6: 1.** Toy gun, bright green, worth 2d6sp/ **2.** .22 caliber sporting rifle with d8 rounds in magazine/ **3.** Pump shotgun with d3 shells loaded/ **4.** Survival rifle, with d6 rifle rounds loaded in magazine/ **5.** Assault rifle, with magazine missing but one round loaded in action./ **6.** Submachine-gun loaded with only d4 rounds of pistol ammo.
19. Pair of relic work gloves, black with knuckle plates and maxi-grip palms. Punches made with these gloves are +1 SV and do +1 damage.
20. Plastic disc, for disc golf, glow in the dark plastic and worth 20+d20sp
21. Fifty caliber cartridge
22. Doggy poop bag contains 4+d6 shotgun shells.
23. Pair of sleek, wrap around black sunglasses, worth 30+d20sp
24. Beach towel, soiled but if washed reveals an image of a cartoon mermaid sitting on a rock during a sunset. Worth 2d4sp if sold dirty or 3d6+10 if sold cleaned.
25. Pack of 4 never used, still shrink wrapped toothbrushes in various colors, medium bristles. Each worth 20+2d12sp
26. Woman's relic purse, fake dark brown leather. Filled with rotten rations, a 500ml flask of whiskey (flask worth 20+d20sp), and a 2 in 6 chance of a relic pocket pistol with d6 rounds in magazine.
27. Folding camp chair, three legged with camo print cushion, weighs 1kg, worth 60+2d20sp
28. Fake plant, apparently worn in a dead traveler's shredded backpack as camo. Tropical, worth 3d6sp
29. Legs of a corpse wearing relic army boots, pair worth

4d6+20sp if cleaned up and sold. Lots of tread left.

30. Ballistic vest on a human rib cage. Will stink of rot for 3d6 months unless new owner pays 14+d20sp to have it properly cleaned.

31. Hand drawn map showing a crude route from the nearest large trade town to an X amid childishly drawn ruins. The word "Bank Vault" written next to the X.

32. Holstered .22 caliber pistol, loaded with d12 cartridges. Spare, empty magazine in separate pouch attached to the black holster.

33. Great sword in finely engraved leather sheath. Sheath alone worth 30+d20sp. Highly recognizable to anybody who new the previous, now dead owner. Could be trouble.

34. Leather hip pouch, torn open. Spread around it are d100 +20 silver coins and d8 standard rifle rounds.

35. Shredded backpack containing moldy clothing, a stained wool blanket, leather sun hat, bottle of unopened red wine (worth 6+d6sp), and a 2 in 6 chance of an advanced fragmentation grenade.

36. Baseball cap from some ancient sports team, nylon, if cleaned will fetch 30+d20sp.

37. Small plastic box containing 6 magnetic ornaments, lady bugs. Never opened and if sold in pristine condition will earn 20+3d6sp

38. Shrink wrapped pack of 6 assorted peel and stick moustaches. Worth 10+d20sp

39. Magnetic banner, yellow loop with the words 'Support the Troops' written on it. Worth 20+d20sp to most uneducated traders, but to a historian or collector, will fetch 100+2d100sp.

40. Communicator wrist watch, battery has enough charge for d6 minutes of conversation.

41. Anti-toxin injector (see page TME 199)

42. Plastic "For Sale" sign, worth 3d6sp

43. Human skull wearing a headlight flashlight, battery nearly dead and offers 3d6 minutes of illumination.

44. Magazine for an automatic pistol, empty

45. Rusty machete, dull and does -1 DMG

46. Human arm wearing a wrist pistol, loaded with one shot.

47. Flashlight, handheld, with d4 minute of illumination in battery charge.

48. Coil of recently manufactured rope, 3d6+6 meters in length.

49. Locally made brass lantern filled with enough oil to provide illumination for 4d6 minutes.

50. Flint and steel

51. Safety goggles, relic.

52. Ballpoint pen, silver plated and nearly full of smooth writing blue ink, worth 30+3d20sp

53. Large oiled sack of drinkable water, d4+1 liters.

54. Doll, a relic, 20cm tall with solar panel on its back. If charged for an hour or more in the sun, and switched on, will talk baby talk and make assorted cute noises for 3 hours. Will be able to stand crawl 1m per round and be move around obstacles and avoid falling down stairs and

so forth. GM: There is a 6% chance this thing is actually a pocket-bot spy for a local mecha. The robotic baby will transmit data back to the robotic hive, especially regarding arms and armor of the characters. Will lead 2d6 light combots to the PC's location or home community. Their intent is to kill organic beings and seek ammo and power sources. Non-mecha baby robot worth 300+2d100sp, possibly double this in a large community like Overpass.

55. Pair of ancient reading glasses, 2x magnification, black with blue flecks, sealed in original plastic sleeve. Worth 100+d100sp

56. Small brown plastic jewelry box. Inside is, roll d6: 1,2. Mini grenades d3+1/ 3,4. 4+d4 High caliber pistol rounds/ 5,6. Golden wedding band, worth 100+2d100sp

57. Wax candle, thick as an arm with three wicks in it, bright red and smalls like cinnamon, worth 20+3d8sp

58. Headset communicator, battery drained but the unit seems operational.

59. Goo coated power cell, drained

60. Shrink-wrapped case of 3 fragmentation grenades

61. Leather pouch containing 3d6 human teeth, several scalps, dried body parts, 3d6 silver coins and d6 gold coins.

62. Purist bible, coated in goop. Inside is a crude hand drawn map of the nearest local free barter town, showing underground passages leading from one cottage to several others, with a large red X at a location leading out of the village perimeter wall.

63. Ancient comic book in a sealed plastic sleeve. Somewhat stained but in remarkably good shape. Subject seems to be some sort of massive green mutant that smashes stuff. Worth 40+2d20sp

64. Odd, bright green, rubbery rod. When shaken for a moment, it lights up and vibrates. Worth 50+d100sp

65. Ancient-made short sword in rusted steel and leather scabbard. This is an alloy replica roman legionnaire's 'Gladius' sword and can be treated as a regular saber that does +2 Damage and is +2 SV. Sheath needs replacing but sword worth 400+3d100sp

66. Ceramic mug, ancient manufacturing, shows a low relief, sculpted city scene of old with the words 'San Francisco' on it. Worth 3d10+20sp

67. Strange, rainbow patterned cape made of nylon, slightly tattered and gooey with the word 'Pride' written across it. Worth 3d6+4sp

68. Large alloy plumber's wrench, worth 30+3d20sp, but as a mace this thing does +2 damage and is +2 SV.

69. Starstruck Coffee, blue barista apron, stained but if cleaned up would fetch 4d6+10sp

70. Plastic box containing d6 standard pistol rounds. Box could hold up to 20 rounds if filled.

71. Tattered, locally made backpack. Inside are simple leather and cotton men's clothing, work gloves and wool socks, along with a day's dried rations and a 16% chance of an advanced fragmentation grenade.

72. A small glass globe showing a brightly colored ancient clown. When the globe is shaken, white flakes of powder fall around the clown figure inside the liquid filled container and the clown spins and a strange song about a circus starts up. Worth 50+d100sp

73. A single fifty caliber cartridge, stained but operational

74. A relic army helmet with sergeant's stripes painted on the back.

75. A plastic sealed paint by numbers set, complete with oil paints, brush thinners instruction and three numbered canvas boards depicting scenes of duck flying over a swamp, a horse, and two kittens. Set worth 40+2d20sp

76. A music disc, featuring 300 assorted 1940's Christmas hits of old, worth 30+2d20sp.

77. Small, cast iron model of an ancient bomber from some ancient war. A B-17 flying fortress on a plastic stand. Fits in one's palm. Worth 40+d100sp

78. Shrink wrapped box of 44, 20mm plastic army soldiers on sprues and in great shape, worth 3d6+20sp. **roll d6** for army: **1.** British Infantry, Napoleonic wars, 95th rifles/ **2.** Vietcong/ **3.** Assyrian chariots with archers/ **4.** 2212 war of Martian Succession, Imperial Terran Marines/ **5.** Medieval knights 12th century / **6.** World War 2 US paratroopers.

79. Plastic Easter egg basket filled with nylon nesting material and 3d6 decayed foil wrapped chocolate eggs. Basket worth 3d6sp

80. Odd orange bucket that looks like a pumpkin but with a triangular shaped eyes and nose and toothy grin. Handle missing. Worth 4d6sp

81. Bright blue pancake flipper, plastic. Worth 3d6sp

82. Wooden pencil, half used, dull, pink eraser chewed. 'F' lead Worth d4sp

83. White, fine toothed plastic comb, needs a cleaning but worth 2d6sp

84. Magazine for an assault rifle containing d4 standard rounds.

85. Large plastic squeeze-clip, possibly for wood working. Black with orange gripper tip. Worth 3d6sp

86. Plastic imitation apple, gala, worth 2d4sp

87. Small jewelry box, ring size. Inside is, **roll d4: 1.** A dried out human eyeball/ **2.** 2d4 kicker berries (see page TME 124)/ **3.** Mini grenade/ **4.** 6 high caliber pistol rounds, taped together.

88. Digital scope, mini power cell will yield 10+d10 more rounds of use before dying.

89. Headlamp flashlight, battery has d3 hours remaining power.

90. Communicator wristwatch, its pill battery is nearly dead, however, offering only 3d6 minutes of communication.

91. Anti-toxin injectors still in original shrink-wrap. Pack contains d3+2 syringes. See page TME 199.

92. Proximity mine, not armed and in nylon sleeve. See page TME 196

93. Canister of pepper spray, never used and in plastic packaging. See page TME 197

94. Army helmet, dark blue with the word 'Police' written across the front.

95. Gasmask in plastic hip pouch and surprisingly clean.

96. Skeletal human hand with a wrist laser strapped to it. The weapon has 2d8 shots remaining

97. Skeletal remains of a human wearing a suit of riot armor, helmet and head missing

98. Assault rifle with magazine, so caked in mud and grit that it will take 3+d2 hours for an untrained person to make it operational, or 30+d20 minutes for a person with the gunsmith skill to get it up and running. Magazine has d30 rounds, all of which need to be removed and cleaned, too.

99. M364 Howitzer shell

100. Fifty caliber sniper rifle in hard plastic gun case. Comes with bipod, cleaning kit and oil, sling and standard scope as well as two empty 10 round mags and one with d10, 50 cal rounds still inside. No other ammo.

CREATURES OF THE APOCALYPSE: 16
Rubble Troll

By William McAusland

Rubble Troll
Also called Junk Giant and Girder Golem
By William McAusland

Defense Value: **base 0**

Endurance: **200 +size and other detail modifiers**

Movement: **base 7m**

Initiative: **-1**

Attacks: **by bite, fist, kick or weapon**

Strike Value: **base 01-70**

Damage: **bite, fist or kick 2d20**+strength modifier/ **by weapon** + strength modifier

Strength: Random see table RT-2

Agility: 20

Accuracy: 30

Intelligence: 3d10

Willpower: 30+2d20

Perception: 20+d20

Appearance: See table RT-4

Valuables: See Rubble Troll loot table on page 98

Experience: Add EF factors from each table

Morale: Random, based on nature table RT-7, page 95

Size: 3 meters base (300cm + any modifiers)

Weight: As END in kilograms +200kg

Implants: Normally none

Mutations: 70% of one, and if so, a 28% chance of d2 more from the rubble Troll mutation list table RT-8 on page 96

Named after a mythological monster, the rubble troll is an enormous, low-intelligence brute. These deviants come in various shapes, sizes and colors and typically exhibit one or even two unique mutations. For the most part, it is safe to assume that any given rubble troll is a bad tempered man eater, although on occasion, certain family groups of peaceful, vegetarian variants will befriend excavators and local human villagers alike, going so far to help dig teams, scavs and travellers in distress.

They have mutated homosapien DNA and a few strains exhibit remarkably human features. In rare cases some of these giant mutants become infatuated with attractive humans and will keep them as pets. Exceptionally rare, the appearance of half-human rubble trolls has nevertheless been documented, although such bizarre specimens are often treated as either very large mutant humans or runts among other rubble trolls, and endure difficult, often short lives.

While determining the details of a rubble troll is something that can be done on the fly during the course of a game, it is advisable that the game master pre-generate several strains of these giant humanoids for handy in-game use. The following tables offer a method to quickly determine the appearance, diet, disposition, unique features and any mutations that a given rubble troll will possess. Generally, any group of these brutes will all be of the same sub-species, with the biggest being the dominant female or male. Should this largest specimen be subdued or killed, the rest will be forced to make a morale check or flee to regroup and establish a new leader.

Table RT-1 Size of Rubble Troll   Roll 2d6

2. Short, corpulent and squat: +2d20cm height, being only +d20 endurance, and slow, moving -1m per round. (EFs +100)

3,4. Modestly sized, but lean: +20+2d20cm height, having an extra 30+d20 endurance, moving faster at +1m per round. (EFs +150)

5,6. Big: +50+d100cm taller, adding 100+2d20 endurance. (EFs +200)

7,8. Huge: +70+d100 taller, adding 150+d100 endurance, and +30 strength. (EFs +250)

9,10. Massive: +100+2d00cm taller, with an extra 200+2d100 endurance and +1 to strength roll below. (EFs +300)

11. Gargantuan, but lean: +200+2d100cm, +300+2d100 endurance, being +1m move per round and +2 to strength roll below. (EFs +400)

12. Truly gigantic, both in height and girth: being +300+3d100cm taller, +500+3d100 endurance, taking great steps thus +2m per round, and +3 to strength roll below. (EFs +500)

Table RT-2 Strength of Rubble Troll
Roll 2d6 plus any size modifiers

2. Skinny limbs, strength of 100 doing +14 damage and able to throw rubble +70% range.

3,4. Modest build, strength of 120 doing +20 damage and +100% throw range. (EFs +50)

5-7. Stout build with a strength score of 130 doing +24 damage and adding 120% range to thrown objects. (EFs +100)

8,9. Goon, with huge build and a strength of 140, doing +28 damage and throwing stuff 140% further. (EFs +150)

10,11. Incredibly well built with a strength of 170, inflicting a crushing +40 damage per physical strike and hurling rubble and rusted cars 200% further. (EFs +200)

12 or higher. Massively built with an incredible strength of 220. Strikes by this monster will do an extra +50 damage while it can throw boulders and other objects 300% further than normal. (EFs +300)

Table RT-3
Commonly Thrown Objects Found in Ruins
Roll 2d6 Randomly Per Throw

2d6	Object	Base Throw Range	Strike Value Mod	Base Damage
2.	Motorcycle	50m	+10 SV	2d20 DMG
3.	Ceramic toilet with pipes	40m	+15 SV	2d12 DMG
4.	Small concrete block	50m	+20 SV	d20 DMG
5.	Medium concrete block	40m	+10 SV	2d20 DMG
6.	Large concrete block	30m	+5 SV	3d20 DMG
7.	Steel pipe	60m	+10 SV	2d20 DMG
8.	Iron beam	30m	+15 SV	3d20 DMG
9.	Steel manhole cover, disc style	100m	+20 SV	2d20 DMG
10.	Truck tire	70m	+12 SV	3d20 stun
11.	Small, rusted car frame	20m	+20 SV	3d20 DMG
12.	Large rusted vehicle	10m	+30 SV	d100 DMG

-10 defense value bonus and +30 endurance improvement. Appearance score: 2d6

6. Tall and stands fully erect like a human. Head is long and eyes wide set. Gains +1 initiative. Appearance score: 4d6

7. Bulbous torso with baggy skin, external organs, glands and tumor-like lumps growing here and there. It has short stubby legs and massive arms (see color cover art for this creature). Appearance d4+1

8. Broad backed with lumpy, watery sacks covering its body like a toad. This specimen can survive in very arid conditions for months, while those who bite it are rewarded with a mouthful of puss-flavoured, yellowish sap that requires the subject make a Type F willpower based hazard check or withdraw from the fight to vomit for d4 rounds. If the sickened victim is forced to fight on, he or she does so at -20 SV and -20 DV easier to hit. Appearance 2d6

9. Bark covered with patches of leaves, moss and whatnot growing from this oddity. The rubble troll has 10+d20% plant DNA in its mix and if hiding in the bush gains +4 initiative when making an ambush, or employs its stealth skill (concealed self or concealed movement) in woodland settings as if of 4 skill points (see stealth skill, page TME 51). Appearance 3d6 and no need to roll color for this rubble troll.

10. Glossy and gooey, like a salamander and covered in bulbous glands and skin tags. This specimen is actually amphibious and can breath in water as if in open air. It also has webbed hands and feet and can swim at 8m per round. Appearance 2d6

11. Reptilian, with scales, claws, lizard tongue, reptilian eyes, and a long, balancing tail. This specimen has elongated claws on its hands and feet and gains +5 damage and always adds an allosaurus-like extra bite attack in melee (3 melee attacks per round, or can throw an object every 2nd round, no need to roll table RT-6). This beast has 20+d20% lizard DNA and an appearance of 2d4.

12. Quite human-like, although with chunky features and a body too large for its head. It exhibits big hands and feet. Appearance 4d6+4

Table RT-4   Appearance of Rubble Troll   Roll 2d6

2. Hideous, hunched, covered in sores, pussy boils, scabs, patches of hair, and a zombie-like, somewhat corpse-like look to it. Sunken eyes, exposed teeth, skull nostrils and discolored skin, and the stench of a cadaver are all features of this brute. (App score 2d4)

3. Hunchbacked brute that when not crushing things flat with its fists, walks on its knuckles like a gorilla. It is somewhat more robust than others of similar size and gains +50 endurance. (App score 4+d6)

4. Elongated arms and short, powerful legs. It has incredible reach double its height and can snatch people off village walls our out of trees. (App score 3d6)

5. Lopsided, knobby, and bark-like husk encase this specimen in an extra layer of hard skin that yields a

Table RT-5   Skin Color of Rubble Troll   Roll 2d6

2. Vomit yellow
3. Chalky, pale dust
4. Charcoal black
5. Olive drab (army green)
6. Human-like, cream
7. Human-like, tan
8. Human-like, dark brown
9. Concrete grey
10. Rust red
11. Two colors, zebra striped, roll d8+1, twice
12. Two colors, spotted roll d8+1 twice

Table RT-6 Main Attack Mode Roll 2d6

2,3. Although able to use a fist attack, this specimen wields a steel girder as a club that has a base damage of 3d20 before any strength modifiers. It also gains a +10 SV bonus.

4. Uses one punch and one bite attack when in melee (treat bite as punch attack). Can throw objects every second round against distant foes.

5-9. Uses a single fist attack per round, but can also hurl an object every second round against distant targets.

10. Uses two fist attacks per round, but can also throw objects at a rate of one every second round.

11. Uses one fist as in roll 5-9, above, but if faced with smaller beings will charge and trample them, running through the victims and attacking up to 6 man sized or smaller beings in a pass. The stomping damage of this attack is considered stun damage. After making a trample, it will turn and fight with its fist attack thereafter.

12. While it can use its fist attack, this specimen holds a bundle of 4+d6 4m long rebar metal shafts that it hurls as spears at a rate of one per round until expending them all. Range, 90 meters, +10 SV doing a base of d20 damage plus the beast's strength modifier.

Table RT-7 Nature and Diet Roll 2d6

2. Peaceful vegetarian. This docile giant will generally ignore other creatures, especially other herbivores and graze right alongside deer, cattle, and livestock. If attacked, even by a smaller creature, this rubble troll is 80% likely simply to run away if possible. If forced to fight, it will turn and either throw logs, boulders and rubble debris or bludgeon any aggressor.

3. Vegetarian, but will aggressively defend its territory from carnivores or belligerent humanoids. If approached by peaceful travellers, this brute may trade with the person, share local info or guide the stranger if befriended, hired or otherwise coaxed by a mutually beneficial deal. It can talk in a very rudimentary version of the local common language.

4. Omnivore, however it considers eating other humanoids repulsive. This rubble troll will sometimes aid, befriend or even work with friendly and fair minded humans and is in fact quite curious about them. If a loner, this specimen may wish to join an adventure party for a few days, especially if the short-ones can supply it with excellent food stuffs, booze and prove themselves as loyal comrades.

5. Omnivore, but territorial, suspicious and inclined to bully, rob and humiliate weaker humanoids. This strain is prone to tricking travellers, ambushing them, double crossing them and often leading to their demise. It is not normally a man eater and tends to avoid outright killing humans unless they put up a fuss when being held-up.

7. Omnivore, but favors flesh above all other foods. It will kill and eat humanoids raw, but something about pure stocks interest it enough to often spare a 'generic human' and keep them around as servants, pets, and a source of entertainment, at least until hunting becomes poor and it loses interest in the captive.

8. Omnivore with a seemingly bottomless stomach. This beast will devour leaves, grass, vines, bugs, carrion and still living animals and people. Although preoccupied with eating, it is not suicidal and will normally leave well armed or very large creatures alone, unless starved. There is a 2 in 6 chance that this specimen hasn't eaten in days and will lose its mind at the sight of other creatures and attack, re-

gardless of the potential prey's numbers or size and risk its life to merely ingest flesh. If killing a person, it will temporarily ignore others and busy itself chewing on the fallen morsel, even as it takes damage from living pack mates of its victim. This brute can consume an adult human in 6 rounds, tearing it into chunks with each gory bite.

9. Carnivore, although it will only eat humanoids if they attack it first, or the rubble troll hasn't eaten in many days (2 in 6 chance). It is somewhat curious about pure stock humans and their look-alikes, and will occasionally greet travelers with a wave, perhaps even with a few words of warning about known hostile creatures or perils nearby. If threatened by humans, it will either run off if the short ones are too many, or else attack them viciously, eating their limbs before moving on.

10. Carnivore, but a skullock eater. This freak has acquired the taste for skullocks, but will also chow down on moaners, warmorts and mutant humans. It sees pure stocks and those that look like them as superior beings, with a semi-divine quality to them. Unbeknownst to itself, genetic programming in this beast have imprinted it with an adoration for generic humans, and it will only hurt one if forced to and then use stun damage attacks whenever possible. Fascinated by pure stocks, it will sometimes follow a group for a few kilometers just to observe them, and possibly protect them – especially from skullocks and the like. Visible mutants are merely food to it and if not travelling with pure stock companions will elicit an attack by this always hungry humanoid eater.

11. Carnivore, and especially likes the meat of horses, cattle and dogs. If it smells or sees travellers mounted on any of these animals, this rubble troll will engage in a hunt. It will try to take a short cut to get alongside a game trail or road, someplace narrow with a blind corner where it and any pack mates can leap out at close range and snap up a horse or other mount. Any human travellers to resist or harm the rubble trolls will be dispatched or driven off to allow the beast to eat the riding animal in peace.

12. Carnivore through and through. This specimen will eat any animal it can jump or chase down, including other species of rubble trolls, and dead pack mates of its own kind.

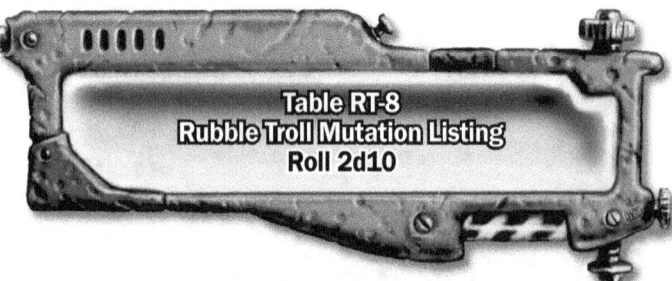

Table RT-8
Rubble Troll Mutation Listing
Roll 2d10

2. Regenerates: This mutant heals from physical injuries at a remarkable rate, recovering d6 trait points per round. The only damage that does not heal at this exceptional rate is that caused by mental attacks, flame, and acid or beam weapons.

3. Studded in bone knobs: Defense value increased by -10

4. Rhino-hide: Armored in a thick series of leathery plates, slowing it by -1m move per round, but improving its defense value by -20 and improving its endurance by +30 points.

5. Encrusted in articulating bone plates: Although this rubble troll is slowed by -2m per round (minimum 1m), it gains +50 endurance and has an improved DV of -30.

6. Spine covered thrashing tail: This tail serves as an additional attack, identical to the rubble troll's fist, but can smash into up to three man-sized targets if they are in a group.

7. Crab pincer arm: This freak will have d3 extra arms growing from its sides. These muscular appendages end in toothy crab pincers which attack as the brute's regular fist attacks, but do an extra d12 damage each. They cannot be used to throw objects.

8. Glue spitter: Three times per hour, this rubble troll can spit a stream of orange gob at a victim up to 12 meters away. SV 01-80, Damage 3d6 stun plus the victim must make an agility based, type D hazard check to get clear of the sticky mess. If failing to get clear, he or she is glued to the spot and any appendages can only be used with great effort, therefore any attacks are conducted at -20 SV. If concentrating on wiping free the glue-gob, a victim can do so in 2d6 rounds. If still stuck in place when the rubble troll, or another attacker, reaches the trapped victim, the subject suffers a +40 DV loss and will make for an easy target.

9. Nail knobs: This odd mutation involves hundreds of bone studs that grow all over the rubble troll. When on the attack and within 15 metes, this creature can focus its muscles on a certain spot of its body to tighten and then release a patch of mature knobs. These knobs resemble the heads of nails, thus their name, and shoot like a hail storm of bullets. Up to three grouped opponents can be fired upon by this wave of bones, strike value 10-90, damage d20 stun plus an additional d10 lethal damage is inflicted on a strike. This mutant can fire up to 10 such assaults per day.

10. Ballistic skin: Clubbing, smashing, and bullets from muskets and relic cartridge firing guns are far less effective on this rubble troll. Against blunt attacks and ballistics, it gains s -30 DV bonus, plus, any bullet that does harm it, inflicts half damage.

11. Mental screen: Mental mutations, mind reading attempts and related psionic activities projected at this rubble troll deflect off, with 2 in 10 coming back to the projector. For example, if a mind crush attempt is used against this brute, there is a 20% chance it is mirrored and instead attacks the sender.

12. Poison blood. Anything to bite this freak must make a type C endurance based hazard check after ingesting a mouthful of toxic blood. Those who fail their hazard check suffer the consequences: Roll d6: 1,2. Heart attack: victim suffers 4d20 stun damage. If more than his or her base, uninjured endurance, then death occurs instantly. If less stun damage, then the victim is allowed a second identical hazard check to merely stay conscious and in the fight. If made unconscious, he or she remains in a coma for 3d6 hours./ 3,4. Sleep venom: victim first goes numb for 2d6 rounds and suffers a -30 SV and is +30 DV easier to hit, then collapses into unconsciousness for 20+d20 minutes./ 5,6. Agony venom: the subject's skin begins to itch and burn terribly, massive pus filled boils pop up after 5 rounds, the subject's face puffs up and makes it hard to see, speak or breath, and finally the sores open and begin to bleed profusely for the next 3d6 hours. The victim takes a permanent -2d4 appearance loss from the scabs and scars. Children will hide behind their parents when meeting the character.

An anti toxin injector successfully delivered right after the ingestion of the venom will ward off these afflictions.

13. Putrid pustules: Whenever this rubble troll is hit, either by a missile weapon or melee ranged attack, there is a 6 in 10 chance that a huge pus filled blister on the creature erupts and spits out a stream of putrid smelling paste. This off-white, foul smelling substance will shoot 6m away often in the direction of the successful attack. If the aggressor is in range, this pus stream may strike the person and coat his or her clothing and armor. Avoiding this pus spray has nothing to do with his or her armor, but instead allows for only the target's agility modifiers and any dodge skill defense value benefits. If one is coated with this pus, the stink will attach itself to the wearer for 3d6 days, in which time carrion eating creatures will be attracted to the victim, thinking he or she is dead and an easy meal, ignoring the subject's companion just to get at the unfortunate stinky subject.

14. Centaur-mutant: This deviant has an extra set of legs and hips, attached to its main body by a secondary rib cage and enlarged stomach and digestive tract. The rubble troll can trot at +2d4m per round, and in melee, rear up on its hind legs, adding 2 meters to its height and getting two extra kick (fist) attacks. Its increased bulk adds an extra 50+2d20 endurance and +50 experience factors if defeated.

15. Enormous antlers, similar to those of a bull elk, grow from the head of this rubble troll. During regular melee attack it can sweep and gore with these growths along with a regular fist attack, however, if angered and given a chance to charge from at least 9 meters away, it will lower its head and plow into either a solitary or group of targets. This vast rack of antlers can potentially strike up to five man sized beings if clustered together, attacking each. A regular melee attack by with this mutation is SV 01-80 and inflicts the beast's regular punch damage +10, but on a charge, is SV 01-90 and inflicts double the random fist damage +20.

16. Two headed, gaining an extra bite attack and increased visual, auditory and olfactory capabilities, resulting in a +2 initiative bonus.

17. Tentacles grow from the back of this monstrosity. These meaty tubes are stubby and only 3m long when not deployed, but when needed, can stretch out to 12m distance to grasp whatever the beast wants to inspect, toy with or eat. There will be d4 such tentacles, all of which can be used as extra melee attacks at +10 SV and

on a hit crushing a man-sized or smaller victim at a rate of d8 damage per round, plus, pulling the victim towards the rubble troll's waiting fists or mouth. The tentacles can be hacked or blown apart and have a defense value of -20 and are considered severed after taking 30 points damage.

18. Chafing particulate ejectors: Across the back and sides of the brute are bugling, fleshy bags with a small orifice in the center. When hurt, enraged, fearing for itself or surprised, this rubble troll will instinctually jettison a burst of purple, agitating micro-grit in a cloud about itself. This cloud engulfs the beast and billows out 6m. Those finding themselves in this cloud suffer from limited vision, and anyone with exposed skin is immediately afflicted by chafe which itches terribly.

Most creatures, such as dogs, will recoil from any attack on the rubble troll to run off and try to rub away the irritating particulate. Humanoids are allowed a willpower based type D hazard heck to try and not itch their bare skin and stay focused on the fight. The particulate can be washed or swept off after 10 rounds of effort. This monster can expel up to 10 puffs of this material per day.

19. Electrical pulse radius: Once per minute (20 rounds), this ruble troll can emit an all-around pulse of electrical energy that has a radius of 9 meters and all those caught with this area, including other rubble trolls, are shocked and suffer d12 damage automatically, plus, each victim must make a willpower based type C hazard check to remain upright on his or her feet and not drop whatever they were holding when the surge of crackling energy swept over them. Dropped items take a round to retrieve, while anyone who falls to their knees loses their next turn and is +30 DV easier to hit.

20. Breaths fire!: Three times per hour, this freak can disgorge a plume of flame in a cone that is one meter wide out to 6m, then widens to two meters wide for another 6 meters, and then fans out to 3 meters wide to a maximum range of 18m. All those caught in the inferno, and not protected by a flame resistant suit or wearing shell class armor, must make an agility based, type D hazard check to try and jump clear. Failure means the subject is 'attacked' SV 01-90, Damage initially d20, but the subject burns for d8 rounds taking d6 damage per round thereafter. Dousing oneself in at least two liters of water will put out the fire.

This rubble troll has flame resistant skin and takes only half damage from incoming fire-based attacks, however, if killed by bullets, explosives or a laser beam, will explode, leveling an area 9m around it and igniting everything in fire. Characters and other non-flame resistant beings are attacked as if caught on fire from the troll's breath weapon.

Table RT-9 Rubble Troll Random Carried Loot Table

*Roll once per defeated rubble troll, using **d10** for items found on vegetarian trolls, or **3d10** for Omnivores, and roll **4d10** for carnivores. Re-roll duplicated results.*

1. Large sack of mushrooms (some with hallucinogenic properties) along with 3d6+6 kicker berries, hundreds of nuts (excellent food supply for up to 10 people for 4 days), and bunches of a mutated marijuana plant that when either smoked or chewed will produce a full body stone (weed and shrooms worth 300+2d100sp if sold in a city or large town).

2. A green walker stuck in a human rib cage. This rubble troll likes the taste of the walker's leaves and every night picked off a few to nibble on. It has snapped off the skull, skeletal legs and arms of the old cadaver so the plant can't get away or bite. There is as 2 in 6 chance that strapped to the rib cage is a old nylon tactical belt with a empty holster on one side and on the other a dual magazine holder with two fully loaded, 20 round pistol mags inside.

3. A pure stock human teenager (50% male otherwise a female) who, since it was rescued as a baby, has lived with the rubble troll. The teen can barely talk the common language of the area and is terrified of mutants and cyborgs, bestial humans or other beings except those who look pure stock. This person is a servant of the troll and its kin, and spent its days grooming, stitching up, washing and preparing food for the huge brutes.

    If this feral person was the property of a vegetarian troll, then the teen was very well treated and will weep pitifully for days if its owner was slain. If the servant of a omnivorous rubble troll, the he or she was treated fair enough, but smacked about a bit and mistreated now and then. The human could be convinced to go with the characters if given food, clothing and shown kindness. If this youth was the property of carnivorous rubble trolls, on the other hand, then he or she lived in constant terror and was kept on a leash. It would have seen what happened to other humans that got into the hands of the trolls, and will happily go along with the characters regardless of their type, and act as an obedient, fear ridden servant unless taught otherwise.

4. A tattered leather backpack filled with grubby commoner clothing, a half filled water skin, some crumbling, moldy rations, a knife, bow string and the land ownership deed to a farm outside the nearest free trade town.

5. A large wooden barrel of recent manufacturing with a strange circular brand marking on the side of it. It is half full with 20 liters of fine red wine. Worth 90+d100sp if sold. Stolen from a missing caravan. Characters could be accused of being raiders and hung.

6. A grenade launcher loaded with 4+d6 advanced fragmentation grenades.

7. Ammo crate filled with d100 standard pistol rounds, d100 rifle rounds, d20 high cal pistol and d20 HC rifle rounds, along with 6d6 shotgun shells and a 3 in 6 chance of d8 fifty caliber rounds.

8. Plastic box of unopened .22 caliber cartridges, still in shrink wrap. Brick of 500 rnds.

9. .22 caliber pistol, an 8 shot revolver, stainless steel finish, fully loaded, rate 1, otherwise same stats as a semi-automatic variant but won't jam – ever.

10. Worn on a rusty steel chain about the troll's neck is an assault shotgun, the drum magazine has d6 shotgun shells remaining in it.

11. Chainsaw, battery operated with 2d100 rounds of use left in power cell.

12. Heavy duty, dark green crate with carry strap. Inside are three M364 Howitzer shells in perfect condition. These shells weigh 47 kilograms each, over a hundred pounds. A person with a strength score under 50 will be reduced in movement by -2m per round, while somebody larger and stronger reduced by -1m per round (GM: if your players have a massive hulking character, reduce movement by half a meter or less, your call).

13. In a crumpled up blue camping tarp is, roll d6: 1,2. A human child, emaciated and in shock, barely responsive and pitiful. If returned to its people, the PCs will be generously rewarded. / 3,4. 3+d3 captive skullocks, all severely beaten, most with broken legs and arms. They seem to be some sort of pet or trophy for the rubble troll. If freed, they will report the character's kindness to their tribe, and later, if the PCs meet a large group of skullocks within 40 kilometers, the excavators will be recognized, bid a good journey, and let pass, if not made honorary tribe members and invited on a raid against a bunker filled with moaners or warmorts. / 5,6. d6+2 male and d6+2 female nubinz, each is threaded to the other by a cable through their ankle tendons. The cable knotted so tightly that these little humanoids could not untie it. They were used as road snacks and if freed, will be astounded and remarkably joyous, but are not loyal to their rescuers and will steal whatever they can and then slip away at the first opportunity. Nubinz are on page 108 of this book.

14. A human skeleton inside a suit of tactical armor, complete with helmet. Person seems to have been tied hand and foot and left to desiccate.

15. Assault rifle, although the magazine is missing.

16. Live pig (see page 78 of the Mutant Bestiary One book if available), if so there is a 2 in 6 chance this pig is actually a bound and gagged Oinker... on the menu for that evening and knows it. He will exceedingly grateful to his rescuers and join the team as a body guard. If a regular pig, this 33kg sow will sequel in panic and try and run off if not tied or butchered. Sow stats: DV -5, END 10+d20, MV 8m, Init. +0, SV 01-40, DMG d10 EFs 6, meat as endurance amount in silver coins.

17. A leather backpack filled with decaying clothes, crumbling rations, a dried out water skin and a coin pouch holding d100 silver coins, d8 gold coins and d3 anti-toxin injectors.

18. A dried out human skeleton wrapped in wires and relic cables. Somebody has made an attempt to paint lipstick and eye shadow on the skullish face. The victim seems to have been a woman as she wears a simple dress. At her waist is a belt pouch containing d12 silver coins and a bead necklace bearing a large jade cross with the initials P. K. on the back. GM note: Locals will recognize this cross, if worn or sold by a PC, as a young woman who went missing from the edge of a farm field months ago. Her name was Peggy Krasher, and her betrothed, the village's top hunter, will believe the PCs kidnapped and murdered her. Guthree, the hunter, and his belligerent friends, will get drunk one night, arm themselves for bear hunting and come after the characters for vengeance. Guthree has a relic compound bow with 30 regular arrows and d6+2 tipped with explosive arrowheads that have been in his family for generations. Treat him as an excavator on the typical humans table and his 3d4 chums as militia soldiers, all armed with bows and machetes. Typical human table on page TME 137.

19. A large wooden crate of recent manufacturing covered in Spanish writing. If opened it reveals a shipment of 30kg of unroasted coffee beans along with a sample of d6 kg of dark and 2d6 milk chocolate individually wrapped in wax paper. The beans are worth 300+2d100sp, and the chocolate worth 100sp per kilogram. GM adventure note: The intended customer for this rare shipment from the mysterious south never received the crate even though he pre-paid the elite airship broker who attempted to import it. The airship flew too low over a ruin filled ravine where this rubble troll hurled a length of rebar up and punctured the airship, brought it down and found both flesh and cargo at the crash site. The powerful warlord who ordered the beans and chocolate will hear of somebody trying to sell them in the local markets, and send out a posse after the thieves.

20. A relic nylon gun case containing a submachine gun and four empty magazines. There is no ammo here.

21. A 4 pack of battle rockets, secured in the original plastic sealed rack.

22. A mesh sack containing the stinking, rotting heads of 4d6 humanoids, including many skullocks and warmorts. One head, however, is blinking and the mouth moving. This is of an attractive female modeled android. She can barely be heard because of maggots filling her mouth, but once these filthy things are shaken free she says "Welcome to Starstruck Coffee. Say, what can I start for you? Today we have a blue cup Special on New Years Blend, goes great with a sparkle bar." GM note: If the PCs say they are looking at the other heads more closely, they will find a cyborg skull fitted with a salvageable optic implant, although disconnected from the power supply that was once housed in the dead person's missing body. Roll d12 on page TME-89 to see what optical enhancement is fitted in the skull.

23. A leather sack containing 3d6 skullock limbs, smoked and salted flavors, along with the left arm of a cybernetically enhanced human victim, the arm held a combo mechanical hand and an assault rifle in one. The assault rifle's magazine has 3d6 rounds inside. If taken to a robotics technician's shop, and given a few days ef-fort, this arm could be attached to a cyborg thus allowing the user to employ the hand like a regular hand, but have an assault rifle at the ready, too.

24. A large red steel trolley with latches on all its doors and cupboards. The tool crate weighs 90 kilograms and is filled with an astounding assortment of mechanical, robotics and woodworking tools, some few have ever seen. If sold in a large town this wheeled trolley and contents intact, it could fetch the characters 2000+2d1000sp. GM adventure option: This cabinet was stolen from a mad technician – hermit who was attempting to cybernetically enhance a gang of slave-chest heads (see page 65 for these nasty humanoids) but his underground facility was raided by rubble trolls. The mad hermit, *Tysuuokis the Magnificent*, and 3d6 chest head cyborg drones, were tracking this particular rubble troll and only hours behind.

25. A leather sack containing smaller bags of dried apples, veggies, meat strips, smoked salmon and 2d6 bottles of rather newly crafted vodka. The contents weigh nearly a hundred kilograms and are worth about 200 silver coins.

There is a 2 in 6 chance that also in the troll's sack is the gagged form of a young woman. If untied and given some first aid, she recovers enough to say that her father's wagon was attacked by the giant, that it ate her dad and took both her and plenty of food away. She says the beast made her dance each night around the fire, and beat her when she did poorly. She has a sprained ankle and needs a crutch to move at least 3m per round. If the PCs can be conceived to get her home, she will introduce the characters to her village. For the PC's heroics and kindness she offers to marry the best looking male PC and allow the whole team to live in their family farm house on the edge of the settlement. Other PCs will also attract unmarried youths of the community. Should the PCs refuse this honor and want to get back to adventuring or travel, the locals might try and make this difficult by drugging the character's beer and food with an ambition numbing, sleep inducing narcotic, at least until the PCs end up married with children.

26. A strange pistol shotgun with four friggin' barrels! It is loaded with d4 unfired shot shells.

27. d3+1 sheep tied together in a ball, almost dead from thirst and unable to make noise or walk until given water. GM note: Once rejuvenated, they will begin to bay and make such a racket that they will attract carnivores local to the terrain type.

28. Santa Claus costume and black felt boots wrapped in original plastic wrap. Worth 40+3d20sp

29. Ammo bandolier, able to hold 50 rounds of rifle or pistol ammo, this one presently holds d6 standard pistol and d8 standard rifle rounds.

30. Pump shotgun, handle missing and void of ammo, but a gunsmith with a few tools could make it serviceable in an hour.

31. d3+1 skinned human torsos, eviscerated and wrapped in pelts. GM note: The stinking things begin to attract scavengers the minute they are pulled out. Above ground: mutant dogs. Below ground: A black centipede.

32. A strange metallic liquid drum with an odd black and yellow warning sticker on it. Disgusting amber liquid seeps out through leaks in the side and whoever holds it gets the stuff on his or her hands. GM note: This is a container of highly toxic waste. The PC who held it is exposed to a contamination that forces a type E endurance based hazard check, with failure resulting in a dreadful illness for 3d6+2 days. The sick person is half all traits and bed ridden. Those who are within 3m of the container at any time have a 1 in 6 chance of catching a breath of the toxic fumes themselves and suffer the same potential fate.

33. A nylon duffle bag holding a .22 caliber semi auto rifle, a shotgun pistol, harpoon gun, pump shotgun and a survival rifle. Both the .22 and survival rifle have magazines, and there are 3d20 .22 cal rounds, d12 standard rifle rounds, and 3d6 shotgun shells present. All of this stuff is loose and dirty and looks like has been exposed to water at one point, but will work.

34. A proximity mine, disarmed and wrapped in bubble wrap.

35. An assault rifle with drum magazine. The magazine normally holds fifty rounds but this one is loaded with 2d20 harmless but noisy blank rounds

36. A newly made leather back pack filled with a commoner's wool pants and shirt, a floppy leather sun hat, sandals, soap, 3d6 silver coins and a crude, hand drawn map of the local region

37. A leather coin pouch filled with 3d6+10 gold coins minted in the Holy Purist Empire and a purist bible. Also present is a human hand wearing a gem encrusted gold ring marked with wavy, burning dagger symbol on the index finger. Ring worth 500+d1000sp just in gold and gem value. GM: Any pure stock human arrested by the authorities of a non-purist land carrying this stuff will have some explaining to do.

38. A leather sack filled with 3d6kg of oats, a still living kitten, d3 strangled ducks and a broken butterfly net.

39. A sealed box containing a pair of night vision goggles, d6 charged mini-power cells, an advanced fragmentation grenade and 3d6 rounds of high caliber pistol ammo.

40. A steel cage wrapped in a tarp made of stitched together human skins. Inside is, **roll d6: 1.** The prize concubine of the local religious leader, who will pay handsomely for his or her return so long as the exchange is handled discreetly so as not to alert the important holy person's spouse or congregation. Payment could be a plot of farm land, a stout two storey home within town, or a money pay out of 300 gold coins and 40 rounds of rifle ammo./ **2.** The daughter of local skullock warlord. The girl is half human, as her mother was a prisoner and forced to marry the warlord. If treated kindly, this halfie may want to join human society and the character party. Skullocks tracking parties are out looking for this particular rubble troll and the much loved skully princess. These trackers will stop at nothing to get her safely home should she be spotted with the characters. If given to the local skullocks, who will learn of her rescue when she tells them of the PC's heroics, local skullocks in the area will be alerted to the PC's identities and let the saviours pass safely whenever in the area./ **3.** The bruised and beaten son of a local water merchant, who the PCs may recognize from hand drawn *Lost Person* posters in a saloon. There is a reward of 1000 silver coins and a 10% share in the ownership of a local pub upon the safe return of the arrogant, hard to like lad./ **4.** Gagged and bound human children from a local village, d4 males, d4 females and 1 hermaphrodite. Villagers who have their young returned will be give the character party d3 goats. 2d6 hens, a cow and lifetime quarters in the largest, newest barn./ **5.** A middle aged excavator who happens to be from where most of the characters originally grew up. He immediately recognizes the PCs and tells them that in thanks for his rescue, he will take them on a great expedition to a site where he and his now dead comrades stashed a heap of relics at the root of a huge high-rise. He is unwell, however, and coughs up blood. One night, he draws a detailed treasure map and by dawn, is found dead. / **6.** A concubine android with flawless skin and the ability to change between a stunningly gorgeous woman, or a handsome man, complete with a change in its malleable, enhanced reproductive parts. It has been the pet of the rubble troll for many months, but desires a more cultured companion, a bath, fresh clothes and tidy quarters. It will gravitate towards the best looking PC in the group, regardless of their type or gender so long as it is not another android.

Snaykin

By William McAusland

Snaykin

Also called: Snakeoid, Snakemen, Hissies or Hissy, and Herpatosapien By William McAusland

Defense Value: **-30**

Endurance: **20+2d20**

Movement: **9m**

Initiative: **+2**

Attacks: **Ranged weapon** or **melee range bite + weapon** (usually a saber), **fist, or a tail slap** if surrounded or fleeing. Can also **constrict** a man sized or smaller creature to make it go unconscious.

Strike Value: **bite, fist or tail slap 01-60, saber 01-64**, base for other **handheld weapon 01-60** Constriction requires a hit by the tail

Damage: **bite d8+4** +venom (see page 104 for random type), **fist or tail slap d8+4**, **saber d20+6** or by ranged weapon (see list on next page). **Constriction does d6+4 stun damage automatically per round** once the tail strikes a target (see description)

Strength: 49 (+4 physical damage)

Agility: 71 (-8 DV)

Accuracy: 77 (+10 SV)

Intelligence: 10+d20

Willpower: 36

Perception: 68 (+2 initiative)

Appearance: 2d4

Valuables: Normally found with a backpack. See Snaykin Loot Table on page 104

Experience: 36

Morale: Excellent

Size: Torso and head 150cm tall, tail extends another 200m: Overall 3.5m long

Weight: 140 kilograms plus 1kg per point of uninjured endurance

Implants: Normally none

Mutations: 1 in 8 exhibit one from the Snaykin Mutations List, page 106

Skills: Wilderness Survival, Stealth 2pts, Junk crafter 3pts

Snaykin get their name from the misspelled title of *Snake-kin*, but are also called *Snakeoids*, *Hissies*, *Herpetosapiens* and the unimaginative *snakemen*.

These reptiles are clearly the work of long ago genetic manipulators and have some unknown quantity of human DNA. They are intelligent, quick witted, resourceful and dangerous. Diversity among this emerging species is considerable, with the coloration and type of venom they possess differing between sub-species. What is consistent about their kind is that they are all carnivorous, prideful, ambitious and nearly always hostile to humans and other mammalian cultures. Snakeoids do make use of other reptiles, however, although their treatment of reptilius lizard men in their service borders on slavery. 6 in 10 snaykin tribes will have a clan of reptilius living within their subterranean or skyscraper based fortress, and serve as laborers, scouts, and cannon fodder when engaging in war on other organized species in the vicinity. In these combined communities, there is often up to twice as many reptilius as hissies, with the lizard folk occupying a subservient role to the snake people in a two caste system. The larger snaykins, being much smarter, more powerful, more ruthless, and often armed with the best relics their dig slaves could uncover, rule by intimidation, guile, and pandering to the base needs and hungers of their less evolved subjects. Regardless of being used as pawns, reptilius tribes that submit to snaykin rule often do quite well, and grow in population, have vast stockpiles of food animals and humanoids kept in reserve, and tend to be better led in battle and win more engagements than they lose.

In a fight, when unable to deploy other reptile pets and servants against enemies, snaykin will first employ whatever ranged weapons they have available, along with any mutational attacks, then rush in to hack, inject venom, or possibly constrict, stun and capture victims for later use. A table on page 103 presents a random list of ranged weapons. In melee, a hissy can both make a bite attack and a saber slash if so armed, however they can also take victims alive with a single tail attack in an attempt to **constrict** and knock out a man-sized or smaller opponent. Any tail hit on a target inflicts an initial d8+4 damage, but each round the subject is held thereafter, allows the snaykin to suffocate and encircle the victim further for d6+4 stun damage. When the victim reaches zero of fewer endurance via stun attacks, he or she passes out and can be killed outright or bound and dragged off to a grim fate. This stun damage heals at the prisoner's normal daily healing rate, but per hour instead of sleep period.

A person being constricted cannot runaway, so too, he or she loses considerable mobility and is -30 SV while attacking the snaykin. To free a person from the constriction, the victim or his or her comrades must either kill the hissy, do at least 20 point damage to it, or use their strength to wrestle free – a strength based type E hazard check is needed to slip free.

Although bent on dominating whatever region they occupy, snaykin do not typically plan to eradicate all humanoids they encounter, and will sometimes conquer a human village or tribe of skullocks just to gather work slaves to undertake some large project. These projects might involve the excavation of underground chambers, building of high-rise or surface fortifications, construction of barges for an invasion fleet, or the whipped and ill-fed workers will merely serve as pack animals and general laborers. When a project is completed, or the hunting is poor, slave populations are sold to other species, ransomed off to the slave race's own kind, or butchered for food. These Snake men have a craving for mutton, beef and horse meat, and would much rather trade a human for a sheep whenever possible, thus all their ransoms and trade deals involve the exchange of prisoners for hoofed livestock. For the most part, snaykin have no use for gold or silver, although will occasionally carry or employ it when travelling to bribe or purchase food, slaves or relics from other intelligent beings.

Snaykin are cold blooded and don't do well below freezing, and if exposed to frigid conditions will suffer d10 damage per ten minutes. They can see in the dark as if wearing night vision goggles, have an excellent sense of smell, but somewhat limited ability to hear faint or distant noises, and can sometimes be surprised by or altogether fail to detect passing travelers moving nearby but out of view. They have a lifespan of about 40 years, reach adulthood at nine years of age, and have a modest rate of population growth. Only the dominant egg queen in a tribe will be allowed to mate, and will produce a clutch of 3d6 eggs each month. Young snaykins will tend to the nests, heaping them with straw and bio matter to keep them warm, yet dry and safe from scavenging rats and insects. Eggs incubate for about two months after the eggs are laid, with the hatching process being a highly celebrated, ritualized event involving most of the local snakeoid population.

The following tables can be used to quickly determine the coloration, venom, ranged weapons, back pack contents and any mutations in both individual and tribes of snaykins. The leader of any hissy group will be the largest female, she who has the highest endurance score, and will also carry the best relic weapons should the group have any at their disposal. The most dominant female of an entire tribe will be the egg queen, having double endurance and strength, always have at least 2 mutations and two relic weapons from table TME-WR, page TME 211, rolled on the mid rank column.

Snaykin Ranged Weapons   Roll 3d6

2. Laser pistol with d8 shots remaining in power cell (+16 SV, Rate 1, d20+10 DMG, range 500m, power cell normally holds 30 shots).
3. Fragmentation grenade (can be thrown 24m, 4m blast radius, up to 8 man-sized targets if in a group, SV 01-70, damage d20+10).

4. Pump shotgun (+20 SV, rate 1, DMG 3d10, range 30m, loaded with d8 shells).
5. Longbow and 3d6 arrows (SV +5, rate ½, d20+4 DMG, range 84m).
6. Pistol shotgun (+15 SV, rate 1 or 2, DMG 3d10, range 20m, loaded with d2 shells but a spare d8 rounds will be found in snaykin's pack).
7-9. Bow and 4d6 arrows (SV +0, rate ½, d12+4 DMG, range 48m).
10. Crossbow (+8 SV, rate 1/3rd, d20+5 Damage, range 72m, has 10+d20 spare quarrels).
11,12. Spear, thrown (SV +0, rate 1, d20+5 DMG, range 18m).
13. Longbow and 3d6 **venom tipped arrows** (SV +5, rate ½, d20+4 DMG, range 84m). Same venom as this snaykin's bite delivers.
14. Bow and 4d6 **venom tipped arrows** (SV +0, rate ½, d12+4 DMG +venom, range 48m). Same venom as this snaykin's bite delivers.
15. .22 caliber pistol (+5 SV, rate 2, DMG d10, range 100m, 18 shot mags with this gun having 3d6 cartridges loaded. 2 in 6 chance the creature has a spare empty mag and a box of d100 extra .22 rounds in pack.
16. Automatic pistol with 3d6 rounds in magazine (SV +12, rate 2, d20 DMG, range 250m).
17. Survival rifle with d10 rounds in magazine (SV +14, rate 1, d20 damage, range 800m).
18. Heavy Machine gun, belt fed with 10+d100 rounds in hip mounted ammo can (SV +15, rate 5, damage d20+10, range 950m, requires strength of 45 or more to heft and use).

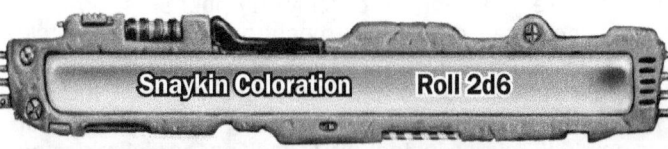

Snaykin Coloration   Roll 2d6

2. Pure white with red eyes and pink tongue.
3. Assorted browns with black triangles, cream underside, rattlesnake-tail.
4. Black back with a gray underside and cobra-like hood.
5. Tan and dull green back with lighter tan underside and chest.
6. White underside with a concrete gray and black spotted back.
7. Yellow underside, chin and chest, with a blue back.
8. Dark red back, pink underside and amber eyes
9. Dark green back, striped with tan and brown, and pale brown underside.
10. Bright tropical green back, pale green underside,
11. Mottled rubble gray, rust-red patches and a dull white underside and chest.
12. Alternating red, black and thinner yellow stripes, with a black snout like an eastern coral snake.

Snaykin Venom   Roll d10

1. Nervous system disruption: Targets bitten by this snaykin are allowed a willpower based type C hazard check. Failure resulting in the subject losing control of his or her body. The afflicted target's limbs jerk about uncontrollably, he or she can only mumble and drool, and any attack it makes is always a fumble on a roll of 01-20. The duration of this condition is 3d6 minutes. All movement is at half speed.

2. Bleeding eye venom: The subject is allowed an endurance based type D hazard check. Failure results in the victim's skin erupting into small spots of blood, but worse, his or her eyes begin to bleed and turn red. After 10 rounds, the subject can't see and fights at -40 SV and moves only 1 meter per round. The duration of the blindness is d4+1 hours.

3. Extreme nausea: Subject permitted a type E endurance based hazard check with an unsuccessful roll meaning he or she suddenly changes color, has an all over body ache, unbearable gut cramps and sudden need to get to a latrine. For the next 2d6 minutes the victim vomits and experiences bowl movements so extreme that he or she suffers d2 damage per minute. After this bout, the subject is weakened to half strength and movement for the rest of the day, requiring a good nights rest to feel somewhat normal again.

4. Skin eruption venom: The subject must make a type D endurance based hazard check or else break out in a hideous, all-over body rash complete with pustules, zits and open, puckered sores. He or she takes 3d10 damage from blood loss and tissue damage, but if surviving this, will begin to recover from the pain. The victim's skin, however, is permanently scared and the subject takes -2d6 appearance score drop (to a minimum of 1 point).

5. Nightmare venom: The subject must make an intelligence based type C hazard check or else commence living a nightmare. Any reptilius or snaykin opponents turn into huge winged red dragons or monstrous crocodiles, while comrades of the victim appear as rotted, animated corpses and their speech slurred and sounding like zombie moans. Subsequent, far stranger and alarming visions persist for the next 4d6 rounds, potentially damaging the victim's mind permanently at a loss of -2d6 to both willpower and intelligence. Another type C willpower hazard check is required to avoid this brain damage.

6. Non-aggression venom: As if designed by the ancient one's to subdue rioters, the bite of this snaykin forces the victim to make a type F willpower based hazard check or immediately become docile and introspective. He or she will simply lower any weapons and step back from a conflict. Only by taking an injury of at least 10 points damage will this subject snap out of his grinning, heavy-lidded, day dream of peace and fond childhood memories. If snapped out of the delusion, he or she returns to normal and can once more engage opponents, flee or do whatever is needed. This non-aggression lasts for 3d6 minutes.

7. Immobilization venom: Bite victim allowed a type E END based hazard check to ward off the venom. Within d4 rounds of being bitten, the victim's body begins to go numb at the extremities. Ten rounds later, he or she loses all muscle control, including bladder and bowel, and collapses. The victim will stay limp and easy to consume for the next 200+d100 minutes, minus the subjects uninjured endurance value. Recovery from this venom is slow and for the first 3d6 hours after being injected, the subject is half movement, irritable, light sensitive and very sick.

8. Proteases: The victim must make a Type E END hazard check or suffer hemorrhaging and muscle-fiber deterioration resulting in the immediate loss of half the subject's movement rate and strike value, plus the loss of d6 points to endurance, agility, accuracy and strength per minute for 3d6 minutes or until death occurs. If surviving this ordeal, the subject permanently loses 1 point from each trait.

9. Heart stopper: Bite victim allowed a Type E endurance based hazard check or suddenly experience heart or respiratory failure, taking an immediate d100+10 stun damage. If the attack is sufficient to make the victim go unconscious, then he or she must make a type C END based HC or suffer a heart attack, pass out, and die within 3d6 minutes. The application of the mutation Heal Touch or an anti-toxin injector will avert this and bring the victim up to 10% endurance. The recovery from this event is arduous and the subject at half movement and -20 SV for 2d6 days.

10. Compound venom: The subject is exposed to two venoms from this table. Re-roll this result if occurring again.

Snaykin Backpack Contents

Snaykins that are undertaking operations, migrating, hunting on patrol or are nomadic loners, carry a leather backpack wherever they go. Within this pack a looter will find 3d6 scalps, d6 dried human, skullock and unidentifiable humanoid hands, ears, and other parts, along with assorted trophies of previous kills, including a few tusks, teeth, strands of hair and other appendages of beasts. These bits are worth everything to the individual hissy, and often passed down generation to generation as treasure items. In addition to these grisly trophies, one will find a rolled up animal hide blanket, water skin (d3 liters), dried meat strips (28% chance human flesh), along with a tinder box, flint and steel, d4 torches and one roll on the following table, re-rolling items that are identical to those found on other defeated or robbed snaykins.

Snaykin Backpack Contents Table   Roll 2d20

2. Pack of six anti-toxin injectors in original shrink wrap.

3. Box of like-new high caliber rifle ammo, 20 cartridges, plastic wrapped.

4. Flashlight, headlamp style, battery offers only 3d6 minutes use.

5. Fully charged power cell.

6. Baggy of 3d6 standard pistol rounds and 3d6 standard rifle rounds.

7. Ballistic vest folded up neatly and looks remarkably new. Words on chest and back say *Federal Californian Army*.

8. Leather bag containing 2d100 silver coins and d100 gold coins.

9. Opaque plastic jug with something scratching about inside it. If opened it contains, **roll d6: 1.** spotted scorpion/ **2.** bog spider/ **3.** small snake/ **4.** venomous lizard/ **5.** stingfly/ **6.** normal rat.

10. Fuel canister 2 liters, full, for a flame unit, chainsaw or similar fire casting or internal combustion relic.

11. Land mine, standard (see page TME 196).

12. Gagged and bound pack of skullock babies, all alive, but malnourished and terrified. They can't be older than a month and weigh only 4kg or so each. 2+d4 in number.

13. Teenage human girl with no legs or arms and bright pink hair. She smiles when rescued and asks if you have her legs and arms around someplace. This is a service industry android named Coworker78B. She used to work in a donut shop and will repeatedly ask what a character wants for a tasty treat. If somehow fitted with limbs, even those of a robot, she will be ineffective as a fighter, but can adapt to camp or motel life and become a cook and maid. There is a 23% chance she is actually an unwilling optic, auditory and location broadcasting receptor for a faction of anti-human Mecha robots. The Mecha do not control her, but do see and hear what she does.

14. Elongated leather case filled with something hard and bulky. **Roll d6: 1,2.** Row of smoked devilkins wrapped in leaves and ready for snacking upon by the snaykin (see page 39 of the Mutant Bestiary One book to learn about these tiny humanoids). There is a 19% chance that d6 other devilkin of the same species occupy a second bag, but these malnourished, gagged and bound morsels are still alive! / **3,4.** A .22 caliber semi auto rifle with a folding stock and a 50 rounds drum magazine attached (empty). / **5,6.** An empty assault rifle, bullpup style with a thirty capacity magazine tied to the side of the well greased firearm.

15. A yet to hatch snaykin egg wrapped in straw and hidden in a leather bag. To sell this in a large city to a bioengineer or gladiatorial arena could fetch the characters a 300+d100sp. There is movement inside the egg.

16. An ancient document in a clear plastic folder. Inside are the Last Will and Testament of an ancient accountant leaving his children a fortune. Tax documents in the file show a sad story. A socialist government of the time applied taxes and fees on the estate to such a degree that the inheritors got nothing and actually owed the government money for processing, filing fees, and social justice and environmental surtaxes.

17. Leather, wide brim floppy hat. In the brim are sewn the teeth of skullocks, moaners, warmorts, oinkers* and reptilius.

See pages 78-80 of the Mutant Bestiary One book

18. Silencer for an automatic pistol (see page TME 197)

19. Small sack made of furry animal hide. Knotted and if opened reveals a change of woman's leather clothing, a simple makeup kit, shard of mirror, and an empty pocket pistol.

20. A small nylon bag made of ancient blue material but recently sewn together. Inside are cotton men's underwear, a flip open replica straight razor, a shard of old world mirror, a pair of wool socks and a smaller coin pouch holding d8 gold coins and 3d6 silver coins.

21. A tattered belt pouch with initials K.G. stitched into it. Inside are 3d6 silver coins, a drained power cell, 2d6 high caliber rifle rounds, some oats, and a pocket flashlight with a fully charged battery inside.

22. The legs and arms of a teenage girl, or rather a service industry android's limbs.

23. Cybernetic weapon arm, freshly severed and twisted from some poor human cyborg. The limb is an assault rifle with 2d6 rifle rounds remaining in the magazine. Removal of the previous owner's bone and muscles must take place.

24. Communicator, standard, battery drained (pg. TME 198).

25. Plastic pack of 6 exploding arrowheads (pg. TME 196).

26. Quiver of 3d8 arrows with special pitted arrow heads filled with a dark, sap like substance - venom of this particular snaykin. Each arrow is able to deliver the poison into a wound only once before being wiped clean.

27. Partially eaten apple. GM note: Anyone eating it exposes him or herself to the venom of the snaykin, who bit into this fruit in anticipation of some enemy getting a hold of its pack.

28. Empty magazine for an assault rifle.

29. Identification Sequence Broadcaster (IDSB), with d100+100 days left in charge. See page 198 TME hub rules for details on this relic.

30. Rad-scanner with d100 days use in mini-power cell (pg. TME 199)

31. Box of 100 .22 caliber cartridges, never opened and in shrink wrap.

32. Live snacks! Gagged and bound Nubinz, d3 male and d3 female all from the same clan sub-species (see page 108 this book for details). These pests will be most grateful to be rescued and inclined to tag along anyone who frees them, eager to be of service or somehow pay back their life debt and save the characters. GM: These little humanoids are inclined to suddenly change from being helpful to being treacherous thieves, who will not only steal valuables, ammo, and relic handguns before leaving, but lead the PCs into a dangerous predicament before bugging out.

33. A digital camera with hundreds of shots of a nearby human settlement. These still images are taken from the bushes outside the place, focusing on the crude towers, walls, zoomed in shots of individual militia personnel, the coming and going of livestock through the main gate, and several large transport wagons. GM: The PC looking at these, who if familiar with the area, recognize the wagons as those that went missing several weeks ago. The snaykin plan to use them like Trojan horses, filling them with reptilius slave-warriors and attacking the community.

The camera itself is worth 400+2d100sp and uses a mini power cell. It contains only 122 pictures but can store 3000. Power cell will last for 3 years.

34. Leather pouch containing d6 mini-grenades, d100 silver coins, d12 gold coins, d6 standard pistol rounds, d6 standard rifle rounds, d6 shotgun shells and d4 high caliber pistol rounds.

35. Battle rocket (see page TME 196).

36. Small, bright orange ammo box containing 10 fifty caliber rounds.

37. Drum magazine for an assault rifle, currently holds d20 rounds, but can hold 100 cartridges.

38. Hand sewn leather bag with shoulder strap. Inside are some rather fresh, human made rations including pepperoni, cheese, hard buns, spices and a bottle of red wine worth 10+d12sp. Also in the bag are d3 standard rifle rounds, d4 shotgun slugs and d20 .22 caliber cartridges.

39. Small knitted human doll, stained with blood and the back crudely stitched. Something rattles inside it. If yanked open, roll d6: 1. Fragmentation grenade, the pin connected to the stitching and when opened, pulls the pin free and detonates the explosive (SV 01-70, afflicts up to 8 people in the 4m blast zone if grouped together, those hit take d20+10 damage)/ 2-4. Advanced Fragmentation grenade, pin not released/ 5,6. Dozens of human teeth along with 3d6 standard pistol rounds and

d20 gold coins from the Holy Purist Empire (See Crossroads Region Gazetteer, page 192)

40. Night vision headgear with d12 hours of use remaining in mini-power cell (pg. TME 201).

Snaykin Mutations   Roll d20

1. Laser reflecting scales: This mutant has extra large, extra shiny scales that deflect incoming laser and other light based attacks in a random direction. To quickly determine the direction that a stray beam careens off to, **roll d6: 1.** back to the shooter. If this is a firearm, it destroys the weapon and inflicts 3d6 damage to the aggressor's hands, however, if the beam came from the eye, hands or other appendage of the shooter it automatically hits the hostile being for random damage./ **2-4.** safely up into the air, into a wall, the ground or some other substance/ **5.** into the nearest flammable substance and if a standard laser (as opposed to a stun or EMP pulse) then a fire erupts/ **6.** into the nearest ally of the snaykin for random damage.

2. Snake infested! This specimen is filled with flabby, sack-like growths in which inhabit parasitic mutant snakes. There are 2d6 small snakes occupying this mutant, which dart out and move to attack anything that threatens their host (DV -7, END 2d6 each, moves 7m, Init. +2, attacks 1 bite, SV 01-40, DMG d3 plus possibly venomous. See page TME 171).

3. An extra arm grows from this freak's shoulder, wielding another saber and adding a melee attack.

4. Two spare arms grow from the back of this snaykin, adding either one more saber attack or in ranged combat, a bow attack (has 20+3d6 arrows in a quiver).

5. Extra head, adding an additional bite attack with a different venom! This mutant is also slightly larger and has a bulkier upper body to support this additional head thus gains +20 endurance.

6. Massive, muscular brute with a strength score of 96 doing +12 damage with any strength based attacks, including bites. It also has thicker scales (gains -10 DV extra) and has an additional +50 endurance.

7. Chameleon powers: This specimen constantly changes colors to blend in with its surroundings. When first encountered, it rolls initiative separately from any regular snaykin or allies, and is +5, plus, has 4 points in concealed movement and conceal self and will not reveal itself until able to take advantage of a rear attack, or else slip away to get help if the battle is going badly for its side. Once it attacks or is spotted, it can no longer hide itself unless leaving the scene entirely and then reacquiring a new color or pattern to hide itself.

8. Bone bladed tail: Adding an additional attack, this specimen can either attack those behind or whip its specialized appendage forward as if it were using another saber attack.

9. Bone plated: DV increased by -30, but the great weight of these growths reduces its movement by -2 meters per round.

10. Song of hypnosis: Once per hour, this specimen will keep back from any hand to hand fighting and unleash a bizarre, multi tonal sonic emission, its mouth agape and issuing forth a musical, bewitching mind influence. All those living beings not wearing ear protection must make a willpower based type D hazard check or cease aggression and merely stand in place to stare off blankly. If engaged in melee, and the song begins, other snake-oids will disengage and slither back a few meters to see if their opponents succumb to the trance or not. Those who shake off the hypnosis can fight on, or smack afflicted comrades and snap them out of the trance. An entranced victim and be disarmed and his or her hands tied or else, an easy, cowardly +40 SV and double damage saber attack applied on the motionless victim. Any hit or metal intrusion on a hypnotized subject will immediately shake off the enchanting effects and return the person to normal.

11. Mind crusher: This snaykin will use mind crush 3 times per day, employing this mutation from a distance while others of its kind engage enemies. Mind Crush: Range 108m, 3x per day, target allowed type B INT based hazard check, or suffer d20 END and d6 INT damage. If reduced to zero or less intelligence, a victim drops into unconsciousness for d100+10 minutes, with a possible death occurring (type B willpower based HC to avoid).

12. Reflective mind: Incoming mental attacks reflect away 80% of the time (01-80 on a d100 roll), scattering into another dimension, otherwise (81-00) back to the person who sent the intrusion or harmful thought wave.

13. Stun ray: From this snaykin's forehead is emitted a ray of blue energy, reaching out to 78 meters. SV 01-70, 3x per day, damage 2d20 stun or double to cyborgs, androids, robots and other machines.

14. Back-up brain and heart: If killed in regular combat and not devoured, burnt to ashes, dissolved by acid, cut in two or decapitated, this Snaykin will rise up again after 3d6 minutes of death, regaining 10+d20 endurance, and either resume the attack or flee to report intruders.

15. Wings: This freak can fly 16m per round using a pair of huge, pterodactyl wings. In melee, it can pummel opponents making two extra attacks at SV 01-60, damage d12+4 stun damage each. While flying, this specimen is also much harder to hit and gains a -20 DV bonus when airborne.

16. Throwing quills: Covering the shoulders, upper arms and back of this mutant snakeoid are hundreds of dark purple throwing spikes. Every round when not in melee, this deviant will shoot d8 quills, range 24m, SV 01-70, damage d10 each

17. Force field: This snaykin has a 10 point per round force field surrounding it whenever excited to combat or fleeing for its life. If surprised, this field of shimmering green light is not available and no such protective shielding exists. This specimen can employ this field 3 times per day, with each use lasting 36 rounds. Note: This is a 10 point reduction from all damage it would otherwise suffer from strikes against it, not a reduction to each hit, nor does it protect the freak from mental attacks.

18. Electrical pulse: Three times per day this mutant snakeoid can shoot a lighting bolt from its forehead, range 40 meters, SV 01-80, damage inflicted on organic beings is d20 or 3d20 to machines, including cyborgs. If needed, this snaykin will use this power to start fires to either block fleeing enemies from escaping, or put up a barrier between itself and superior opponents allowing it to make its escape.

19. Scorpion stinger tail: Besides this freak's venomous bite, it has a sleek black bone spur on the tip of its tail that it uses as an extra melee attack per round. SV 01-60, Damage d12+4 plus different venom from whatever the snaykin's bite injects.

20. Extra mutie, plus bulked up brute: This freak has an extra 30 endurance and thick, knobby hide giving it a defense value bonus of -10. Likewise, it has one additional mutation from this table. Re-roll this roll if duplicated.

Nubinz

By William McAusland

Nubinz

Also known as Butcher Babeez, Nubz, Nubbers, Tunnel Turds, Rubble Robbers and Pipe Thieves

By William McAusland

Defense Value: **-20**

Endurance: **3d6**

Movement: **4m**

Initiative: **+2**

Attacks: **1 bite or by weapon** (knife or blowgun)

Strike Value: **bite 01-40, knife** or **blowgun 01-50**

Damage: **bite d2, knife d6, blow gun d3 +venom**

Strength: 10+d12

Agility: 52

Accuracy: 38

Intelligence: 10+d20

Willpower: 28

Perception: 44

Appearance: 3d6

Valuables: 1 in 6 carries a satchel. See Nubinz Satchel Contents table, page 115

Experience: 12

Morale: Poor

Size: 20+d20cm tall

Weight: As END in kilograms

Implants: Normally none

Mutations: 1 in 10 chance of one from the Nubinz Mutations List, page 112

Skills: The typical nubinz will possess the following skills; however, chieftains and rare individuals will have a wider range of talents. Stealth 4 pts, Pick locks 2 pts, Junk Crafter 1 pt, Lying 3 pts, Dodge 1 pt (applied to stats above), Climbing 3 pt, Pick Pocket 2 pts, Tacking 3 pts.

The diminutive, knee-high, humanoid race of nubinz is both plentiful and widely hated. This is because they purposefully come into contact with humanoid communities as these opportunistic mutants seek to exploit their exasperated hosts in a parasitic relationship. Nubinz, who go by a dozen different names, including tunnel turds, dwell in different clans which vary in the degree of trouble they cause a settlement. This mayhem ranges from occasional thefts and making a mess, to the extreme of eating pets and babies and disrupting a settlement so badly that they force the citizens to either pack up and move, or hire pest-controllers such as excavators, devilkins or skullock mercenaries to go underground and rid them of the nubber infestation.

In a fight they employ a knife as if it were a sword, often held in two hands, or else for ranged shots, use dart guns made from lengths of plastic pipe or reed. These blow guns are armed with a small poison dart, have a range of 12m, SV 01-50, rate ½ and inflict only d3 damage, but the subject is exposed to potential toxins. Once each Nubz shoots a dart, it will either flee, or if these creatures greatly outnumber their enemy, will draw their knives and charge in to kill or capture the target. Roll 2d6 here to see what poison a target is exposed to only after being punctured.

Nubinz Blow Gun Dart Venom Table   Roll 2d6

2,3. Extreme paralysis venom: Victim must make a type E endurance based hazard check or collapse instantly, remaining incapacitated, but awake and feeling, for the next 3d6 hours. He or she can still employ mental mutations.

4-9. Nerve venom: Subject must make a type C endurance based hazard check or after d6 rounds, begin to loose the feeling in his or her hands and feet, moving half speed and being -30 SV and +20 DV easier to be struck at for the next hour.

10,11. Sleep venom: Victim must make a type B endurance based hazard check of begin to stagger about and wilt. On the 4th round after being exposed, he or she will be forced to kneel, being -30 SV and +20 DV easier to hit. On the 10th round thereafter, if not already swarmed and taken prisoner or killed, the victim will drop into unconsciousness for d6 hours.

12. Hallucinogenic toxin: The victim must make a type G willpower based hazard check or else begin to hallucinate and see all his or her comrades as goat headed devils, and the nubinz as naked human babies with little wings and bows shooting love arrows. Needless to say, the PC's ability to take the fight to the enemy is reduced to -20 SV, half movement and being +20 DV easier to hit. This and a growing selection of weird hallucinations persist in the victim for the next 3d20 minutes.

These leathery, wrinkly and unattractive mutant men and women are considered vermin in many areas, and often have a bounty of up to ten silver coins per head. Nubz, as they are also called - usually said with a hateful spit, a rude gesture and a curse following the pronouncement of their name - are known to be thieves, pests, troublemakers, pranksters and a constant annoyance to the inhabitants of all humanoid species. Even mighty warmorts, who are far too big to pursue these tiny, chuckling, shrieking and giddy ankle biters into their pipes, cracks and crevices, suffer and chafe at the presence of nubbers and seek to rid themselves of them any way they can.

Nubinz are basically a line of mutant humans and rarely possess animal DNA. Slight color, body shape, hair growth patterns and facial shapes vary between clans. Each clan will give itself a name based on some underground structure, sign, beast-god or nearby population of victims. For example, one group might call themselves the Cheese Stealers, another the Waiting Room Jackers, while others names such as Pie Pilfers, Toy Harvesters, The Airporters, The Dwellers of the Silo, or Eaters of Man-Children, etc.

For the most part they are colored like junk, with a dusty, tint of brown, amber, olive green, or rust red. The following table can be used to quickly generate the eye, skin and hair color of a clan's populace:

Nubinz Eye Color   Roll d8

1. Glossy black orb
2. Red
3. Purple
4. Amber
5. Pink
6. Glassy gray (cataracts)
7. Blue
8. Orange

Nubinz Hair Color   Roll d8

1. Straw blond
2. Orange
3. Rust red
4. Charcoal gray
5. Jet black
6. Concrete powder white
7. Snot green
8. Dull brown

Nubinz Skin Color   Roll d8

1. Dusty brown
2. Chalky white
3. Soot black
4. Dull green
5. Rust red
6. Caucasian human pink
7. Neutral gray
8. Dark gray

As mentioned previously, each clan of these little pests operates differently when exposed to a host community. They prefer human villages above all else, particularly rural farming and fishing villages where there are plenty of crops to steal and where the town site is built over ancient ruins. In large human communities and emerging slum cities, however, food is harder to come by, but the opportunities to pilfer interesting items increased. Urban hives of nubz will occupy a vast network of structures, with family units concealing themselves in the basements, attics, between walls and in whatever ancient subway tunnels, ventilation pipes and other spaces that may exist below street level.

The way they interact with a human settlement's occupants differs based sometimes on the nature of the nubinz clan, yet at other times their behavior depends on how the big folk respond to them. If villagers tolerate the nubz occasional thefts of muffins, cheese and eggs, and no serious thefts or kidnappings of babies occurs, then the nubz will generally maintain the status quo and try to keep the level of mayhem, practical jokes, property damage and noise to a tolerable level. On the other hand, if the nubbers are more predatory and begin to kill livestock and pets, swarm an elderly or homeless person and pick clean his or her flesh to the bones, or worse of all, steal a baby for a subterranean banquet, then all hell breaks loose. Most humanoids, especially humans, will not tolerate the butchery of their young, and will employ such measures as poison, leg hold traps, snares, carnivorous animals and ambushes to rid themselves of the tunnel turds.

In nearly every case, however, an attempt to wipe out a nubber infestation sees things go from bad to worse. An angry nubz colony can destroy a host humanoid community, especially if the nubz start to loose and feel that their cohabitation with their benefactors is coming to a close. In such dire circumstances when all is lost, the nubbers might set fires to the town granary, kill all the milk cows, release the hens, and ultimately open up underground passages into town to allow black centipedes, spiders and even enemy humanoid forces into a settlement. Such acts of vengeance by nubinz on their former hosts are never forgotten, and humanoid survivors of the devastation will make every effort to warn others of their kind to eradicate a nubber hive the moment it is detected.

Only rarely are nubinz beneficial to a host population. In the very few cases where these small humanoids have been helpful and kind, the union of the two races has been remarkably rewarding for both sides. In one case, nubbers occupied the buried passages and chambers below a farm village, and traded relic arms, armor and medical wonders to the humans living above. In return, the humans provided plentiful meals, seasonal feasts, and booze to their tiny 'cousins' below. In another case, several nubinz from an all-but eliminated clan joined forces with an excavation team and served them as scouts, camp guards, cooks and humorous entertainment, living in special backpacks worn by the dig team as they travelled the region.

Sadly, the cases of cooperation and harmony are rare between most humanoids, and nubinz in particular are at odds with larger mutant species. On the next page is a random rumor list that game masters can use to better establish what clans of nubz have done to a small human community. These rumors could be related to the player characters when they arrive in a town and talk to locals at the slop house or saloon, or else events that happened as the characters grew up in a place.

Random Rumor Tables regarding Nubinz in a town Roll 2d8

2. "Them butcher babeez came 'n stole my cousin's kid from his crib. I am sure of it, although we ain't yet found the bones to prove it. Just found a hole in the floor leading down into God knows where."

3. "Nubbers stole my master's keys. They then freed all the slaves and it took months to catch his rightful property. Some slaves were never found... either taken deep beneath us into the ruins and eaten, or they fled to the city."

4. "Them fricken nubs keep stealing the eggs from the coop. The chickens go nuts and wake us but we can't find where the nubber's escape to. They must have a hole near the pens."

5. "I guess my cat had a fight with a nubber as we found blood all over the floor. Next night, found my cat hanging by wire and nearly dead. Now, poor Mr. Whiskers sleeps in a cage next to my bed. Got to kill them tunnel turds before they try to murder him again!"

6. "God damn nubinz sawed right through the wall of my wine cellar and stole every last friggin' bottle I had stored there. Gonna make them little shits pay, mark my words, friend."

7. "Other people hate the nubz, but my daughters think they are cute and my youngest swears that they came into her room when she was little and tried to coax her into a hole in the floorboards to have dinner date with them. She said she couldn't go with 'em because she had to make sure she had something to contribute to dinner, like bread. Isn't that cute?"

8. "I know most people hate the bloody nubz, but I kid you not, when I was sick as hell in bed, and couldn't get up to get some food or water, they gathered around me by the dozen and just watched over me. One brought me some water and food and they got me better again. I was worried, though, as a few had knives and seemed to be arguing amongst themselves in their chattering talk."

9. "Aw, whatever. Nubinz won't hurt you if you don't hurt them. I leave some cheese and bread out for 'em at Christmas and on most Sundays. They once left me a basket of eggs. Nice, eh?"

10. "Don't listen to what these fools around here tell you about the nubinz. They ain't cute or cuddly or good luck if you rub their bellies. They are cannibals and baby eatin' freaks and If I could, I'd kill every last one of the little f'n thieves!"

11. "The nubz around here live right below your feet, friend. They're listening to us talkin' right now! There are ruins and tunnels, and treasure filled bunkers all around this area. The nubinz, however, are so small that they can move around in the rubble and twisted junk passages with ease. If you are I ever tried to go down there, we'd have to crawl on our hands and knees to get around... and that's when they would ambush your ass and eat you alive."

12. "Nubber's are just undisciplined mutant vermin. Think of 'em as humanoid rats, okay? Just leave them some scraps of food, keep your valuables locked tight and you'll be okay. If you treat 'em with some respect and have a sense of humor, they won't kill your kids or devour your dog."

13. "Guess what? My neighbors, aunt's cousin was dragged from her bed and yanked into a hole only as big around as her head. They found her night gown and blood and that's all. Wherever they yanked her down to... there was no way she got there without every bone in her body broken. They terrify me and I can hardly sleep anymore."

14. "Did you know that them nubinz have never forgiven me for kicking one of them when I caught it in my pantry? Ever few nights the same one comes to me and does something awful to either me, my spouse or my poor terrified kids. One night I woke and it was standing on my chest and pissed on me before I knew what was going on. I've set a few steel traps now, and bought a pitbull. Gonna get that freak."

15. "Now that I am grown up, I hate and fear nubz. They taunt me and steal my stuff and poop on my plates and knock everything over. But, when I was a kid, I used to crawl into a hole in the earth outside of town, go down some old steps and into a series of ancient machine encrusted rooms. The nubinz were always waiting there for whatever snacks I could steal for them, and we used to play for hours and hours. I loved them then... but they changed. When I became a grown up, they caught me and hurt me. I don't know why they did that."

16. "I hear that there is a nubinz city below us. There are thousands of them down there and more being born all the time. They hoard relics of every kind. I also hear that our leaders and the clergy must pay tribute to them every week, sometimes with a goat, a cow, or even a stranger to town. We must be careful of getting arrested, too, as a few people who were taken to jail, never came out again. I bet there is a hole in one of the cells where the nubz come to collect their due."

Nubinz have short life spans of about twelve years, reach adulthood at two, and nearly every birth yields twins. Roughly half the population is male, with another 25% being genderless, and the other quarter females. A female will produce offspring three times a year, on average, although some very large, bloated breeder queens have been discovered which deliver quadruplets six times annually. With their massive population growth potential, and their ability to hide in spaces well out of reach of most other creatures, they can very quickly over populate a hive.

Normally, a growing supply of nubz flesh attracts the attention of subterranean predators; many that move into a den very close to the nubber infestation to take easy advantage of the bounty. Besides frequent predation, nubinz often get themselves killed off by the dozen when digging new passages under a town. Here they will cause a collapse, or discover a pocket of methane gas, stumble into terrible predators, open up radioactive zones, or die by countless other perils, including the bullets and blades of human excavators.

Likewise, nubz are eaten by many creatures once reaching the surface during a heist. Dogs, black owls, a wide range of large mutant bugs and other hunters take many of these humanoids as they surface or try to flee for the safety of one of their holes. Humans, once alerted to the presence of these pests, will eradicate them as best they can. Offering a ten silver coin bounty on the head of a nubinz has proven to be the best solution, as village teens with sling shots and bows, snares and falling box traps claim plenty of nub lives.

When the tables are turned however, and the nubinz get the better of a captured humanoid, especially human excavators, the prisoners are severely mistreated. The punishment differs depending on the crimes of the big folk. If an excavator has not killed any of the clan's populace, nor done much damage by the time he or she is captured, then the intruder will merely be robbed and left naked, his or her head shaved, body painted with deeply staining berry juice, and possibly worse humiliations. The naked prisoner is often left tied to a tree, wagon or slab of concrete somewhere near a village entrance to maximize the embarrassment of the subject.

Prisoners who have previously killed nubinz of a clan are almost never seen alive again, and dragged to the central hall of a clan hideout, tied down, tortured for days, then eaten while alive. So few people have witnessed or survived such dreadful encounters that this truth about the savagery of nubinz is often disputed, for most cannot believe such tiny, goofy looking little people can resort to such cruelty.

One in ten nubinz will be a mutated specimen, having a deviation from the following list. A nubz leader – often referred to simply as 'boss' – directs any heist gang of twenty or more raiders. This leader will have a relic handgun, a grenade, +10 endurance, 2 or more mutations from the following selection plus a totally random prime mutation from table TME1-57 on page 58 of the hub rules.

Nubinz Mutations List   Roll 2d12

2. More human: For whatever reason, this specimen seems to be a half breed and is an extra 30cm taller, has +10 endurance, and is somewhat more attractive with an appearance score of 10+2d20. It is particularly curious about its human side and is likely to be less hostile and cruel to humans it either meets or captures. There is a 4 in 10 chance that this being is a secondary leader among its kind, and armed with a relic handgun (roll d6 for gun: 1-3. Pocket pistol loaded with d6 rounds ammo. / 4. Mini laser, d12 shots left in battery. /5. Shotgun pistol with 2 loaded and d6 spare shot shells. / 6. Automatic pistol with d12 rounds ammo.

3. Spidery freak: This nubinz has two extra arms and two extra legs. In an attack it will wield two additional knives and can climb at a rate of 6 meters per round with climbing skill of 6 points.

4. Two headed specimen: This extra alert, somehow more robust freak has an extra +2d6 endurance and an additional +2 to its initiative (now +3). As it often serves as a leader and a scout, there is a 2 in 6 chance this freak has been given a .22 caliber pistol in which are loaded 3d6 cartridges.

5. Acid bloated: If shot, stabbed, bitten or otherwise punctured, this bag-like specimen will erupt like a pimple, gushing a spray of bright pink acid back at the source of the injury. Range of acid spray is 4 meters, target attacked like a ranged assault with an SV of 01-70, damage on a coated subject is d4 per round automatically for d6 rounds, and however, washing off the acid with a liter or water, beer or other neutralizing fluid will end this painful contamination.

If this nubinz is killed, it explodes and sprays acid in a 3m radius. Anyone in the radius, including other nubinz, is coated in the pink spray and is afflicted by the acid as noted above.

6. Winged: This humanoid has a pair of leathery bat-like wings as arms, with a rudimentary hand at the peak of the growths allowing it to climb and use tools as others do. These wings are small, however, even for the size of this creature, and will propel it through the air at only 12m per round.

7. Gills and webbed hands and feet: This nubber is coated in slime and glistens like a wet frog. It will prefer to employ sewers, creeks and ponds as a pathway to and from any raid. If threatened, will dive in the depths to escape pursuers, swimming at a rate of 9 meters per round and able to stay submerged indefinitely.

8. Bladed limb growing from the thing's hunched, upper back. This is muscular fella, having an extra +6 endurance and with this blade, able to slash foes for d12+1 damage (SV 01-50).

9. Giant headed freak: This nubinz's head is twice the normal size and contains a far more complex brain than regular specimens. It has an intelligence and willpower bonus of +20 each and a 19% chance of the mutation telekinesis (page TME 75, a 32% chance of the mutation telepathy (page TME 75), and a 41% chance of the mutation mind crush (page TME 70). This mutant is nearly always the leader of a heist gang, if not a whole tribe.

10. Armored and spiked: This robust nubz has articulating bone plates and rows of short but stout bone spikes growing from its shoulders, back and rump, giving it a DV bonus of -20 (now -40), a reduction of movement of -1m (now 3m) and an increase in endurance of +12. If provoked, it can make a bowling ball attack once per encounter, getting a run at an opponent and ramming them at SV 01-70, Damage d20+2 stun.

11. Elongated tail: Similar to a spider monkey, this nubz has a strange, two meter long tail that it can use to pilfer items off desks, through cages, from holsters, tabletops and even out of open backpacks... all without forcing the humanoid to get dangerously close nor expose itself in the open. In a fight, it will use the tail to clutch a separate knife and make an additional, normal blade attack

12. Tentacles: This nubz has no arms or legs, but instead 4+d6 fleshy, sticky tentacles a meter in length each. The creature can climb at five skill points, swim 6m per round, leap up to 4m in height or distance, and in an attack, adhere to a target and whirl around to the back of the opponent and bite at the subject's throat or eyes. Any critical hit by this nubz on a person always results in the victim having a grievous injury, roll d6: 1-3. One eyeball sucked out and swallowed by this nubz/ 4-6. The tentacle mutant bites the throat open of the target and then leaps away to either escape or attack another foe. The victim of the bite must use a hand to clutch the open, blood gushing wound or suffer d6 damage automatically per round until dead. While holding one's open neck, the subject is +20 easier to be hit by enemies and makes attacks at -20 SV. Bandaging the open wound will stop the bleed out, but take 2d4 minutes to accomplish.

13. Fanged freak: This nubz has a massive jaw filled with the teeth of a pitbull. It goes berserk in any fight and only uses its powerful jaws, making two attacks per round at SV 01-60 inflicting 2d6+1 damage per bite. This monster is entirely carnivorous and is prone to murdering and eating weaker members of its tribe when able to get away with it.

14. Poisonous blood: This little deviant's blood is toxic as hell, although at the time of consumption tastes the same as any other nubz. After 3 minutes of exposure to the blood, the eater must make a type E endurance based hazard check or suffer extreme nausea and be half all traits, barely conscious, and vomit painfully for 3d6 hours. There is a further 2 in 6 chance that this specimen was radioactive and anyone to consume or bite it is exposed to a mild dose of radiation (see page TME 125).

15. Shock tendril: A two meter long, clear, glowing tube grows from

the belly of this bloated little freak. In a fight, it will whip this tendril at an opponent and try to electrocute the subject. Any hit on somebody in metal armor automatically transfers a jolt of juice that inflicts 3d20 stun damage, while those in other armors are allowed an agility based type C hazard check to inadvertently deflect the tendril so that the connection cannot be made. This nubz can produce one shock every 4 turns, to a maximum of 6 delivered shocks per hour.

When not electrocuting people or prey animals, this monster will use the tendril to swing between rafters, beams and branches and travel 7m per round. Although it can control the tendril quite well, it is not agile enough to use as a grasping appendage.

16. Advanced regeneration: This more rubbery variant of the species will heal 1 endurance point per round, likewise, any legs or arms cut from its body will regrow in 3d6 days. If shot, stabbed, crushed or squished by normal attack modes, and 'killed', its limp body will remain dormant for 3d6 hours before miraculously commencing to heal itself. If burnt by acid or fire, or ingested, it will be killed, so too if it is decapitated.

17. Fur covered: This nubz has the pelt of a Persian cat and at first glance, if seen in the half dark or at a distance of over ten meters, looks like a large rodent, raccoon-thing, small dog or some other easily dismissed ani-

mal. Besides offering warmth and some ability to mimic common animals, this pelt does offer a -5 DV bonus.

18. Spits bone clusters: Once every 3rd turn, this big bellied deviant can hork up a fist sized, rock-hard chunk of crushed bone that it previously swallowed and cached in a special stomach pouch. The projectile is spit with great velocity, much phlegm and a sickening sound, range 9 meters, SV 01-60, damage 2d4+1. The nubz has 3d6 such bone-balls available to it per day.

19. Venomous bite: Instead of attacking with a knife in melee, this specimen has a set of fangs like a small dog and bites at SV 01-60 doing d6+1 damage, plus, anyone bit must make a type C endurance based hazard check or succumb to paralysis venom. Those who fail the check collapse after d6 turns and while able to see, hear and feel everything that happens to them thereafter, cannot move for 3d6+10 minutes.

20. Spiker arm: This deviant's left arm is a muscular, mace-like appendage covered in dozens of yellow, bone spikes. Besides using this arm as its primary melee weapon (SV 01-60, DMG 2d6+2), it can fire a volley of these spikes out 15m, SV 01-60, damage d6 per spike with d4+1 spikes shot per volley. It can unleash a maximum of 20 spikes per day.

21. Suicide bomber: This Nubinz is covered in odd, translucent fatty sacks and glands and carries a tinder box and set of tiny torches. It will usually precede an attack on a troublesome humanoid tribe, often going for leadership targets, or else toward the spouse and offspring of the hated leader. When able, it will rush ahead of its pack and ignite its oiled skin on fire and simply run into the midst of the enemy, often trying to clutch onto the leg of the primary target. Once ablaze, this nubz has a 2 in 6 chance of exploding per round. Once it explodes it will erupt in a bright orange fireball that engulfs a 6m radius around it in shards of bone, sticky flammable fat and fire. All those in the area are attacked twice, once by the general blaze: SV 01-70, damage d10, and the second attack, which is a more lethal but less likely result of the blast, with a shard of bone or large sack of flammable substance clinging to a victim: SV 01-40, damage 2d20.

Needless to say, if this suicide attack occurs in a wooden or canvas structure, or near other flammable substances like ethanol fuel tanks, things could get much worse.

Should a burning nubz be killed before it explodes, or a bucket of water is poured on it as it attacks, the detonation can be avoided – although, puncturing or shooting a burning nubz of this sort will immediately detonate it. Also of note is that some tribes of warmorts have leaned to recognize these explosive mutant specimens, capturing them, biding them and using them as projectiles to either drop down on attacking forces or load and launch these suicide nubinz in catapults.

22. Screaming lunatic: This nubinz has misshapen head, flabby cheeks and a barrel chest. When alarmed, needing help, wanting to alert its pack or tribal pets, it can unleash a deafening wail. Anyone within 6 meters of this shriek must make a type C willpower based haz-ard check or drop whatever he or she is holding to cover his or her ears. Those without hearing protection will be deafened for d6 minutes, even after instinctually covering their ears.

In most cases, the use of the scream allows the nubinz and its heist mates to flee, or else, gather in numbers and attack intruders. If a village has captured or killed members of this nubinz tribe, this specimen is likely to sneak into a community at night, around three in the morning, and unleashing this scream repeatedly to ensure that night after night, the citizens of the village are kept awake and miserable. This punishment will continue for d6 weeks or until the nubz captives are freed, some wrong has been corrected or this freak is eliminated.

23. Fart of misery: Although tribe mates are immune to the stench caused by this bloated, balloonish nubz's gaseous discharges, other beings are less lucky. If needing to escape, inflict misery, enjoy tormenting humans or otherwise requiring that extra touch to a situation, this nubinz can fart once every hour, propelling a noisome burst of faintly green gas into a 6m radius about it. Anything inhaling the stink cloud must immediately make a type G willpower based hazard check or become sickened. Animals and NPCs are forced to make a morale check or else depart the area for fresh air, while player characters who wish to remain in the afflicted area must make a type C endurance based hazard check or collapse to their knees and vomit repeatedly for d6 minutes, taking 2 points damage per minute. Regardless of getting ill or not, those who remain in the fart cloud fight at -20 SV and any attempt to use a mental mutation has a 44% chance of failure, expending one use of the mutation in the attempt.

The fart cloud will remain potent and airborne for 10+d20 minutes in an enclosed space, but outdoors, become dissipated in the wind after 3d6 rounds.

24. Extra mutated!: This nubz is already a bigger, more muscular and athletic specimen (+10 endurance, +1 damage from any physical attack modes, and +1m movement per round. In addition, it has another mutation rolled on this same table. Re-roll this result if occurring again.

Nubnz like cool little objects, food and anything stolen from bigger humanoids. Their possessions are trophies, and often brought out during quiet moments at home to boast about, rub, lick, eat, toy with or trade for breeding rights, food stuffs, better sleeping arrangements or some other perk. A nubz property, or lack thereof, shows their status among tribe. 2 in 6 nubinz will be found wearing their crudely made leather or plastic bag satchel.

The common possessions in a nub satchel include an oil skin of water (100+d100ml) tinder box, crude knife, d6 small portions of dried fruits, mushroom slices, nuts seeds and a few bones for casual chewing. Each will also contain a rolled up tattered rag that serves as a blanket, a vest-like shirt with a single button on the chest, and a filthy washing rag that smells of feces. Also in a satchel will be 2d6sp worth or plastic bits, such as old toys, electrical parts, straws, pens, dice, cutlery, and unidentifiable but colorful shapes. These plastic bits serve as currency among their kind, although gold and silver coins are also valuable.

These carrying cases are often made from skullock or human skin and besides being filled with the personal belongings of the nubinz each will have at least one roll on the following table. Leaders will have 3 rolls.

Nubinz Satchel Contents Table   Roll 2d20

2. A Prisoner! GM: Either a very attractive, vegetarian Devilkin (see page 39 of the Mutant Bestiary One if that book is available) otherwise **roll d6: 1.** A newly born bi-pedal rat. / **2.** A baby skullock. / **3.** A human baby, stolen from the nearest village. / **4.** A muto-harpy baby, its wings stitched together so it can't fly off when toyed with (see page 80 this book for Muto-Harpy description). / **5.** An unhatched reptilius egg. / **6.** A spotted scorpion (pg.TME 169) in a jar, mad as hell and will attack the nearest person to it if the jar is broken or opened.

3. The dried husk of a human baby. GM adventure idea: Perhaps this sad discovery could still wear the night robes it wore when stolen from the nearest village's CEO. A bracelet on the dried cadaver's hand will identify it as the missing child. If the PCs return the cadaver and bracelet, or worse, are found trying to sell the bracelet in the missing child's village the authorities accuse the PCs with the kidnapping and murder of the baby. A determined and blood thirsty posse are sent on the PC's trail.

4. A block of cheese wrapped in authentic ancient aluminum foil. Freshly stolen from somewhere and worth 4+d4sp.

5. A zippy bag of 3d6 standard pistol rounds.

6. A moldy cinnamon bun.

7. A pair of relic prescription glasses, recognizable to nearby villagers as once belonging to the town priest. Worth 10+d20sp to a relic dealer, but to the priest worth 200+2d100sp.

8. A magazine for an assault rifle with 0-10 (d12 minus 2) rifle rounds inside.

9. A headlamp flashlight, battery has only 3d6 minutes worth of illumination.

10. Strips of dried meat. 100+d100 grams. Could be anything.

11. Bottle of recently brewed red wine, worth 6+d12sp.

12. The bald head of a robotic mannequin. The battery is drained but not so long ago it talked in a sultry woman's voice speaking of recent fashion trends and then "How good you too could look in this ensemble, new for fall 2217" A pill power cell will reactivate the facial expressions, blinking and motion activated statement list for 500 hours. Worth 100+2d100sp.

13. Tattered, recently made rag doll. A girl in the nearest village will claim the PCs stole it if the characters are seen with the item.

14. Pair of woman's leather slippers, worth 3+d3sp.

15. Bone smoking pipe with leather pouch filled with a mix of marijuana and tobacco. Flint and steel also in satchel. Set worth 4+3d6sp.

16. Zippy bag containing 3d6 silver and d8 gold coins.

17. Small bronze cross on a simple leather and bead necklace, worth 3d6sp.

18. Dried out baby hands, assorted humanoid species.

19. ID swipe card, "Mall Security: Maximum Clearance".

20. Small tattered book of old. Pocket Guide: English to Spanish Translation, worth 3d20+20sp.

21. Folded wool blanket with locally recognized pattern showing sheep and salmon shapes, worth 4+d8sp.

22. Anti toxin injector (see page TME 199).

23. Empty pocket pistol.

24. Full magazine for a high caliber pistol.

25. Land mine, in original plastic wrap.

26. Tattered copy of the Holy Purist Bible, bound twenty or so years ago in the Holy Purist Empire of the Cross-roads Region.

27. Relic T-shirt, sports logo of old painted on it. A bit tattered and stinky, but if washed would fetch 3d6+10sp.

28. Teddy bear made of deer skin with bone button eyes and stitched face. Name stitched on the back reads *'Tabatha's Best Friend'*.

29. Small glass boot, some sort of ancient shot glass. Worth 4d6+3sp

30. Package of 6 mini grenades wrapped in original plastic seal (see page TME 195).

31. Bright blue wig, woman's bobbed hairstyle. Fits in clear zippered bag and in remarkable shape, worth 30+2d20sp

32. Gold wedding band, crudely made by local goldsmith, worth 50+d100sp to a trader, but original owner who had it stolen years ago will pay twice that plus d6 sheep and 2d6 chickens to get it back.

33. Crudely made, 4 cup teapot with lid. Wrapped in a skullock's torso skin to secure it. Worth 6+d8sp.

34. Leather pouch containing 20+d20 assorted skullock and human teeth, 3d6 silver coins, d12 gold coins and a fist sized metal cylinder with a grip and a pin running through the top (fragmentation grenade).

35. Relic compass, made of alloy and in excellent condition. Needs to have filth cleaned off but could sell for 100+d100sp, triple this to a barge or airship captain.

36. Pottery, mug, locally made, chipped and worthless. The word 'Mutants Rise Up' carved into it.

37. Large relic button with a rainbow pattern and the word 'Pride Parade 2112' printed on it. Worth 10+d20sp.

38. Large relic candle in original plastic, vanilla scented. Worth 3d12+30sp.

39. Small brass bell, crudely cast and says 'Made in Overpass' on handle, worth 4d6+6sp

40. Advanced fragmentation grenade, see page TME 195.

CREATURES OF THE APOCALYPSE: 19
ApoCalypse Moth

By Danny Seedhouse

Apocalypse Moth

Also called the Scissor Man, Spire Daemon and the Limb Taker
By Danny Seedhouse

Defensive Value: **-30/-55** flying

Endurance: **200+2d100**

Movement: **2m/ 12m air**

Initiative: **+3**

Attacks: **1 mandible and 2 wing talons**

Strike Value: **01-98** or 108 on unaware targets

Damage: mandibles **2d20+10** and type **C paralysis venom, wing talons 1d12+10**

Strength: 80

Agility: 77

Accuracy: 84

Intelligence: 15

Willpower: 63

Perception: 108

Experience Factors: 285

Morale: excellent to poor

Size: Body 5m including tail

Wing span: 8m

Weight: 450 kg

Mutations: 1 in 10 table AP-1, this page.

Relics: none

Implants: none.

Valuables: none unless its lair is found

The Apocalypse moth is a bio engineered horror built to be a silent assassin and terror weapon in some long ago war. There hunting grounds are always carefully chosen and share some basic characteristics. Enough space to open its wings and do its usual swooping attack, so 9 meters wide by 20 meters long. They are found across a wide range of terrain but require a high perch for its lair, with its preference being cliff side caves of either natural or man made formation. Capable of riding thermals, the moth can float above silently and unseen due to its natural, adaptive and ever changing sky camouflage. A soaring moth has an effective stealth rank of 4.

Once prey is selected this beast silently glides in, camouflaged skin patterns giving it 3 skill points in stealth on its approach. Its first attack is always a called shot to amputate a limb, (roll d20, a result of 1 and 2 is neck, 3,4 upper right arm, 5,6 lower right arm, 7 right hand, 8,9 upper left arm, 10,11 lower left arm, 12 left hand, 13,14 upper right leg, 15 lower right leg, 16 left foot, 17,18 upper left leg, 19 lower right leg, 20 left foot.) at a SV 98 or 108 on unaware targets, this includes the called shot penalty. If the bite does at 30 points of damage or more, there is a chance that the limb is severed, the target is allowed a type D endurance or agility (targets choice) hazard check to save the limb. To keep the target from sounding any alert or running, the limb taker's mandibles also deliver a dose of type C paralyzation venom. This

substance requires any victim to make an endurance based type C hazard check or go limp and defenseless for d6 hours.

Often the moth will do multiple passes over a small group attempting to paralyze the targets before returning to feast with impunity. If taking over half its endurance in damage an apocalypse mouth will flee back to its lair to hide and heal, trying to at least take a paralyzed victim or at vary least a severed limb with it.

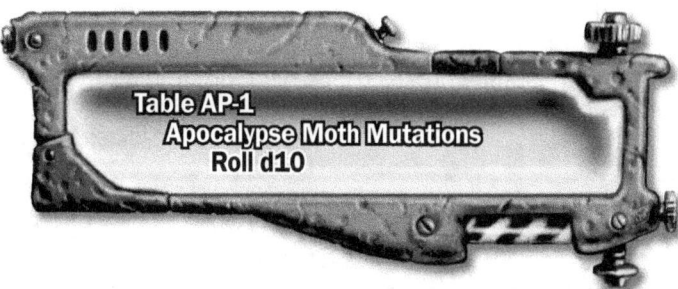

Table AP-1
Apocalypse Moth Mutations
Roll d10

1. Youth about 1/2 the size of a full grow adult but still dangerous. Good news reduce END by 100, SV by -10, reduce damage by 5 and it only has a type A paralyzation venom. Increase DV by -10 and add +2 meters of flying speed and 0.5 meters of ground speed.

2. Roll on table TME-1-58 creature mutations, pg TME 59.

3. Roll on TME-1-59 ghost mutations, page TME 59.

4. Massive: Add extra 70 END, +10 to all strike values and +5 to all damage inflicted. Has a 12m wingspan and is 8m long.

5. Bladed tail: 1 extra attack at SV 01-90, DMG 1d20+10.

6. Stinger tail: 1 extra stinger attack at SV 01-98, DMG 1d6+10+ type B paralyzation venom (20+d20 minutes incapacitation).

7. Tail spikes: Rate 3, SV 90, DMG 1d10+5, range 100 meters, 1 in 6 chance of the spikes being venomous just like the bite.

8. Aquatic: This version has mutated to be at home underwater, it has no fly speed but swims at 10 meters a round. Its skin is camouflaged for aquatic environments and its breaths equally well on land as under water. Still hunts as an ambush hunter. It lurks just under the water surface, eyes barely visible, dragging its paralyzed prey underwater. GM: Re-roll if moth already appearing in a terrestrial game situation.

9. Two heads... are defiantly better then one. This horror has a second bite attack at its full normal SV, venom included.

10. Acid spray: This creature has lost its poison attack but can spit a spray of acid. Rate 1/2, can spray a group of 1d4 targets, SV 01-98 DMG 2d20 and 1d20 for the next 1d4 rounds. Immersion in water will neutralize acid.

The Apocalypse Moth Lair

The easiest way to find the moths lair is to follow it back after it has been driven off or is returning to its lair with its latest victim. The other method of finding the lair is smell. The lair stinks overwhelmingly of rotting meat. Anyone passing within 100 meters gets a type B smell based perception hazard check, within 50 meters its a type A and with in 25 meters this is automatic. At this point, most creatures are smart enough to leave this site well enough alone.

Each lair is somewhat different due to its location but all feature a pit of some sort and it is in the cavity that all unconsumed parts of the moth's victims are thrown. The apocalypse moth grows its young in the pit and each hole contains, 1d8 larva, 2d6 rolls on the body part table (AM-2, below), as well as several rolls from part eight of the TME hub rules starting on page TME 206: 1d6 primitive weapons (WC-P), 1d6 standard street weapons (WC-SS), 1 in 4 chance of 1d3 relics from WC-RC and a 1 in 4 odds of having 1d3 from WC-R. Also present are stationary valuables from page TME 209 with 1d6+1 rolls on the corpse chart (C), 1d4 un-looted corpses (UC) saved for later, as well as various chunks of meat and scraps of torn clothing.

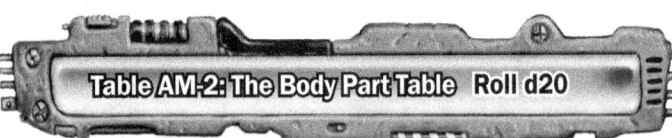

Table AM-2: The Body Part Table   Roll d20

Roll 2 to 12 times per larva pit. When needed, roll a dice with an odd number result meaning right and an even result as left, or odd for male and even for female.

1. 1d6 toes, 1 in 8 chance there are painted toe nails, roll on TME-1-18 for a random paint color.

2. 1d6 fingers. 1 in 10 chance of having a ring on one finger worth 2d20sp.

3. A normal hand.

4. A humanoid creature's hand. Moaners hand (odd) or a skullock hand (even) or what ever is the common type in the current campaign setting.

5. A strange hand. **Roll d10. 1.** Odd color (see table TME-1-18)./ **2.** leather-like skin./ **3.** scales./ **4.** fur covered./ **5.** only 3 fingers./ **6.** 1d3 extra fingers./ **7.** claw like fingernails./ **8.** extra finger joints./ **9.** robotic./ **10.** thumb on wrong side of hand.

6. A normal arm.

7. A odd arm, roll a **d12. 1.** strange color TME-1-18 mutant skin color./ **2.** its a tentacle (roll for color)./ **3.** robot arm still partially covered in android flesh./ **4.** oversized hand and forearm./ **5.** covered in tattoos./ **6.** has two elbow joints./ **7.** hand is on backwards./ **8.** covered in fur. / **9.** from a bestial human./ **10.** cyborg weapon arm with a weapon still attached, see implant 50, page TME 92./ **11.** really large (re-roll 1d10 on this chart)./ **12.** really small (re-roll 1d10 on this chart).

8. Arm from a humanoid creature, moaner (odd) or a skullock (even).

9. Limb from random creature, roll on TME 4-2 Street Level from Ancient Ruins Encounter Matrix, page TME 130.

10. 1d4 larva.

11. A regular foot.

12. An odd foot, roll a **d12. 1.** odd color TME-1-18./ **2.** its a tentacle (roll for color)./ **3.** robot foot still partially covered in android flesh./ **4.** over sized foot./ **5.** covered in tattoos./ **6.** is a hoof./ **7.** add 1d3 extra toes./ **8.** missing 1d3 toes./ **9.** foot from hydraulic walker legs./ **10.** is from a bestial humanoid. /**11.** really large (re-roll 1d10 on this chart)./ **12.** really small (re-roll 1d10 on this chart).

13. Foot from a moaner (odd) or a skullock (even).

14. A regular leg.

15. A odd leg, **roll 1d10. 1.** odd color TME-1-18./ **2.** knee joint is reversed./ **3.** robot leg still partially covered in android flesh./ **4.** over sized foot and ankle./ **5.** covered in fur. / **6.** covered in bone plates. / **7.** covered in scales. / **8.** is from a bestial human-oid./ **9.** really large (re-roll 1d8 on this chart)./ **10.** Really small (re-roll 1d8 on this chart).

16. Leg from a Moaner (odd) or a skullock (even).

17. A regular head.

18. An odd head. **Roll d10: 1.** odd color TME-1-18./ **2.** strange hair color TME-1-18./ **3.** odd colored eyes TME-1-18./ **4.** from a bestial human./ **5.** horns./ **6.** mandibles. / **7.** huge jaw./ **8.** roll on physical alterations table, re-rolling inappropriate results (mutation 98)./ **9.** a bestial humans head./ **10.** cybernetic implants: (**roll 1d4: 1.** armored, implant #3 pg. TME 85./ **2,3.** optical enchantment, implant #30, pg. TME 89./ **4.** panoramic optic node implant #32, pg. TME 89.)

19. Head from a humanoid creature, moaner (odd) or a skullock (even).

20. Head from a random creature, roll on TME 4-2 Street Level from Ancient Ruins Encounter Matrix, page TME 130.

What's on the discovered Body Part?

A **hand** 1 in 4 hands have a glove on them, for type of glove roll d10

1. Cloth work glove.

2. Camouflaged glove.

3. Fingerless glove.

4. Hand woven winter mitten

5. Leather work glove

6. Scrap armor

7. Plate gauntlet

8. Scrap relic armored glove

9. Still has a death grip on weapon from WC-SS, pg. TME 206.

10. Death grip on a relic weapon from WC-RC, pg. TME 207.

Most **feet** have boots, 1 in 4 are bare. Roll d10 for what's on the foot.

1. Rag wrapping.

2. Cloth wrapped

3. Sandals.

4. Leather home made shoes

5. Leather boots

6. Leather knee boots

7. Junk armored boots

8. Plate armored boots

9. Relic work boots

10. Relic combat boots (a pair gives -2 DV).

Arms and legs, are usually covered in something. 1 in 4 are bare otherwise roll d10.

1. Torn cloth rags

2. Homes spun wool

3. Rough cotton

4. Furs

5. Leather

6. Junk armor

7. Plate armor

8. Sports padding

9. Scrap relic armor.

10. Re-roll covering, but has a concealed holster, roll d6: 1 to 2 is a knife, 3 to 4 a dagger, 5 is a relic switch blade, and 6 is pocket pistol on a leg or a wrist gun on an arm.

1 in 4 **heads** have a wig, hat or helmet on, 1 in 6 have some sort of eye covering on, and 1 in 8 have some sort of face covering:

Hats and helmets d20
1. Hair is a wig
2. Rags
3. Cloth bandana
4. Relic cap from some long forgotten sports team
5. Straw hat tied on with twine
6. Wide brimmed leather hat
7. Plastic rain hat
8. Felt cap
9. Hand woven hat
10. Fur hat
11. Cowboy hat
12. Beanie
13. Relic fedora
14. Leather helmet
15. Junk helmet
16. Iron cap
17. Iron helm
18. Iron full helm
19. Sports helmet
20. Army helmet

Eye coverings d8
1. Monocle
2. Scrap built glasses
3. Relic glasses
4. Welding goggles
5. Sun glasses
6. Diving goggles
7. Safety glasses
8. Military goggles

Face coverings d6
1. Facial tattoos
2. Pierced nose
3. Rags
4. Bandanna
5. Filter mask
6. Gas mask

Apocalypse Moth Larva
Defensive Value: **-4**
Endurance: **4+1d6**
Movement: **4m**
Initiative: **-1**
Attacks: **1 bite**
Strike Value: **01-45**
Damage: **1d4**
Strength: 11
Agility: 47
Accuracy: 25
Intelligence: 2
Willpower: 30

Perception: 30
Experience Factors: 4
Morale: Excellent
Size: around 50cm
Weight: 2 to 5 kilograms
Mutations: none

These horrid worms resemble jaw worms, leading some to speculate a relation between the two species.

Spider Lord

By William McAusland

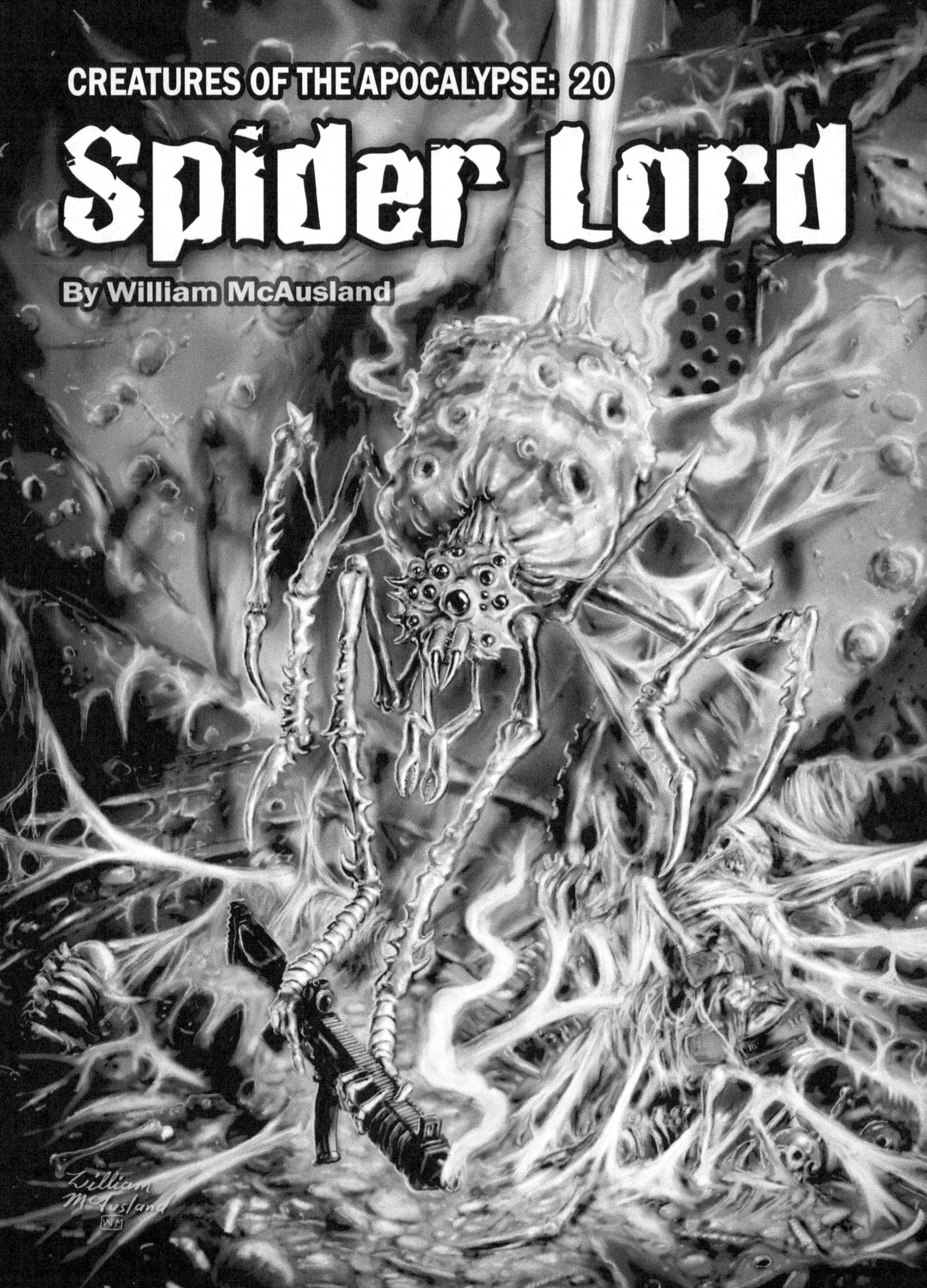

Spider Lord

Also known as Arachadus, Demon Spider, God Spider and Crawl-God *By William McAusland*

Defense Value: **-44**

Endurance: **110+2d100**

Movement: **15m**

Initiative: **+4**

Attacks: **Random metal attacks**, **relic weapon** or **in melee: venomous bite and two leg stabs**

Strike Value: **Base for weapons 01-70** or **01-80 for bite** and **leg stabs**

Damage: **By mental attacks** (see description) **by weapon*/ bite 2d6+10+venom**** and **leg stabs d20+10 each**

*If using a strength based weapon, such as a crossbow, club or sword, it gains +10 damage due to strength.

** Type D paralysis venom: Type D END based HC or immobilized.

Strength: 83 (+10 DMG)

Agility: 136

Accuracy: 98

Intelligence: 88

Willpower: 92

Perception: 124 (+4 Init.)

Valuables: See spider lord hoard Loot table, page 124

Experience: 496

Morale: Average

Size: body is 1cm long per point of uninjured endurance (100cm =1 meter)

Weight: As END in kilograms +100 kg

Implants: none

Mutations: Always one random from the Spider Lord mutation list plus the following: Mind Crush, Stun Ray, Electromagnetic Pulse, Mental Mine, Electrical Pulse, Reserve Mind, Reserve Heart, Telepathy, Empathy, Immunity: to radiation and poison/venom. Special mutations: Gaseous Diffusion, Mimicry, Rapid Healing, Heightened Intelligence, longevity.

Skills: Lying 3pts, Negotiating 4pts, Climbing 9pts, stealth 4pts, Tracking 4pts, Wilderness Survival, Navigate by Stars, Junk Crafter 2pts,

Although there are many larger nightmare monsters in the Mutant Epoch era, few are more feared than the spider lord. This intelligent, cunning, and long lived being is viewed as a demon or deity to many who are unlucky enough to live near them. Both human cultists and sub-humans such as moaners, skullocks, chest heads and the diminutive nubinz are all known to treat one of these bizarre mutant arachnids as either a minion of God, or an actual deity. In these cases of god spider worship, the supplicants sacrifice victims and animals to the giant arachnid, and its guardians. These offerings are made daily and worshippers must scour the ruins and wastes around their lair-shrines on a never ending quest to find worthy victims to throw to their bad tempered god. These religious devotees are often more terrified of their divine master than they are of excavation teams or other invaders, and will fight like fanatics to feed or defend their lord, often resorting to suicide attacks to ward off infidels long before they can even get close to the temple of their eight legged deity.

When forced to fight their own battles, a god spider will first conceal itself and launch a series of mental attacks at intruders. It prefers to do this while the invaders are already under attack by its worshippers or mutant spider guardians and are as yet unaware of the spider lord's presence high above in a ledge, hanging in mid air by a web, or stuck the side of a concrete wall out of direct sight. This creature will unleash one random metal attack per round, directed at a separate, random target per round. The exceptions to this is a mutation with an area effect, such as mental mine, or if a cyborg android or robot is spotted and randomly selected, in which case the spider lord always emits a electromagnetic pulse attempting to neutralize the fully or partial mechanical being. What follows is the random list of discharged mutations with a brief detail overview of each, the mutation's number, and the page number in the hub rules where it can be looked at in more detail if needed.

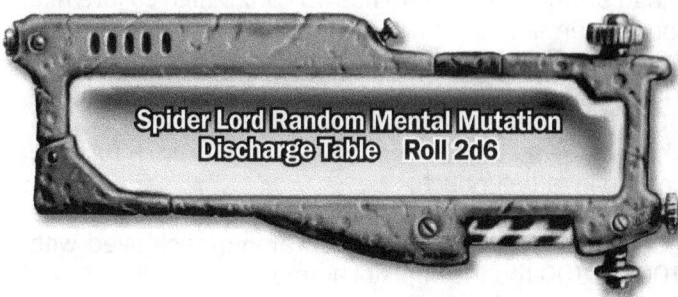

Spider Lord Random Mental Mutation Discharge Table   Roll 2d6

2. Mental Mine 54, page TME 70: Range thrown 92m or left 50m away to detonate, Blast Radius 5m, SV 01-80, DMG d20+12.

3,4. Electromagnetic Pulse 32, page TME 65: Range 176m, SV 01-100, DMG d10 to organics or d100 to electronics including robots and cyborgs.

5-7. Stun Ray 82, page TME 74: Range 176m, SV 01-80, DMG 2d20 stun or x2 (4d20) to machines and cyborgs.

8,9. Electrical Pulse 31, page TME 65: Range 264m, SV 01-90, DMG d20 to organics or 3d20 to machines and cyborgs

10-12. Mind Crush 56, page TME 70: Range 264m, harms organic brains only, Victim allowed a type B willpower or Intelligence based hazard check to avoid d20 END damage and d6 Intelligence damage. If reduced to zero or less endurance the victim must make a type B willpower based HC or slip into death. Those knocked out remain unconscious for 10+d100 minutes.

Once detected and taking fire, a spider lord will resort to whatever relic or archaic ranged weapon it has at its disposal, preferring not to get into melee combat if at all possible. When shooting at opponents, this demon spider will employ darkness and cover, gaining an extra -20 DV bonus if such cover is available to it. Although the beast may have a stockpile of other relic weapons, it will choose the one with the most ammo, that it can hold easily and has the most spectacular rate of fire or brilliance when discharging. Use the following table to see what a spider lord carries when encountered, rolling 3d6:

Spider Lord Relic Weapon Table   Roll 3d6

3. Laser carbine: SV 01-95, rate 1, DMG 2d20+10, range 2km, ammo: 3d6 shots left in power cell, but 4 in 6 chance it has d4 spare, fully charged cells as backup.

4. Pulse rifle: SV 01-90, rate 4, DMG d12 each, range 800m, ammo: 15+d10 bursts remaining in cell, but 3 in 6 chance it has d6 spare, fully charged cells in reserve.

5. Advanced frag grenades: carries a pouch of 3d6 of these deadly explosives: range 32m, burst radius 10m, SV 01-80, DMG 2d20+20

6. Heavy machine-gun: SV 01-85, rate 5, DMG d20+10, range 950m, ammo drum has 40+3d20 high calibre rifle rounds remaining, with a 1 in 6 chance of a spare full 100 round drum carried by the spider lord.

7. Assault shotgun: SV 01-90, DMG 3d10, rate 2, range 30m, drum loaded with 20+d20 shot shells, with a 3 in 6 chance of a spare, fully loaded 40 round drum magazine carried in a belt pouch.

8. Submachine gun: SV 01-80, DMG d20, Rate 5, range 250m hooked to back mounted ammo pack filled with 100+2d100 rounds of pistol ammo.

9. Fragmentation grenades: (with satchel filled with 4d6+8 more of these grenades: range 32m, burst radius 4m, SV 01-70, DMG d20+10.

10. Pump shotgun: SV 01-82, DMG 2d20+12, range 100m, rate 1 loaded with 8 'slug' type shell's loaded and a pouch filled with 40+d20 spare standard shot shells.

11. Assault rifle: SV 01-90, DMG d20, rate 3, range 900m, magazine holds 20+d10 rounds, with d6 fully loaded 30 round mags carried in a nylon shoulder bag.

12. Rocket launcher: With 4+d8 battle rockets: SV 01-90, rate ½, DMG direct d100+20, blast radius 2d20, range 4km, blast radius SV 10-80 within 5m radius.

13. Sniper rifle with silencer, bipod and standard scope: SV normal shooting 01-108, or carefully aimed (taking two rounds +60 SV and using scopes +20 SV) SV 01-150 (add +10 SV if using the bipod), rate 1 or ½, DMG d20+10, range 2km, 20 rnd magazine loaded with 10+d10 high calibre cartridges.

14. Assault rifle with 50 round drum magazine, fully loaded: SV 01-90, DMG d20, rate 3, range 900m

15. Heavy laser carbine: SV 01-105, DMG 3d20+20, rate 1, range 4km, ammo 3d6 shots remaining in power cell, with a 2 in 6 chance the spider has d3 spare, fully charged batteries in a pouch.

16. Heavy pulse rifle: SV 01-95, DMG d20 each, rate 4, range 1km, ammo 10+d10 bursts left in power cell, with a 3 in 6 chance of d4 spare full cells carried in a leather bag.

17. Fifty calibre sniper rifle with standard scope, bipod and 4 fully loaded 10 round magazines: SV 01-110 or carefully aimed shots SV 01-160 (add +10 SV if using the bipod), DMG 3d20+20, rate 1 or ½, range 3km.

18. Chaingun, belt fed with 50+d100 rounds pistol ammo: SV 01-80, rate 10, DMG d20 each, range 220m

If forced to enter into melee combat, or a group of attackers are driven off after taking casualties and the intruders need to be chased down and wiped out, the spider lord is fully capable of killing in close quarters. In truth, when needing the succulent juices of prey animals, especially humans and all their off shoots, this creature prefers to leap upon and defeat its prey alive. In an attack it will pounce on a potential victim with a venomous bite as well as two stabbing attacks with two of its lethally sharp, lance-like legs. **The bite of a spider lord injects type D paralytic venom into a subject** (victim allowed an END based type D hazard check otherwise become immobilized), which after two rounds reduces the victim to a quivering, muttering heap on the ground. While paralyzed, the subject can still hear and feel everything, but is unable to control his or her muscles or nervous system; therefore any cybernetic implants are offline. The only option to such a doomed victim is to rely on mental mutations, should he or she exhibit any.

Once a victim is paralyzed, the spider lord will either commence to puncture it and drain the subject of all body fluids, if hungry (2 in 6 chance) or else wrap the morsel in a cocoon of web and hoist it someplace high above the floor in the darkness of the ceiling, and devour it hours or even days later. **The paralysis venom will immobilize a creature for 300+2d100 minutes minus the kilograms weight of the prey animal to a minimum of 3d6 minutes.** This means that very large victims are not cocooned for later consumption and instead stabbed to death and only partially consumed by the god-spider, the rest of the kill being dragged to feeding area of any lesser arachnids to enjoy.

Should a character wake from paralysis while cocooned the subject will be allowed a type D strength based hazard check to break free of the hardened web, but will be hanging 3d6 meters above the concrete rubble far below and either need to climb up among the dozens of past cocooned victims and reach the rafters above, or else take a chance and drop down, which is noisy and possibly lethal.

Each spider lord will have acquired the loyalty and obedience of other spiders. These guardians will live in the ruined structures or chambers within a kilometer or less of their master, and are telepathically linked to the spider lord, although only dimly. If any spider guardian is hurt or killed, it will alert the spider lord that trouble has occurred. Their master arachnid will know immediately which of its guardians has been afflicted, and send other minions to inspect the area while it grabs a relic weapon and prepares a defensive position deep in its lair.

A spider lord will have 4d6 rubble spiders and d3 freakish spiders as guardians, although freakish spiders are often hard to control and wander off for days at a time to hunt, mate and tend to young.

If a cult has emerged around the worship of a specific spider lord, the shamans of this spider worshipping religion will be telepathically alerted, too, and instructed to kill or capture intruders. For the most part, spider cultists will be only too eager to accost and capture alive excavators or other travellers, instead of outright killing them, as their spider deity is always eager for offerings of warm flesh and fluid, and if it isn't an outsider who is fed to their god, then one of the cultists must volunteer or draw straws to submit to the divine honor of being sacrificed... and earning a place in paradise.

Given their ability to surround themselves with lesser spider guardians, as well as convince humanoids and savage humans that they are indeed supernatural beings, spider lords are thus not easy to get close to and kill. Even if getting within combat range of a spider lord, these creatures are incredibly powerful and able to eliminate almost any single adversary or squad of attackers foolish enough to challenge them. Not being mindlessly brave, however, god-crawlers think nothing of abandoning a lair, their treasure hoard, status as a god or hunting grounds if it means surviving, and always have an escape tunnel.

If assaulted and its pets and worshippers seriously depleted or the spider lord is driven from their nest area, it will become obsessed with revenge. Should this extremely intelligent arachnid observe those responsible for the insolent attack against its temple-lair, it will plot the destruction of the interlopers, along with whatever families and community the upstart, trouble making, pesky vermin call home. It will even make a brazen night time raid into a human town or city, using stealth and speed to locate and eradicate those who defiled its sanctuary.

Spider lords have no set lifespan, and if not killed by an accident, larger predator or highly experienced diggers, will in theory live for countless centuries. Nearly every crawling god alive in the current era is a first generation specimen from an original hatch site. This site, is rumored to be in a vast bio-weapons facility outside the former city state of Atlanta, Georgia. Hundreds of these creatures were created, broke loose, devoured their human overseers, and defeated the automated and robotic security measures and spread across the continent and soon after, the world. There are no accounts of more than one of these spiders cohabiting with another of its kind, and it is speculated that they hate each other passionately and are unable to tolerate their own kin even long enough to mate. Eventually, the ultimate extinction of their species seems certain.

Other mutations these beast exhibit include gaseous diffusion, mimicry, rapid healing and heightened intelligence. All over the back of this arachnid are crater-like orifices that can disgorge a cloud of brilliant green haze. This putrid smelling miasma is usually discharged when the spider is either angry, surprised or being defeated and it needs to cover its retreat. Like a squid exuding ink to confuse and blind its attackers, the spider lord can unleash a billowing cloud of this substance in a 6m radius around it. Once obscured, it gains an extra -40 defense value and can vanish down any number of pre-planned escape tunnels, or merely shoot a web at the ceiling and crawling up above the enemy to either flee or attack from another angle with mental mutations or relics. The stinking green cloud irritates the lungs of other creatures and leaves them coated in a spray-paint like green dust, but is actually not harmful in itself. Often, first time opponents of a spider lord believe they have inhaled poison gas, and flee the battle, sometimes splitting up in their retreat and making for easy targets for the god-crawler or its minions.

The ability to mimic any voice it has heard, or sound of animals, allows the spider lord to trick, terrify or toy with intruders. One of its favorite harvesting ploys is to call to excavators in the voice of a distressed child or young woman, pleading for help. The would-be rescuers follow the voices into an ambush, trap lined corridor, or the gun sights of a well-aimed relic weapon, behind which is concealed the ready, trigger-happy spider lord.

Besides not growing old, this mutant arachnid has the mutation of rapid healing, specific to its species. Any damage it suffers heals at a rate of 1 trait point per minute, so even if seriously harmed one day, it will appear the next day fully recovered.

The geneticists who designed this monster made special effort to imbue it with an uncanny level of intelligence. Their hope was to create a bio weapon capable of fighting robotic units, using EMP and other organic offensive measures, but so too, the ability to employ cunning tactics and learn from both experiences and simulators. They achieved their aims, to their detriment, and created a being smarter than most humans. Although having very high intelligence scores, their brains and way of thinking are quite alien. They have no sense of humor, fail at creativity, make nothing new, and are unable to predict tactics that they haven't already seen before. In short, they suffer from a failure of imagination and have a very difficult time understanding the mutations exhibited by mutant humans, or any sort of enemy attack that doesn't involve the intruders coming straight through the main passages. They therefore cannot foresee that a hostile dig team might look for and employ its own escape tunnel, or come from deeper ruins beneath it instead of from street level, and so on. Likewise, for all their smarts, spider lords can't seem to figure out that if its cult worshipping humanoids continually raid nearby farms and villages for sacrificial victims, that those abused populations won't rise up and seek to destroy the cult and so too, its deity. Time and again, the spider lord's temple is eventually located, attacked and ultimately destroyed, forcing the god-crawler to flee and take up residence in another area. It is these times of migration, often with only a few rubble spiders for company, that it is most vulnerable, and often encountered by unsuspecting dig teams.

The driving off or killing of a spider lord will leave its considerable hoard open to looting. Herein will be found a mix of bones, dried humanoid and animal husks, shredded clothing, backpacks and adventure gear along with silver and gold coins, archaic arms and armor, and highly prized relic wonders. There will be 3000+3d1000 silver coins here, some of it loose but much of it contained in the purses and pouches of the dead. Also present are 300+3d100 gold coins, 2d6 random jewelry items and 2d12 random gems (see table bottom of page TME 209 in the hub rules). Scattered about will be 3d6 suits of leather armor, 2d6 suits of junk armor, d6 suits of scrap relic armor, 3d6 machetes, 4d6 knives, 2d6 bows, 2d100 arrows, d100 crossbow quarrels, d10 crossbows, d6 sabres, d6 musket pistols with enough shot and powder for 10 rounds each, 3d6 water skins (dried), d6 bottles of assorted booze, d100 days of eatable dried rations, d6 lengths of 10m rope sections, 4d6 troches, 5d6 candles and 1000+d1000sp worth of plastic trinkets worth selling.

Spider Lord Hoard   Roll 2d20

Each excavators looting the hoard will find one item from the following table (to a group maximum of ten rolls). Reroll duplicated results.

2. A bog spider guardian, which has been waiting for its chance to leap up at the face of the nearest person: DV -5, END 2+d4, MV 6m, Init +0, attacks 1, SV 01-30, DMG d3+ type B death venom, but even if surviving, then a type C weakness poison risk. See page TME 171

3. Red plastic tackle box filled with ancient fishing lures, lines pliers, and gear. Set worth 300+2d100sp

4. Desiccated corpse in a suit of olive green combat armor, no helmet.

5. Razor sword in original nylon sheath

6. Plastic wrapped set of three power cells, drained but otherwise like new.

7. Ammo pouch holding two fully loaded 30 round magazines for an assault rifle.

8. Survival rifle loaded with d10 rifle rounds.

9. Mountain bike, relic, urban camo paint treatment.

10. Advanced Binoculars (pg. TME 201)

11. Ammo pack, built for rifle rounds and filled with d100 cartridges

12. Set of night vision headgear with d12 hours of operation remaining, plus, a side pocket contains d4 spare, fully charged mini-power cells.

13. Box of 20 50. caliber rounds

14. Pump shotgun with folding stock and sling. D8 rounds loaded in weapon and another d6 slug style shells in the sling's own ammo sleeve.

15. Ammo can filled with a belt of 100+d100 standard rile rounds.

16. Spotlight flashlight with 40+d20 hours of light remaining.

17. Dried human skull with headlamp flashlight still attached (3d6 hours illumination remaining). Victim had gold teeth which if pulled will be worth 40+d20sp when sold.

18. Substance reader with d3 years of battery life remaining.

19. Rad scanner with 3d100 days of use left in charge.

20. Handy six pack of anti-toxin injectors in original protective packaging.

21. Ammo case made of green plastic containing d100+10 pistol rounds.

22. Military crate containing a tactical missile (see page TME 197)

23. Missile launcher, with no missiles, in carry case and ready to be folded out and deployed see page TME 198).

24. Stack of 8 land mines, not armed, in shrink wrap.

25. Plastic box containing never before opened, sealed selection of 24 fragmentation grenades, 8 advanced frag grenades and 8 nerve gas grenades.

26. Assault rifle hard plastic carry case. Folding stock with silencer and two empty thirty round magazines, sling and cleaning kit.

27. Sniper rifle in nylon fabric carry case. Comes with sling, standard scope, bipod, and two fully loaded ten round magazines.

28. Cocooned victim: There is somebody jerking about inside a web cocoon, their muffled cries of panic clearly audible. If the head area of the wrapped victim is exposed, **roll d6: 1.** a skullock. / **2.** warmort./ **3.** chest head (see page 65, this book). / **4.** Just one of 4+d4 nubinz all packed together in a single cocoon (see page 108, this book). / **5.** A human woman from a nearby village. / **6.** A human man, a farmer from the nearest village.

29. Combat helmet, olive green, human skull still inside and needs a good cleaning.

30. Gasmask still attached to a human skull.

31. Force field generator in original plastic carry case. Two power cells included but both drained (pg. TME 195).

32. A attractive human in a white jumpsuit laying bent and twisted awkwardly, but its eyes are open and watching the PCs move about. This android is patterned after a twenty-something year old male 50% of the time, otherwise female. "Hello," it says, smiling. "I'm Jo-99, a personal assistant. I've been left here for several decades and if you would be so kind as to supply me with a fresh power cell, I could be very helpful. I would love to get to know you and sort out your habitation or work space. Would you like some coffee? Perhaps an espresso? By your perplexed facial expressions, I see that you were not expecting a new employee at this time."

Joe or Joanne is clerical android with only a 9% chance of being infected with a mecha command and control virus. If infected, it may not be aware that it is serving as the eyes and ears of a local robot hive. If given a power cell and helped to its feet, it will readily help the PCs in their mission, but has a violence inhibitor program running and will not engage in combat except against spiders and non-humanoids, and then only with a limp wristed fist attack.

33. Rocket launcher loaded with one battle rocket.

34. Stun stick with 20+d20 'hits' of energy remaining in battery

35. Laser carbine with 3d6 shots remaining in power cell.

36. Solar generator unit enclosed it its backpack. Pack holds d6 standard, and 2d6 mini and 3d6 pill power cells, all drained but in good order.

37. Heavy pulse rifle with 3d6 bursts left in power cell.

38. Flame unit with full 1L canister of fuel attached to it yielding 20 streams of flame.

39. Chain gun with attached belt of d100 rounds pistol ammo.

40. Suit of heavy combat armor with helmet, worn by dried out previous owner. Suit is black with the word SWAT written on shoulders, forehead and back in dull gray lettering.

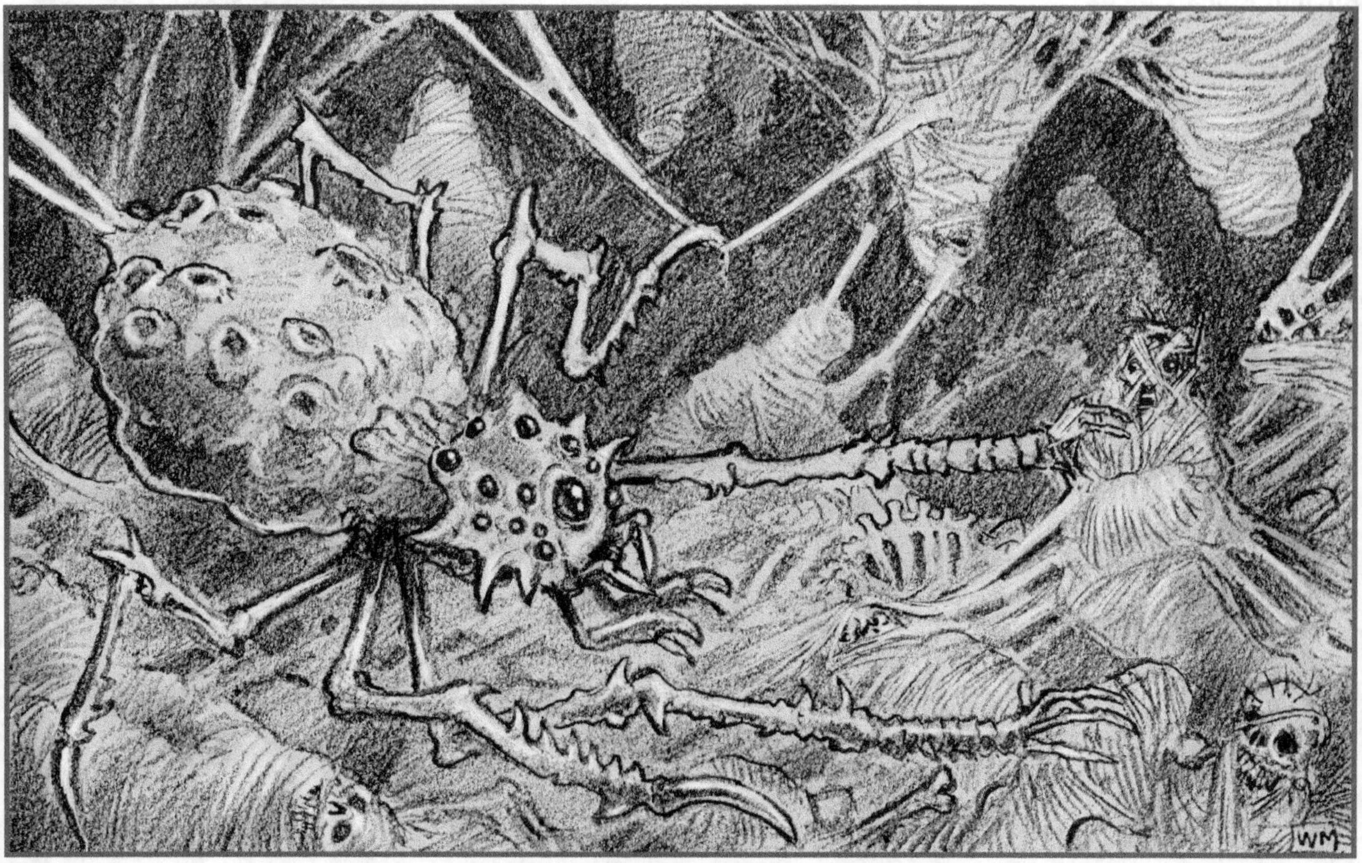

Encounter Tables

PC Rank Tiers for encounter strength:
Low Character Ranks 1-4
Mid Character Ranks 5-9
High Character Ranks 10 and up

Terrain	Odds of Encounter per Check	Daytime * Check Frequency	Nighttime ** Check Frequency	Range of Encounter Daytime / Night
Plains	1 in 10	every hour	every half hour	50+d1000m/ d100m
Desert	1 in 10	every 2 hours	every hour	10+d1000m/ d100m
Badlands/ Scrub	1 in 10	every hour	every 45 minutes	10+d100m/ d20m
Forest	3 in 10	every 45 minutes	every 30 minutes	d20m/ d12m
Jungle	4 in 10	every 30 minutes	every 20 minutes	d12m/ d8m
Swamp	3 in 10	every hour	every 45 minutes	d20+2m/ d12+1m
Hills/ Old Battle Zone	2 in 10	every hour	every 30 minutes	2d100m/ 2d20m
Mountains	2 in 10	every 2 hours	every hour	d1000m/ d100m
Ruins, street or skyscraper	4 in 10	every 20 minutes	every 10 minutes	d100m/ d20m
Ruins, underground	5 in 10	every 15 minutes	every 5 minutes	by Chamber or 2d10m
Water, swimming/ wading***	6 in 10	every 30 minutes	every 20 minutes	d10m/ d6m
Water, via boat or ship	2 in 10	every hour	every 45 minutes	Special (see below)
Air, while flying	2 in 10	every 45 minutes	every 30 minutes	300+2d1000m/ d100m

*Add +2 to the chance of an encounter if any member of the group, including livestock and pets, have bleeding wounds or infections; or if exposed meat or cadavers are being transported; if a team member fires a ballistic weapon or uses an explosive (musket, assault rifle, pistol, grenade, etc.); or if one is making noise louder than conversational talking.

**At night, as above in '*' all the above circumstances apply, plus, if a fire is not concealed in a sheltered pit, add +5 to the chance of an encounter due to predators seeing the fire from afar.

*** This applies to each crossing if one is wading a river or stream, or between sandbars or reefs, etc.

Ancient Ruins Roll d100

Number of Beings Encountered

Street Level	Skyscraper	Underground	Battle Zone	Encounter Result	Low Rank	Mid Rank	High Rank	Page
01-07	01-03	01,02	01-06	Sickle Foot	d2	d3+1	2d6	5
08-11	04-09	03-11	07	Red Harvester	1	d3	2d4	9
12-17	10-15	12-15	08-11	Spikeback	d2	d4+1	2d6+1	14
18-22	16-20	16-19	12-16	Junk-Mobster	1	d2	d4+2	19
23,24	21-26	20-33	17,18	Bog-Billy	d6	2d6+1	3d6+5	25
25-27	27-31	34-36	19,20	Scraplurker, Juvenile	3d6+2	3d6+10	3d10+18	30
28-33	32-34	37-40	21-24	Scraplurker, Adult	2d4	2d6+6	3d6+7	30
34-38	35,36	41-43	25-27	Scraplurker, Brute	d2	d4+1	2d4+2	30
39,40	37	44	28	Back Hatcher	1	d3+1	d6+3	37
41-43	39-46	45-50	29,30	Quasi	1	d6+2	2d6+6	43
44-47	47,48	51-53	31-36	Spiker, Wild	1	d2+1	d4+2	46
48-51	49,50	54,55	37-41	Spiker, Armored	1*	d2	d3+1	46
52	51-53	56-58	42,43	Wailing Jhonny	1	d4	2d4+1	51
53-55	54	-	44-53	Tyrannosapien	1*	d2	d4	56
56-60	55-61	59-64	54-61	Chest Head	d3	d6+2	3d6+3	65
61,62	62-66	65-68	62-66	Talontessa	2d4	3d6	6d6	70
63-66	67-73	69	67-71	Muto-Harpy	2d4	3d6	5d6+4	80
67-73	74	70	72-77	Walking Mouther	1	d2+1	d4+1	84
74-80	75	71,72	78-84	Rubble Troll	1*	d3	d6	92
81-87	76-80	73-77	85-88	Snaykin	d4	2d4	3d6	101
88-91	81-90	78-93	89,90	Nubinz	4d6	6d6+20	d100+50	108
92-96	91-95	94	91-99	Apocalypse Moth	1*	d3	d6	116
97-00	96-00	95-00	00	Spider Lord	1**	1**	1**	120

* This creature is a deadly foe for low rank characters, and will most likely kill several if not all. GM's should perhaps re-roll.

** Spider Lords will often have guardian cultists (50+d100 humanoids or human savages) plus other spider companions. See Description on page 121.

Wilderness Areas Matrix COTA-1   Roll d100

Number of Beings Encountered

Plains	Hills	Mountains	Badlands	Desert	Snow	Encounter Result	Low Rank	Mid Rank	High Rank	Page
01-09	01-05	01-04	01-05	01-08	01-06	Sickle Foot	d2	d3+1	2d6	5
10	06-08	05	06,07	09	-	Red Harvester	1	d3	2d4	9
11-16	09-17	06-14	08-15	10-17	07-12	Spikeback	d2	d4+1	2d6+1	14
17-23	18-21	15-18	14-18	18-22	13-18	Junk-Mobster	1	d2	d4+2	19
24	22-25	19	19,20	23-27	19	Bog-Billy	d6	2d6+1	3d6+5	25
25,26	26-29	20-22	21,22	28,29	20-24	Scraplurker, Juvenile	3d6+2	3d6+10	3d10+18	30
27,28	30,31	23,24	23,24	30,31	25-30	Scraplurker, Adult	2d4	2d6+6	3d6+7	30
29,30	32,33	25,26	25,26	32,33	31-34	Scraplurker, Brute	d2	d4+1	2d4+2	30
-	34	-	-	-	-	Back Hatcher	1	d3+1	d6+3	37
31	35-39	27-31	28-31	34-39	35-38	Quasi	1	d6+2	2d6+6	43
32-34	40-47	32-38	32-38	40-45	39-42	Spiker, Wild	1	d2+1	d4+2	46
35	48,49	39,40	39,40	46,47	43	Spiker, Armored	1*	d2	d3+1	46
36-39	50-56	41-59	41-49	48	44-66	Wailing Jhonny	1	d4	2d4+1	51
40-53	57-80	60-68	50-55	49-53	67-72	Tyrannosapien	1*	d2	d4	56
54-61	61-65	69-76	56-62	54-56	73-77	Chest Head	d3	d6+2	3d6+3	65
62-70	66-69	77-81	63-69	57-59	78,79	Talontessa	2d4	3d6	6d6	70
71-79	70-74	82-87	70-74	60-65	80-84	Muto-Harpy	2d4	3d6	5d6+4	80
80-84	75-78	88,89	75-78	66-69	85	Walking Mouther	1	d2+1	d4+1	84
85,86	79-83	90-94	79-86	70-75	86-90	Rubble Troll	1*	d3	d6	92
87,88	84-87	95	87-92	76-88	-	Snaykin	d4	2d4	3d6	101
89	88-93	96	93,94	89-94	91-00	Nubinz	4d6	6d6+20	d100+50	108
90-99	94-99	97-00	95-98	95-99	-	Apocalypse Moth	1*	d3	d6	116
00	00	-	99,00	00	-	Spider Lord	1**	1**	1**	120

This creature is a deadly foe for low rank characters, and will most likely kill several if not all. GM's should perhaps re-roll.

*** Spider Lords will often have guardian cultists (50+d100 humanoids or human savages) plus other spider companions. See Description on page 121.*

Wilderness Areas Matrix COTA-2   Roll d100

Number of Beings Encountered

Aerial	Forest	Scrub	Swamp	Freshwater	Saltwater	Encounter Result	Low Rank	Mid Rank	High Rank	Page
-	01-04	01-07	01-04	-	-	Sickle Foot	d2	d3+1	2d6	5
-	05-08	08-10	05-18	01-69	01-24	Red Harvester	1	d3	2d4	9
-	09-13	11-17	19-22	-	-	Spikeback	d2	d4+1	2d6+1	14
-	14-16	18-26	23-25	-	-	Junk-Mobster	1	d2	d4+2	19
-	17-24	27-29	26-35	70-72	-	Bog-Billy	d6	2d6+1	3d6+5	25
-	25,26	30-32	36,37	-	-	Scraplurker, Juvenile	3d6+2	3d6+10	3d10+18	30
-	27,28	33-35	38,39	-	-	Scraplurker, Adult	2d4	2d6+6	3d6+7	30
-	29,30	36-38	40,41	-	-	Scraplurker, Brute	d2	d4+1	2d4+2	30
-	31-44	39	42-59	73-93	25-31	Back Hatcher	1	d3+1	d6+3	37
-	45-49	44-48	60-62	-	-	Quasi	1	d6+2	2d6+6	43
-	50-55	49-56	63-65	-	-	Spiker, Wild	1	d2+1	d4+2	46
-	56	57,58	67	-	-	Spiker, Armored	1*	d2	d3+1	46
-	57-59	59-61	68-71	-	-	Wailing Jhonny	1	d4	2d4+1	51
-	60-63	62-66	72,73	-	-	Tyrannosapien	1*	d2	d4	56
-	64-69	67-70	74-77	-	-	Chest Head	d3	d6+2	3d6+3	65
-	70-76	71-75	78-81	-	-	Talontessa	2d4	3d6	6d6	70
01-64	77,78	76-80	82	94-96	32-88	Muto-Harpy	2d4	3d6	5d6+4	80
-	79-82	81-83	83-85	-	-	Walking Mouther	1	d2+1	d4+1	84
-	83-88	84-88	86-88	-	-	Rubble Troll	1*	d3	d6	92
-	89-93	89-92	89-93	-	-	Snaykin	d4	2d4	3d6	101
-	92-96	93-95	94,95	-	-	Nubinz	4d6	6d6+20	d100+50	108
65-00	97	96-99	96	97-00	89-00	Apocalypse Moth	1*	d3	d6	116
-	98-00	00	97-00	-	-	Spider Lord	1**	1**	1**	120

This creature is a deadly foe for low rank characters, and will most likely kill several if not all. GM's should perhaps re-roll.

*** Spider Lords will often have guardian cultists (50+d100 humanoids or human savages) plus other spider companions. See Description on page 121.*

Sickle Foot   Copyright 2015   OutlandArts.com The Mutant Epoch

William
McAusland
WM

Spikeback Copyright 2015 OutlandArts.com The Mutant Epoch

William McAusland

Junk-Mobster   Copyright 2015   OutlandArts.com   The Mutant Epoch

Back Hatcher   Copyright 2015   OutlandArts.com   The Mutant Epoch

Tyrannosapien   Copyright 2015   OutlandArts.com The Mutant Epoch

Chest Head

William McAusland

Talontessa   Copyright 2015   OutlandArts.com   The Mutant Epoch

Walking Mouther   Copyright 2015   OutlandArts.com The Mutant Epoch

Apocalypse Moth   Copyright 2015   OutlandArts.com   The Mutant Epoch

Discover
THE MUTANT EPOCH
TABLETOP ADVENTURE ROLEPLAYING GAME

THE MUTANT EPOCH
TABLETOP ADVENTURE ROLE-PLAYING GAME
GAZETTEER 1
The CROSSROADS REGION

Excavator Monthly COMPENDIUM

THE MUTANT EPOCH
TABLETOP ADVENTURE ROLE-PLAYING GAME
The Mall of Doom
Adventure TME-1

THE MUTANT EPOCH
TABLETOP ADVENTURE ROLE-PLAYING GAME
Beyond Red Crater
Adventure TME-2
For 6 to 10 1st Rank Characters

Created by
William McAusland

THE MUTANT EPOCH
TABLETOP ADVENTURE ROLE-PLAYING GAME
Mutant Bestiary One

PITFORD
GATEWAY TO THE RUINS
THE MUTANT EPOCH

THE MUTANT EPOCH
TABLETOP ADVENTURE ROLE-PLAYING GAME
Flesh Weavers
Adventure TME-3
For 6 to 8, 2nd to 4th Rank Characters

THE MUTANT EPOCH
TABLETOP ADVENTURE ROLE-PLAYING GAME

Created by
William McAusland

OutlandArcs.com

WWW.MUTANTEPOCH.COM